BRATVA KING'S SECRET TWINS

A FORCED PROXIMITY DARK MAFIA ROMANCE

VIVY SKYS

1

GWEN

"Well goddamn, darlin', you keep spinning like that you might just take my whole paycheck," Jacob, a regular with graying hair and a worn smile, yells to me.

I roll my hips, arching my back while I slide down the pole. My black curls cascade over my shoulder, and a sultry smile spreads across my lips.

"Baby," I purr, swinging my hair over my shoulder. I slide to the floor and crawl closer to the balding man holding a wad of 5's, "it'll be the best check you've ever spent."

He howls like a maniac, and his friends happily shower me with bills. *That's right, keep them coming. Your paycheck will definitely put me ahead of payments for Mason.*

I lean back, letting the pink light from above wash over me. The music fades, and Justin's sorry-ass voice comes over the loudspeaker. "Give it up for the delicious Cinnamon!" I roll back on my heels, licking my lips at the older men. "But hold onto your bulges, boys, because next up is a sweet little slice of heaven. Welcome Angel!"

I gather all the money I can, stuffing it into my panties and bra and make my way off the stage. "What the fuck, Dylan? I had at least ten more minutes in my set!"

Dylan, the club's owner, rolls his eyes as he lights a cigarette. "Gwen, you were boring the crowd."

"How fucking dare you—"

"Aye, watch your fucking mouth, or I'll take you off the books for a week!" I press my lips firmly together, crossing my arms over my chest.

"That's illegal, you know."

"And *you* know I don't like legal chat in my club." Dylan flicks the cigarette ash on the floor, giving me an annoyed look.

I smile, grabbing the cig out of his hand. "I see. I can only talk legalese when I'm getting you out of trouble." Dylan gives me a humorless laugh as I take a long pull. "Go figure."

Two years ago, I was at the top of my class at Georgetown Law, with dreams of becoming the best defense attorney in Washington, D.C. But then Dad disappeared after Mason threatened to break his legs. Mason had told Nana Rose that Dad's debt was her debt. Despite everyone telling me not to, I dropped out of Law School to help pay off the debt because no one hurts Nana Rose, not if I can help it.

So when Dylan's club was facing the threat of being shut down due to rumors of illegal activities in the secret "peek-a-boo" rooms upstairs, we made a deal: I would use my legal expertise to help him, and in return, he would allow me to work on the main stage at Dream Palace until I paid off my father's debt.

"Ha. Ha. Funny." Dylan snatches his cigarette back. "Now go out there and offer a dance to some of Mason's crew. They haven't spent any money yet."

Fuck. I shift my weight from side to side, biting the inside of my cheek. Mason probably sent some of his men to collect the measly 500 dollars I pay towards my father's quarter of a million-dollar debt. "Come on, they love Angel way more than me." I roll my eyes, trying to count the bills in my hands quickly.

"Chop. Chop. You know you're Tyler's favorite." I roll my eyes, continuing to count. 15. 20. 25. Fuck, I only got 375.

I push my breasts up and take a deep breath, steeling my nerves. "I thought I was boring," I mock, sticking my tongue out at Dylan.

"Don't pick a fight with me. Get out there." Dylan points the cigarette at the door behind me, and I huff, sharply turning around on my six-inch stilettos.

I add an extra sway in my hips and make my way to the main floor, sliding just out of reach of some of the handsy men. I get wolf calls and "Hey baby," but there is one set of eyes that silently weigh on me.

I look up to the left corner of the club, my eyes locking with a set of deep blue eyes. His gaze burns into mine, causing a thrill to ripple through me. I can feel his eyes tracing every curve, every dip of my silhouette, as I make my way through the club. I am drowning in his bright blue eyes.

He holds my gaze and lazily sips the amber liquid from his tumbler. I lean forward, eyes hooded behind the rogue strand from his slick back, dirty blonde hair. I can't help but keep my gaze on him, his presence drawing me like a moth to a flame.

"Goddamn, you are fine!" Tyler's whistle breaks the man's trance. I look up at the smug motherfucker in a white tank top and dirty blue jeans. His buzz cut is colored green but looks purple under the neon lights, and despite all the ways he could be cute, he is just shy of being good-looking.

I stare at the angry pink scar pulsating on his face, but I mask the shiver of disgust with a seductive smile. "Well, I heard you boys were looking for me?"

"Hell yeah, baby!" An eager member who looks a little too young to be in here smiles, looking at the rose tattoo that spirals up my legs and gathers on my left butt cheek.

"Come sit on Daddy's lap, Gwen." There is nothing more unattractive than a man calling himself Daddy. Major ick. That honor should be bestowed upon you, not self-titled.

"Oh, come, Ty. If you want to take me home, you need to try harder than that." I walk closer, almost between his thighs, crossing one foot in front of another, sliding my hips side to side like a snake charmer. Tyler leans back in his chair, legs wide, eyes hooded with a visible tent growing in his jeans.

"You know Mason won't let none of us touch you." I give him my best pout, squatting between his legs and peering up through my eyelashes.

Leaning up by his ear, I whisper, "Well, ain't that too damn bad." I'm not fucking Mason. I'm not fucking anyone, never have, but Mason claimed me as if I was his future wife. He knows if I had it my way, I'd have him swimming with the fishes before I would ever voluntarily call him husband.

Tyler swallows, his eyes running over the curves of my body. When his eyes land on mine, he licks his lips and says, "Jordan is waiting outside for this week's payment. Side door."

"Thanks, love." I wink, blowing Tyler a kiss that makes his eyes lower.

With a flamboyant flourish, I turn around and switch my hips over to the side door when my eyes drift up to that man again. The tumbler he was drinking out of is abandoned on the side table next to his empty seat, glittering under the dance lights. I huff, blowing air between my lips. You need to get it together, Gwen; no paying attention to the hot, mysterious stranger's absence when Venom is waiting for payment.

Maneuvering through the crowd and keeping out of Dylan's eyeline, I make my way to the side alley. Knocking my right shoulder into the metal door, I stumble into the side alley where the midnight air bites at my exposed flesh. I gaze to my right, where Venom lazily smokes a cigarette.

"Venom, buddy!" I laugh, holding the metal door open with my hip and crossing my arms under my chest. "How the hell are ya?"

Venom, a big, burly man with thin lips and a bald head so shiny it gleams in the streetlights, smiles at me, flicking the ash from the cigarette at my feet. "Well, Gwendolyn—"

"Ew, not my full government." I grimace. Venom smirks, looking at me from the corner of his eye, and if I didn't watch him break my father's kneecap with his bare hands, Venom would be just my type. He is the enforcer in Mason's inner circle, and if I ever stopped paying my payments, Venom would be the one to track me down and kill me after he has all the fun he wants with me, and from his gaze, I can tell I would be in for a long night.

"From the tone of your voice," he takes another pull of his cigarette, "you're missing part of your payment." I cross my legs, giving my most innocent smile.

"Oh, only by 125 dollars."

Venom lets out a low whistle.

"But I have three hours left in this shift. I promise I'll have it by the end. I mean, come look at these." I motion to my breasts with a clever grin on my face.

Venom finally turns his body to me, his eyes shamelessly ogling my chest. His smile widens, showcasing his pearly whites, while his eyes move from my breasts to the curve created by my tiny waist and wide hips.

I place my left hand on my hip. "Woah there, Venom. Keep looking at me like that, and I'll charge you."

Venom tosses the cigarette on the floor and places both of his large hands on my hips, dragging me into his chest. I yelp, scrambling to fight him off before the door closes, but I am too late, and he is too strong. "You know there is an easier way to work off that debt, Gwen."

"Oh," I giggle nervously, trying to wiggle out of his embrace, but Venom pulls me in closer, forcing me to inhale his stink of cigarettes. I almost gag on the smoke still spilling out of his lips. I make my voice firm, losing all of my playfulness as I make eye contact with his black eyes. "Venom, if you are looking for a lap dance, go inside the club."

"Baby, I don't want no fucking lap dance," Venom's smile is sinister, "I want you on your knees sucking my dick," he whispers heavily.

"Venom, what the fuck?" I jerk back in his arms, moving to knee him in the dick.

"You're right; that's only worth like fifty." His hands run from my waist, and he grips both of my cheeks, kneading my ass.

"I'll fuck you in the ass after. We can call that an even 200, what do you say?"

"Mason will fucking kill you-"

"Nah, because you are going to be a good girl and not say a word." He pulls me in closer and licks my cheek.

"Venom, you bring your dick anywhere near me and I'll bite it off," I growl, slamming the heel of my stilettos into the toe of his combat boots; he doesn't even flinch.

"I always knew fucking you would be rough." Venom spins me around, wrapping my hair around his hand. He tries to push me down to my knees.

No. No. No. I can't lose my virginity like this and definitely not to a guy named fucking Venom. I dig my heels into the ground, using my body as leverage to keep me from hitting the ground, but Venom is too strong. My knees buckle, and I am left panting and praying to Gods I don't believe in for any solace.

A shot whizzes through the air. Venom jumps back, looking for his weapon, and tosses me to the ground as if I am nothing. "Fucking hell," Venom growls, searching the area for the assailant.

"I don't miss twice." A thick Russian accent rumbles through the air, but I am in too much panic to appreciate it.

The minute I hit the ground, I pat the area around me, looking for a weapon to defend myself. My fingers wrap around the neck of an empty beer bottle. I grab it, smashing it against the concrete wall and stumbling over to the other side of the alley, out of Venom's reach, brandishing the broken bottle as a weapon.

"When a lady says no, the answer is no." The silky tenor of the voice causes a shiver to run down my spine. My eyes lock with the same bright blue eyes I almost drowned in.

2

GWEN

With bright blue eyes, a man emerges from the shadow of the alley, caressing the pipe of his pistol as if it were a loyal dog.

Venom sneers, "You better fuck off before Mason has your fucking head."

Blue Eyes's lips spread into a sinister smile as if he was a kid playing with his favorite toy. "Oh, and this Mason lets you run around and rape young women?"

"Mason owns this city and everyone in it." Venom laughs as he points to me. "Especially her, so I'd mind my fucking business if I were you."

Blue Eyes shrugs. "You see, I would if she didn't say no, and well-" He winks at me. "When a beautiful girl says no to a jackass like you, I can't help myself."

It all happens in a flash. Blue Eyes reaches for Venom's gun, twisting his body so Venom's head is on the sidewalk, underneath Blue Eyes's knee, and his arm bent back so that Blue Eyes could easily break his arm.

Underneath the streetlight, I can see his slick back, dirty blonde hair, with a rogue strand dancing above his right eye, which is brown. I want to tuck that strand back so it can spring back and have a reason to touch him again. His blue eyes are vibrant and deep like the ocean, and he has swirls of intricate black tattoos peeking out of his button-up and up his neck. I swallow as my eyes land on the vein popping on the forearm that stretches to put pressure on Venom's shoulder blade.

When he looks up at me, there is a sparkle in his eye, and his lips are in an easygoing smile. "Normally, I'd break your arm, but since you were bothering the lady, I think it's only right that it is her choice what we do with you."

I twist my lips as if I am in deep thought because the idea of Blue Eyes breaking Venom's arm for me makes my panties wet. "Well, before you break anything in my honor, how about you tell me your name?" I purr, leaning forward to his eye level. Venom struggles beneath him, a slew of curses leaving his lips.

He brandishes a bright smile, rolling his name off his tongue like we are meeting in line at a coffee shop. "Nikolai Petrov, pleasure."

"Nikolai? Petrov?" Venom whimpers.

"In the flesh." Nikolai's cocky smile flashes in my direction with a flourish.

"Petrov, wait, I-I-" Venom begins to beg, but Nikolai clicks his tongue, silencing him.

"No. No begging now." Nikolai twists his arm, causing

Venom to yelp, but he brings his eyes back to me. "Our handsy friend is getting a little impatient..."

"Gwen. I would shake your hand, but they seem full right now." I smile, flipping my curls over my shoulder, the broken bottle still swinging between my fingertips.

"Well, *Gwen." Fuck, I love the way he pours over my name.* "What would you like me to do with the handsy guy here?"

"Hmmm, you see, a broken arm can heal."

"Continue." Nikolai nods, intrigue flashing across his eyes as a devilish smile spreads.

"And I think this fucker needs a permanent reminder to keep his hands to himself." I purse my lips as if contemplating before looking down into Venom's eyes. "Don't ya' think, Venny?"

"Gwen, I swear to God-"

"Threaten her, and I will take your tongue as a souvenir," Nikolai growls, and heat rushes straight to my core. "Continue, love."

"Thank you." I beam. "I vote for a pinky finger, not too significant, but he'll miss it."

"I like the way you think, Kotik." Nikolai pulls a knife out of his back pocket, flipping it open. He looks at the hand he is currently twisting away from Venom's body, pressing the knife to the base of his pinky. He looks down at Venom with a nasty grin. "This may hurt a tad bit, mate."

The alleyway fills with the screams of Venom, and I think I am in love with a psycho.

Venom shakes in the fetal position, vibrating from the pain as he holds his bleeding hand. Nikolai looks at me with a mischievous smile, with the pinky in his hand. "For you, Kotik."

"How romantic," I deadpan. "Normally, men get me diamonds and dinner first."

Nikolai throws the pinky away as far from Venom as possible. "Those men are carbon copies of each other. At least you will remember my name," he teases.

A smirk dances on my face. I cross my right arm under my chest and placing an inquisitive finger on my chin. "I'm sorry, what's your name again?"

He laughs in his low voice as he grabs my hand, kisses it, and whispers, "My name is yours if you want it to be."

My cheeks heat up, and electricity sparks where his lips connect with my skin. There is no reason for one man to be so sexy and smooth with eyes that make me so weak in the knees. The smirk he gives me while he looks at me through his eyelashes will end me.

"Jeez, you're too much of a charmer for your own good."

The laughter that rumbles through his chest causes me to catch my breath, wishing to hear the sound again and again. "And you are too beautiful for your own good. A girl like you should be throwing the tips, not dancing for them."

I pop my hip to the right, my nails wrapping around my hip. "What? You didn't like my dancing?"

Nikolai's eyes heat, his tongue poking out to brush over his lower lip before poking his inner left cheek and looking away.

"Oh my God, do you think I am a bad dancer?"

Nikolai's hand loops around my waist, his hand spreading over my lower back, pulling me into his chest. The motion startles me and I drop the beer bottle. The scent of leather and fresh rain invades my senses. His eyes flutter to my lips, the boyish smirk spreading across his lips before he makes eye contact with my breathless body. "No, my love, I love your dancing." His voice lowers. "I just would rather you do it in private for me."

I can't breathe. I can't think, not with Nikolai this close, and for the first time since the fourth grade, I fucking stutter. "W-well, i-if you wanted a d-dance. All you had to do was ask." *Jesus. Fuck. Get it together, Gwendolyn.*

His nose grazes mine. "Dance for me."

"When?" He slides his phone into my hand.

"Tomorrow. Let me take you out and show you the lifestyle you're supposed to be living." My mouth parts mindlessly, and I gather all the shallow breaths I possibly can as I type my number into his phone.

"Pick me up at 8," I say. Nikolai lets me go, and I immediately feel the chill of the night consume me.

He winks at me, not even checking if I gave him my real number, the cocky bastard.

3

NIKOLAI

Gwen, my little hellcat, stands in a thin, skin-tight black dress adorned with sparkles in the bay window of the little two-bedroom house she and her grandmother Rose live in.

I am supposed to be here at 8, but I can't help myself from getting here early when all I could think about was her ass in that sparkly emerald green lingerie set with fishnets and neck-breaking heels.

She looked magnificent as she stood in an alley, with a cracked beer bottle in her hand and mouth too sharp for her own good.

If she talked to me the way she spoke to half of the guys in that club, I'd have her writhing over my knee, her perfect bottom stained with my handprint as she begged for me to fill that filthy mouth of hers with my cock. I smile at the image of her big hazel eyes, almost brimming with tears, so turned on and frustrated with me that she curses my name, and I, in turn, punish her for it.

I bet she's a brat. *Fuck.* I adjust myself in my slacks as I stare at her, continuing to mess with her curly hair. She keeps fluffing her black curls, spilling down her back in spirals. They are more airy and free than they were at the club, swaying along her spine as she smiles at herself in the mirror. I keep flexing my hand in and out, waiting to thread my fingers in her hair and pull her into me.

I've wanted to run my hands along the curve of her waist, grip her hips, and make her feel what she has done to me since I saw her dancing. She had every man's eyes on her. Every man was fixing their cocks in their pants. Every man under her siren song, like the little minx she is.

She could be a modern-day Cleopatra, have men killing themselves just for a moment in her presence, and I could be her Caesar, but then I heard our modern-day Cleo speak, and she spoke like a warrior.

Men fawned over her, and she kept them where they belonged, kissing at her feet, so of course, when I saw that fucker try to rape her, I took his pinky. Fuck, I would have taken his life if she asked, but Gwen is a merciful queen.

I look at the time again: 7:55, which is early but a respectable early. I slide out of my Rolls Royce, adjust my suit jacket, and grab the bouquet of pink roses because Gwen texted me that *I better not be fucking unoriginal* and bring red. Bringing pink was a minor submission, anticipating when I had her on her knees begging for me.

I knock on the peeling white door. A pair of wide eyes and the slick smirk of an old lady greet me.

"Oh my." She fans her face, her eyes roaming over my body as I flash my most parent-friendly smile. "You must be Nikolai."

"Yes, ma'am," I say, kissing Nana Rose's hand. "And you must be Nana Rose?"

I wink at her, and a warm smile spreads on her wrinkled face. A gasp leaves her lips. "Oh." She points at me with her other hand. "You're good. I bet you're a charmer."

"Not as much as your granddaughter." I rise, smiling as she turns her body to the side, letting me into the small living area.

"Well, she got it from me!" Nana Rose claps. "Back in the day, I was a brick house. That's old lady talk for I was the shit."

"I bet you were," I laugh as Nana Rose's slippers click past me.

"Oh, I got the pictures to prove it! But make yourself at home while I see what's taking her so long." I nod, looking around the living room, cast in the soft glow of an aged lamp in the corner. From down the hallway, I hear Nana Rose call out, "Gwen, that man is fine, and he is waiting! Don't keep good-looking waiting!"

I look around, my curiosity about Gwen only growing as I take in more of her house. A pink and cream flower couch and a worn wooden coffee table adorned with colorful delicate lace doily sit in the room's center.

I roam over to a weathered brown bookshelf peeling tan against the far wall, its shelves filled with an eclectic mix of novels and a family photo of Gwen as a child sitting on the lap of a smiling man with a salt n' pepper mustache. I pick up the image, focusing on Gwen's wide, toothy smile.

"Well, shoot. If I knew you were going to go snooping, I would have told Nana to leave you outside." Gwen's snort breaks me out of the trance of the photo.

I return the frame and remark, "Consequences for keeping me waiting." When I turn around, her hazel eyes are hooded, her pink lips are glossed and slightly apart in a smile, and her hands are holding a small clutch in front of her.

She whispers, "Are there always consequences with you?"

Nana Rose comes back in, a slight squeal leaving her lips. "You brought flowers!" I hand them to Nana Rose as Gwen peaks at the bouquet with a smug smile.

"Pink?" Gwen questions.

"You said no red," I counter.

"And they are beautiful!" Nana Rose smacks Gwen's arm, narrowing her eyes at her before smiling at me. "I am going to put these in water."

As Nana Rose walks away, Gwen steps forward. The scent of coconuts and jasmine invades my senses. I swallow dryly, my eyes roaming over her now that she is in front of me. "Are you going to answer my question?" I arch my eyebrow, looking down at her. "You said that your snooping was the consequence for keeping you waiting, so I asked, are there always consequences with you?"

"Only when earned." I wink. She gives me a mischievous smirk, taking another step forward.

"Did I earn one?" she whispers breathlessly.

"I don't know, can you follow directions?" Gwen raises an eyebrow, challenging me.

"*You* can follow directions; thank you for the *pink* roses." Her lips pop on the letter p in pink as she wiggles her eyebrows.

"I follow directions very well," I purr, pushing a curl behind her ear, watching the blush rise to her cheeks. "That's why I rarely have consequences, but the question was: can you follow directions?"

She shrugs, giving me her faux innocent eyes. "Depends on the direction." *Oh, so my little hell cat wants to play a game of chicken.*

I lick my lips. "Spin for me."

"What?" Her eyes widen, and she looks around the room.

"You said you would dance for me privately." I lean over to whisper in her ear, "So do it."

"I am not dancing for you with my nana in the other room." Her voice and eyes are firm as she pushes back, but when she places her right hand on her hip, my smugness reappears.

"I am not asking for my dance yet." I bend over so I am at eye-level with the scowl she dawns on her lips. "Just a taste, or don't tell me," I almost brush my lips against hers, whispering, "you're a brat who can't take directions."

Gwen's nostrils flare, but her eyes dart to the doorway her grandmother walked down in excitement. She takes a small breath, and I lean back, watching as she crosses one of her strappy black heels in front of the other and quickly turns. When she looks at me again, she pulls her lips into a smug grin. "There. Are you happy?"

"No." Her brows furrow, but before she can protest, I whisper, "Slower."

"Nikolai!" she huffs.

"Call me Nik." I take a step back to see her whole body easily. "And I said slower."

Gwen bites her lip nervously, looking at the doorway again, but when her eyes land on me, they sparkle with determination. She crosses her heel over the other again, turning slowly, and I smirk, admiring how beautiful she looks tonight.

She's stunning in that tight strapless sparkle long dress, the slight slit in the back teasing at what lies beneath. Her big black curls tumble down her back, framing her face in a way that makes me want to mess them up. Those pink glossy lips, smoky eyes—everything about her is intoxicating.

Her eyes cautiously make contact with mine again, and she crosses her arms behind her back, accentuating her chest, as she sways from side to side. "So?"

"Fuck, you are gorgeous, Kotik." She blushes, looking away from me. I lean in again, my breath fluttering over the shell of her ear. "Tonight is going to be fun."

4

GWEN

Nik bought out an Italian restaurant in town. The *best* Italian restaurant in town. This guy is rich, and I mean stupid rich. I mean so rich that the only other person in this restaurant is our waiter and the chef who both jump at the slightest movement from Nikolai.

I mean I should have known from the Rolls Royce or the fact that this guy sits in front of me in an Armani suit tailored to perfection over his muscular body, and despite the smooth, velvety rumble of his Russian accent, he speaks Italian to all the staff. He doesn't let me order; instead, he tells me he knows what I would like as if he didn't meet me yesterday. So hot, dominant, multilingual, rich guy casually takes me out to dinner. *Great.*

I twist in my seat in my dress drop shipped from Amazon and nibble on my bottom lip.

The waiter takes away our second course; Nik leans forward, placing both elbows on the table, his right fist in his left open palm, raising an eyebrow. "Kotik, what's wrong?"

I clear my throat. "Nothing, I-I just-" I point to the room around us. "I wasn't expecting all of this for a first date. What are you going to do for our second? Fly me to Mars?"

"No, but what do you think about Rome?" He reaches to grab my hand, but I pull back.

I scoff, "I was joking."

"I wasn't." He fixes the napkin on his lap, and I lean forward, splaying my fingertips in the middle of the table.

"Nikolai-"

"Nik," he corrects, and the firmness of his correction makes me swallow and cross my legs from the heat.

"Nik, this is insane. Are you a secret billionaire?" I whisper, looking around.

He laughs, leaning forward and lowering his voice. "Something like that."

"You're either from old money, a tycoon, Jeff Bezos's secret child, or a criminal." I cross my arms under my breast. His eyes flicker to them, dazed with lust and sin. I flick my wrist, gesturing to the table, my mind running with the possibilities of this man. "Which is it?"

"Kotik-"

"What does that even mean?" I snap at how he purrs the name as if to distract me, and boy, he could distract me if he wanted.

"Little cat." His lips spread in amusement. I rub my thighs together, looking around.

"You think of me as a cat?" He leans forward, his hand gripping the seat of my chair, as he pulls me closer to him. My eyes flutter at the invasion of his fresh rain scent, and he groans.

“I think of you always, ever since I last saw you.”

The smooth caress of his voice makes me cross my thighs tighter, and he growls in my ear.

“Why are you fidgeting so much, Kotik?” His fingers trail from my calf, over my knee, and along the outer thigh of my crossed leg. “Do I make you uncomfortable?”

I do not dare look at him; instead, I shake my head no. “Use your words.”

“No,” I gasp. Nik grips my dress in his fist, a smile spreading on his lips. I don’t have to look at him to feel the curve of his smile against the shell of my ear.

“Good girl.” My breath catches in my throat. Nik pulls the dress up slowly, allowing his breath to feather over my heating skin. “Now, explain why you fidget in your seat so much?”

“I was not fidgeting in my seat,” I whisper breathlessly. Nik tsks at me, tightly gripping my exposed thigh.

“Liar.” I twist to look at him but freeze once his fingertips start to caress my inner thigh, closer and closer to my core. I shift in my seat, my eyes darting around nervously as I try to pull at the hem of my dress, but Nikolai lightly smacks my hand away, a smirk playing on his lips as he watches me.

“Nik, what if the staff see us?” My voice is more breathy than I intended. I swivel my head to look around the restaurant again; Nik pinches my chin and makes me look at him.

"Relax, Gwen," he murmurs, his voice low and soothing. "No one's going to notice."

I bite my lip, heat running up my neck and blossoming over my cheeks. "But what if they do?"

Nikolai chuckles, and the sound sends goosebumps across my skin. "Then we deal with it. Besides, I can tell this turns you on." His breath feathers over the column of my neck. "Doesn't it, Kotik?"

My heart pounds in my chest; all I can hear is ringing in my ears and the crescendo of my heavy breathing. I bite my bottom lip trying to stifle the moan coming out of my lips. My eyes flicker down Nik's face from the swirl of his blue eyes to his pink lips.

"Answer me, Kotik. You like being played with in public, don't you?"

"I like it," I gasp barely above a whisper. His nails dig into my inner thighs, and my legs fall open. I can't believe he is touching me like this in public. I can't believe I am just letting him. The closer he gets to my core, the wetter I am, and fuck, I have never been so turned on.

Nikolai's eyes darken with desire as he pushes my dress around my waist, almost leaving me bare.

"Good," he says, his thumb stroking my inner thigh. "Because I have plans for you tonight."

"What are you thinking?" I ask, my voice trembling with anticipation.

My breathing shallows at the heat of his touch. The way his eyes shine when they land on mine makes my mouth dry. He wants me, and I want to give him all of me. I want him to touch me in ways I have only imagined.

Shit. I can't tell him I'm a virgin right now, not while his hands run up my body and search for more of me. Not while his eyes turn so dark they look like the depths of the sea. Not while he is growling as if there will never be enough.

"W-what are you planning for me tonight?"

Nikolai's smirk widens as he leans in closer, his lips brushing against my ear. "I'm thinking about how much I want to taste you," he whispers, sending a shiver down my spine. "How much I want to feel you come apart under my touch."

My cheeks flush with heat as I imagine his fingers exploring my body, teasing me until I can't take it anymore. "Nik-"

"Mi scusi, signore, è pronto per il prossimo piatto?" My eyes widen, and my breath catches in my throat as the waiter clears our appetizers.

Despite the waiter clearing his throat, Nik doesn't take his eyes off me, steadily drawing circles on my inner right thigh. He leans in towards me, his lips grazing along my jaw as he whispers against my flushed cheeks, "What do you think, Kotik? Should I have him bring the next course?"

Nik's fingers graze along the thin barrier of my black lace thong. He hisses once he feels how soaked I am through my underwear. My cheeks burn in embarrassment as he presses his finger against the wet spot.

"Kotik, unless you want him to watch you cum which will force me to pluck out his eyes, I'd advise you to tell him no."

I want to speak, but my voice is caught in the back of my throat as his pointer finger slides up to put pressure on the bundle of nerves between my legs. I shake my head no and let Nik's chuckle roll over me. Without stopping the small circles he draws on my clit, he speaks to the waiter with an amused grin.

"Non tornare qui dentro finché non te lo dico io o perderai la vita."

The waiter shoots up straighter than before, saying quickly, "Sì, signore," as he escapes.

My heart pounds in my chest as I glance around the room for any more prying eyes, but all I see is the escaping waiter, a tray of appetizers balanced expertly in his hands. I watch him disappear into the kitchen, the tension in my body easing slightly, and I relax enough to let a moan roll from my lips. Nik moves my panties to the side, presses his thumb back to the sensitive bundle between my legs, and rubs his pointer finger along my slit.

"W-what are you touching?" I whimper, my thighs fighting to close.

Nik slaps my thighs, the sharp pain running right to my core. "Kotik, don't tell me you don't know what your clit is?"

The amusement is so clear in his throat I want to smack it off, but the rush of need silences my annoyance. I mean I know about sex. I know how it all works on a logical level, penis, vagina, hymen, all simple, but this fire shooting through me? The way my body is just dripping with a primal need from more? No, I did not know anything like this existed. I shake my head no, pulling my bottom lip into my mouth.

"Kotik," he purrs. "My naughty little kitty never had someone make her feel good. I bet I am the first man who's made you this wet."

I push my pelvis forward, wanting to feel his finger inside me press harder on my clit. A pulsing in my stomach clenches with a need for something more, like this small touch isn't enough and I want more. I shudder against him as his finger grazes my opening.

"Don't tease, asshole," I gasp. Nik's nose grazes my neck.

"Such a dirty mouth." Nik removes his hand from my dripping pussy and sticks two fingers inside his mouth. His eyes drop and his Adam's apple bobs. I can't catch my breath. He looks like every woman's wet dream sucking my juices into his mouth. "Kotik, you're so fucking sweet, like candy."

"Nik," I gasp, my voice barely audible. I can't take the teasing, the things he is saying and the danger that anyone can walk in and see what we are doing at any minute. "If you are going to do it, do it."

Nikolai sharply slaps down on my pussy, light enough to elicit pleasure but firm enough to make me jump in my seat. "You are so bossy when you're needy, baby."

He rubs down firmly on my clit, causing my deep groan to fill the dining area. His fingers continue to punish me, encouraged by my ever-growing wetness. I arch my hips, desperate for more, but he holds back, teasing me with his touch. I don't even realize my eyes are closed until he growls for me to open them.

"Open your eyes, Gwen," he says, his voice firm yet gentle. "I want to see your reaction."

I obey, despite the pleasure building. All I want to do is buck against his hand and throw my head back, eyes closed, but I obey. I can't say no to him when he says things in that tone. I can't say no when he has me in a position I've never been in before. My eyes flutter open to meet his gaze.

His eyes almost look midnight under his scorching gaze, and my breath comes in short, ragged gasps as I feel his two fingers slide inside of me. He fills me completely, and I moan, my head falling back as I surrender to his will. His fingers stroke my insides, pushing me closer to the edge.

"Please," I beg, and I never fucking beg for anything, but when he slowly fucks me with one finger inside of me and his thumb drawing small circles on my already overly sensitive clit, I can't do anything else but beg for him. For release. For more. "Don't tease me. I need to...I need to..."

"What, baby?" His deep baritone rolls over the shell of my ear, making me shudder. "What do you need to do?"

"I need you," I whimper, my nerves killing my need to ask for my release.

Nikolai's eyes darken with lust as he leans closer, his lips brushing against my ear once more. "You have me."

With the flick of my clit, the dam breaks. My body convulses under the crashing orgasm, rolling over me like a tidal wave. I bite down on my lip to muffle the sounds, but it is futile. The pleasure is too intense, too all-consuming. I have never given myself an orgasm like this, never crashed into a thousand pieces like this before. Nik holds me up so I can make eye contact with him.

"Good girl," he praises softly, a wide smile on his face. Nik lazily fingers me through as I come down.

Once my body stops trembling, his fingers withdraw, and he quickly shoves them both in his mouth, his eyes never leaving mine.

"Mmm, you taste even sweeter after you've cum." Nik leans over and smooths my dress back down, and without missing a beat, he snaps his fingers twice to get our waiter's attention. "Now, let's finish our dinner."

For the rest of dinner, Nik feeds me after he leaves me too dazed to eat the most amazing bolognese I have tried, and he laughs when I timidly say thank you. It unnerves me how eagerly I accept each bite from Nik's fork. I've never allowed anyone to feed me before, yet here I am, demurely opening my mouth like some lovestruck teenager. I could almost scream at myself for how stupid I must look.

When dessert is served, I finally regain my ability to breathe evenly, and I grab my own fork and gasp, "Tiramisu? How did you know all my favorites tonight?"

"A little research does wonders, don't you think?" Nik winks, lifting his glass of whiskey to his lips.

I pause mid-cut of my tiramisu, eyeing Nik suspiciously. "You did research on me?"

His lips curl into a smirk. "I told you I'd show you the life you deserve. Had to know what I'm working with, didn't I?" He leans back, swirling his whiskey. "Come on, don't tell me you didn't try to dig up dirt on me."

"Oh, I had to," I retort, savoring a bite of dessert. "I met you in an alley. For all I knew, you could've been a serial killer with great hair."

Nik's laugh is rich and deep, sending an involuntary shiver down my spine. He licks a spot of cream from the corner of his mouth, and I catch myself staring. "So," he says, leaning forward on his elbows, eyes glinting mischievously, "what did you find?"

I tap my fork against my lips, feigning nonchalance. "Well, you have one sister - gorgeous, by the way - and a brother. Though weird, I couldn't find any pictures of him after age five."

"It means he's doing his job." Nik winks when I raise an eyebrow. "What else did you uncover?"

"Nothing," I admit with a shrug. "You're a ghost."

"Or," he counters, "you don't know where to look."

I lean in closer, unable to resist the challenge sparkling in his eyes. "Oh? And where should I be looking?"

"That's not fair if I tell you. Besides, a man needs his secrets."

"So does a woman, but clearly, you know where to find all my secrets. So spill."

"I learned you were raised by your father, Randolph, and Nana Rose. Riverside High valedictorian, top of your class at Georgetown in criminal law until..." He pauses, his tone softening slightly. "Your father disappeared. Now you're at the Midnight Howl, paying off...something."

I whistle, impressed and unsettled. "Wow, you've got my whole transcript. Should I be flattered or creeped out?"

"Both?" He winks. "I also know your best friend is Kelsey - pre-K buddies, cute - and your last boyfriend was that sleazeball Jacob. Gotta say, dumping Fireball on his head? Brutal, but brilliant."

I can't help but laugh at the memory. "He had it coming. So, I'm guessing you also discovered my love for Italian cuisine?"

Nik's smile turns softer. "That was a hunch. Your grandmother went to culinary school, specializing in Italian. I figured some of that passion might have rubbed off."

I stare at my empty plate, my stomach turning like a storm. Part of me knows I should be terrified by how much he knows. But another part - a part that's growing stronger by the minute - is intrigued, even excited.

Looking up, I meet Nik's gaze head-on. "Well, Mr. Detective, you've certainly done your homework. But trust me, you've barely scratched the surface."

His eyes light up at the challenge. "Is that so? Well then, tell me something I don't know."

I curve my lips into a smile, and let the words run off my tongue before I can think twice about it. "I'm a virgin."

Nik's smile falters for a moment, a shadow passing over his eyes. He leans back in his chair, studying me intently.

"Being with me might not be what you expect," he begins, his voice low and serious. "If we were to...go further, I might not be able to stop myself. And I don't want to hurt you."

I feel a shiver run down my spine at his words, but I move to the edge of my seat, not breaking eye contact. "Who said you can hurt me?"

Nik smiles with his teeth, a gloriously scary occurrence that makes me want to run as much as it makes me want to rub my thighs together. "Kotik, I could break you into pieces."

My breath catches in my throat, but I thrive on the suffocation and keep pushing him for more, a phenomenon that only occurs when he looks at me as if he knows everything about me. Despite every fiber of my being telling me to run.

I look him in the eyes and say, "Try me."

5

NIKOLAI

The night I've planned for Gwen is perfect. She's perfect. My perfect little virgin.

How the hell did a girl this beautiful, with that mouth and a knack for drawing in danger, stay a virgin for so fucking long? Maybe that's why she has that type of mouth on her. No one has taught her how to properly use it.

I would teach her all the ways to properly use that lethal tongue of hers. My cock throbbed just at the thought. Fuck, it's been so long since I've wanted someone so bad. She was so tight while I was fucking her with my fingers and so beautiful as she came apart. When I have her on my cock later, she is going to feel fucking divine, because she will be mine, all mine.

As we leave the restaurant, I can't help but steal glances at her. The soft glow of the streetlights catches in the curls of her hair, illuminating her features in a way that takes my breath away. I've met countless beautiful women in my line of work, but Gwen? She's in a league of her own, even with her hair a little frizzy from the sweat of her cumming. She looks fucking radiant and sexy with the smell of sex on her.

I open the passenger side to my car. Her eyes beam a bright gold as she slides in and I run to enter the driver's side.

"So, Mr. Mysterious," she says, a playful lilt in her voice. "What's next on this grand tour of yours?"

"How do you feel about dancing?"

"Dancing?" She giggles.

"Yeah, a little jazz club on Wilson."

Gwen, with those mesmerizing hazel eyes, leans over, her hand lightly grazing the curve of my neck, sending a jolt of electricity through me. "I like dancing, but I thought after what you did in the restaurant, you would want me all to yourself."

Her other hand glides across my thigh, edging ever closer to the growing bulge in my pants. "There will be more than enough time for that after—"

Before I could finish, Gwen's hand strokes the bulge in my jeans. I suck in a sharp breath, my grip on the steering wheel tightening. The car swerves slightly, caught off guard by the sudden surge of adrenaline.

"Gwen, what are you doing?" I speak through my gritted teeth.

"Just repaying the favor for earlier," she whispers, her hand firmly in place.

I take a deep breath and try to focus on the road as she teases me. My little hell cat giving me a taste of my own medicine, and it is fucking delicious. She cautiously zips down my pants and pulls out my throbbing cock.

"Do you even know what you're doing, Kotik?" I tease.

Her hand can barely fit around my cock, a scoff escaping her lips. "Nik, that is not going to fit...anywhere."

I chuckle, one hand curling up the side of her face and running across her jaw. "Don't worry, Kotik. You were made for me."

My fingertips massage the back of her head. Her fingers grip tight around me, but it is nothing compared to her mouth wrapping around me. Shit, she's so warm. So wet. So fucking made for me.

Gwen's lips envelop me, causing me to grip the steering wheel tightly as the city becomes a blur of lights and sounds around us like a kaleidoscope. "God," I hissed, quickly changing lanes to exit the highway.

Her lips are dangerously soft, her tongue teasing and tormenting in equal measure. I bite back a groan, my hands trembling on the wheel as I navigate the chaotic streets.

"Fuck, Gwen," I manage to gasp, my voice barely audible over the hum of the engine and the distant honks of traffic.

She pulls back, her eyes locking onto mine, a sexy smirk on her lips, and for a moment, everything else fades away. I can't remember when a woman made me feel like this. "Change of plans," I say, my voice steady despite the lazy stroking of her hand. "We're going to my hotel."

Gwen's lips curve into a knowing smile, her hand still working its magic as she leans back in her seat and spreads her legs. Her eyes never leave mine.

I speed up the car, weaving through traffic as I try to make it to my hotel before I bust. Her strokes come in slow, and she squeezes the base of my cock. I damn near see fucking stars. I grab Gwen's wrist. Her eyes bulge, but I ease her nerves by kissing her palm. "When I cum, it will be in your pretty little pussy, understand?"

Gwen bites her glossy lips, a shit-eating smile spreading across them. "Yes, sir," she teases.

"Kotik, don't test me," I growl, white-knuckling the steering wheel.

The car's engine roars as I push it to its limits; every second feels like an eternity. The anticipation is killing me - the thought of having Gwen writhing beneath me, desperate for my touch - I could hardly fucking contain myself.

She sits next to me, her hands roaming over her body, over the curve of her breast, down her stomach, and hovering over her soaked panties. "Gwen, if you touch yourself, you will be over my knee the minute we get upstairs," I growl, and she giggles.

This fucking girl laughs in my face after watching me cut off a man's pinky when most men, without seeing what I am truly capable of, fall to their knees and stutter, but Gwen? She openly defies me and thinks my anger is laughable.

"Promise, cutie?" she moans, her fingers rubbing her slit through her panties. Her eyes light up before becoming hooded. I can feel my heart pounding in my chest, my breath growing heavier with each pass of her thumb over her clit.

I park my car outside the dimly lit hotel. My breathing becomes heavier by the second as I cut off the engine and look over at Gwen teasing herself. My hand itches to be on her body. I watch her rub her pointer over her folds, and she sucks the bottom lip I want in my mouth into hers.

Her lips part and a small whimper escapes them. I curl my hands into a fist to stop myself from running my hands through her hair. Her eyes land on mine, a fury of desire from the edging she keeps doing to herself. I look at the valet attendant, who is contemplating whether or not he should knock on my window to take my keys, and signal for him to come closer.

"Nik?" she sings. Her other hand follows the curves up her body, but I grab her wrist before she can cup her breast.

I whisper between heavy breaths, "Do you have a safe word, Kotik?"

Finally, she sits up and stops rubbing her fingers over her pussy. *Thank God.* "A safe word?"

My lips curve into a smile. "A word that will make me stop, no matter what."

"Umm. No, I don't have one. Do I need one?"

"With you," my eyes outline the curves of her body, "looking like that. Yeah, you need a safe word."

She takes a deep breath, looking around, but her gaze avoids mine. My thumb runs along the side of her wrist, and I try to gently talk, but her nickname comes out like a growl, "Kotik."

"I'm thinking." She places her other hand flat on her thigh, pressing her fingertips into the fabric of her dress. I watch her for a moment, focusing on the flex of her hand and my deep breaths. "Okay," she whispers, "Pickles."

"Pickles?" I smirk.

"I hate them. They gross me out so...I would never think about them during," she shrugs, her ears turning bright red as she points between the two of us, "ya' know."

Her innocence, the way she acts as if she wasn't cursing me out ten minutes ago or didn't threaten a man's life with a broken bottle a day ago, turns me on so much my cock beads with precum. This girl with her naughty mouth and need to be corrupted will be the fucking end of me, I swear.

I tuck my cock back into my pants. "Go to the penthouse."

"What? You're not coming with me?"

Her eyebrows furrow, and her bottom lip slides from between her teeth into a pout. *Jesus Christ, what is she doing to me?* I release her wrist and dig my nails into the palm of my hand to keep myself from dragging her over the middle console onto my lap and bite her lip until she screams.

"Nik?" she snaps.

I take out my phone and text security that a girl with big black curls and a sparkle dress will be rushing inside and under no circumstance should anyone stop her.

"You need to make your way upstairs before I fuck you in this car and then kill that valet boy for seeing you naked. Is that what you want, Gwen? You want me to take your virginity on top of a fucking corpse?"

Her body goes bone straight, her eyes wide like a doe, and she slowly shakes her head no, reaching to unbuckle her seatbelt.

"Good girl." I lean back, crossing my hands over the painful tent of my cock and close my eyes. "Now run your little ass all the way to the top. Don't let me catch you."

6

NIKOLAI

I've never felt this way about anyone, and trust me, I'm no stranger to women, but something about Gwen - the way she controlled me in that car, the way she obeyed me in the restaurant, the ways she combats me at every turn - it turned me on in ways I never knew possible. It makes me want to possess her, make her mine.

I can't control myself with her, but I must learn to. The future king of the Russian Mafia can't be brought to his knees by a woman, not even a wickedly sexy woman like Gwen. I take measured steps towards the penthouse, surely giving her a hefty head start because the idea of anyone but me seeing Gwen naked makes me trigger happy.

As I enter my hotel, guards nod silently at me and nod in the direction of my squealing kitty. I walk over to the elevator; the one on the right shows she already made it to the top. A smirk tugs at the corner of my cheeks, because my smart little kitty probably thinks she made it, that she's safe. But baby girl is so wrong.

I press the button for the second elevator and lean against the far wall once I enter, the coolness of the metal walls easing the heat in my skin.

This is my Kotik's first time. A part of me is screaming that I have to be gentle, or as gentle as I can be, because no one should be fucked the way I like to on their first time. Another part of me is telling me I could fuck her the way I want and mold her pussy to my cock, make so that she never wants to fuck another because nothing will feel as good as me.

The elevator doors open and Gwen is standing in front of the door of the penthouse looking for a key in the dirt of a plant in the hallway. She has already slipped off her heels and is kneeling on the floor, just the way I wanted her. I exit the elevator and slowly start to clap.

"Congratulations, you saved that valet boy's life."

"I should send him a fruit basket." She rolls her eyes and shakes the dirt off her hands.

I stalk down the hallway towards her and she gets off her knees. She tries to slip away, but my hand is already curving around her waist, pulling her into my chest.

"I couldn't find the key. Do I at least get a consolation prize?"

"I'll only make one of your ass cheeks red."

Her breath catches in her throat as I press my thumb into the scanner next to the door. "No fair, there was no key."

I push us inside the penthouse, already zipping her dress down. My fingers graze her bare back, and I groan in her ear. "No bra?"

She holds the dress with one hand, as I snake my hand around her to open the door, shaking her head no. "Didn't go with the dress."

I slam the door shut behind me with a growl and turn Gwen around so that her back rests against it; her hazel eyes shine golden with desire. I cup her face in my hands, tracing her lips with my fingers before capturing them in a biting kiss.

Her lips part, allowing my tongue access to her warm, sweet mouth. I devour her, hungry for her taste, needing more of her. She melts under my tongue, moaning in my mouth. *Fuck me.* I've never been kissed like this either. My hands slide down her body, gripping her waist as I lift her onto the entryway room table.

"God, Nik," she moans, spreading her legs wide so I can stand between them.

I pull away from her lips, kissing down her neck. "I love it when you say my name, Kotik. It should be the only word you ever say again."

Unable to resist tearing off the barrier of her dress any longer, with a swift yank, I tear the dress from her body, leaving her standing before me in nothing but her back lace thong and high heels, her chest heaving.

I take a step back and admire her, and she closes her thighs demurely, heat rushing to her cheeks, and I can't help but groan at the sight of her, the way her eyes meet mine. "Kotik, you will be the death of me."

She looks at me through her eyelashes. "That good, huh?"

"You're kidding me? How did a girl like you, with a body like that, stay a virgin for so fucking long?" I lightly pull Gwen's legs open again and step between them.

"I would never let anyone get this far," she breathes heavily, stars in her eyes. "I guess I was waiting on you."

The smile that spreads across my face is feral. Gwen whimpers softly, arching into my touch as I trail my fingers down the smooth skin of her back.

"Kotik, I may have to kill every other man who saw you like this before me."

I can feel her pulse quicken under my kiss, but she moves her hips into me, and I trail my fingers along her chest, pinching her nipples.

"You don't have to kill anyone. It's only been you."

I smirk and take one swollen peak in my mouth, sucking hard and rolling it with my tongue, hearing her gasp and feeling her fingers digging into my shoulders.

She groans. "I may have to kill every woman who has ever had your tongue before."

"I will write you a list," I mumble against her nipple.

My hands move lower, sliding under the lace of her thong, feeling her heat through the thin fabric. She sighs quietly, and I know she's ready for me. I thread my fingers in the delicate lace and rip them in half, revealing her wet, pink center.

"I'll buy you another pair," I growl, staring at my new salvation, my Kotik's pussy. The sight of her swollen clit glistening with her juices pushes me further, making me desperate to feel her come undone beneath me.

Gwen's body trembles under my touch. The sounds that come out of her make all other music pale in comparison. I just want to hear her moans again and again. My tongue slides across her slick folds, tasting her sweetness.

"You're so wet, Gwen," I whisper, my voice thick with arousal. "I can't wait to feel you around me, baby."

My hand reaches up, tracing gentle circles around her nipples, eliciting soft mewls from her. I press two fingers inside her, curving up, the tips of my finger gliding along her barrier. "Nik," she whispers.

"Shh, baby, just let me."

Her walls pulse around my fingers, begging for more as I continue to press forward. The tip of my tongue traces her clit, causing her to jolt up, her hips bucking against my face. I push my fingers inside her fully, feeling the barrier that separates her virginity from her new world, my world. I pause, my fingers stilling inside her as I watch her eyes squeeze shut as she waits for the pain.

I start to kiss up her inner thigh and whisper, "Gwen, look at me."

"No. It's going to hurt."

"You mean it's going to hurt like this?" I shush her, biting her inner thigh lightly. She hisses and her core tightens around my fingers. "Or is it going to hurt like this?" I lightly smack her clit.

"Nikolai," Gwen hisses, and I bite her thigh again.

"Gwen, I doubt it will hurt more than this." I flip her around, pulling my fingers out of her and pulling her ass into the air. "Don't I owe you a punishment?"

"Punishment for what?!" Gwen huffs, looking back at me, her neck flushed with red and her lips pink from her biting on them.

I run her arousal all over her plump ass and tap her thigh lightly. "I believe I told you not to touch yourself in my car."

"You made me cum in a restaurant." I smack her ass harder, reveling in the yelp from her lips and the vibration that rings through the room from the impact of my hand on her ass.

"Yes, and I should be the only one who makes you cum, Kotik." Gwen's eyes widen, but I keep a firm grip on her ass. I gather her hair in one hand and gently tug it, pulling her head back to expose her bare neck. "Remember your safe word."

"Nik-" I squeeze her ass, and she yelps.

"Safe word," I command, palming her ass.

"Pickles."

"Good girl." I raise my hand, quickly bringing my palm down, connecting with her ass. The sound of the slap slices through the air.

Gwen yelps. "Fuck!"

"Now how about we do three more? Seems like a good enough punishment for me." I fix myself behind her reddening ass.

"Fuck you," Gwen snarls.

"Well, kitty, don't get ahead of yourself. We're almost there." I smile.

I raise my hand again, watching the tremble in her thighs as she anticipates the next blow. This time more forceful, I strike Gwen's ass with a sharp crack. The heat from her skin sears my palm. I can't help but smile as I watch my smack leave a bright red mark.

"Blyad!" I cuss, rubbing my hand over her blossoming ass. She leans back into my touch, finding comfort in the small kindness I offer. "Now, Gwen, do you like being a naughty little kitty?"

A devilish smile crosses her lips, but she purrs, "No."

I pinch her ass. "Liar."

My hand descends once more; she cries out, her body arching with the strike. My lips graze the back of her neck, whispering, "You are mine, Gwen. No one else's. And I am the only one who gives you pleasure, isn't that right?"

I watch as her spine straightens, her ass cheek still red from my latest spank. "Yes, Nik."

"Good kitty," I say, my voice low. "Now, let's see about this aching pussy." I pinch her throbbing clit.

Kneeling before her, I can't help but marvel at the sight of her glistening pussy, beckoning me. My fingers trace the outline of her swollen lips, and I feel her trembling, yet so driven by desire she is offering herself to me. "Look at my good little kitty offering herself to me."

With my lips now in sight of her pussy, I dive in. I lash my tongue against her clit, causing her to cry out. My fingers join the dance, slowly entering her aching pussy.

She moans, her body bucking against my touch, as her fingers run through my hair, messing up the slick back hairstyle. My fingers graze against her barrier again, but this time when I pause and look up at her, she is staring at me, her eyes shining gold like she is the first stop to salvation, and I, a sinner, have come to worship at her altar.

"Make me yours, Nik," she whispers. My entire world explodes. I can't breathe with her looking at me like that and saying what she knows I want to hear.

I dive back into her pussy, and with a slight push, I break through her barrier. She gasps, her eyes widening with a mix of pain and pleasure, and her fingers pull sharply at the strands of my hair.

"I got you, Kotik," I murmur against her folds as I lick her up, a mixture of honey and metallic. My skin feels on fire as I feast on her, and she swallows my fingers like I was always supposed to be inside of her.

Her hips buck against me, begging for more. I groan, feeling the rush of desire coursing through my veins, knowing that this is what I've been waiting for, the moment when our bodies become one. "That's my girl."

I pull her lips to mine, biting her bottom lip. She trembles and moans, but pulls away and mumbles against my lips, "It's not fair. I am naked, but you're still dressed."

"My apologies," I say as Gwen reaches for my suit jacket, her hands gliding over my shoulders as I shrug out of it. I waste no time with the rest of my clothing. Gwen's eyes roam over my body, licking her lips like a predator who just found its prey.

She should know by now that I am the apex predator. I scoop her up in my arms as she lets out a squeal.

"What are you doing?!" She giggles, twisting in my arms.

"Cleaning you up." I grip her ass, holding her in place against me. "I told you I would show you the life you've always deserved, so I am going to give you a bath. Treat you like my little princess."

Her cheeks flush to the delicious shade of red I love. Gwen mutters, "I'm more of a queen."

I kiss the top of her forehead. "My apologies, my queen."

I relish in the shiver that rips through her body and pull her in closer as I carry her to the bathroom.

Once we enter, I set her down on the black, marble toilet and I can run a hot bath. Gwen crosses her legs tightly and squirms as her juices run tacky down her thigh. She squirms, trying to hide her breast in her crossed arms and make herself smaller.

"You're absolutely beautiful like this, Gwen," I reassure her softly. "It's a sight I wish to witness every day. Do not hide yourself from me."

She looks up at me, her eyes a stormy mix of embarrassment, desire, and vulnerability. I tug at her arm, urging her to stand up and step towards the bathtub. She reluctantly rises, the gentle curve of her hips and the swell of her bottom on display just for me. I push away the swelling feeling of my cock and focus on the small smile on her lips.

"You really want to see me everyday?" she whispers. Adjusting the water temperature, I take some of the lavender bath salts from the counter and sprinkle it into the water.

I get in first and offer Gwen my hand. My eyes glaze up her body, and I lick my lips. "Every second of every day."

She takes it, face tinged with pink, and nestles her petite frame into my more built one. "You are such a flirt," she sighs.

"Only with you, Kotik," I mumble into her hair, inhaling the scent of cocoa butter and vanilla that seems to follow her everywhere.

We are back-to-chest, sitting in the tub. I take her thick curls and gather them to the side so I can mouth against her neck. The smell of her sweat slicked skin mixed with the lavender is intoxicating, and I kiss her there hard enough to bruise. My hands, previously limp against my side, run against the smooth expanse of her inner thighs and her breasts. She's so perfect. She rivals even statues of Aphrodite in museums. So perfect and all mine. I take one of her pert nipples and roll it in between my thumb and forefinger.

"Ngh—Nik, please." Her cheeks turn a pretty shade of pink that only rivals that of the plush shade of her pussy.

I lean back on the edge of the tub, my fingers hovering over her curves in the water. "Please what, Kotik?"

She spreads her legs as an answer. I raise my brow, laugh rumbling from deep within.

"You want to cum again from my fingers? How many times do you need to cum before the main event? So greedy kitten." My fingertips run up the outline of her inner thighs, and she switches slightly, a dark smile on her lips.

"I—no! Just clean me like you said you would." Her bottom lip slides between her teeth in the pouty way that makes me want to slip my cock in her mouth, and her eyes shine with need like she wants me to take her again.

She looks up at me through her fanned out lashes, supple and pliant in my arms. I run my fingers through her softest part, washing her cum away with water, and think about how only I get to see her like this. My hands roam lower, grazing against her clit.

"This pretty little pussy has been waiting on me. To clean. To lick. To fuck."

"Ah, Nik, I'm sensitive from earlier just—ah!" I press down a little harder and her cheeks inflate in frustration. Shit, even the way she scrunches her nose and inflates her cheeks makes me hard.

But what the hell am I doing bathing her? I don't do this. Gwen makes me feel like a different person, makes me do so many things out of character. She turns to face me suddenly, water splashing out of the tub.

"Careful, Kotik." Her eyes drop to her breast, and I follow a drop of water that curves from her neck to between her breasts and then scoops underneath the left one.

"Sorry," she whispers, and I look back at her bowed head. "I just wanted to wash you too."

"My little kitty wants to roam her hands over me?" She dips her head, the pink in her cheeks deepening. I pick up her chin and smirk. "Go ahead."

Gwen nods sweetly and lathers some shampoo in between her hands to then work the soap into my hair. Her delicate fingers make sure to work the shampoo into every strand of my hair. She catches my eye and giggles as some of the suds go into my eye as she rinses it off, fingers never leaving my hair.

"You aren't even a little afraid of me?" I ask.

She frowns. "No. Why?"

"I did lop off a man's pinky in front of you."

"Yeah, but you did it for me. Because he was trying to hurt me. You protected me." Her eyes bore into mine. "I trust you."

I grab her by her pert ass and foist her up from the tub. Her legs instinctually wrap around me.

"Oh my God, Nik!" she squeals.

I throw her on the bed and crouch down in front of her.

"We're still wet from the bath!" She giggles, wrapping her arms around my neck, her eyes golden with lust and something else I can't quite name, but I know I want her to keep looking at me like that.

I nuzzle her neck, whispering, "And you're going to be wet in other ways once I'm done with you."

7

GWEN

"It should be a crime to cover up your body," I whisper, my hands running down his abs, stroking at the dark ink patterns.

"I know it's a crime to cover yours."

"Who says?" I giggle, pulling Nik closer from his crouching position, my hands gently scratching the scalp I just shampooed.

"Me." We kiss and he slowly dips one finger into my silky wetness. "Kotik, you ready for me?"

"Damn right, I'm ready," I breathe into his ear, making my voice a silky whisper. It's part truth and part lie. The truth is I want him. The lie is I don't think his thick cock would fit. I can barely wrap a hand around it. That monster of a cock is going to split me in half. I can't fucking wait.

Nik slowly pushes himself into me, my back arching.

Shit. I knew it. Death by dick. I guess the last 24 years were great. Nice knowing you, world. My voice sounds like it's coming from underwater. "Oh, oh God. Nik—"

"You're taking me like such a good girl, Gwen," he whispers into my ear.

I stare into his glossy and unreadable eyes. His chest rises and falls rapidly. He's holding back for me. The sight of such a powerful man trying to not hurt me causes me to shudder. I want to tease him, but no words come out.

"What? My dirty-mouthed girl doesn't have anything to say?"

Inch by inch, he pushes into me. "Fuck me," I gasp, feeling restless.

I hear the smack more than I feel it on my ass, every nerve still alight on my pussy. I tighten reflexively around him. "You can be nicer than that Kotik."

"Nik." I try to move, but Nik's large hand comes down to rest on my ass, forcing me to stay perched on his cock. I push against him, only to be met with another smack on my ass. "Nik, please. Please. Fuck me."

"Well, since you said please."

He gently presses his lips against mine and slowly pulls out to the tip, only to catch me off guard again. He slams himself back into me, previous gentleness non-existent. My nails sink into his back as he begins to fuck me in earnest, sinking deeper with every stroke.

"Nik, don't stop. Right there."

He continues to pummel my pussy relentlessly, and my body arches to meet his. The hotel bed creaks in rhythm. He's so fucking good at this. I've heard of stories of men being too timid, leaving my friends unsatisfied. But Nik was going at it, no-holds barred. He steadies himself against my waist and picks up the pace as if he can't help himself.

"You feel so good, baby."

I watch my pussy stretch and swallow his length. It's still not enough. I need a stronger sensation. I want to drown so deep in him that I would refuse a lifeboat. I wrap my legs around him, pulling him deeper into me.

"Fuck, that's right, milk me dry."

I gasp, my body trembling involuntarily beneath him. "Nik, I'm so close, please."

My fingernails dig into his warm skin. "Good girl, mark me, Kotik."

He slaps my ass again, and I let out a moan. Embarrassed by how much I like the sensation, my face digs into the crook of his neck. He pumps in and out with no mercy. I feel a coil tighten in my stomach. His blue eyes are looking at me, and I let go, the knot coming undone with feral screams of pleasure.

"I'm not done, baby," he whispers; slowly, he pulls out, and I whimper, overstimulated. His strong arms spin me around, pushing me onto my knees, ass in the air, head lowered on the bed. He gives it a squeeze and I hope it leaves a mark. "You have the most perfect ass, Kotik. Did you know that?"

I moan, positioning myself on all fours. "You're gonna need more than a dinner at some fancy Italian restaurant to fuck me in the ass, Nik."

He kisses my reddening cheeks as I turn my upper half to see him stroking his cock. "I am perfectly fine with this glistening pussy right here." He thrusts inside with no precursor this time. “I want you to know that this is my pussy, and I say what happens to this pussy. Right, Gwen?”

My moans grow even more wrecked, increasing in volume. I turn to jelly against his touch as he pinches my tortured clit. “Nik!” I whimper.

“Right, Kotik? This pussy is mine.” I clench around him in an attempt to gain the upper hand again. He responds with longer strokes that turn my brain to mush.

“Yes. Yes. This pussy is yours,” I whine. He resumes rubbing my clit as I hop up and down on his cock, his deft fingers meeting me with every thrust.

My moans become more broken and incoherent. The scent of my arousal fills the air, a heady mix of sweat and desire. Between my babbling, I manage one sentence: "Nik," I gasp, "I'm going to cum. Fuck. I’m going to-”

“Not till I say you can.” He growls and suddenly pulls out of me, and I swear I want to scream. But before I can think of anything to say, he picks me up like I weigh nothing and flips onto my back...

Instinctively I let my thighs open, and reach for his arms, “Nik please...” I whine desperate for him to fill me. He lets out a low rumble that sounds like a mix of a growl and laughter lighting every inch of me on fire. Keeping his eyes on mine, his hand slides between my folds and I can’t help but tilt my pelvis up, silently begging for him to be inside me.

“Fucking beautiful, Kotik,” he leans down and nuzzles my neck whispering in Russian, as he peppers kisses along the curve of my neck. My pussy clenches under his touch, begging for more attention, and like always he reads my mind ramming into me giving me what I want. Giving me what I need. I scream so loud I'm sure the entire building can hear me.

"Nik please..." I gasp. "Please...I, I need to..."

"What do you need Kotik?" He whispers into my ear between long deep thrusts.

Before I can respond, Nik's mouth finds my collarbone and he bites me gently. His other hand pins my hips in place leaving me no choice but to wrap my legs around him taking him deeper inside me.

He speeds up the ministrations on my clit. "Cum for me, Kotik. Cum for me." His cock pounds into me. My body offers no resistance this time, completely enraptured by Nik. I attempt burying my face into his chest.

"No. You look at me when you cum."

I swear it's his eyes that do me in. Those damn blue eyes. I convulse against him, bringing him over the cliff with me this time.

The only sound in the room is our labored panting. After a while, he slowly pulls out of me, his cum dripping out of me on the sheets. I pout at the emptiness he's left me with.

"Nik?" I whimper as he rubs my ass idly.

"Yes, Kotik?"

"We have to do that again."

"You read my mind, Kotik. Give me ten."

I AWAKE TO NIK'S SOFT SNORES. HE LOOKS YOUNGER when he sleeps, the rays of the morning kissing the stress of the world from his brows.

Nik and I went for two more rounds after the first, collapsing on each other out of exhaustion. It was amazing sex. Maybe even the best sex I'll ever have. I smooth his hair back, and he nuzzles into my hand, moving closer to me.

I could stay here looking at him like this for hours. I could get used to waking up next to his soft blue eyes and hearing the rasp of his voice in the morning, but I can't. It's probably around 6 a.m. and I need to go before he wakes up. If he still wants me in the daylight, then I will never leave.

I would be in love if I wasn't already. But my life doesn't fit into Nikolai's. I have debt from my father. I can't leave my nana alone to follow him. I want to go back to law school and get my degree from Georgetown. I mean this time I might not be top of the class, but I would be achieving my dreams. Dreams that have to wait for Papa's debt to be paid off, and despite the power Nikolai seems to have, Mason runs DC. If Mason found out I was with Nik, he would do worse than cut off a pinky. Probably cut off his head and make me watch.

A shiver runs up my spine as the image of a decapitated Nik flashes across my eyes. No, I can't do that to him, not when he would be the closest thing I will ever have to a love story. I grab a dress shirt out of his closet, my phone off the floor, and the shreds of my dress from last night. The soft fabric of his button-up makes me quiver, and I inhale the familiar musky, wood scent of Nikolai.

I freeze when Nik rolls over onto his back, deciding it is better for me to just grab my shoes and abandon my underwear, because it's not like it's intact anyway. On my tip-toes, I make my way out of his penthouse, closing the door lightly behind, thinking I made it out safe when a throat clears next to me.

"Oh my god!" I grab my chest and scowl at the security guard eyeing me. "You scared me."

"Ma'am, does Mr.Petrov know you are stealing his clothes as you leave?" he asks me, bored, as he glances over my clothing.

"I don't think he will mind," I say, rubbing the cuff of his shirt between my thumb and forefinger.

"Should I wake him up and check?"

The guard shifts to open up the door, and I launch myself at him, grabbing his forearm. If he wakes Nik, I know I won't be able to leave. One look. One word in that panty dropping accent would make me fold, and I would never leave his arms again.

"Wait, look." I show him the shredded pieces of my dress. "Surely he won't miss one shirt. I mean look at what he did to my dress!"

He eyes the pieces of fabric and smirks. "Seems like a good fuck to me."

"Fuck off," I snap, taking a step back from him. "Look, I have to go. I wouldn't steal his shirt if he left me anything to wear, okay?"

The guard takes a deep breath and rubs the bridge of his nose in annoyance. "Fine."

"Thank you," I huff, and scurry to the elevator, entering the doors as soon as they open. When the guard keeps staring at me, I give him a small wave and a wide smile. He just nods, staring forward. Once the doors close, I lean against the furthest wall and take a deep breath.

I can't believe I am doing the walk of shame after a night with Nikolai. I want to go back upstairs. I want to wake him up with a kiss. I want his hands on my body the way they were last night. *Shit, I just want him,* but I can't have him. I can't make his life ten times more complicated. I can't force him to be with me. It doesn't matter anyway; men like Nik meet women like me everyday. He'll forget about me soon enough.

The doors open, and to my delight, I don't see anyone immediately. I press my phone power button to order a cab, but the thing is so dead the dead battery alert won't even pop up. I huff, running my hand through the mess of my hair as I look around.

"Are you alright, ma'am? Do you need me to call someone?" A warm voice breaks me out of my panic, and I look back with a sheepish grin on my face. It's a woman with big red hair, brown eyes, and a hotel uniform on.

"Uh, yes... Can you order me a cab?"

"Sure thing." She beams. "Who were you rooming with? Or what room number are you?"

"Oh," I wave my hand, "that doesn't matter."

"Oh well, since our residents are wealthier, sometimes they bring their...unsavory business home. We have a service that brings people...like you home in the morning." The lady leans in across the counter a little. "We will even give you coffee and a pastry."

This realization hits me like a bat to the head. Nikolai is used to handing out exorbitant meals at Italian restaurants and getting girls to come home with him. Last night was like any other night for him, and I as I hoped wasn't special, so why does knowing I'm not special hurt? "Nikolai Petrov...the penthouse."

"Oh! You go, girl! You got the owner of the hotel. I've seen him. He is so hot." She wiggles her eyebrows and licks her lips. "With looks like that, he has to be the best in bed. Tell me he is the best in bed!"

"One of the best." I grin. Probably the best I'll ever have. The woman fans her face as she types and my stomach drops as I think about the amount of women Nik has probably wined, dined, fucked and said nasty things to before me and the thousands that will come after.

"Okay! So your cab is out front. He will take you to get breakfast and then take you home." She smiles and I wince under the happiness she cascades over me. "Is there anything else I can help you with?"

"Yes, can I leave Nikolai a note?" I ask.

"Of course." She smiles and grabs me a pen and paper. I take it from her and lean against the counter as I write out the note that will protect my heart.

Nik. I'm sorry. I can't see you again.

8

GWEN

T*wo weeks later*

"Bitch, spill everything!" Kelsey squeals, kicking her legs in the air and rolling over onto her stomach. Kelsey is my best friend from Pre-K. We were practically made for one another, the yin to my yang; without her, I don't know who I would be or where, but I promise you, nobody would have liked it.

Kelsey is all bubbles, sunshine, and rainbows; literally, she has golden blonde hair and bright green eyes that shine whenever she laughs, and she is always laughing. We're sitting on her baby pink couch with sour gummies, popcorn, and fuzzy pajamas. A must whenever boys are involved.

"Okay, so he is hot, Kel." I grin.

Kelsey has her legs on top of mine, looking at me with the intense gaze a housewife gives a murder mystery podcast while popping my award-winning concoction of sour gummies and warm, buttery popcorn into her mouth. She questions with her mouth full, "Like Taylor hot?"

"No, like every single romance book you have ever read hot."

I lazily drum on her knees, avoiding Kel's growing eyes. She sits up, glaring at me. I nod my head, a wide grin spreading on my lips, "Like Daddy status."

"Shut up," Kelsey whispers as she very calmly places the popcorn concoction on the coffee table and levels me with a look that says, *I must see this man ASAP.*

I place both of my hands up in front of me, blocking her. "Before you ask, he has no social media."

"Oh, that's fine." She smiles, pulling her legs from on top of my lap. "Because you're going to give me a very detailed description or drawing."

"Kel, I can't draw." I lean back as she sits on the heels of her feet.

"Okay, then get to talking." Kelsey's eyes are crazed, and a scarily happy smile spreads on her face.

"Kelsey, what would David think about you asking for a real life portrait of my date?" I ask. David is my childhood boy best friend and Kelsey's fiancé. They had the perfect *'it's been you all along'* moment in high school, and it was totally rom-com worthy. Especially with Kelsey being bubbly and sweet, while David was the complete boy next door package, with the football abs, messily perfect sandy brown hair, golden retriever energy, and girl-swooning smile to match.

"Oh, he won't mind." Kelsey leans forward, not blinking.

"What will I not mind?" I look over at David entering the house as he shakes out his hair and tosses his baseball hat on the opposite chair.

"Gwen went on a date with a book boyfriend." David smiles, looking between us. "And she refuses to describe the handsome devil."

"Oh, come on, Gwen, no fun." David slides onto the couch cushion behind me, matching his fiancé's crazed look.

I shake my head and make a zip motion over my lips. "Nope, the date goes to the grave because it's not happening again."

"The hell it will!" Kelsey attacks me, jumping five feet in the air monkey-style. Her fingers automatically get to work, running over my skin, and I contort to dodge her fingers, but David holds me in place to allow his fiancée to get her dirty work done.

"Guys!" I laugh, squirming under Kelsey's relentless tickling while David's grip keeps me pinned. My laughter turns desperate as Kelsey's fingers find all my most ticklish spots.

"Mercy! Mercy!" I gasp, but Kelsey's only response is an evil grin as she keeps tickling. My laughter becomes breathless, and I can feel my stomach churning. "Kelsey, stop! I'm going to—"

I can't finish my sentence as a wave of nausea washes over me. Panic flares, and I wriggle free with a sudden burst of strength, bolting towards the bathroom.

"Gwen?" David calls after me, concern lacing his voice, but I'm already halfway down the hall, pushing the bathroom door open and making it to the toilet just in time.

Kelsey's laughter fades behind me as I retch, my stomach heaving. I hear David's footsteps approaching, and a moment later, his hand is on my back, rubbing soothing circles as I empty my stomach.

"Gwen, are you okay?" he asks gently.

I nod weakly, resting my forehead on the cool edge of the toilet seat. "Yeah, you two deserve each other."

Kelsey appears in the doorway, her eyes wide with guilt. "Gwen, I'm so sorry! I didn't mean to—"

I wave her off, still catching my breath. "It's okay, Kelsey. Just a little...sensitive today."

David's brow furrows, and he glances at Kelsey before looking back at me. "Sensitive, you're like the least sensitive person I know." Kelsey smacks the back of David's head, and I elbow him in the rib. "Ow! I meant, you can stomach anything."

"Gwenie." Kelsey kneels next to me on the bathroom floor and flushes the toilet for me. "What do you mean by sensitive? Did your book boyfriend hurt you? Do I need to kill him?"

I take a deep breath, shaking my head, on the edge of the toilet seat. "No, I've been feeling off for a few days now. Nausea, fatigue and my breast hurt."

"Maybe we should go to the hospital." Kelsey starts to get up and drags me with her, but I pull her back down. "I mean, you said a few days so that it could be-"

"You know my period always makes me ill." I wave her off.

Kelsey gets into complete boss mode. "Oh, you're on your period! Okay, so let's get you a heating pad, and David, you're on the couch tonight and-"

"No, no, I don't have my period yet. It's like a week late." I brush her off. Kelsey huffs, leaning against the cabinet and David walks away towards the kitchen, reappearing with a glass of water in his hand.

"Sounds like you're pregnant." David shrugs, leaning against the door. "Hey when my sister was pregnant I was the only one who knew!" I roll my eyes because sometimes stress, like paying off a quarter million to a gang who keeps threatening your life, would possibly make my period a little late. "The club has been stressing me out, that's all."

"Stress totally makes sense because if you were pregnant that would mean you lost your virginity, and you would have totally told me," Kelsey nods in agreement.

I lean up and grab the glass of water out of David's hand. "Well, about my virginity-"

Kelsey pops up, her eyes doing that crazy thing again, ripping them from that Everclear green to dark mossy green. "You are painting me a portrait of this man, stark naked."

"I'm right here." David points at himself smirking, but Kelsey just kisses him on the forehead and rolls her eyes. I sip the water, urging the liquid to calm my nerves.

"You used a condom, right?" Kelsey raises her eyebrows at me, but I just shake my head no.

"What can I say? Heat of the moment." I blush, and David chuckles as my cheeks turn a level of crimson I didn't even know was possible.

Kelsey's jaw drops, and she looks like she's about to explode. "Gwen, you didn't use protection?"

I shrug, feeling the heat rise to my cheeks. "It was a moment of weakness, okay?"

Kelsey looks around the bathroom, and her eyes light up. "Hold on." She stands up and opens a drawer, rummaging through it until she pulls out a small box. "I thought I saw one of these in here. You never know when you might need it."

I stare at the box in her hand. "You keep a pregnancy test in my bathroom?"

Kelsey shrugs, glancing at David. "You never know when you might need it," she repeats with a smirk.

David winks, then winces when I elbow him again. "Hey!"

"All right, let's get this over with," I mutter, taking the box from her.

Kelsey and David exit the bathroom but hover by the door, peeking in anxiously as I read the instructions and follow the steps. After placing the test on the counter, we wait, my heart pounding.

"Whatever happens, we're here for you," David adds from the other side of the door.

I take a deep breath and follow the steps. I remove the cap and place the absorbent tip in the stream of urine for the required five seconds, then replace the cap and set the test on the counter.

"Gwen, are you okay in there?" Kelsey asks, knocking lightly on the door. My heart pounds in my chest, and my hands shake as I step back and open the bathroom door.

"Yeah, just...waiting," I reply, my voice shaking.

David enters with Kelsey right behind him and immediately looks at the stick with confusion. "How long does it take?"

"Just a few minutes," I reply, wringing my hands. I take my phone out of my back pocket and put on a timer for three minutes.

Kelsey grabs my right hand, entwines it with hers, and whispers, "What do you want it to say?"

I shake my head. For the first time ever in my life, I don't know what to say to Kelsey because a part of me feels a flicker of excitement. I think about the bond between a mother and child. A bond I've never had and don't know how to forge. What type of mother would I be when I have never known mine? I'm only 24, and my life is far from stable. What life could I give any child?

I look into the mirror and see an empty gaze growing in my eyes, the same I bet my mother had when she looked at me. The gaze I bet I'll have looking at my child. I'm in debt to a gang for fucks sake and I am still figuring out my career, finances, and relationships. Raising a child requires so much—time, energy, money—all the things I never got as a child. I look over at my timer and sigh at the minute to go.

Kelsey squeezes my hand twice and I break eye contact with myself. "Gwenie, you never answered my question, what do you want it to say?"

I shake my head and pull my hand away. "I don't know, Kels."

When she gives me a sad smile, I look over at David's identical look of sympathy. And then my stomach drops when the fear of doing it alone comes in. Sure, I have Nana Rose, but she is getting old. Kelsey and David would definitely help me and think of it as practice for the future twins Kelsey is sure she is having, but they have their own lives and responsibilities. I don't know where Nik is, and I don't know if he even wants to be the father of some random stripper's baby. He was in DC on business, not to find a baby mama. I would never want to ruin his life like that, but the thought of facing this alone makes me want to scream, but then my timer goes off. I hold my breath and don't dare look, neither does Kelsey, or David.

"Do you want me to look?" Kelsey whispers, and all I can do is audibly open my mouth and dry swallow. "Okay we'll look at the count of three."

I nod and whisper, "One."

"Two." Kelsey lifts the pregnancy test, the results flipped away from us.

"Three," I say, and the minute she flips over the results, my head spins. All I can hear is the ringing in my ears which drowns out the laughter from Kelsey and the pats on my back from David.

They both pull me into a hug, but they feel miles away, and when she pulls back, I can see the word on her lips.

Kelsey's voice pulls me back to reality. "Congrats, you're pregnant!"

Two Months Later

I sit in the back room of the strip club, playing with the straps of my garter as I look at my text to Nikolai for the fourth time today and the thousandth from this month alone. I keep looking at his messages from after that night as I pull the skin off my bottom lip.

Nikolai: Naughty Kitty, leaving in the middle of the night without even a goodbye.

Nikolai: I am in town for two more days, see me off. That's an order.

Nikolai: Don't make me get you from your bed tonight, Kotik. My offer still stands.

Nikolai: I can see you reading my messages.

Nikolai: Naughty Kitty gets her virginity taken and ghosts me, you better hope I am nowhere near that ass ever again, because I am going to make my handprint permanent on your ass, Kotik.

The last message always makes my core clench. Normally, I'd say something like: "Yeah, your handprint on my ass to match the one I'll put across your face." But I know what Nik does to me. When I am around him, I can't fucking think straight and now pregnant with his baby. I can't think at all.

Nikolai even showed up to my house once, and he waited for me with Nana Rose playing card games until like 2 am, but like the coward I am, I hid out at Kelsey's until I knew he had left. For a few weeks, he sent me every rose color that wasn't red with notes that ranged from sweet to commanding in a way that makes me want to obey mindlessly.

What am I supposed to say: "Hey Nik sorry for ghosting you, by the way I'm pregnant so don't worry about me ever leaving your life because I'm like a permanent thing now. LOL." I type out another text for Nik, one I think is nice and to the point.

Gwen: I'm pregnant.

The words look so empty on my screen. So damning. I don't know what else to feel, other than my stomach sinking to fucking hell.

"Earth to Cinnamon," Angel's high pitched, scratchy voice claws in my ears, and I glare at her from the corner of my eye.

"What?"

"Cinnamon," she whines. God, I hate when she says my stripper name. "You're up, bitch!"

I roll my eyes and click my phone close as Angel tries to look over my shoulder. "Stop being nosey, Rebecca."

Angel gasps, "You are not allowed to use real government names! I am telling Dylan!"

"While you're at it, tell him you're cheating on him with the fucking DJ," I snarl and Angel stomps her foot, her straw blonde hair stiffly flying behind her. I groan and slide on my strappy black heels to complete my outfit as I make my way backstage and signal to Justin, the sleazy DJ, that I'm ready.

"Ladies and gentlemen, give it up for your favorite spice," the lights swarm around before landing on me at the opening between the curtains, "Cinnamon."

Immediately, Justin starts to play *Drop it like it's hot,* and I swivel my hips as I make my way on stage.

The bass thumps in my chest, drowning out the leering stares of the audience. I plaster on a dazzling smile, but my mind is already miles away. As I twirl around the pole, I search for the quickest exit strategy. The acrid smell of desperation and cheap cologne fills the air, making me want to gag. I glance around the room, and my eyes land on the regular who loves me.

I lean down in front of him putting my tits on display. The regular old man, with a stack of 5's and hair only behind his ears, smiles as I crawl over and run my hand over the bald part of his head.

"Hey pops, you came here to see dirty little me?"

"You know I can't go a week without my dose of cinnamon." He smiles, sliding a five into the left cup of my bra. As I leaned in closer to the regular, his breath tinged with whiskey hits my face. I force a giggle, a hollow sound that mingles with the throbbing music. A wave of nausea washes over me, but I push it down and sling my body around so I am sitting on the heels of my feet.

"Well, you know I am always happy to oblige, Pops." I smile, but the minute I get up, another wave hits me and I almost stumble back. The room feels too hot, too crowded, and I can't shake the feeling of suffocation that threatens to overwhelm me.

Pops leans over and smacks my calf as he wiggles a five in his hand. "Make it good for me."

I nod and maintain my seductive smile despite the nausea churning in my stomach. As the music blares on, driving pulses of adrenaline through me, I dance with practiced ease. I smile at the right times, but the minute I hook my knee around the pool and swing, I gag for the first time.

"Baby, don't tell me you don't have a gag reflex?" a rando in the back who I can't see yells over the music, but I ignore him, shimming down the pole and flinging my hair back. I attempt to do my signature move again, hooking my right leg behind the pole, but then a wave of dizziness that sends the stage spinning before my eyes. I stagger mid-twirl, barely able to keep my balance as bile rises in my throat.

"Fuck," I cough, flinging my fingers up at Justin and running off stage as fast as I can. I barely make it past the curtains when I vomit all over the floor backstage.

"What the hell?" Dylan snaps but stops mid-sentence as he watches me heave over my pile of vomit. "You know you are not supposed to come into work sick. What would have happened if you threw up on a fucking customer, Gwen?"

"I'm not sick," I heave, taking as many deep breaths as possible.

"The fuck you are," Dylan scoffs, pointing at me and the vomit.

"I'm pregnant!" I snap before standing up and wiping my mouth with my arm.

"Shit," Dylan whispers, shaking his head.

"I know."

9
NIKOLAI

F*ive Years Later*

"Nikolai, you open up this instant, or so help me," Nadia, my little sister and second in command of the New York Russian Mafia, growls.

"Didn't I tell you five minutes?" I grunt, loud enough for her to hear, my slowly softening dick sitting in the mouth of a blonde who's been working on my cock for the last thirty minutes.

The memory of her soft skin, loose black curls, her taste on my lips, her eyes filled with adoration, desire, and innocence waiting to be corrupted invades my mind, and for the first time since this girl got on her knees, I can feel the pressure in my balls growing. For the past five years, this is the only way I can cum, with the image of Gwen invading my mind. My Kotik. My obsession. The woman who I should have tied to my bed and refused to let her escape me. *Fuck, I'm almost there.*

Nadia's impatient rattling of the doorknob grows louder, startling the blonde beneath me, and I grimace when the blonde's teeth scrape against my length. I wrap my hand around her hair, jerking her off of me.

"Watch your teeth." I lower my gaze, my voice a deadly sweet tone I usually use before taking someone's finger as a souvenir.

Tension spreads throughout her spine as she jerks to attention, but I keep my eyes closed, focusing on the images of Gwen that I can still conjure. I can see how perfectly Gwen and I fit together, and I try to remember how she moaned my name that night. *Fuck.*

"Nikolai! ты, чертов идиот, открой дверь!" Nadia's voice rings through the door, but I drown it out.

I swear I can hear Gwen whispering Nik into my ear right before breaking apart. The blonde taps my thigh.

"Nikolai," she whispers, her voice that cautious steady you use when cornered with a predator, but with Gwen this close to me, I don't hear her again until she mumbles, "M-my jaw..."

The images of Gwen fade away from me, and my cock falls limp again as the blonde comes back into focus. I pinch her jaw, a defeated look on my face as my thumb runs sharply down her jaw.

I whisper, "Go," pulling my completely softened cock away from her lips.

Her face twists up in confusion, and she reaches forward. "What? Give me one more chance."

"No need..." I trail off because I can't remember the girl's name for the life of me.

"Isabel." I snap my fingers and nod, a devilish smile spreading on my lips.

"Oh, I'm sorry, Isabel." I reach over my table, grab a napkin to clean my member, and press a button under my table that unlocks the door Nadia frantically rattles. "I'll call if I need you again."

I smile, knowing the words I am saying are a lie. Nadia stumbles in mid-shake of the door and scowls at me. "You fucking asshole."

"That's what you get for not waiting five minutes." I roll my eyes, looking back down at the blonde, who patiently waits for something to clean her face.

She sits like the good girl she has been trained to be: on her knees, with her hands flat, face up, and head bowed. Before Gwen, I'd admire a girl like this, even try to remember her name, but now I just incredulously stare at her for still being here when it is clear I would rather be with someone else. I'd rather be with Gwen.

"Is there something you need, Isabel?"

"Mr. Petrov, I can be a good girl. I can do it," she nods, lunging at my limp cock.

My balls almost suck themselves back into my body, and I swiftly turn around, my eyes darkly on hers and a humorless grin on my face as I catch her chin between my thumb and forefinger.

"People have lost their lives for less. I would hate to get blood on my new Armani suit because you can't take a fucking hint." I bring a napkin to her face, wiping the saliva from the corner of her mouth. "Now go."

Nadia leans over, grabbing more napkins for the girl, and she snaps her fingers sharply, looking impatiently. "Come on, sweetheart, move it before I move you."

Isabel looks at me with wide eyes as she stumbles to stand. "I'm sorry, Mr. Petrov." I nod as Isabel bows before scurrying out of the room, not even grabbing the additional napkins Nadia so kindly offered.

"Alek, I never knew you were the type to watch your siblings fuck," I tease. Aleksandr flips me off, an empty look in his eyes, and I smirk, grabbing another napkin and continuing the work of cleaning myself up.

Aleksandr's humorless voice cuts through the room, "Since when did you have your mistress bow? Isn't the protection and fuck me package enough?"

"It's not a fuck-me package; it's a thank you because, unlike you, Nik is a gentleman." Nadia smacks Alek in the chest and nods her head at me.

"Thank you. Besides, she's not my mistress and did the bowing herself. I like to see it as a sign of respect." I shrug, tucking my member back into my slacks and throwing the used napkin into the bin under my desk.

"I don't need to be a gentleman when I can actually fuck." Aleksandr's voice, despite the attempt at humor, is so even it slices like a knife.

"Oh, Alek, let him have this," Nadia said. "It's obvious he had us waiting over a very important failed blowjob," Nadia snickers, and Aleksandr offers her a fist bump with a smug smile on his face.

I roll my eyes, leaning back in my seat. If the small act of offering the blonde a napkin or the light bickering between us, makes you think Nadia, or as most of us call her, Nadi, is kind, then think again. She is the first woman to be second in command of the Russian Mafia, not because of her kindness. She was made my right hand after the unfortunate 'disappearance' of my father and was known for her ruthless yet efficient torture techniques. While I lob off a pinky or two, she takes pleasure in carving up her victims and leaving them permanently disfigured, if they ever live to tell the tale, or more likely, leave a message that she is coming for more.

Nadia has the temperament of our father and the looks of our mother, with straight, butt-length blonde hair cascading down her slim, athletic build and bright blue eyes that have slowly faded over the years.

"Come on," Aleksandr's robotically even voice sighs. "Nik has always thought with his dick. You would think with so much access to pussy he wouldn't need to."

I throw a pen at Aleksandr, but he catches it, staring at me with the same empty eyes. I avoid looking too deeply into his eyes, not wanting to fall victim to his void. Despite being the youngest, Aleksandr is massively built and looks exactly like our father.

While Nadia and I share our mother's blonde hair, Alek's is jet black and always neatly slicked back without a strand out of place. He is always neat, measured, and well-disciplined, making him perfect for running numbers and the legitimate side of the Mafia business. He isn't prone to violence like Nadia and I are. Alek prefers numbers and order to the mayhem of flesh and blood, only killing when all other options have been exhausted and he sees no other way out.

"Oh, you didn't know?" Nadia drops down into the chair on the other side of my desk and kicks her combat boots on my desk. Nadia wears her signature cropped leather jacket, black ripped jeans, and a lacey skin-tight camisole. "Nik's dick is broken."

"Your ankle is about to be broken if you don't get it off my custom desk." I smack her boots. She drops them to the floor, flipping me off.

Nadia isn't wrong because the last five years have been fucking torture. I can't find Gwen anywhere, and trust me, I've tried. She left the strip club where she worked three months after I visited. She moved houses two months after that, and despite all of my power in Washington, D.C., my resources have found nothing. The only reason I am sure she is not dead is because my mole in social security hasn't seen her death certificate yet, and she checks for it every day. It's like she was a ghost or a figment of my imagination, but I know she wasn't because I could have never conjured someone as glorious as Gwen.

I lean against the edge of the desk and scowl at Nadia, but Alek sits beside her, unbuttoning the jacket of his navy blue three-piece suit. I can see the tattoo we share poke out from beneath the sleeve of his right arm, a rose tattoo with a viper wrapped around the stem. Nadia has the same tattoo on her neck, and I have mine on my spine.

"Nik, it's time." Alek sighs.

"We saw our father last year," I deadpan as I walk over to my whiskey bar, pulling out two tumblers and a twenty-year-old bottle of Macallan.

"I know. That's why it's time again," Nadia whispers.

I pour a cup for Nadia and me, since Alek doesn't drink, and walk over, handing her one of the tumblers as I tentatively take a small sip of mine.

"He's not going to tell us anything." I look at Nadia from the corner of my eye, and she avoids my gaze to sip her drink.

"He will tell us something." Alek nods as if declaring a statement like that will make the outcome true. "Long-term isolation can result in heightened activity in the amygdala, increasing susceptibility to anxiety, depression, and other mood disorders, while also disrupting neurochemical balances such as dopamine and serotonin levels."

"Layman terms, Einstein." I roll my eyes, taking another sip.

"That means he will be paranoid enough to make any deal to stop his isolation. We are social creatures. We need human interaction in order to maintain ourselves." Alek steadily speaks as if he has memorized a psychology book.

He ignores my gaze and stares at the shine of my desk in front of him, continuing to mentally calculate the probable outcome of the man we have locked in our basement finally telling us anything of value.

"It's been three years," I say, staring at the picture of our mother and the three of us I had commissioned on her last birthday. Instead of being in her living room like I imagined, it now sits on the wall to the right of my desk. "How much longer does he need to tell us where the rest of our mother is?"

"It may be taking him longer because he was already mentally imbalanced," Alek comments

I grimace, flinging the rest of the whiskey down my throat. "I vote that I can start breaking bones this year."

I slam the tumbler on the table and look over at the emptying gaze of Nadia, who is the only one who has prevented the full violence between Aleksandr and me because, despite everything he has done, she still loves our father. Nadia nibbles on her bottom lip, the glass still full and barely between her fingertips.

I whisper, "Nadia?"

Her glossed-over eyes meet mine, and I reach out to smooth down her hair. Alek takes the tumbler out of her hand and places it on a coaster on my desk. "I get to pick which bones."

10

GWEN

"Mia! Come on!" I stand at the end of the hall off the kitchen, calling out my daughter's name for the third time. She doesn't respond, and I mindlessly wipe the pancake batter on my slacks. "Shit."

I glance at my son, Gio, his black wavy hair covering his eyes as he almost sleeps in his pancakes.

"Gio, baby." I walk over to the sink, wetting a paper towel to clean the syrup off his face. "You've got to wake up."

He looks up at me with a lazy smile, and I rub a little harder to get the syrup off his face, whispering, "I thought I told you to go to sleep at 8?"

"Mommy, I had to finish my book before the first day." His voice is small but earnest.

I look into his big blue eyes and immediately soften like I did when his father looked at me. Gio's luscious locks cascade in soft waves. His deep black tresses, which match mine, are striking against Nikolai's deep ocean eyes and mischievous smile.

But it's his brains; I don't know where he got that. At only five years old, Gio possesses the intelligence and savvy of a twelve-year-old prodigy, making him a mini Einstein in the making. He is currently teaching himself about every primate he can get his hands on because he has a deep passion for animals. Right now, his favorite is the lemur.

His eyebrows furrow, a frown on his face. "Did you know orangutans are going extinct?"

"I did. That's really sad." I give him a sympathetic smile.

He huffs like an old man who has seen too much of the world. "I don't like that. People keep wanting them as pets, and they weigh 285 pounds as adults, so that's just dumb." His pout turns into a yawn, and I kiss his head. "Plus, the places where they live are being destroyed."

"That's terrible, baby. Let's make a game plan to help them out tonight." I ruffle his hair, and he smiles at his cold pancakes, which reminds me of my daughter.

"Mia!" I scream again, but Gio sighs.

He looks up at me with wide blue eyes and a sad smile.

"Girl, if you don't stop all that yelling; it is 6:36 in the morning!" Nana Rose's slippers click down the hall, holding her hand to her forehead in annoyance.

"Mia doesn't want to go to school," he says matter-of-factly, stuffing a hefty forkful of pancake into his mouth.

"What do you mean Mia doesn't want to go to school?" Nana Rose snaps. "Back in my day, kids didn't have a choice if they went to school or not."

"Is she sick?" I question, sliding two pancakes on my plate.

"No, but she didn't like summer camp, so she doesn't think she'll like school." Gio shrugs, picking up his orange juice and taking a huge gulp that leaves some OJ dripping onto his green t-shirt. Genius or not, my baby is a mess.

"Nana, please clean Gio up. I have to talk to Mia." I sigh, walking off down the hallway toward the twins' room.

I find Mia sitting on her bed, clutching her favorite stuffed animal, a well-worn bunny named Mr. Floppy. Her hazel eyes are downcast, and she looks up at me with tears gleaming in her eyes.

"Mia, honey, what's wrong?"

She hugs Mr. Floppy tighter. "I don't want to go to school, Mama." She speaks into the head of the stuffed animal, tears cresting her hazel-green eyes. "I'm not smart like G. Everyone will make fun of me."

I take a deep breath and smooth down her curls that match mine. Her dirty blonde color resembles Nikolai; sometimes, I can't help but stare at how much she resembles him.

"Mia, we do not say mean things to ourselves. What do we say?"

"I am smart," she whispers. "I am pretty. I am great."

"You are everything and more," I whisper into her hair and kiss her forehead, pulling her into my chest. "I promise everyone feels that way on their first day, and everyone will be learning and growing. No one knows everything, not G, Nana, or me."

"You don't know everything?" she asks with wide eyes.

I giggle, a bitter sound escaping my lips. If I knew everything, I would know where their father was. If I were truly growing, I would have told him years ago that we have two of the most wonderful kids in the world. I tried once when the twins were one, right before we moved out of D.C. to Maryland, to escape the pressure of the debts my father owed. No one knew I had children, and I never wanted Mason to find out and use them against me, so we moved in the middle of the night.

But before we left, I wanted to tell him. I wanted to let Nik know, but most importantly, I just wanted to see him again, to have him look at me like the world revolved around me, the same way he did that night when he rocked my world. The memory of his gaze, filled with warmth and adoration, haunts me. It's a look I've longed for every day since I snuck out of his hotel room.

I knew Nikolai owned that hotel we went to, so I went back and asked if I could get his email or number, and I was practically dragged out of the lobby. They thought I was a stalker or just trying to exploit their boss for money. After that, I tried googling him, but Nikolai Petrov is a pretty common name, and he was a ghost before I met him. Now, he's a figment of my imagination. The only proof we ever met are the twins and the button-up I stole and kept underneath my pillow because it used to smell like him.

Mia crawls into my lap with Mr. Floppy, breaking me out of my trance. I smile and nuzzle her cheek.

"I am always learning new things because nothing is better than learning."

"Really?"

I tickle her chest. "Really? Besides, you'll learn, have much fun, and make many new friends."

Mia pushes Mr. Floppy closer to my face. "Do you think Mr. Floppy can come with me?"

"Of course, Mr. Floppy can come. He'll be your brave buddy."

A small smile forms on her lips. "Okay, Mama."

"Alright, get dressed in whatever you want except the princess gowns." I kiss her forehead.

Mia's eyes light up with excitement as she jumps off the bed and rushes to her wardrobe. She rummages through her clothes, pulling out a pair of bright pink overalls and a sparkly blue t-shirt. With a toothy grin, she holds them up for my approval.

"Perfect choice! You'll be the coolest kid at school in that outfit."

Once Mia is dressed and ready to go, she grabs Mr. Floppy's paw tightly in her hand. I smile and take her hand, leading her out of the room and back to the kitchen.

Gio looks up, his face brightening when he sees Mia. "Ready to go, Mia?"

She nods more confidently this time. "Yeah, ready."

After pouring an obscene amount of syrup on top, I slide her the plate of pancakes I made for myself. "Alright, eat quickly; the bus will be here soon."

As the twins finish eating breakfast, I pack their new backpacks with notebooks, pens, and snacks and zip up the bags. I hoist them onto their little shoulders and adjust the straps for a perfect fit just as the school bus pulls up out front.

"Okay, are we ready for school?" I ask, ruffling their hair.

Mia takes a deep breath, squeezes Mr. Floppy, and nods.

Gio laces his hand with hers. "Don't worry, I got you, Mia."

I pull them into a bear hug, kiss their foreheads, and watch as they rush from the front door to the bus.

Nana Rose is leaning against the wall, an expectant look on her face as she taps her ruby-red nails against the mug of her coffee.

"What?" I question, moving towards the kitchen sink to wash the pancake batter off my pants. Nana Rose follows me.

"You know this would be easier if you just told Nikolai that he has children." Her voice is sharp and demanding, as it always is when discussing this. "That man would not leave you to raise them alone."

"Nana, I told you. I can't find him," I snap, wetting a paper towel and rubbing out the drying tan stain on my black slacks.

"Bullshit, you could have called him." She uses the same firm voice she did when I was lying as a kid. I throw the paper towel onto the kitchen counter and huff, slouching over the sink.

"He changed his number. All I get is dial tone now." I sigh, but she clicks her tongue and roughly places the mug on the table. "Besides, I don't know what he does for work, but it is not legal."

"So you are so righteous now that you will work yourself into an early grave?"

I spin around and narrow my eyes on her. "I am working this hard only because your son still owes 200,000 to the fucking mob in D.C. If I don't make those payments, they will come for us, Nana. Do you understand?"

I walk closer, but Nana squares her shoulders and looks me dead in the eye with a sharp pointer finger.

"Do not talk to me as a child," Nana says, her voice leveled and stern. She takes a deep breath and continues speaking a little softer. "I am worried about you, Gwen. You work all night at that bar and all day as a receptionist. You don't sleep. You barely eat. Shit, you don't even have time to wash your ass."

"I don't know what else I am supposed to do." I sigh, leaning against the kitchen sink.

"Find him. Make him listen, not only so you can get a break, but because that man deserves to know he has children," she pleads, and I avoid her eyes.

I whisper, "I know."

11

NIKOLAI

Ever since I was a child, the basement of our house has been a makeshift prison. Soundproofed so my mother wouldn't hear the endless screams and the type of cold that cuts straight through to the bone. My father always said the cold is meant to suck the warmth from your body with every step. It was his last act of kindness to his captives, an early introduction to the chill of death's touch—the perfect place for a monster—the perfect place for my father.

Despite all the cells down here, there is no one else. I don't believe in the messiness of keeping captives longer than a week. If they don't break under the torture of Nadia, then they will never break and deserve the emptiness of death, like we all do.

A sharp gust of breath from Nadia's lips fills my ears. This time of year is the hardest for her. She was, and sometimes still is, a daddy's girl. She visits him every other month to chat, but when we come with her, she knows the only conversation we will have will end in violence.

I reach back, open my hand to her, and she laces her fingers with mine.

"It's okay. I got you, sestrichka," I whisper, but the hollowness of the makeshift prison makes my voice sound louder than it needs to.

Nadia squeezes my hand twice as we approach the metal door at the end of the hall. Aleksandr goes into the cabinet to the right of the door, slipping the black bag of torture items underneath his arm and giving me a sharp nod. A guard stands to the left in riot gear, staring straight ahead.

Every Father's Day, we follow the same routine. Aleksandr is the torturer because the last time Nadia tried, she cried. Nadia doesn't cry, not even when our mother died. Not even when her first love broke her heart; it is the only time I have ever seen her dwindle into sadness, and Aleksandr is so separate from his emotions that he can easily separate the man who raised us from the monster who looks at us now. His torture is methodical, systematic, and precise. He deals the maximum pain in the quickest ways possible.

I alone have the courage to meet his gaze and witness the madness rippling through his eyes. Unlike my brother Aleksandr or our sister Nadia, I do not hold onto any memories of kindness from our father. From a young age, I knew the darkness lurking inside him. And now, as I face him once again, I ask the same three questions that consume my thoughts. Where is she? Why did you do it? How could you? These are the only things that matter to me when it comes to him, and the minute he tells us, I will gut him like a fish.

Nadia watches so that she remembers the monster our father is. If things get too intense, she stops us, and we wait until next year as she nurses him back to health.

I nod at the guard. He positions himself at an angle with an AK-47 pointing straight at the door.

The door hums with a low, electric buzz as the security system engages. A sleek, touch-sensitive control panel beside the door lights up with a soft blue glow, displaying a complex interface of biometric scans and security protocols. My fingers dance across the surface as I input the code, my mother's birthday, and authorize my access with a fingerprint scan. With a faint beep of approval, the panel's light shifts from blue to green. A soft, mechanical click echoes through the corridor, and the door slides open in a smooth, almost silent motion.

I step through the threshold, and the door automatically closes behind us with the same silent efficiency. The guard keeps the gun trained on my father, who sits in the middle of the cement floor, legs crossed. The dim light from a single, flickering bulb casts long, haunting shadows that dance across the walls.

An eerie silence crawls across the room, only broken by the subtle sound of pages turning. My father, Boris, continues to read, his eyes flicking up to meet mine for a brief moment before his gaze darts away. He sighs as if we have caught him at the wrong time.

"Son, what can I do for you today?" Boris grumbles, boredom invading his features.

He is wearing gray sweatpants and a white cotton long-sleeve t-shirt with matching white socks. The gray in his hair almost erases any evidence that it was ever jet black. His face is weathered and lined, yet there's a sharpness in his eyes that I've wanted to cut out since we locked him down here.

"The same thing you can do for me every year." I shrug, entering the room more.

Nadia moves to the corner of the room, leaning against the wall. Aleksandr walks over to the metal table bolted to the floor of the cell and unravels the black bag, an assortment of knives, hammers, needles, and anything else he might need to extract pain from Boris.

Despite the harsh fluorescent lighting of the prison cell, Boris's resemblance to Aleksandr is striking. Though softened by age, his broad shoulders and solid frame still hint at the powerful man he once was. Even in this confined space, he is still the man that haunted me as a child. The red dot from the guard's gun shines brightly on his chest.

He looks down and smiles. "Oh, is it this time of year again? You're going to threaten to kill me and then fail to do so."

"Dad," Nadia whispers. He looks at her from the corner of his eye, placing the book open on his knee. "Just tell us where Mom is."

My breath catches in my throat, and I fail to stop the rolling of my jaw. He looks at me, lifting his chains that connect to the cuffs around his ankles. His eyes stay on me as he speaks. "Aleksandr, did you receive her left foot this morning?"

"No, the right." He wipes down his knife methodically and looks at us from the corner of his eye. "Your guy must be slacking."

"Must be; the right is supposed to go to Nikolai. My right hand. The heir to my throne." His eyes narrow on me. I don't move. I don't want him to know that he still gets to me. "The one who betrayed me."

"Betrayal is a funny word coming out of your mouth." I click my head to the side.

"Why?" Boris rises to his feet. "Is bastard better?"

I hold my tongue, and Aleksandr stiffens, his head slowly turning to me. "What does he mean by bastard?"

A low chuckle comes from his throat, and he gives me a toothy grin that makes my skin itch. A shaky finger is brought to his browning lips as he shushes Aleksandr. "That's a secret between Nikolai and me."

My body is so stiff I am afraid to breathe, yet no one knows from the smirk I have on my face as if Boris amuses me. I mastered my poker face young because he always said, 'To show any sign of weakness as the head of the Petrov Family is to show yourself to be an unfit king.' That was one of many violent lessons from Boris, the first of many that ended in me spitting blood out on concrete and wishing I was never born. Now, I am nothing if not a man fit to be king.

Nadia's shaky voice breaks me out of memories of my childhood. "We don't keep secrets from each other."

I can feel her eyes burn in the back of my head. The laughter that leaves his lips is nothing but cruel, yet his eyes light up like a child on Christmas morning. "Nadi, you know a man is nothing without his secrets, even from his little sister."

Her voice is harsher this time. "I am his right hand."

For the first time since we entered the cell, Boris looks at Nadia with his nostrils flared, eyes hardened, and voice laced with venom. "You have never been acknowledged as a member. Do not fool yourself."

Nadia steps deeper into the corner of the room, looking down at her hands and pinching the inside of her wrist like she did when we were kids.

My eyes whirl on Boris, a sliver of emotion showing on my face. "Speak to her like that, and I'll take another finger."

He raises his hands up, revealing his right hand, which is missing his thumb and middle finger, a crazed smile on his lips. "This time, take the ring. I'll bleed more."

Nadia shakes her head. "I can't."

"Nadia," I warn, my voice stern and sharp.

"No, if you can keep secrets from me, then I do not have to be a part of this," she huffs, pushing off her wall. "Neither will Aleksandr."

"This is why we don't allow women into the mafia," Boris sighs. "You're too emotional."

Nadia storms across the room, snatching the knife out of his hand, and throws it perfectly into Boris's shoulder. He grits his teeth, looking down at where the knife is lodged in his right shoulder. Laughter bubbles in his chest, and I look over at Nadia. Her lips twist into a snarl, her eyes wide, and her brows furrowed. She looks like she wants to vomit.

"Go," I command firmly.

"I can do it, Nik," Aleksandr responds, unfazed by anything that happened.

"No." I flex my arms in front of me. "He's all mine."

12

GWEN

I drag my feet behind me as I walk from the bus stop to Mia and Gio's after-school program. The only thing on my mind is the countdown to my next shift. I have three hours to get them home, shower, change, and get to work. Maybe Nana is right. I don't have enough time. I am working myself into an early grave, but if I don't work, no one will, and then all of our lives will be on the line.

The sound of children laughing makes me smile, erasing the tired expression that Gio will surely see the minute he looks at me. I approach their teacher, a smiley young woman with honey-blonde hair, thick black frames, and an unlimited collection of rainbow dresses.

"Hey, Mrs. Taylors, I'm here for Mia," I say, smiling as I look around for her blonde curls.

Mrs. Taylors looks at me with a confused expression. "Ms. Sharp, didn't you send your friend to pick Mia up?"

My heart skips a beat, a cold wave of panic washing over me.

"No, I didn't send anyone," I reply, my voice trembling slightly. "What friend? Who picked her up?"

Mrs. Taylors' face pales. "A man came by about an hour ago. Last night, he was added to the system to be on the approved pick-up list."

I look at her with wild eyes. "What?"

"Yes, he is under the friend category and uploaded everything needed to be an official pick-up."

"I'm sorry, can I?" I ask, reaching out for her tablet, dread settling in the pit of my stomach.

"He said his name was Mason," she answers, her eyes wide with concern. The name sends a shiver down my spine. Mason, the leader of the mob my father owes money to. The man who wants me to be his. He wasn't supposed to know I have a child. He wasn't supposed to know where we moved to.

I stare at the photo and ID that were uploaded into the pick-up system. His straight, thick, black hair is pulled into a man bun with two thick braids in the front. His black eyes, which look like the pits of hell, glitter, and his lips are curved into a knowing, lazy smirk that makes my body feel like ice.

I try to steady my breathing, my mind racing. "Yes, of course, I remember. It's just mom brain," I manage to say, my voice barely above a whisper. "Sorry for the panic."

Mrs. Taylors nods, a wave of relief washing over her features as she digs in her pocket. "He told me to give you this if you forgot he was doing pick up. He said that as your new boyfriend, he wanted to take some things off your plate, and I thought that was the sweetest thing in the world."

I give her a tight smile. "I know, he's the best." She hands me a neatly folded note, and I unravel it so quickly I almost give myself a paper cut:

"Meet you at home, Pretty Girl."

I rush to the opposite building where Gio has his gifted classes, my mind racing a mile a minute. Mason wouldn't hurt a child. He's trying to scare me, but I bet he doesn't know I have two children because Gio is in a gifted part of the school with a completely different system.

I sprint towards Gio's classroom, my thoughts a blur of fear and anger. Mason has Mia. I have to get her back, but first, Gio. I have to make sure Gio is safe.

As I reach Gio's classroom, I see him sitting at a table, hunched over a book. He looks up and beams when he sees me, but his smile fades when he notices the panic in my eyes.

"Mommy, what's wrong?" he asks, his voice small and worried.

His teacher, Mr. Henderson, a man with pale skin and dark brown eyes, approaches me with a worried look. "Ms. Sharp, is everything okay?"

"Yes, yes," I frantically nod, walking towards Gio's backpack and putting away any materials I find that are his. I pause, my mind racing ahead of me, and I look at him cautiously. "Um... by any chance, did a man named Mason come here and try to pick up Gio?"

Mr. Henderson tilts his head to the side, furrowing his brows. "No, not today, at least."

"Okay, good," I nod. I was right. He doesn't know about Gio, only Mia. "Can you put him on the do-not-pick-up list?"

"Certainly," Mr. Henderson agrees, following me to Gio's cubby. I grab his jacket and smile at Gio, handing it to him. "Are you sure everything is okay?"

I put on my most convincing smile as I reach my hand out to Gio. "Come on, Gio," I say, trying to keep my voice steady. "We have to go. Now."

He grabs my hand, and I quickly lead him out of the building. "Mommy?" he questions, almost falling over his feet as he runs to keep up with me.

I bend down and hoist him onto my hip as I rip my phone out of my pocket.

"Gio, Mommy needs you to listen very carefully." I open the Uber app and put Kelsey's, my best friend since birth, as the first stop and then my address as the second.

"We are going to get in this Uber, and you are going to Auntie Kelsey's and stay with her tonight, okay?"

"Mommy, everything is not okay."

"Mommy will never lie to you," I say carefully. "But I will make sure everything is okay. Trust and believe that I will always protect you and your sister. Okay?"

He nods. "I trust you, Mommy."

The Uber pulls up to us, and I slide both of us inside. "Twenty extra dollars if you step on it."

The driver nods, and I don't even look at him as I call Kelsey. Her voice rings joyfully through the phone, "Hey, girly pop!"

"I need you to take Gio for the night and maybe even longer," I say in one breath. I look out the window as the car speeds down the highway.

Her voice gets serious as she speaks, "Gwen, what's wrong?"

I whisper harshly into the phone, hoping Gio isn't listening too closely, "Mason has Mia."

"Shit. Do you know where?" she questions, and a ball of salt builds in the back of my throat.

"No, I don't," I say. "We'll be there in two minutes. Be downstairs."

I hang up, trying to keep myself from crying or vomiting. Gio reaches over to my lap and places his small hand in mine. I look at his big, bright blue eyes, and the image of Mia flashes into my mind. I keep telling myself Mason won't hurt a child, but the more I say it, the less I believe it. What if I never see her again? My chest tightens, and for a second, I think of Nik. A wave of nausea makes my skin tingle. What if he never meets his daughter? He'll never forgive me.

The car pulls up to Kelsey's apartment complex on the outskirts of DC, where she moved after I moved to be closer to me and not make me go back to Mason's territory for no other reason than payment. I look over at Gio. "Be good."

He nods, and Kelsey opens up the door with a fake smile on her face.

"Hey, buddy," she exclaims, but worry infects her eyes when they meet mine, and I look away.

"Keep Gio safe," I whisper, looking straight ahead.

"With my life," she nods, closing the car door.

I look at the driver in the rearview mirror, my eyes like steel. "Drive."

As the car accelerates, my thoughts spiral into a whirlwind of panic and fear now that I know Gio will be safe. Mason has Mia. How did this happen? What does he want with her?

I close my eyes, trying to steady myself but seeing only Nik's face. What if when I tell him about our daughter, I have to tell him that our little girl is gone? I swallow hard, forcing back the tears.

The car weaves through traffic, the city lights blurring into streaks of color as we speed toward my house. I rip out my wallet, throwing the twenty-dollar bill onto the passenger seat.

"Thank you."

I don't even wait for the car to completely stop as I rip open the door and rush up the steps to our house. I hear cartoons the minute I open the door, and a wave of relief washes over me until I round the corner.

Mason is hunched over on the floor with Mia, a Barbie doll in one hand, and a gun poking out of his waistband. He still has the same long black hair braided into a man bun, just like how he would wear it in high school, making his chocolate brown hair look black. Intricate black tattoos run up his arms, and a raven's wing peaks out from underneath his black shirt on his neck.

Mia sees me first and runs up to me with a wide grin, singing, "Mommy, look what Uncle Mason got me!"

Mason's black eyes turn to me with a wide smile, and he shakes his Barbie in his hand. His slick Irish accent drenches me in a cold sweat.

"Welcome home, pretty girl. Long time no see."

13

GWEN

The presence of danger triggers a primal response in humans, causing them to flee, fight, or freeze. But with Mason, it's different.

He exudes danger in every fiber of his being, yet I never feel the urge to run or hide. Instead, he ignites a dangerous fire within me. It's as if his very essence defies all logic and instinct within me.

My mouth goes dry, my palms slick with sweat, but most dangerously, he brings out an unnerving level of confidence within me. A false bravado that convinces me I can survive the depths of hell because I am confident that he would drag me down there kicking and screaming.

You could call that fight, but I think of it as a twisted tango because I know I will never win, but something within me won't let me show my fear because if he is a beast, then I am a monster. With Mason, I can always go lower and be faster and wiser, but never stronger. It's been like that since we were kids, and even if I leave every battle black and blue, it's okay because he becomes less of a man every time we do this violent dance, and it is my sick pleasure to make him feel like the insecure boy I know he is.

His obsidian eyes glitter with a dangerous gleam as he slowly roams over every curve of my body in my grey polyester pantsuit. The intensity of his gaze sends shivers down my spine as he licks his lips and clicks his tongue in disapproval.

"What a shame," he purrs, "to hide all this beauty from me. How disrespectful."

Mia is still wrapped around me, giggling, swinging a brown-skinned Barbie doll with a '70s outfit at me. I tuck a loose strand of hair that has fallen out of my bun behind my ear, plaster on a smile, and bend down to Mia's eye level, "What's that, baby?"

She giggles. "I am going to name her Jasmine. She's so pretty! Uncle Mason got me her and three others."

She laces her hand with mine and drags me across the living room to sit next to Mason. I take a deep breath and instantly regret it because he smells precisely like he did in high school: leather and spice. The difference between the Mason who gave me my first kiss and the Mason I know now is that I watched him murder a man and he relished in the violence. That is why I got my bachelor's in California instead of staying in D.C.

When Mia pulls me down, I sit on my knees next to Mason. He places an arm behind me, leaning back slightly, and leans over my shoulder. His breath spreads across my skin in heavy gusts, causing the hair on the back of my neck to stand at attention.

"I've missed you, G."

I speak low, smiling as I pick up a tanned-skinned Barbie with long, straight, black hair, and act as if I am happy to play Barbies because Mia can't know how much danger we're in.

"*Uncle* Mason?"

He darkly laughs, his lips brushing over the curve of my neck. "I would have preferred Daddy, but it seems my girl has been a little slut."

"I'm not yours," I growl, keeping my eyes on Mia.

"Oh, come on now, pretty girl," he sighs as if he is exhausted. "You know you can't be no one else's. I'll make you watch me kill them."

I inhale sharply, and he nips at my flesh, and I flinch away, leaning in closer to Mia, "Hey baby, why don't you introduce Jasmine to your other doll, Hannah?"

Mia's eyes light up, and she jumps to her feet. "Hannah is going to love you, Jasmine!"

She giggles and runs to the twins' bedroom, and once I hear the door slam behind her, I feel as if I can breathe. Mason is still breathing down my neck, but instead of the welcomed heat, it feels like the breeze of the Arctic consuming me, chilling me to the bone. He inhales me violently, his lips forming into a satisfied smirk as he exhales, a content sigh leaving his lips.

"You have been very naughty, pretty girl."

His fingers tangle in my hair and pull it loose from its tight bun. It's a gesture that feels too familiar as if he's done this every night when I come home from work, as if being with me is second nature to him.

"You deserve punishment, pretty girl, for leaving D.C., for sending me money without a return address, and for making me hunt you down like a fucking animal." His growl deepens with every word, and a spray of spit is shot out onto my face.

The strands of my hair fall in large, loose curls down my back, and Mason wraps them around his hand, yanking sharply. "But the worst thing you did was get knocked up by someone else. Did you really think I wouldn't find out? Who was it that got to taste your sweet little pussy?"

Mason jerks my head back, and my scalp feels like it is on fire. My head is throbbing as if each strand of hair is being plucked from my skull, but I refuse to cry or beg. I can't give him the fucking satisfaction. Instead, I keep my mouth shut, and I grunt, jerking against him as if I want him to pull harder.

I speak through gritted teeth, "None of your goddamn business."

He yanks me down to the ground with a brutal force, pinning me beneath him. His face contorts into a starving animal, his obsidian eyes glinting with a manic hunger that makes my blood cold. A small whimper leaves my lips, and his coal eyes brighten as if he has found his next meal in me. His voice comes out like a spider's caress along my skin, and my neck stretches to escape the delight on his face.

"You know I always loved it when you put up a fight, G; it always made breaking you so much better."

My body freezes as he licks up my face from chin to temple and moans at the taste of my sweat on his tongue.

"Now, tell me who I have to kill for tasting you first, for ruining my precious pretty girl."

My ears are ringing, my breathing is coming out in harsh, sharp gusts, and I feel like, for the first time, I may experience what other humans do. I may not be able to break him down because he is threatening Nikolai. Mason would never kill a kid, but he would make me watch as the first man who ever made me feel like my skin was electric died, and then Mason would want to fuck me next to his corpse. I could never do that. Something within me crumbles, and I growl, flattening my hands against Mason's chest and pushing. He doesn't move.

Instead, he chuckles, "Oh, you'd rather have me go to Mia's room? I would hate to kill my daughter, but we can always make another."

I freeze, my eyes widen. "Mason, you wouldn't dare."

His face contorts into a snarl, and he knocks against mine. "You want to bet?"

I fall into the black hole of his eyes and find no humor or fear, and then I realize I've been lying to myself. Mason would kill my kids, but I stare, voice gritty as I growl, "You lay a finger on her, and I will bathe myself in your blood. I will kill you so slowly that you beg for death."

Mason's laugh is boisterous and light, as if he did not just threaten my babies, and he rips my hands off his chest and presses them into the rug above my head, locked together.

"Oh, there she is." He searches my face with a grand smile. "My little psycho."

"I am not yours," I whisper, but Mason just smiles, nuzzling his nose against my neck, and for the first time, I can feel a bulge against my thigh growing.

"Oh, but you always have, and always will, pretty girl. You will always be my little psycho, but it's not like you have a choice anymore," he coos, and my body becomes so stiff I feel like I can't move.

"What do you mean I don't have a choice?"

"I gave you six years to pay off this debt, and you still owe me one hundred and ninety five thousand dollars," he whispers as his nose trails my neck to his ear. "It's a bad look for me to have such an outstanding balance."

"Then go find my fucking father and kill him," I growl, but he clicks his tongue at me.

"I don't want your father, pretty girl," he purrs. "I want you."

"You can't have me," I say with hardened eyes and my voice a deep rasp I have never had before this moment.

"You need to learn how to play your cards right because I have a royal flush right now, and your hand is bad." He laughs. "You see, either you get me my money by morning, or you become my little mistress, and if you fight me on this, I will take little Mia in there and sell her to the highest bidder." My body becomes ice cold, my mouth dry, and I stop breathing, but Mason continues with a humorous smile, "And then you hate me and still have to be mine."

"You have to give me more than a night, Mason," I whimper, the tears in the back of my throat vibrating with the need to run down my face. "Please."

"Well, since you asked so nicely," he inhales me again, "48 hours."

"Not enough time," I say, locking eyes with his empty abyss.

"Make it enough," he snarls, his grip on my wrist tightening to a crushing level that sends shockwaves of pain through my entire body. I grit my teeth and refuse to let out a single cry, knowing it will only fuel his rage.

The front door slams with a deafening force, and Nana's heels clicking against the hardwood floor fills me with relief. My eyes squeeze shut as I struggle to catch my breath as the sound of her rustling through her purse gets louder. When she rounds the corner, all the sound she is making stops, and I can feel her heavy gaze on Mason on top of me.

He doesn't flinch or even try to move; instead, he makes that boyish smile of his as he stares at me head-on and says, "Hi, Miss Rose."

"Boy," she greets, walking forward and placing her bag on the end table closest to her. "Get up off my granddaughter."

Mason laughs into a scoff as he rolls his eyes. It is as if we are teenagers again, and she just walked in on us making out when he was about to get to second base.

He sits up, still straddling me, and places both hands on his lap with a lazy smile. "Oh come on, Miss Rose, we're grown now."

My grandmother clocks her head to the side and stares Mason down. "You don't fool me, Mason. I know your daddy. I know how you boys get down."

Mason's eyes harden into an icy glare as he looks Nana up and down, sizing her up like a predator assessing its prey. A smirk tugs at the corner of his lips as if he's already planning his victory.

"How do we get down?"

"By beating your women into a pulp," she declares, running her tongue across her gums with a chilling smirk and a humorless laugh. "But you see, I'll tell you what I told your granddaddy when we were young."

Mason laughs, a smirk playing on his face. "Oh yeah, and what did you tell him?"

My nana reaches into her coat pocket and brandishes a gun, pointing it directly at Mason. "I told him that I am a sharpshooter who will kill him and you dead without hesitation."

Mason's humor leaves his face, but he looks my nana square in the eye and scoffs out a warning: "Miss Rose, you're not the only one with a gun."

Nana smirks, her finger resting on the trigger. "I bet," she says calmly as she cocks the gun. "But I am the only one with their gun cocked and ready to blow." Her voice drops lower, almost a guttural growl. "So as I said, get the fuck up off my granddaughter and mosey yourself up out of this house."

Mason's eyes narrow, but he doesn't meet her challenge. Instead, he slowly rises from his position on top of me, maintaining eye contact with Nana the entire time. His hands are up in the air as a sign of surrender, and his voice is calm but firm.

"48 hours, Gwen, not a minute after," he says, not backing down. I don't dare look in his direction but feel his gaze streaming down on me.

Nana Rose shakes her head, her gun hand steady. "We'll be, Mason, but if you ever try to pull this garbage again, I won't hesitate. Understand?"

Mason bares his teeth in a smile that isn't quite a smile, then turns his gaze to me. "Neither will I."

Nana Rose keeps the gun trained on him as he walks past us out the door. I stay lying on the ground, my hands above my head and my breathing unsteady. Nana's breath comes out shaky, but she doesn't make me move because I feel completely human for the first time in my life, no more bravado or slick comeback to defend me.

I am terrified and frozen on my living room floor.

14

GWEN

Nana sits on the couch next to my idle body, but after about ten minutes, she whispers, "Gwen, what happens in 48 hours?"

My chest tightens, and I want to pull my hair out and scream, but I don't have the energy to do so because everything feels so out of reach, so out of control that I want to crawl into a ball and sob.

"In 48 hours, either I get him the 197,000 dollars, or he wants me to himself," I respond, not daring to look at her because I know her heart is shattering into a million pieces.

"You can't be his."

"I can't get one hundred and ninety seven thousand dollars in two days." I finally sit up.

My head feels heavy, and my chest is so tight with the need to cry that I am practically shaking as I look over at Nana, whose eyes glisten with tears, but her lips are in a straight line with a confident look.

"Then you need to run." She slaps both of her thighs with her hands and gets up, walking towards the kitchen. Her statement sends a spark of electricity through me, and I shoot up, trying to follow her quick movements into her bedroom.

"I can't go on the run with two five-year-olds!" I whisper yell, afraid Mia, who is still playing with her *Uncle Mason's* Barbies, will hear me arguing.

Nana Rose looks over her shoulder, narrowing her eyes at me as she lowers to her knees as if she is about to pray, but instead reaches underneath the bed. She reveals a pink, rosy box I remember from childhood because I couldn't touch it.

"Nana?" I question, cautiously moving forward, but she doesn't respond.

Instead, she whispers to herself as if she is talking herself into whatever she is about to reveal to me. "Nana, you're scaring me."

Taking a deep breath, she begins to speak, "Your grandfather was a terrible man. He was just like Mason, quick-tempered and dangerously possessive."

She opens the box, revealing stacks of neatly bundled cash, along with important paperwork like birth certificates and social security cards and a small, silver revolver.

"Gwen, when I was a young girl, I made the hardest decision of my life, but I did it to protect my family, and it was the smartest thing I have ever done."

Nana places a stack of cash on the floor next to her, and speechlessly, I fall to my knees slightly behind her. My eyes stuck to all the money she had that we could have used over the years. I reach forward to touch the most money I have seen, but she swats my hand away and turns to me, leveling me with a serious glare.

"Gwendolyn, I ran to protect my family, to give them a chance at a better life, and now you must, too," Nana speaks with a certainty I have never possessed, and tears crest in my eyes.

"W-where will we go? Mason will find me if I travel with two kids and they have school and friends. I can't. I can't-"

My breathing comes out in sharp gusts as my chest tightens to the point where I can't breathe. I bend over my knees, trying to control how my lungs burn for oxygen, but the ball in my throat won't let it in.

"Now, you can't run with both Mia and Gio, so I think you need to leave them behind, leave them somewhere safe." I shake my head. The word *"no"* creeps across my tongue, but I hold it in, shaking the tears out of my eyes.

"You should ask Kelsey to visit her family in California with them. Give her some of this money."

Nana places one of the stacks in my hand, and despite the weight and awe I feel in having so much money in my hand, I drop it to the ground as if it has burned me.

How could she ever ask me to do this? To leave everything I know, to abandon my children, and run with no end in sight. When will they ever be able to come home? When can I ever hold my babies again without fear of revealing their location to Mason? Nana grips my hands in hers, but I can't bring myself to look her in the eye because she would give me that look that would mean this is real and it is something I have to do.

She shakes my hands lightly against her thighs and whispers, "You are strong enough to do this. You are resilient. You can get through anything. Isn't that what I always told you?"

I nod, the tears creating rivers down my cheeks and dripping off my chin. Nana leans in closer, her forehead against mine. "Tell me what we say when we are afraid."

A sob leaves my lips, and I can feel myself quivering as if it is freezing, but I feel ten and afraid of going to school and having my crush call me ugly. I feel like I am small enough to crawl into her lap again, which makes the tears fall even faster. The words come out between gasps of breath, but I repeat the mantra the same way I always have.

"I am brilliantly beautiful, able to withstand dragons and defeat armies because I am the princess that saves herself."

Nana kisses my forehead, whispering, "That's right, baby, and now you have graduated to a queen who defeats the villain and saves her kingdom, but first, you need to get the right army behind you."

Tears blur my vision as I lean into her lips, still pressed against me. "How did you manage it? How could you just run away?"

Nana's face softens, a hint of a sad smile tugging at her lips. "I had help from people who cared about me, just like you have, and I had faith that I would get through this."

I nod, almost believing that I, too, possess this same strength. "This money will get you started in a new location, somewhere where Mason can't find you while you get your bearings and figure out a game plan."

I look at the box's contents, the world seemingly crashing around me. "Where will I go? I don't even know where to start."

"You've always wanted to go to New York, be in the Big Apple with all those lights?" I nod in agreement. "Well, there is the bright side. You can finally go."

The smile in her voice makes me chuckle lightly. "Okay, you call Kelsey, and I will start to get you packed up."

The sweetness in her voice lulls me into action. I head to the kids' room, my mind racing, but the minute I see Mia playing with her dolls, I smile, leaning against the doorframe. Nana walks up behind me with a child-size suitcase, and I realize that if I run, she will be here and vulnerable to Mason's wrath.

"Nana, what about you?"

Nana Rose smiles, her eyes filled with a mix of sorrow and determination. "I'll be fine. I'll tell Mason whatever he needs to hear to buy you more time. But you have to go now because, by morning, he will have so many eyes on you that you won't be able to run."

I lace her hand with mine, squeezing tightly, the tears threatening to spill over again. "Thank you, Nana. I don't know how I'll ever repay you."

"Just keep those babies safe," she whispers, holding me close for a moment longer before pushing me gently away. "And when you go, find a way to come back to me."

15

NIKOLAI

I stand in the middle of my father's prison cell, sweat and blood drenching my white button-up, but that motherfucker still has the gall to spit onto the floor and smile.

My father, Boris, is slumped over to the side, hands tied behind his back to the metal chair that the rest of his body is strapped to. His eye is swollen, and he wears a bloody smile from the teeth I have ripped out, but regardless of all the pain I know I have inflicted on him, he laughs as if I only made fucking paper-cuts.

I despise how this man gets under my skin, and it makes me want to crawl up the goddamn wall with his pure psychotic tendencies. Who knew having an ex-military father turned criminal would be such a fucking headache?

"Come on now, Nikolai, I've taught you better than this," he scolds, narrowing his eyes at the hammer I have dangling between my fingertips. "Maybe you should have Aleksandr come; at least his ways of torture are creative."

"Trust me, Papa, we are only getting started," I counter between gritted teeth, my voice low and simmering with barely contained rage. "I was thinking of carving that stupid smile into your face. How does that sound?"

Despite every conscious fiber of my being screaming that I am in control, there's a part of me—a dark, vicious part—that feels like a caged animal, one rude remark away from tearing my father's chest open and ripping out his still-beating heart.

It has taken years of self-control and patience to learn how to contain this beast within me. The countless nights spent honing my mind, restraining my impulses, mastering the art of control. I've walked the razor's edge, balancing between the man I strive to be and the monster lurking in my blood. Because there is nothing worse than a mad king, a ruler so consumed by his own rage that he is willing to sacrifice every man who dares look at him the wrong way.

Boris's laughter grates against my nerves, a sound that seems to mock my every effort to remain composed.

"Now that's the spirit, Nikolai," he says, his voice dripping with condescension. "Show me that fire. Show me you're not the weakling. Be my bastard of a son."

"I am nothing like you," I snarl, my grip on the hammer tightening until my knuckles turn white. "You've built an empire on people who would rather betray you than stand in the pits of hell alongside you. I am better than you. My people would die for me."

Boris's eyes flash with anger, but the twisted smile never leaves his face. "And yet here you are, Nikolai, standing in the pits of hell with me. What does that make you?"

I throw myself at Boris, my nails digging into the flesh of his cheeks as I grip his jaw, placing the hammer on his chin. I know I fucked up when I see the light in his eyes, as if he recognizes this version of me as kin.

"Ahh, there you are. A Mafia King who is willing to kill." Boris chuckles, adjusting himself in his chains as if this is a Sunday afternoon and he is getting comfortable on the couch. "Maybe a lesson or two did get through that thick skull."

I push air through my nostrils and push myself off the madman. My laugh is humorless, making my way to the weapons adorning the table and evaluating which knife would cut the slowest out of the bunch. I would have to scold myself later for that outburst. No one man should make me this violent. My breathing steadies as I run my finger along the edge of a machete, and I respond.

"If I listened to all your lessons, I would have killed my wife in cold blood and then cut up her body and sent them to my children. Seems like you're a fucked up teacher to me."

"Ahh, you see, you were always a terrible student."

I peek at him over my shoulder, unwilling to show him how eager I am to still learn from the infamous Boris Petrov, once called the Demon of New York.

"If you were a better student, you would see the lesson was in loyalty and what to do to those whose loyalty falters."

My jaws click as I run my teeth together and turn my attention back to my examination of torture tools. I run my fingers over a scalpel, and I turn to look at him over my shoulder, "How does a scalpel sound?"

He clicks his head to the side and gives me that toothy smile I fucking hate. "Splendid."

"You were always so caught up in lessons that you never knew where you faltered." I spin the scalpel across my knuckles and smile in that toothy way that makes others think we are blood-related. I wag the sharp end of the scalpel at him as if he is a naughty child and continue, "Because let's make one thing clear: you are a failure."

His face smooths out to the scowl I got accustomed to in my childhood, the wrinkle between his brows, his eyes hardened, and his lips plastered into a straight line. This makes me laugh in a way that isn't to show that I can match his madness. No, this laugh is pure pleasure that I've hit a nerve.

"You see, I did learn from you because I know all about loyalty," I say, taking a dancer's step closer to him as if we are doing a psychotic version of the tango. "I learned loyalty to the Mafia. Loyalty to your followers. Loyalty to the grunt worker who may see a thing or two he wasn't supposed to." I allow the mask of my control to slip ever so slightly so that family resemblance really gets under his skin.

I drop my voice down to a whisper, "But what about loyalty to family, huh? What about loyalty to the ones you supposedly love?"

I mock him, tapping the knife to the apples of his cheeks that are already swelling from earlier activities, but he doesn't give me the satisfaction of a flinch.

"You see, that's where you fall short because those people could be the end of you. That's a lesson you should have learned, or do I need to teach you again?"

Boris's eyes flash with something—anger, perhaps, or amusement but he shakes his chains as if he could break free like the Hulk, and I step back, clicking my tongue. "Don't be mad at me that you don't follow your lessons."

"A lesson in love," he spits. "Love is a weakness. I taught you that too, didn't I? I showed you what happens when the facade of love clouds you. You leave yourself open to be taken for a fool. You then have to let your bastard run the Mafia you built from ashes just to save face, or if given the chance, you have to kill him too, just like his whore of a mother."

My nostrils flare, but I maintain composure. "Funny. You wish you could kill me so you don't have to look into the eyes of the man who actually loved my mother," I taunt, gripping the scalpel's handle so tightly my knuckles turn white.

"What are you ashamed of, Boris? That when she got tired of your shit, she found someone else? Someone worthy. Someone who wasn't a limp dick piece of shit."

Boris's face darkens, his bloody smile fading for a moment.

"Your mother was a weak whore who lived her life thinking about the next nut she could get," he says with a look of excitement on his face as if he hasn't said something just as cruel thousands of times.

"She betrayed the Mafia and paid for it with her life, and I will make sure she never rests in peace so that I can torment her little betrayals until my last breath."

"Is that what I am?" I press, feeling a sick thrill as his eyes narrow. "A reminder of her betrayal?"

Boris sneers. "You are a reminder of the only regret I have ever had. I should have killed you when I had the fucking chance."

"Aw, could've, would've, should've. Those things will haunt you," I say, laughing, stepping closer to him, the knife glinting in the dim light. "You know what really pisses you off," I sing, gliding the knife across his shoulder blade. "You aren't certain that you have an heir. You don't know if any of your children are actually yours, but her bastards get to carry on your legacy. That's pathetic."

"You see, you are a weak king, Nikolai, still searching for his mother's tit," Boris growls. "You were never fit to be king because you have a bleeding heart. I should have gutted the organ when I had a chance."

I toss the scalpel into the air, catch it, and dig it into the thigh of Boris as he rings out in frustration. "I won't make this easy on you, but since you are so convinced that you and I are similar, let me tell you the cardinal difference between us." I yank the scalpel out of his leg and watch the blood gush from the wound. "When I get a woman, she will be treated like a queen. That way, I know my heir is fucking mine."

Boris laughs, leaning over from the pain, but grits through his teeth. "And that weakness will get you killed."

"Maybe," I say, leaning in close so he can see the fire in my eyes. "But I'd rather be dead with a son who will avenge me than wish me dead."

Boris laughs, a harsh, grating sound. "Where's the fun in that?"

"You're right about that. This is so much more fun." I lift the tip of the scalpel to his lips and smile. "Now say cheese."

As usual, Boris didn't crack. When I exited the prison beneath our building, I was greeted with my mother's left rib cage. I guess he was right; I am a bleeding heart because the idea of holding the part of my mother that once housed her heart almost made me fall to my knees. But I can't break until I have her entire body in my hands. Only then will I allow myself the solace of crying over her death.

After changing my blood-soaked button-down into a white cotton T-shirt in my office, I decided to walk home and clear my mind. I still have to tell my siblings the truth—that we may all be bastards, and I don't know who our true father is. I just know Boris isn't. Or I could take that to my grave and let them believe I am not their blood brother. But what would that mean for the crown of the Mafia? That would mean it rightfully belongs to Nadia or Aleksandr, and I have stolen it from underneath their noses. They will never forgive me for stealing the kingdom for myself. But I can never let this go. I was made to be king, no matter the blood in my veins. I was made to rule over New York.

I walk down the dimly lit streets, my body still slick with sweat, the ghost of Boris's laughter echoing in my mind. The night is thick with the scent of rain and dirt, the city's neon lights casting eerie reflections on the wet pavement. I feel myself spiral as I always do after being covered in blood. The excitement courses through my veins, and in this state, I believe I could take down a bear and defeat an army. My God complex runs at an all-time high as I look up into a diner, ready to make the world bend to me. That's when I see her.

In the window of a small diner, illuminated by the soft, warm glow of the interior lights, I see her curly black hair and tanned skin as she reaches for a salt shaker. She sits with another girl, laughing, her delicate features framed by her dark hair, her expression serene as she sips her coffee. My heart squeezes in my chest, and I swear the world stops. This must be what it feels like when a sinner is given the option of heaven. I am seeing an angel for the first time. My heart pounds, and before

I know it, I am running towards her, desperate to steal this little slice of heaven all for myself.

"Kotik!" I call out.

The woman turns around, her hair bouncing in the air, and my heart plummets. The girl isn't Gwen. In fact, her hair is brown, not black, and her lips are painted an awful shade of red that isn't glossed the way Gwen likes to gloss her lips. Her eyes aren't that intoxicating honeyed brown; the woman's eyes are a cool blue.

I stare at her. The disappointment hits me like a physical blow, and I feel as if I've been yanked from heaven and thrown back into the depths of hell where I belong. The woman's eyes widen in surprise and confusion, and I mumble an apology, stumbling back onto the street, unwilling to look at the imposter any longer.

When I hit the streets, my city is colder, its lights harsh and unforgiving. This walk is no longer a comfort for my mind and is now a vehicle to torment me further. I lean against a lamppost, struggling to catch my breath. Seeing that woman makes me think that the sickening smell of vanilla invades my nostrils, and I want to hunt for my darling kitty all over again. I want to drag her back into my arms, and tie her to my bed, and never let her leave me again.

The beast within me roars, demanding release, but I clench my fists and hold it back. I have to be stronger than this. I have to be the king I was meant to be, and no woman who is slowly drifting into a figment of my imagination can bring me to my knees. I cannot allow myself to be a lovesick king, no matter how much I want her.

16

GWEN

As a little girl, I dreamed about New York as a place of glamor and excitement. But after my first night in the city, being curled up on the dirty floor of the subway train, with the stench of urine filling my nostrils, I couldn't believe I wasted so many birthday candles in this place. My first night in the city, and I was already living like a homeless person.

I always dreamed of living in a god-awfully small apartment with roaches and a naked neighbor who did things like yoga with all their lights on. I would make friends in a coffee shop and not flinch whenever a dark figure came into my eyeline, thinking it could be Mason. I would have wine nights and basically relive an affordable version of *Friends* or *Living Single,* but not this.

With nothing to my name but the trusty suitcase, duffel bag combo, and a photo of Mia and Gio in my pocket in case I lost my phone, this was my New York experience, and I loathed it. It had taken me twenty long hours to convince the owner of a rundown hotel on 42nd Street and Twelfth Avenue that I wasn't a prostitute, drug dealer, or drug addict, just a girl in desperate need of a shower. After numerous threats and the mention of 'Big Joe' - whoever that was - the lady finally believed me and let me stay for only $15 a night. As I settled into my dingy room and lay in bed, I considered my next steps. Still, I could only think about my children, who were currently in California with Kelsey and David on an indefinite vacation.

My fingers tap restlessly on my phone screen until I find Kelsey's name. My makeshift living space - a cluttered and dimly lit room adorned with cheap furniture - serves as the backdrop for our video call, but I desperately hope she won't notice. Kelsey answers on the second ring, her golden hair illuminated by the warm summer sun. My heart swells at the sight of her face on the screen. Attempting to keep my emotions in check, I smile before speaking, but Kels can see through it with her big, concerned eyes.

"Gwen, what's wrong?"

"Nothing's wrong." I beam as if not a ball of salt is forming in my throat.

"No, I can see it in your face. Don't lie to me. Besties don't lie to each other," she scolds, her eyes narrowed as she tries to look over my face.

"Kels," I whisper. "Nothing is right. I am in New York. You are raising my children, and we are all on the run from a horny, obsessed, probably murderous Mason."

Kelsey sighs, lying out on her bed. "I know, but you are doing what needs to be done to protect your family, right?"

"Yes, but I-" My voice catches in my throat, and tears threaten to pour. "I don't know what to do next, Kels. I mean, I am living in a hotel that I am pretty sure is a front for a drug ring, and the owner already threatened me with the presence of Big Joe."

"Wait, why are you living in a motel?"

"Because where the hell else am I supposed to go?"

Kelsey's eyes bug out of her head, and she sits up, looking at me as if I had just grown a second head. "Taylor."

I sit up with wide eyes and shake my head feverishly. "No, I am not calling Taylor."

"The hell you are not!" Kelsey yells back. Another screen pops up, and I can hear the ringing of another call to join Facetime.

Taylor is my best friend from law school because he was always in second place to me until I left to deal with my dad's debt. We also have done some strip study sessions, which always ended with him butt naked and me with just one shoe off. We even attempted to date once, but our relationship felt more like a legal battle than a romantic connection. So we made a pact to be best friends instead, but now I can't help but feel a twinge of regret every time his name flashes across my screen.

"Kels, I haven't talked to him since I dropped out," I scold, balancing my phone on my thigh and pulling my hair into a ponytail.

Kelsey clicks her tongue at me, and the deafening sound of the ring vibrates on my lap. The call clicks, and I see Taylor's shaggy brown hair enter the frame, a big smile on his face. He is in his kitchen, cutting up an array of vegetables.

"Well, if it isn't my two favorite ladies!"

"Tay Tay, how are you, darling?" Kelsey pops up, talking to Taylor, and the phone almost tumbles out of my hand as I try to hide my dingy hotel room.

"I'm well, just missing two of my favorite people in the world." He smirks, looking at the camera from the corner of his eye. "Hey, Gwen."

"What's up, Tay?" My voice sounds more awkward than cool and confident, as I intended, and I want to smack my forehead in frustration.

Taylor's smile falters as he catches the strained note in my voice. "Gwen, are you okay? What's going on?"

He sets down the knife and leans closer to the camera, his eyes searching mine for any signs of distress. Kelsey shoots me a pointed look, silently urging me to spill the truth.

I fall silent, and Kelsey huffs in frustration, looking at me with knitted brows. "Taylor, guess what?"

"What?" Taylor sings, obviously confused, but that playful golden retriever smile radiates across the screen, and I catch myself smiling at him.

"Gwen is in New York!" Kelsey says as if we are teenagers, and she is telling him I have a crush on him.

Taylor stops cutting his carrot and looks at the screen with so much excitement that my heart somersaults my chest.

"And she needs a place to stay."

"Yes. Gwen, where are you?" Taylor brings the phone close to his face as if he can look around the room and determine my exact coordinates.

"Taylor, you don't have to worry about it," I say through a gritted smile as I plan Kelsey's funeral.

"No, no, send me the address where you are, and I will pick you up," Taylor demands, and I hear the clink of keys as he makes his way to his front door. "And you better text it to me because I am already on my way."

Taylor hangs up the phone, and when the call is just Kelsey and me again, my eyes narrow on the screen.

"I am going to kill you."

"You are going to kill me freshly dicked down on Egyptian cotton sheets. I think that is a good death my mother will be proud of." She nods, waving her eyebrows as she teases me.

"Don't you dare kiss my children with that dirty mouth."

"I'll wash my mouth out with soap first, Mama Bear, don't you worry!" She winks, and I hang up the call with an I love you and a promise to call tomorrow to talk to the children.

I send Tay the address and he promises to be there soon. I walk around my room and pack the few items I have taken out, ready for his arrival. As I make my way out of the room and into the hallway, I see a flier for a job at a club called *Johanna's*. I steal the paper off the bulletin board and stand out front.

Taylor pulls up in a sleek, black Mercedes Benz and immediately hops out with a swoon-worthy smile.

"As gorgeous as ever, Gwenie." He beams, walking over to me, and his arms loop around my waist. He then brings me into a large hug and spins me around. "God, I missed you."

Taylor opens up the passenger side car door for me, closes it, and leans in through the window. "Baby, Georgetown was shit without you."

I buckle my seatbelt with an unladylike snort. "With you as valedictorian, I bet."

Taylor laughs, putting my suitcase in the trunk and sliding into the front seat of his car. "Hey, I was just as smart as you."

"Taylor, I know the exact girth and length of your dick, and that was just from study and strip." I roll my eyes, and the engine roars with his laughter.

"I was distracted by the most beautiful girl on the East Coast." He leans over to me, his caramel eyes rolling over me with a relaxed laziness as if he has done this a million times before.

I lean in close with a small smile on my face. "You are still not fine enough to ride this ride, honey."

"Well, besides you trying to destroy my ego," he peeks at me from the corner of my eye, "why are you in the Big Apple? Did you get into NYU's law program?"

I take a deep breath. "No, I didn't, but I got in eight years ago, and Georgetown is still my first choice."

"So what's up? Are you on the run?" he jokes, and I swallow deeply, looking out the window and away from his eyes. "No shit, you're on the fucking run! From who? Not the police because I cannot lose my license because I harbored a fugitive."

"I am running away from Mason," I breathe out.

"That creep who stalked you all the time? What the hell did he do now, Gwen? I told you to get a restraining order years ago," he snaps as he pulls into a spacious, underground garage of a sleek, sixty-story tall glass tower.

"Taylor, my dad owes this man one hundred and ninety five thousand dollars, and if I didn't give it to him by yesterday morning, he was going to take me and my kids for himself." I avoid eye contact as I look at my cuticles and bite my lower lip.

Taylor pulls the car into a parking space and turns to me with concerned eyes. "You have kids? Where are they?"

"Gio and Mia are with Kelsey in California until I can get the money or figure out a plan," I mumble. "And I know this is a lot, so if you don't want me here, then I can figure something else out."

Taylor interlocks his hand with mine and kisses my knuckles. "No, I always want you here, Gwen. Don't worry about it. You can stay here as long as you want. I got you, always have, always will."

As sunlight streamed through the blinds, I woke up to the smell of freshly baked biscuits and bacon. Taylor had left breakfast for me in the microwave before heading off to work. I couldn't help but admire his dedication and ambition as he was on track to become the youngest New York assistant attorney general.

As I ate my breakfast, I thought about my goal for the day: getting a job at *Johanna's* as a bartender or dancer. Despite Taylor offering me a job as his personal assistant to ease back into the legal world, I knew I needed to lay low and take jobs where Mason wouldn't easily find me. After all, there was only one Taylor McKibble that Mason knew I knew, and there were hundreds of clubs where I could dance.

As I stood outside *Johanna*'s imposing doors, my eyes flicked back and forth between the flier in my hand and the lavish club before me. The golden script on the glass doors spelled out its name: *Johanna's*. Despite the sleek exterior, I could practically feel the pulse of temptation emanating from within.

I couldn't help but wonder if it would rival the raunchiness of my hometown strip club Nikolai first saw me in or perhaps even surpass it for those with deep enough pockets to afford such luxuries. A velvet rope lined the entrance, manned by two imposing bouncers in tailored black suits, their stoic expressions adding an air of exclusivity.

Before I shift to make my way inside, my phone buzzes, and Kelsey's name pops up on the screen. I quickly answer, ready to chastise her for calling Taylor yesterday, even if she was right about his Egyptian cotton sheets.

Mia's bright hazel eyes and wild blonde curls pop into the screen, and my scowl immediately turns into a bright smile. "Hi, sweetheart! How are you?"

"Hi, Mommy! We went to the beach today! Gio and I built a big sandcastle!" Mia's voice is filled with excitement as she turns the camera to Gio, who is messing with the edges of the sandcastle to make it as perfect as possible. For a moment, a pang of guilt shoots through my chest for being so far away from them.

"That looks amazing, baby! I wish I could have been there with you."

"Mommy, when are we going to see you again? Gio and I miss you!" Mia asks, her face too close to the camera.

"I will be back with you by the next shooting star."

As I speak to Mia about her new school in California, a sleek black town car pulls up sharply to the curb. My heart pounds against my chest as a tall man in a tailored suit steps out, exuding an air of power and menace with his slick, dirty blonde hair and cold, calculating expression. His piercing blue eyes seem to sparkle with malice and intrigue, a combination that reminds me instantly of Nikolai. The guy's black suit is accented with subtle shades of gray, giving off an air of sophistication and danger. But it can't be him as my heart races at the sight of him approaching. As he locks eyes with me, a surge of fear and longing overwhelms me - it couldn't be Nik after all these years. But his narrowed gaze betrays no recognition as I watch him disappear into the back entrance of *Johanna's*, my mind reeling before I force myself to focus on Mia again.

"And Gio's new animals are chimpanzees. We went to the zoo, and he told me not to smile at them. I said that was rude." Mia huffs as she sticks her tongue out at Gio.

"If you smile at them, they think it is aggression. They think you are being mean," Gio says in frustration, almost yelling at Mia as if he has told her this thirty times today alone.

"Gio, no yelling at Mia. Mia, Gio is right. Chimps are different from humans; smiling isn't nice to them."

"Told you," Gio mumbles.

Mia sticks her tongue out at him before returning her attention to me. "I love you, Mommy, but it is *Bluey* time."

"I love you, Mia. Give each other a big hug from me, okay?" Mia runs up to Gio and tackles him in a big hug.

"Done, Mommy. Bye!" Mia hangs up, and I take a deep breath, steeling myself in front of the club.

My heart is racing with anticipation as I reach for the door handle, but the bouncer, with a silver stud in his ear and glass blue eyes, stops me swiftly with a hand stretched out in front of my chest.

"State your business," he growls.

I swing the flier up in my hand and cock an eyebrow. "I am here for the dancer position."

"You don't seem like a dancer to me," the other bouncer with a bald head snorts, crossing his hands over his chest.

"I know this doesn't look like much, but get me in a room alone, and I promise you my legs can reach my ears with the right incentive," I whisper, giving both bouncers a seductive smile while trailing my eyes up their bodies.

"I don't know, Bruce; she sounds like a stripper to me." The bouncer with the stud opens up the door for me with lust dancing across his eyes. "Oscar's office is up the stairs and on the left."

I nod, swaying my hips as I enter the club. The interior is more intimidating than the exterior, and I don't have my jaw on the floor.

Rich, dark wood and plush, velvet seating dominate the space, creating a level of luxury I have never seen before inside a strip club. The dim lighting is placed strategically to create intimate pockets of light that dance off the mirrored walls and reflect on the polished marble floors. Crystal chandeliers hang from the ceiling, casting a soft, seductive glow that bounces off the glitter-adorned dancers' bodies as they do their warm-up routines.

I make my way toward the bar, my eyes scanning the room. The main stage, the focal point of the room, is framed by heavy, red velvet curtains and adorned with golden accents. The few dancers are already on stage, moving with an unnatural level of grace that seems almost ethereal under the soft spotlight. A girl jumps up into the air, her legs dropping into a split as she swings down the pole, and for a second, nerves run through me because that girl up there is good, treating stripping like the art form it is.

As I approach the bar, I can't help the second wave of nerves that prick over my skin as I touch the smooth dark wood that feels like a pornstar martini never spilled on it. The bartender, a tall, muscular man with dark hair, a chiseled jaw, and piercing blue eyes, looks up from polishing a glass. He lets out a low whistle, his eyes raking me leisurely.

"Well, well, what do we have here?" he says with a playful smirk. His voice is smooth, dripping with charm. He leans on top of the bar, closer to me. "Darling, you know this is a gentleman's club, right?"

I slide into one of the chairs with my own flirty smile on my lips. "Do I not look like a gentleman's wet dream?"

"I try not to be so forward with a girl when I first meet her," he says, placing the glass on the table and taking a long look at my breast peeking through my v-neck t-shirt.

"Why not?" I ask, a sly smile playing on my lips.

I cross my right leg over the other, feeling a surge of confidence rush through me. My body feels electric, every inch of my skin tingling with anticipation. It's a feeling I haven't experienced in years. A feeling I thought I would never feel again because I had kids and worked so many hours that I couldn't always be bothered to run a brush through my hair or not have some type of stain on my clothing.

As I sit here across from a hot bartender in a city where no one knows my name, I am reminded of the woman I used to be – confident, sexy, untouchable. My hair falls in loose curls, freshly brushed and styled. My white v-neck falls right below my belly button, and my jeans caress every inch of my curves.

For once, everything feels perfect, and I can't help but revel in being truly good again.

"Girly, you are playing with fire." He slides me a rum and coke which works in his favor because it's my favorite drink.

"How'd you know I was a rum and coke girl?" I smile, pulling the straw to my lips and taking a light sip.

"You look like a classic with a little fun." I roll my eyes at his blinding smile and slowly turn on my stool.

"So flirty boy, what's your name?" I tease.

"My name is Hudson." He winks.

"Like the river?" I counter.

"I was named after my ability to make things wet." He winks, and I laugh because no one other than Nikolai can flirt with me like this. Never missing a beat. Surprising me. I think back to that guy I saw outside of the bar, his deep oceanic blue eyes, dirty blonde hair, and black suit. He looked like Nikolai, and my body tingles with the need to see that guy again.

"Well, if I get a job here, we can test your namesake." I wink, reaching my hand across the bar. "My name is Gwen."

"Sexy name for a sexy girl." He brings my hand to his lips as he tilts his head towards the double doors to his right. "The manager's office is through those doors next to the bar, first door on the left."

"Thank you." I smile. I start to pull my hand away, but he holds on with a little pressure.

"Do a good job, would ya? I want to see your fine ass here every day." He releases my hand, and I snort, rolling my eyes.

He laughs to himself, and I shimmy through the double doors to my right.

I knock on the door with a shaky hand, my heart pounding in my chest. A rough, commanding voice booms from inside, ordering me to enter.

"What's your business?" he barks, wasting no time on small talk.

"I'm here for the dancer's job." I lean on my right hip and present my resume from my bag.

The man's piercing gaze sweeps over me, lingering on my curves and less-than-perfect figure. "You don't exactly look like a dancer," he says bluntly, a smirk playing at the corner of his mouth.

Normally, I would tell him he doesn't look like much of a man, but I really need this job, so I close my mouth.

My teeth grind together as I try to force a smile, pushing my resume onto his cluttered desk. "I am sure the men that frequent this place all have different tastes in ladies, and I have experience dancing in two jobs, and despite my lack of visible muscle, I know my way around a pole, and I am really bendy, I promise."

His gaze narrows on me, a sharp edge of dismissal on the tip of his tongue, but the phone on his desk rings before he can respond. He hesitates for a moment, his eyes still locked onto mine, before finally reaching for the receiver with an exasperated sigh.

The low murmur of voices filters through the line as he answers with a curt: "Boss?"

The man's face contorts in annoyance, his eyebrows furrowing and lips tightly pressing together. But then, as if a light switch has been flipped, his expression shifts to one of surprise.

"Actually, there is a young woman here inquiring about a job," he finally admits with a nod. In the blink of an eye, he snatches up my resume from the desk and scans it quickly, muttering, "Her name is Gwendolyn." He nods a string of yeses and nos under his breath. With a skeptical look in his eye, he looks back at me and lets out a heavy sigh. "Alright, sir," he concedes reluctantly.

"You must have friends in high places. The boss wants you to start tonight."

"Or your boss must have more taste in ladies that look more like me?" I smirk, placing a hand on his desk as I lean over.

The guy gives me a once-over again and snorts. "I doubt it. Be here at seven pm sharp. Tell Hudson your size on the way out."

"Oh my god!" I squeal. "Thank you. You won't regret this."

The manager sighs, muttering, "I already do."

17

NIKOLAI

It's her. My Gwen, at my bar, looking to be a dancer when she truly looks like a goddess who has descended from the heavens. My heart feels like it's going to burst out of my chest because the minute Oscar said Gwendolyn, I knew it was her. Shit, I knew it was her when I saw her outside, but this time I had to make sure.

And now it is taking every inch of my willpower not to run down those stairs and grab her, hold her close, and inhale the sweet vanilla scent that I remember that lingers in her hair.

My eyes don't leave her body as I watch her on the security cameras in my office. She looks fucking delectable. Her wild black curls cascade down her back in perfect spirals, begging me to run my fingers through them. Her pink lips, full and plump, taunt me with their smirk, reminding me of all the times they've wrapped around my length and made me bust without savoring the velvet feel of her tongue.

But then my gaze falls on her ass, round and full, practically begging to be squeezed and spanked. Her thighs still have a sinful level of thickness that makes her jeans damn near look painted on.

And I realize that Hudson must have had a better view of it than I did from up here. The surge of anger that courses through me is almost suffocating as he laughs at something she says and his eyes linger on her curves.

How dare he even look at my girl? I should skin him alive. I never liked his face anyway; maybe I could rearrange it for him. That would help the anger coursing through my veins, or maybe a more fitting punishment for the stupid kid is for me to gouge out his eyes. That way, he can never look at her again.

I hear the low wolf whistle as Gwen does a little dance before leaving, happy that she got the job. A blush creeps up Gwen's neck, and I snarl. *Fuck. Maybe I should cut out his tongue as well.*

Hudson calls after her, "Don't be late, girly! I'll be waiting."

A low growl escapes my throat as I watch Gwen leave, Hudson's admiring gaze fixed on her form. She may have gotten the job at the bar, but she's mine.

My fists clench so tightly that my knuckles turn white, and I imagine smashing them into Hudson's smug face. But I know better than to let my emotions control me. I take a deep breath and try to calm myself before grabbing the keys to my Escalade and storming out of the building.

My security team is hot on my heels, but I shake them off with a stubborn shake of my head, as I trail behind her. She walks down the street and slides her headphones in her ears.

I watch her walk down the crowded street, my muscles tense and my heart racing. My gaze follows her every step, scanning for any potential threats, or if she will do that disappearing act where one moment she is nuzzling my neck and the next she disappears for the next five years. She can't do that to me again.

I flex my fingers, trying to loosen the urge to throw her over my shoulder caveman style, make her know she is mine again. The thought of any other person having what I did makes my skin scorch and my joints tight with the need to pummel said person into the ground.

My eyes never leave her body as she dances carelessly down the street, oblivious to the world around her. I can't help but feel the need to hide her from the world, keep this little piece of heaven just for me, but then a flood of shame runs through me as I think about Gwen being hidden, and I want to let her out again. I want to be selfless with her. I don't want to drag her into the depths of hell with me unless she wants to, but all that nice guy talk leaves my mind the minute a man purposely gets in her way to touch her.

I almost groan aloud when I watch her two-step into the fucker with a large smile, and she just giggles out an apology, not noticing when his eyes trail her as she walks, his eyes following her every step. My heart beats frantically like a caged animal, wanting to lash out in protection and dominance. But I force myself to keep control, running my hand through my hair in frustration as I fight against my instincts. When I pass by the man who still can't take his eyes off Gwen, I shoulder check him so hard he stumbles back.

As Gwen turns the corner and walks down Eleventh Avenue, she pulls her curly black hair into a messy bun and the scent of her sweet vanilla wafts down the street. I almost buckle at the scent, my will to keep my distance until tonight slowly faltering as she spins, her hair whipping in the wind. As she continues down the residential street, she greets everyone with a bright smile and bounces around people who don't give her the light of day. It is as if she doesn't know this is New York, and the nasty looks she gets from some people make me want to grab them by the throat and force them to bask in her light.

She skips towards one of the buildings on 34th street, a familiar building that is mostly glass and screams bachelors with too much money. She can't afford to live here if she just got a job at my club. I know this because Aleksandr owns all the buildings on this street, and the rent is fucking astronomical, but as Alek puts it: perfect for the rich douchebags that live here.

She turns to see a tall man with shaggy brown hair sneaking up behind her. Before she can react, he wraps his arms around her in a bear hug and spins her around.

Gwen's headphones fly out of her ears as she clings to the person hugging her, her wide smile lighting up her face.

She playfully squeals out, "Taylor! Put me down!"

My heart constricts and my blood boils at the sight of them together. The anger bubbling inside me is enough to make Jeffery Dahmer seem like a friendly neighbor in comparison.

Taylor finally sets Gwen down, their laughter mingling as Taylor tucks a loose curl behind her ear. She seems to beam at the interaction.

"What's got you in such a great mood, baby girl?" Taylor says, his eyes lingering on her.

"I got a job at Johanna's!" she replies, her smile softening as she looks at him.

He bends slightly, excitedly grabbing her arms. "Oh my God! We have to celebrate!"

She giggles as he spins her around, "Not too much. I have to work at 7!"

Taylor checks his watch with a smile. "That means I have three hours to get you drunk and sober you up! More than enough time." His hand intertwines with hers, and he drags her into the building. She giggles as he pulls her along.

I step forward, ready to follow them into the building, rip Gwen from his arms, and pull her right into mine where she belongs. But just as I'm about to enter the building, my phone vibrates in my pocket. I glance at the screen and see Aleksandr's name flashing.

I answer the call, my voice taut. "Yes, Aleksandr?"

"Office, ten minutes," he says, his voice curt and to the point.

I take a deep breath, forcing myself to calm down. "I am handling something. Can it wait?"

"Ten minutes," Aleksandr snaps, and then I am greeted by the dial tone. *Fucking great.*

I grit my teeth, my eyes flicking back to Gwen and Taylor as they wait for the elevator.

As much as it kills me to walk away, I turn on my heel and make my way to Petrov's office because I know, despite whatever happens in the next three hours—and if Taylor wants to live, it better involve everyone's clothes on—I'll see Gwen tonight. And after tonight, she will be mine. No one else will touch her. No one else will make her smile like that. She will be back on her throne where she always belonged.

18

GWEN

As I stepped into *Johanna's Gentleman Club,* the pounding bass and colorful neon lights assaulted my senses. The men here were a far cry from the usual rowdy crowd back home - they exuded wealth and sophistication, their designer suits and expensive cologne marking them as successful businessmen. And then there were the women – not just strippers, but skilled contortionists who twisted and turned their bodies in seductive poses for the mostly male audience, with a few women scattered throughout. It's clear that everyone here has money to spare, unlike me with my mountain of debt to Mason.

I couldn't help but feel envious of their easy access to money, knowing that any one of these patrons could easily wipe away my debt to Mason with a flick of their wrist. But as I make my way through the club, I couldn't help but feel a set of eyes on me. I walk through the side doors to the back where the manager's office is and Oscar, the manager, is staring at me with an impatient glint in his eye. "You're twenty minutes late."

I give him a sheepish smile and shrug slightly. "I'm not from New York. I didn't know a twenty minute train ride really meant forty." Oscar rolls his eyes at me walking ahead of me and I jog to keep up with him. My belly rolls and I curse Taylor under my breath because only he would send me to work four drinks in and full of Korean fried chicken when he knew I'd be dancing around a pole tonight. The thought of all the food I just ate coming up in spades makes my body lurch as if I am seconds from throwing up, but I swallow it down. *Do not throw up on your first night, Gwen.*

"Okay so you will be working the floor tonight unless someone personally asks for a private dance," Oscar says opening the door to a huge dressing area complete with private rooms and a huge gust of *Victoria Secret* perfume invading my nostrils.

"By private dance, you just mean dance, right?" I question, following after Oscar as he slides between two topless girls, not even sparing them a second glance.

"This is not a prostitution ring," he responds in a bored tone. "If you want to fuck a patron, do it after hours during your own time. Here is your locker." He points to a dark pink locker with my name scripted on the front in a sparkly gold print. "Inside, you will find your uniform. At the end of the night, put it in the black hamper over there and it will be cleaned by your next shift. Any questions?"

Before I can respond, a voice pipes up from behind me, "Don't worry Oscar! I got her."

Oscar lets out a quiet "thank god" as he hurries out the door, leaving me face to face with a brown-skinned girl. She has a large puff of hair on her head, artfully styled with swooped baby hairs around the edges. She's wearing a red satin bodysuit with a built-in corset, and looks just like Betty Boop. "Hey there, I'm Kimberly. You can call me Kim. Go try on the outfit and I'll give you a tour when you're ready."

I nod and grab my outfit out of my locker, and go into a small private changing area, sliding the curtain closed behind me. Once inside, I strip and start dressing in the gorgeous uniform. I carefully slide on fishnet stockings that sparkle in the light, followed by a vibrant emerald green satin corset bodysuit that embraces every inch of my curves, accentuating my figure in all the right places. Lastly, I slip into sleek black kitten heels, adorned with glittering jewels. I slide the curtain of the changing area. With each confident stride, my hips sway and cause my ample bosom to peek out from the top of the suit.

I take a deep breath before stepping out of the dressing room. Kim is waiting for me, a smile on her face as she looks me up and down.

"Wow, you look amazing!" she exclaims. "That outfit was made for you."

I do a little turn at her compliment and smile. The outfit itself seems way more classy than my green two piece I wore at my old gig; this outfit screams class and had a lot of sass. "Thanks, but I totally think this outfit was made for you. You look like Betty Boop." I point to her outfit and she pokes her left hip out and places her hands on her hip.

"Girl, I like you." She laughs, reaching her hand out to drag me in closer to her.

"Alright, think of me as your *Johanna's* study guide. I have been here the longest and I know the most about everything," Kim says, leading me out the side doors to the main area of the club.

A high pitch whistle rings out from the bar, and Hudson yells over the music, "Looking sexy, ladies!"

Kim smirks, smacking her ass. "Don't I know it!" She leans back in whispering to me, "I'm assuming you met Hudson, sweet as pie with a huge dong."

I giggle. "No way!"

"Girl, I've seen it and used it." Kim stretches her back from side to side. "It almost put me in the hospital." She points to the main stage where a blonde-haired girl swings around the pole in slow motion in a hook spin, waving to the patrons before flipping down. "That is the main stage." She points to a hallway lit up in purple lights. "Those are the VIP rooms if someone requests you for a private dance, and that up there," she points to a large glass room that gleams blue, "That is where the big boss sits. He is one fine man, and one good time to party with if you find him on a low-key night. Most of the girls are scared of him, with good reason, but I've known him for eight years. He's a little shit but he is a good person."

I stare up at the glass office, the strange feeling of someone making direct eye contact creeping up my body. I keep staring up until I hear Kim laugh in my ear, "You can't see him, silly. One-way glass." She turns me around towards the bar. "Your job while you are on the floor is to look good and entertain the masses." Kim waves to a patron and smiles at me, her pearly white teeth on display.

"Hey, Kimmy baby," a light skinned man with sparkling brown eyes walks up. Kim immediately cuddles up to him against the bar and he wraps an arm around her waist.

"Hiya, handsome. Gwen, I'll talk to you later." The man scoops Kim closer to him and Kim disappears into the shadows with her new companion. I turn my attention back to the pulsating energy of the club. The thumping bass shakes my chest as I survey the crowded club. My body moves to the rhythm without conscious thought, my eyes scan the room until they lock onto a figure approaching me from the dance floor. The guy is tall and lean, with dark hair that falls messily over his forehead, and he moves towards me with smooth, confident steps, his piercing brown eyes never leaving mine as they peer into my very soul. I shift my weight, crossing one leg over the other and smoothing out my lips into a sly smirk.

"What are you drinking?" the man says, sliding up next to me at the bar. I laugh a little to myself, because this guy does a classic move that shows not only is he in control, but that he has been watching me.

"I wasn't drinking, but I'll have a rum and coke." I lean my head to catch the light shining in his caramel eyes, and he chuckles, running his tongue across his lower jaw. He signals for the other bartender to come over and orders my drink along with his own, a Pina Colada.

"Seriously?" I chuckle, but the sound comes out sharp as I can feel the eyes on me from Boss's quarters again, almost narrowing in on me, constricting my reactions. I clear my throat and lean my hip against the bar as the bartender slides my drink into my hand.

"Have you never had one?" he teases, his eyebrows wiggling at me. "I can order you one."

I bite my straw before wrapping my lips around and taking a quick sip. He watches my every move, even when I pull my lips away to respond. "Of course. I was just expecting whiskey."

The guy coughs, shaking his head no as he reaches for the Pina Colada and slides a fifty dollar bill across the bar. "Oh hell no. I don't like to drink gasoline."

"Oh, I never said it tasted good, just that is what I expected." I turn back away, and he leans his butt against the bar with me, pointing to a man who looks like the human version of Scrooge Mcduck. "See, that dude is a multi-billionaire, and he is into tickling."

I snort, my drink dripping slightly from the corners of my mouth. "No fucking way."

"Oh yea," he exclaims, pointing to a woman with copper hair, "And she is a huge Wall Street mogul who likes to be degraded."

"Oh, I can totally see that." I shrug. "Rich and powerful man wants one part of his life he does not control."

"So you can believe that, but not that I would drink a Pina Colada?" He laughs.

"Sorry, the weirdest thing here is the Pina Colada," I tease, knocking him in the hip.

He leans forward, his mouth grazing my ear. "Is it as weird as me asking you for a private dance?"

A sly grin spreads across my lips as I notice his clever maneuver, and I nod in agreement. "I see what you did there, but yeah, let's go." Our hands intertwine, and I can't help but look up to the office windows above my skin feeling as if it's on fire, and this is my last warning before I get my punishment. As we approach the private dance room, my skin prickles with anticipation to be alone with a guy who would probably make me laugh more than wet, and I appreciate that for my first lap dance. I confidently make my way through the bustling crowd, following the trail of purple lights that lead to the secluded private dance rooms. The air is thick with the scent of perfume and sweat, a heady combination that fuels the energy of the room.

I pull the guy forward when a bodyguard stops me a stern look in his eye as he pushes in his headpiece, listening in closely to the message coming through the piece. The bodyguard shakes his head no at us. "You can't come in here with this patron."

"Excuse me? I am a dancer here and he asked me for a private dance," I huff, trying to push past the guard.

"You have already been booked, Ms. Sharp." He nods toward someone behind me, and I let go of the patron's hand.

Taking a step back, I look up at the other bodyguard coming up behind me. "A VIP upstairs."

I nod, shooting the Pina Colada guy a sympathetic smile as I follow the bodyguard's lead, my heart pounding in my chest as we make our way up the stairs to the glass office overlooking the dance floor. The echoes of music grow fainter as we ascend, replaced by the muffled sounds of conversation and laughter from below. My palms grow clammy and I wipe them against my thighs. I can't help but wonder who this VIP could be who has been watching me all night. The pit of my stomach twists as I think this could be the eyes I have been drawn to all evening. The irises that seem to be magnets to my own.

As we reach the top of the stairs, a sleek wooden door stands before us, guarded by another imposing figure. The bodyguard nods at him, and without a word, the door swings open to reveal a lavish private room bathed in soft, colored lights that dance across the walls. There is velvet across the mini-stage and the room is circular, so that there is nowhere for the dancer to hide.

Inside, sitting on a plush leather couch, is a figure shrouded in shadows. My breath catches in my throat as I step into the room, my eyes adjusting to the dim lighting. The VIP's features slowly come into focus—a sharp jawline, piercing eyes, and a predatory smile that sends shivers down my spine, but I steel myself. I pull my shoulders back and swish my hips in a slow seductive way that could have someone mistaking my walk for me swimming through molasses. I step up the stairs to the main stage, arching my hips away as I grab the pole and stretch. I then spin around, my back arching off the pole as I stare at the figure, eclipsed by the shadows, and slide down the pole slowly. I give him my best pouty face as I say, "You know you are my first dance in a while."

"Is that so?" I pause my descent, the cheshire like tone to his gravelly voice purred against my skin, reminding me of the rumbling voice of Nikolai as he nuzzled my neck in before demanding we fuck again. I stand up, lazily walking around the pole as I caress the curve of my body.

"Yup, I took a little hiatus." I smile, jumping in the air as I hook both knees around the pole. "So excuse me if I am a little rusty.

The figure lets out a low laugh as he adjusts himself to lean back, deeper into the darkness. I continue my dance, as the figure in the shadows watches me intently. His eyes follow every movement, every twist and turn of my body as I loop and swing with grace around the pole. He groans when I slide down slowly into a split and shake my ass a little and I lean in forward towards him. "You don't seem out of practice to me," he comments.

"Well, let's just say I love to be watched." I wink, flipping myself up and wiggling my ass as I roll up, flipping my hair back dramatically.

My body twists and contorts around the pole, my eyes locked on the shadowy figure watching me. A shiver runs through me as a flicker of recognition ignites in my mind. It's him - Nikolai, with his unmistakable presence branded onto my consciousness. My muscles tense as I stare at him, staring lazily at me from the shadows. He leans in just so I get only half of his face in the light. He licks his lips with hooded eyes as he purrs, "Dance for me, Kotik."

19

GWEN

"Come on now, beautiful. Dance for me. Make me proud." Nik's husky voice cuts through the music as he runs his tongue over his lips. Heat radiates from his eyes as they bore into me, setting my skin ablaze. I feel his gaze tracing every curve and contour of my body as I move to the rhythm of the melody. As he leans back further into the darkness, his predatory gaze rolls down my body, sending shivers down my spine.

"Good girl, Kotik," he growls with satisfaction as I whimper at his praise and the use of my nickname. My heart races with fear and arousal, and I silently curse myself for revealing my weaknesses so easily to him.

My body betrays me, uncontrollably drawn to him like a masochist to pain. I crave to satisfy all of his dark desires. I crave to let his imagination run wild all over my body.

"E-enjoying the show?" My voice comes out in a stammer.

"Of course, Kotik. It's you." My heart flutters in my chest as he takes another pull from his cigarette.

I writhe my hips in a circle, eliciting a low whistle from him that morphs into a dirty chuckle, and my core clenches. "Do that again," he commands, and I do so without even a second thought, because that is what Nikolai does to me. He makes me want to obey. He makes me want to make him proud. No other man has such an effect on me.

The pulsating beat throbs through me as I grind my hips in time to the music. Then I feel it—his hand reaching forward, his fingertips tracing up my inner thigh.

"Mmm, Nik," I moan. He smirks playfully, the spotlight illuminating his face. And I feel something I've been missing all these years—a heat, a scorching, unyielding fire, that crackles all over my body.

He takes another pull from his cigarette, allowing the smoke to flow from the corners of his mouth as he talks. "You know, Kotik, I made this room just for you."

"Oh yeah?" I whisper, keeping my eyes on the darkness that belongs to him and his dangerously alluring grin.

Fuck, even with the cold metal of the pole gliding down my spine, my skin flushes with heat, with want.

"You see, you owed me a dance," Nikolai states. "And I was hoping you weren't the type of girl who doesn't hold up to their side of a deal."

I laugh, taking a step closer to him. He spreads his legs open so I can stand in between them. I slide between his thighs and cup his chin, covered in a five o'clock shadow and a drunken smirk. "I always keep my promises, Nik." I lean in close, my lips hovering over his. "You should know that."

A sly smile plays on my lips as I spin around. Holding on to both of his thighs—and with deliberate slowness—I shimmy down, my ass brushing against his growing member.

Nikolai groans in my ear as I sink into the plush carpet. I spot Nik's hand shooting out to grab me, but I swing around into a tantalizing crawl just out of his reach, a playful smirk dancing on my face.

His voice is husky with desire as he warns me, "You're treading on dangerous ground, Kotik." But there's a glint of amusement there that fuels the fire burning between us.

Playfully batting my long lashes at him, I tease, "I was under the impression this wasn't a whorehouse." I twirl back into his embrace. "And yet here we are."

Pressing my body against his, barely grazing his nose with my heaving chest, I hear him mutter, "Whoever made that stupid fucking rule must be an idiot."

I chuckle, dropping back down with my best innocent pout. "Boss, I believe it was you who made that stupid fucking rule," I purr, squatting between his legs and looking up at him with hooded eyes.

"Then clock out," he commands, but I just chuckle and continue teasing him with my touch.

"Nikolai, this is my first night. I can't just clock out." My fingers trail up the seams of his slacks as he rolls his chiseled jaw, the joint clicking slightly as my fingertips graze against the bulge in his pants.

With a low growl, he pulls me roughly onto his lap, spreading my legs wide and holding them open with his feet. My hands are pinned behind my back against his chest while his free hand pinches my cheek with a bruising grip.

His hot breath washes over my collarbone, making me tremble in anticipation. "You're off the clock now, Gwen," he says through clenched teeth.

I let out a gasp before pulling away in protest. "Nikolai, you can't just clock me out like that."

But he's not having it. He pulls me back onto his lap, a wicked smirk on his face as he pins me with his strength. His legs cross over mine, locking them in place as his hand moves from my chin to curl around my neck with just enough pressure to make me squirm. His other hand trails down and cups my breast. Heat blazes between my legs.

His breath blows out hot and unsteady once more across my collarbone, and I moan at the sensation. A giggle leaves my lips. "Nikolai, come on! You can wait four hours until my shift ends."

He lets out a humorless laugh, leaning in close to whisper in my ear, his lips grazing against my neck. "Do you really want to play this game, Kotik?" His voice is low and dangerous, sending chills down my spine. "You expect me to wait, after you disappeared from my bed five years ago, leaving me wanting?"

I bite back a groan as his hand trails down to tease my center. I smirk, my voice dripping with fake sympathy. "Aww, Nikky had to take care of himself because I left him with morning wood."

Nikolai's smile grazes against my neck, inhaling me, before he trails kisses down toward my chest. He moves his hand from my chin to wrap it around my throat with just enough pressure to make it hard to breathe. His other hand moves down to the front of my bodysuit and yanks the corset down, my breasts spilling over the bodice. A growl rolls through his chest as he cups my breast, and I instinctively arch into him.

His voice enters my ear as he speaks again, "I've been patient for five years, waiting to taste your wet cunt. And I won't wait another damn minute."

His teeth gently graze against my skin, causing a rush of heat to travel throughout my body. I hiss at the intrusion of his teeth, my breathing shallow and unsteady as he marks me. "Kotik?" he says as I whimper against him. "Do you remember your safe word?" I nod mindlessly as he sucks on my lower lip and reaches around, unfastening the tie at the back of my corset, slowly allowing it to slip from around my waist onto the floor. "What is it?"

"Pickles," I whisper.

"Remember to use it if this becomes too much." I give him a subtle nod, too drunk off the way his hands feel as they run across my skin. I'm left with nothing on but my black thong, garter belt, fishnet stockings and stilettos.

He whispers, "Use your words."

"Yes, Boss." He freezes for a second, and I don't know why I decided to push him at this moment, but I do, feeling no shame when his bulge deepens into my ass.

"Bad girl, Kotik. If you're going to play that game, call me sir."

I bite my lip and shift my weight a bit, not knowing what beast I'm about to unleash as I whisper, "Yes, sir."

"Now, let's get rid of those fishnets and heels. Show me my beautiful body." His voice comes out in a gravelly whisper. I feel his hands move to the clasps holding my sparkling fishnets in place, unfastening each one deftly at the same time with a single hand.

Normally, I'd swing off of a guy's lap and slap him clean across his face if he ever insinuated that my body was his, but with Nikolai, I can't help but shiver at the command. I *want* to obey him. I *want* to be his.

I bend over in his lap, rubbing my ass deeper into his growing member. He groans, gripping my right hip with bruising strength. I take my time unhooking the buckle for both of my heels before sliding them off. I hear Nikolai say in a strangled voice, "Faster, Gwen."

I giggle but obey, looping my fingers through the tops of my fishnets, rolling each one down seductively before kicking them off. When I am done, Nikolai pulls me back into his chest, breathing heavily as his hand wraps around my throat.

"Fuck, you're so beautiful," he mutters as his fingers trace the curve of my spine, sending shivers down my body. "Did you think I'd forget how good you feel under me?"

With a swift move, he spins me around so that I'm facing him and straddling his lap. His hand comes down swift and sharp across my ass, sending a shock through my body, heightening my senses. "Fuck, Nik!" I whine, arching my back, my breasts grazing against his chest.

I look into his eyes and gasp. Nik's eyes are a deep blue that I can only compare to the depths of the Atlantic as he stares at me. I can't help but drown in them.

Without reprieve, his hands are everywhere, urgent and demanding, as if he is trying to reclaim me or planning to later draw my body from memory. "Did you think I'd ever forget how you were made perfectly just for me?"

A gasp escapes my lips as his rough hand slides lower, pulling aside my panties and exposing my entrance, dripping with liquid heat. The cool air hits me like a shock, baring my overwhelming desire for him.

"Nikolai, please," I beg, my voice trembling.

He chuckles darkly, his finger sliding inside me, making me arch into his touch. "Please what, Kotik? You want me to fuck you? You want me to make you scream?"

His finger moves faster and harder, sending electrifying waves of pleasure coursing through me. I can't help but hold onto his arms tightly, digging my nails into his skin as I lose control to the overwhelming sensation. "Y-yes."

But just as quickly as he inserted it, he removes his finger, leaving an empty ache behind. He brings his glistening digit to his mouth and savors the taste of me before speaking in a low, sultry voice. "First things first, Kotik." Nik pushes me to my knees and I find myself face to face with his throbbing cock. "You have to take care of the raging hard-on you left me with five years ago."

20

NIKOLAI

My Gwen sits between my thighs, continuously licking her lips as she stares at the bulge in my slacks. Her eyes flicker up to meet mine, a look of defiance sparkling in those hazel eyes. "You've had a hard-on for five years?" She smirks. "I doubt that."

Her fingers dig into my knees, her breath hot against my skin as she leans in, her eyes dancing with desire. I try to maintain composure, but my body betrays me as she moves closer and closer. Her hand travels up my thigh and wraps around my pulsing member. A soft moan escapes her lips as she feels its heat, but I resist the urge to pull her onto my cock, and instead, I give her a wicked smirk.

"No one compares to you, Kotik," I growl, pressing myself closer to her. "No one even comes close to how good your pretty little mouth feels." She flexes her fingers against my bulge, and I let out a low hiss, unable to resist the primal desire coursing through me. "Now unzip my pants and use that mouth of yours on my cock."

"What if I-" Gwen's eyes twinkle with disobedience and I growl at her, her bratty mouth twitching in a smirk. She says in a snarky tone, "I am so sorry, sir."

I ignore her, finding satisfaction in the way my little kitty looks at me with widened eyes as if she forgot how big I am. The anticipation shows in the way her fingers tremble as they reach for the button of my pants. I guide her hand gently, making sure she knows what to do.

Her fingers manage to unfasten the button and pull down the zipper, and she strokes my cock out of my pants. A smirk crosses my face as I watch her. Her lips are slightly parted, her pink tongue flickering across them. "Do you like what you see, Kotik?" I ask playfully.

"Yes, sir," she mumbles. Her eyes are glued to my cock as her fingers wrap around it, gently stroking as if testing its reality.

I let out a guttural groan. My breath hitches as her touch sends electric shocks shooting through my veins. "Fucking hell, girl."

Her lips part and she leans forward, her breath warm against my skin. She hesitates for a moment, then her tongue darts out and licks the tip, tasting the precum that has already begun to bead at the slit. "Mmm."

My head lolls to the side. "You like how I taste, baby?"

Instead of responding to me, she grips my cock tighter, a strangled noise crawling up my throat. My breath hitches as her soft lips press against me. "Mmm...that's it, Kotik," I growl through gritted teeth.

Her velvet tongue circles around my head, and I damn jump off the fucking couch. "You're going to be a good girl and swallow me down, aren't you?" I say in a rushed breath.

My words are met with a throaty moan from her as she sets a punishing pace, driving me fucking wild.

My hand threads through her hair, pushing her down my shaft, and just like I taught her, she relaxes, opening her throat for me. I see goddamn shooting stars flash across my eyes.

Her cheeks hollow as she sucks harder, her tongue swirling around my length, massaging every sensitive spot. The sensation is overwhelming, building a pressure deep within me that demands release. But I won't let her off that easily. Not yet. Not after I've been stroking myself while savoring the memory of her velvet walls wrapped around my cock.

I grip her tangled curls tightly in my hand and pull her off of me, strands of saliva stretch between our bodies. Her eyes widen in surprise.

"Was I doing something wrong?" she gasps, her breath coming out in short pants.

A dark smirk spreads across my lips as I run my fingers through her hair, massaging her scalp with just enough pressure to make her moan. "No, baby," I purr into her ear, "you've been so good to me." She whimpers as I tug on her curls before pulling her head back and looming over her. "And now, it's time for me to be good to you. Get on your hands and knees," I command, my voice thick with desire.

She turns around, arching her back for me as she sinks her hands into the carpet with her glistening pussy on display.

"Fuck," I whisper under my breath. I move behind her, my hand trailing down her spine, feeling the slight tremble in her muscles. My other hand reaches out and firmly grips her hip. "That's it, perfect," I murmur against her neck. I can feel her pulse racing, matching the rhythm of my own accelerating heartbeat.

Leaning forward, I press my body against hers. "Remember the last time we were together? Remember how I did everything I wanted to you?" My voice is a low growl that makes her twitch in my arms.

"Yes," she groans, wiggling her ass at me.

"Well, I have one regret," I say, my fingers tracing the delicate crease between her thighs and teasing the sensitive skin around her asshole. "I regret not owning every single part of you." I press a finger against her puckered hole, feeling it clench in response. "You want me to own every part of you, don't you?"

"Yes," she breathes, her voice barely audible. Gwen arches into my touch with a moan, begging for more. "Please."

"Please what, Kotik?" I tease, my index finger running over her slit, grazing over her throbbing clit, my finger wet with her juices. She whines every time I glide past where she really wants me. With a hungry glint in my eye, I press my finger inside her tightness and she inhales sharply.

"Please fuck me, Nik. Please." She pushes her head into the carpet, her knotted hair partially hiding the blush flooding her cheeks.

I push gently, feeling her tense up for a moment before she releases. Her body shudders under my touch as I slowly work my finger in and out, coaxing her to accept me. "That's it," I murmur, my voice heavy with lust. "Relax for me, Kotik. I'm going to make you feel so good. You trust me to make you feel good?"

I relish the frantic way she nods and the whimpering noises she makes. "Yes, Nik. I trust you," she pants.

"Good girl." I move my finger in and out of her in long, slow strokes, allowing her to get used to me.

Her body undulates beneath me, her arousal drenching the carpet. "Naughty girl," I taunt before pressing a second finger into her puckered ass, stretching her out. She whimpers, pushing her cheek deeper into the carpet. "You are soaking the carpet, Kotik. I am going to have to make you clean it."

She makes desperate whimpering noises, her muscles clenching around my digit as I slowly penetrate her. I add another finger, stretching her, preparing her for my cock.

"Look at you, taking it like a good girl," I whisper, watching her face contort with a mix of pain and pleasure. Her eyes are closed, her lips parted, and her breathing erratic. I lean down, my lips brushing against her ear. "You ready for more?"

Her response is a muffled yes, her voice so low I almost miss it. I withdraw my fingers, leaving her momentarily empty, and rub lube on my cock. I position myself behind her, my cock pressing against her pucker, and push forward, slowly entering her, feeling her muscles stretch around me.

Gwen gasps, her hands gripping the carpet tightly. I pause, giving her a moment to adjust. "Gwen, are you okay?"

She groans in response, her eyes shut tight. I move a curl from her slick forehead. "Remember your safe word and breathe for me."

Her breath comes out shakily, tension still riddled throughout her body.

"Gwen, I need verbal confirmation."

"Y-yes, Nik. I'm okay." She shudders. "You're just...so big."

A chuckle rumbles in my throat as I wrap my hand around her, sliding my fingers to her clit. The tension in her body ripples away like stone dropped in a pond. I kiss her shoulder, slick with a salty sweet flavor. "You are doing so well for me. I know you can do this."

I begin to move, the rhythm of my fingers on her clit matching my slow thrusts.

Then I build up speed. Each thrust is deliberate and deep. Her moans turn into cries, her body arching back to meet each thrust. As I push inside of her, every inch of me is consumed by her tightness, sending a surge of pleasure through my body. She lets out a cry, a mixture of pain and pleasure that echoes through the room, igniting a primal desire within me. I let out a strangled groan. "Fuck, baby, you feel so good. You like feeling my cock inside you, filling you up?"

"Yes, yes," she chants, her words broken by her gasps for air. She relaxes, arching further into me as I build up speed. Each thrust is deliberate and deep. My fingers increase their speed on her tortured clit as her moans turn into cries, her body arching back to meet each thrust.

I reach around, tweaking her nipples, causing her to arch further into my touch. "Tell me how much you want it," I demand, increasing the pace, thrusting harder, deeper.

"I need it, Nik, I need you," she cries out, her voice raw with desperation.

I pull out, making her whimper in protest, then position myself at her puckered entrance again. This time, I push in faster, deeper, eliciting a sharp cry from her. We move together, our bodies a dance of sweat and skin, our moans, grunts and the clapping of our bodies a symphony filling the room.

"You're so tight, so perfect," I groan, my hips slamming into hers. "Take it all, take everything I give you."

Gwen's body responds to my every command, her nails scraping the carpet. I feel her orgasm building, the tension coiling tighter with each thrust. "Nik, I'm going to cum."

"No," I growl.

"No? I can't...I can't stop it," Gwen whines, grinding herself down on my hand.

"Hold it a little longer. I want you to cum with me."

She presses her cheek into the carpet. Her eyes roll back, her mouth opening wider, and her body undulating with each thrust. "Nik," she groans into the floor. "Please."

I pinch her clit, focusing on the small circles I am making. I pull her back by her shoulder, arching her back even further. "Cum for me, Kotik."

Gwen's body convulses beneath me, her muscles gripping me so tightly it feels as if she's trying to pull me deeper inside her. As she climaxes, her ass tightens around me, milking my cock of every last drop of pleasure, her voice reaching a high pitch of ecstasy. "Oh fuck, Nik!"

"Fuck, Gwen!" The sensation is intense, and I follow her over the edge, pouring myself into her as wave after wave of ecstasy crashes over me.

We collapse together, our breaths ragged, our bodies slick with sweat. I lean back on the floor against the couch and she turns, crawling over, and lays her head on my chest; her breath comes out in unsteady gusts. "You know, a simple hello would have been great."

I laugh aloud for the first time in a while and pull her deeper into my chest. "Kotik, that was me saying hello. Give me ten minutes and I'll tell you how much I miss you."

21

GWEN

Nikolai hasn't let me leave this room since I entered it. His hand stays firmly on my hip, drawing small circles as he stares into my eyes. I run my hand over his dirty blonde hair that was slicked back when we first started and now it lays a mess. He leans into me, softly, his eyes falling closed at the way my hands seem to bring him peace. "Gwen," he whispers, grabbing my wrist from smoothing back his hair again.

"Yes, Nik?" I respond, my voice like a feather, too afraid to break the peace we have found.

"Stay," he pleads, his eyes shut like a child. Just like Gio when Mia doesn't understand something he learned or his head hurts from reading with a nightlight instead of going to bed. "Don't leave this time, love."

"Where am I going, Boss?" I tease, scooting my body closer so that our noses barely touch. "I got another shift tomorrow."

He lets out a light scoff, bringing my wrist to his lips. He kisses my pulse point softly, lingering for a moment, before continuing. "Kotik, you have mastered the art of disappearing."

I smile to myself, because at that moment I could tell him. I could show him photos of Gio and Mia. Tell him I've been searching for him, and the right words, but I could never find them. I could tell him that we are on the run and beg him to go get my children, our children. I could ask him to pay off Mason, or strike a deal. Shit, he could scare Mason shitless for all I care. Right now, I can ask him to be my prince charming. I open my mouth, ready to spill that I am not disappearing. In fact, if he wants me, he can have me for as long as he wants, but then he sighs like he has the world on his shoulders. His ocean blue eyes flicker to mine, and he yawns, "Please, Kotik. I don't trust you not to leave when I go to sleep. I need you to be here when I wake up."

A knot forms in my stomach, but I push through with a laugh. "You know Cinderella left Prince Charming at the ball and he found her." I poke his nose and he scrunches it, scowling at me. "Now they live happily ever after."

"Gwen, I am serious." He levels me with a glare, and I try to shift slightly away from him but he grips my hip tighter and stares me in the eye.

"Nik, I don't see myself going anywhere anytime soon, so chill." I kiss his lips lightly, but he doesn't really kiss me back.

Nik's grip tightens even more, his eyes hardening. "I can't just chill, Gwen. You don't understand. I looked for you everywhere. I told you I wanted you to come back to New York with me."

"And I told you I couldn't because I needed to take care of Nana and that is non-negotiable." The knot in my stomach twists tighter.

His eyes flash with frustration. "I told you Nana could come with us."

"Nik." I roll my eyes and push away from him, a cold dose of reality washing over me. "No offense but I had just fucking met you. I still know jack shit about you. So sorry I don't want to follow some guy back to their hometown and be their live in sex slave."

"Some guy? I am really some guy to you?" His eyes narrow as I walk over to my thong, and despite the cold wetness, I pull them on. "So that night meant nothing to you?"

"Nik, oh please you have a system to get girls out of your hotel! A great one by the way, five stars! You really know how to make a girl feel special." I look around the room, finding the corset but no ribbon to lace it up, as if I had the fucking energy to even sit here and do that right now.

"Gwen, I would have gotten you room service while I'd eaten you out for breakfast. You didn't have to leave that way. You chose to," Nik snaps, his nostrils flared, eyes hardened and chest heaving as if he has just ran a marathon.

"Because, Nik, I am not some random whore. I have responsibilities. I can't just stay locked up underneath you forever." I grab his button up off the floor and roughly slide my hands into the arms. "The clock struck twelve. My carriage was now a pumpkin and my dress was shredded. The night where I was yours was over."

"So you admit it?" he scoffs, moving to grab his underwear.

"Admit what?" I roll my eyes, and he lets out an annoyed groan.

"For one night, you were mine and no one else's." He slides his underwear on, a wicked smirk playing on his lips as he strides over to me with a predatory gleam in his eyes. My heart races as

I remember how it felt to be completely his, mind, body and soul. But I can't give into those thoughts now, not when Gio and Mia are still in danger, not with Mason hunting me down. I can't be anyone's, especially his.

His gaze pierces through me, demanding an answer, but I look away, feeling the heat roll over my skin as his eyes rake over my exposed breast under his crisp button-up shirt. I am tempted to surrender and admit that I am his, even if it was just for that one stolen night. The desperation in his eyes makes me ache to be claimed by him again and again, but the weight of the danger that will follow makes my chest feel heavy. My lips tremble as I struggle to find the words, knowing that the truth could shatter everything between us.

"You wouldn't understand," I whisper, trying to pull back, but his hold on me is unyielding.

"Try me," he challenges, his voice cold. "I've been nothing but patient, waiting for you."

"Nik," I snap back, feeling my own frustration rising. "You don't trust me, and I know that can't be good for you. A big Mafia guy like you needs people he can trust."

His jaw tightens, and for a moment, I see a flash of hurt in his eyes. "Gwen, I want you here, but I will not beg."

"Who's asking you to beg? I am telling you I can't stay here with you forever." I push back, my voice rising. "You can't keep me locked away because you're scared I will leave again. You can't demand I be yours!"

He takes a step back and runs a hand through his messy hair. "Do you have to be this fucking difficult?" he growls, his voice dripping with frustration and need to lash out. "You want

Nana Rose here? Done. Kelsey? Done. A job running the whole fucking club? Done. Anything you want. Just...stay, Gwen. Fucking stay."

I take a deep breath, feeling the tension, and a part of me wants to build the bridge between us brick by brick. A part of me wants to tell him to defeat the dragon and fight my battle, but I can't. I won't. I lower my voice, softening my tone, "Nik, I can't just be yours. You don't trust me, and I don't really know who you are. It's that simple."

He looks at me, his eyes searching mine, but I can see the doubt still growing as he sighs pulling away. "What aren't you telling me, Gwen? Because something is wrong, and you just need to tell me."

I hesitate, the urge to spill everything warring with my need to protect my children. "I can't... Not yet," I say finally, feeling a pang of guilt. "It doesn't matter what you do; the answer will be the same, Nik."

He shakes his head, a bitter smile on his lips. "Then how can I trust you when you can't even be honest with yourself?" He takes a step forward, taking a deep breath and closing his eyes before they open on me, cold as ice. "You don't feel anything between us? You want to lie? Fine. But when I have you on your knees screaming for me, know you could have had this the easy way."

The silence between us is heavy, the air thick and I almost feel like I can't breathe, as if I am equal parts excited and scared for my fucking life. I feel my heart breaking, or racing itself to exhaustion.

"Nik, I don't mean to-" I say quietly, but he stops me with a slow shake of his head.

"Gwen, you made your bed," he says, his breath feathering over my face, "now lie in it."

My breath catches in my throat, and before anything else can be said, Nik walks out the room, leaving me alone, half-naked in his button up just like I left him the first night we spent together.

22

NIKOLAI

"You're late," Nadia hisses the minute I walk into my own office back at the Petrov buildings. She is sitting with her combat boots crossed on my desk, and she is filing her sharp claws down to an even finer point with a knife.

For the past two weeks, I have been late to everything and spacing out in meetings.

My mind is constantly consumed with thoughts of Gwen - wanting to pull her close and carry her back to my bed. I yearn for one of us to apologize and for her to acknowledge that she belongs to me and that she also feels this intense connection between us.

I know she feels it too. I see it every time her body quivers when my fingers trace down her spine or our eyes meet, showing me that she feels the same irresistible attraction towards me. But something is holding her back, and the side of me that craves pain wants to understand hers. I want to kill whatever is making her run away from me. That is the thought

I'm most consumed with. How do I stop her from running away again?

The squeak of Nadia shifting her boots on my desk brings me out of my thoughts and I roll my eyes, making my way over to her, tapping her calf. "What about custom do you not understand?"

Nadia slides her boots off of my desk, leaving a small trail of dirt along my desk. "I'll understand custom when you tell me what our father meant by bastard." She takes the knife she had been filing her nails with and plunges it into the wood of the desk.

I PAUSE, TAKING A DEEP BREATH THROUGH MY NOSE, not looking Nadia in the eye, because despite our meeting with Boris being three weeks ago and I have told Nadia Boris meant nothing by the term bastard, she is like a dog with a bone. Nadia asks me every chance we get. Last time, I told her there is bliss in ignorance and she tried to fucking stab me.

A PART OF ME DOESN'T WANT TO BE THE ONE TO POP the bubble of our "Angelic Mother." Nadia and Aleksandr still don't know the venom our mother had for Boris. They don't know the only way she could get back at him was by cheating and making him a cuckold. They don't know that there is a possibility we are all someone else's. And if they find out that I am a bastard and then we find out that they're not, Nadia with a bloodbath the size of Manhattan, or Alek if they were to play into the politics, should be the rightful head of the Russian Mafia. I should be nothing. I should be a glorified bodyguard for my siblings, or a punching back, or a weakness. If I have it my way, they will never know and this will be a thing I take to my grave along with so many other secrets Boris has left me to carry.

"Nadia, do you trust me?" I look at her from the corner of my eye, and she shifts in her seat, eyeing me suspiciously. She pauses and I narrow my eyes at her, rolling my jaw. "It's a simple question."

"It used to be, Nik. I could easily say I trusted you with my life." Nadia leans forward, her fingers wrapping around the handle of the knife lodged in my desk. "But you are hiding something."

"Have I ever put your or Aleksandr's life in danger?" I growl, turning so that I am hovering above Nadia with my fingertips sprawled against the desk. "Have I truly given you a reason not to trust me? When I asked you to be my right hand, you pledged your life to mine. What did I tell you?"

She swallows sharply. "That if any of us go down, we all go down together."

I give her a wide, creepy smile. "Just like the string orchestra that played as the Titanic went down. You, me, and Aleksandr go down with the fucking ship, Nadia. It's that simple. Now I am keeping my promise, but baby, if you want to jump ship." I tap the desk and her crystal eyes gloss over. "Then allow me to help you."

. . .

"Was that a threat, Nik?" she snarls, the knuckles around her knife handle turning stark white.

"Was that knife in my desk a threat?" I give her the smile that only showcases my top layer of teeth, and I lower my eyes at her. She laughs, biting her lip and contemplating her next moves. If I was an enemy, she'd pop that knife out of the desk and slice my neck open, faster than I can get my gun out. Lucky for me, I am her brother, even if it is truly just by a half.

Her voice comes out in a sadistic whisper, "We can't fight right now, bro, there is a war outside those doors."

"I agree." My head shoots up to see Aleksandr leaning against the doorframe of my office. "It would be stupid of us to kill each other with the Yakuza and Italian breathing down our necks."

Nadia doesn't keep her eyes off me as she speaks. "So we just let him lie to us?" I don't take my eyes off of her as Aleksandr shifts against the frame of the door, staring at me from across the room.

"No." Alek crosses his arms over his chest and kicks off, walking closer to us. "All secrets come to the light, Nadia. It's only a matter of time, but until then, the Irish are coming to discuss how we keep the Yakuza at bay."

. . .

I SCOFF, DROPPING INTO MY DESK CHAIR AS NADIA pulls the knife out of my desk and closes it before tucking it in her bra. "You think it's smart for us to get in bed with the Irish?"

"THE YAKUZA DESTROYED ONE OF OUR WAREHOUSES by the Hudson, left a calling card and everything. They want us to go to war, and they are sure they are going to win," Nadia says, tucking the arm of the chair underneath her knees.

"THE IRISH ARE STILL RECOUPING FROM THEIR WAR with the Polish last year," I say, but before Aleksandr can counter me, a knock is at the door. Aleksandr doesn't keep his eyes off me as he yanks the door open and my secretary, a petite brown-skinned girl with a slick back ponytail and big glasses, peeks her head in. "Yes, Lily?"

Aleksandr's intense gaze shifts down to Lily, almost piercing through her. She startles when she notices him looking at her and grips my door frame harder. "Jeez, Alek," Nadia scolds. "You're going to give Lily a fucking heart attack. Stop looking at her like that."

Nadia's voice is stern but Aleksandr doesn't flinch. Instead, he leans in closer to her. Lily was sort of a childhood friend of ours, always quiet with her nose in a book. After her father passed away four years ago, I paid for her to finish college at Yale with a double major in political science and British literature. She now works for us as my secretary, thanks to a hefty salary that I offered as an incentive, but why Alek is looking at her like he would bite her head off is beyond me.

"Nik," Lily squeaks, trying to blend into the wall. "Mr. Doyle and a group of Irishmen are here."

"Thanks, Lil," I nod, and she gives me a tight smile before slipping out of the room. Aleksandr's eyes remain fixed on the spot where Lily had been standing instead of returning my gaze.

Nadia leans forward, pulling my attention back. "Well, boys, it's time to go down with the ship."

The boardroom is a battlefield, with the Irish positioned around the perimeter like a well-oiled army ready for battle. Their eyes are sharp and their muscles tense, exuding an aura of confidence and power. Many other men would shit their pants at the show of power they have, but I know I am the safest man in this room.

Nadia is a fucking beast who could possibly have the highest body count of murders in this city, maybe even this country. If provoked, we would unleash a wrath that these men can't even imagine. One whistle and five of them would be dead, while Alek crushes Doyle's skull in a headlock with a purpling black eye. We are not just murderers; we are sadistic killers who revel in every drop of blood spilled. And if these men dare to start something, it would only give us the perfect opportunity to release our pent-up frustrations towards each other, and maybe some of the frustration I had towards Gwen. Missing teeth and destroyed suits would be a small price to pay for the adrenaline rush of a good fight. I'd probably be thankful for the opportunity.

“Mr. Doyle, I see you and your men have made yourself comfortable,” I remark, smiling as I walk in, unbuttoning the middle of my suit jacket as I make my way to the head of the table, opposite Doyle.

Doyle snorts through his nose, looking over as his right hand man Edward speaks on his behalf, "Better safe than sorry, gentlemen and lady."

"Oh Eddy, honey, we both know from my high school days I am no lady." Nadia laughs, taking her comfortable position to my right and swinging her boots up on the desk. Edward gives her a short snort, and she gives him a wicked smile that on anyone else would be charming; on her, it's downright sadistic.

"Stop with ya' flirtin', Edward, we are here on business," Doyle scolds, shifting in his seat.

"I always say business and pleasure go together." I smile, and Doyle growls, flexing his muscles, before spitting on my floor and leveling me with a glare. The room is silent for a moment, but I continue to smile. "Don't you worry, the cleaning lady will get that."

Aleksandr jumps in, "I am sure you have been aware of the increasing pressure from the Yakuza on our operations." His voice is steady and commanding as I lean back my chair, eyeing the Irish leader across the table.

Doyle nods, his expression serious. "Aye, we've been keeping tabs on them. It's strange, though, for them to come after you."

"Why is that, Doyle? We are the biggest fish in the pond," Nadia chides in a teasing manner before pouting her bottom lip out at him.

Doyle's nose flares, and Edward cuts in, "Your father Boris always had a close relationship with the Yakuza. You both have had a truce for years, and we don't understand why they would back out of that deal if your transition to power was so smooth."

Aleksandr shifts in his seat, his eyes narrowing. Nadia's body stiffens slightly but she masks it with a whistle. I, on the other hand, come up with a lie quickly. "It's precisely because of that relationship we're in this mess. They know our weaknesses. They think they can dismantle us."

Nadia catches onto the lie quickly, tapping her fingers against her thighs, her eyes cold. "We need to change the game. A truce between us and the Irish, and possibly the Italians, could turn the tide."

Doyle clicks his head to the side, his tone skeptical. "And why should we trust you? Boris was intimate with the Yakuza. What makes you different?"

I lean forward, my gaze intense. "Because Boris is no longer calling the shots. I am. And I intend to protect what's ours and our allies at any cost."

Nadia kicks her boots off the table with a wide smile. "Besides, you don't think we came here without incentive, did you?"

"You've wanted the Upper East Side for a while, right?" I say with a smirk because Doyle shoots up straight in his seat.

"What about it, Nikolai?" Edward's eyes narrow.

"Join us and we'll call it neutral territory for just us," I say.

Doyle smiles toothily, leaning in forward. "Let negotiations begin then."

By the end of the meeting, we agreed upon a temporary truce with a neutral Upper East Side and we gave them 10% of our property in the Bronx. The minute we were sure they were out of earshot, Nadia turns on me. "Is that it?

Did you fucking know Dad was in bed with the fucking Yakuza?"

I wring my hand through my hair, my eyes wide. "No, I did not fucking know!"

"So, this war is starting on behalf of Dad?" Nadia growls, her lips tight and eyes murderous.

"I would bet money on it," Aleksandr responds calmly. Nadia lets out a guttural scream, breathing heavily, and I walk closer to her.

"Nadia," I breathe.

"Move. I am going to kill him." She speaks through tight teeth, and I believe her. Daddy's little girl is going to kill her Daddy and as much as her doing that would solve like three problems for me, I stop her.

"I'll meet with Boris. Get the full picture. Once I have the information, we'll solidify our plans," I speak, and she narrows her eyes on me.

The room falls silent, with only the sound of her heavy breathing. She breaks the silence with a low, icy whisper. "If I find out you knew about the Yakuza, or you are working with Dad against us, I will have your fucking head, Nik. I won't hesitate, brother or not."

23

GWEN

For the past two weeks, I've been a complete disaster. Nikolai is nowhere to be found, and I miss him. I fucking miss him. It feels like he's gone off to war, leaving me alone and uncertain of when or if he will return. Every moment without him is like a knife twisting in my chest, and I can't shake the deep ache of longing that consumes me. But this is what I wanted, right? I don't want to be his because then it will be easier if Mason finds me and I disappear. He doesn't have to worry about the threat looming over our children and he doesn't have to be my prince charming because I am the girl who saves herself, always.

I WALK OUT INTO THE LIVING ROOM IN PINK leggings and a matching pink and green sports bra as I swing my work duffle bag over my shoulder. Taylor works from home on Fridays so he sits in the living room, shirtless with his computer on his lap. I snort at him, pointing at his naked chest. "So what happens if your boss calls for an emergency Zoom meeting?"

. . .

"I THROW ON MY POLO SHIRT IN TEN SECONDS OR less." He points to the white polo hanging on the back of the couch. Wiggling his eyebrows, he says, "You want to time me?"

"ABSOLUTELY...NOT." I LAUGH, RUNNING MY HANDS through his shaggy hair before walking into the kitchen. "Please tell me you made biscuits this morning?"

"NO, DARLING, YOU ARE ON YOUR OWN FOR breakfast..." He looks down at his Apple watch. "Well, lunch now."

"DARN IT." I POUT, AS I GRAB AN APPLE OFF OF THE counter. "I'll just be healthy. I guess."

TAKING A BITE OUT OF MY APPLE, I LEAN AGAINST the kitchen counter. Taylor speaks without looking at me. "Are you done pouting about your 'one that got away'?"

I choke on the unchewed chunks of apple as I force it down my throat. My stomach churns with guilt as I recall how I left out crucial details to Taylor about Nik's true identity as Gio and Mia's father. Instead, I told Taylor about how I saw my 'one that got away' and screwed it all up again. In a haze of alcohol provided by Taylor, I cried uncontrollably, forgetting all restraint. Who was I to shed tears when I had rejected him so cruelly?

I straighten up, trying to compose myself as he turns around, his piercing gaze boring into me. I shake my head no, allowing my curls to fall in my face. "Aw, Gwen." He places his laptop on the couch to walk towards me but I take a step back.

I didn't tell Taylor that Nik owns the club I work at, and that every night I reject every client and just stare up at his office, never feeling any eyes back on me. I don't even know if he is up there, but I know I want him to be. I want him to watch me and keep his promise to pull me back to him kicking and screaming. A part of me can't let go of that possibility.

"Don't wait up for me tonight!" I call out as I make my way to the front door. "I'll be at *Johanna's* all night, picking up an extra shift."

I don't wait for Taylor to respond as I leave the apartment. Desperate to escape my racing thoughts, I shove in my headphones and blast "Dance Dance" by the Fall Out Boy at ear-splitting volume. I drown myself in a flood of music, trying to numb the pain that threatens to break me.

My feet pound against the pavement as I sprint to Johanna's, each beat of the music pushing me further into a frenzy. Every song that blares through my ears becomes a lifeline, drowning out the painful reality that threatens to bring me to tears. But I can't cry, not here, not now, not when I'm about to step onto the main stage for my debut performance tonight.

I refuse to let this break me, even as my heart feels like it's shattering into a million pieces with each step I take.

When I get to *Johanna's,* Kim is sitting on the edge of the main stage talking to Hudson, waiting for me. Kim is laughing, her head thrown back as Hudson stands between her thighs whispering into her neck. I call out from across the room, "Am I interrupting something?"

HUDSON LOOKS OVER HIS SHOULDER WITH A flirtatious smirk on his face. "You are not interrupting anything you can't join."

KIM SWATS HIS CHEST, LAUGHING. "BOY, YOU better stop. That is the Boss's girl." Kim squeezes his cheeks with a pouty lip. "Nikolai will kill you and your face is too pretty for a closed casket."

I MAKE MY WAY ACROSS THE ROOM AS HUDSON smiles drunkenly at her. "You think I'm pretty."

KIM LOWERS HER VOICE, CLICKING HER TONGUE AT him. "Boy, get out my face. You know you're pretty."

HUDSON DONS A SHINING SMILE AND WINKS AT HER and me before making his way back to the bar. "Kim," I sing and she shakes her head laughing.

"INNOCENT FLIRTING, THAT'S ALL." KIM STANDS UP, stretching. "But I heard you were fucking the boss in the upstairs private room?"

"What," I scoff, tossing my bag on the floor. "No."

. . .

"Don't lie to me." She laughs, crossing her right arm over her chest and pulling. "I said I heard which means I heard you screaming *Nik! Oh, Nik! Please....just--"* I rush over, covering her mouth from mocking my moans.

"Oh my God, Kim! Why didn't you say anything?!" I whisper-scream. I have been working with Kim almost every night since then and I had not heard a word about this. She has acted like she knew nothing, just like everyone else. She licks my hand and I remove it from her mouth.

"I would never expose you like that to the other girls, but you work fast." She looks at me with admiration and a wide smile.

"Nik doesn't show anyone the light of day," she comments, "I mean there was this one girl years ago he was completely obsessed with and couldn't find her anywhere. It drove him crazy, and then his mom died so that drove him crazy, and then he was like a dormant volcano, just waiting to erupt."

"His mom died?" I question, stretching my back against the pole.

"Yeah, no one knows how, but this used to be her place. I knew her, she was a firecracker. The best boss literally ever, but don't tell Nik I said that," Kim warns before she shakes her muscles out.

"THAT'S TERRIBLE," I WHISPER.

"YEAH, YOU SHOULD HAVE SEEN HIM. IT WAS LIKE something broke. He lost everything and then he was the head of the Russian mafia overnight." Kim sighs.

"Crazy," I respond automatically, but my mind is in overdrive. Nik's pleading eyes haunt me as guilt gnaws at my conscience. I selfishly refused his desperate plea to stay, and now I am left with the realization that my absence was a catalyst for his downfall. The weight of my actions crushes me, a suffocating pressure building until a surge of adrenaline courses through my veins. Every fiber of my being screams for me to find him and beg for forgiveness, to make things right before it's too late. I turn my back, ready to jump off this stage and tear this city apart looking for him, but then Kim claps her hands together, dragging me out of my spiral. I shoot up, looking at her.

She says in a cheer-like manner. "Now, let's get you main stage ready!"

24

NIKOLAI

Boris's cage is colder than normal. He sits in the middle of the cement floor, legs crossed, eyes flicking up from his book to meet mine as I step inside.

The guard keeps his gun trained on him, the red dot of the laser sight dancing on Boris's chest. He looks down at it and smiles as always, a gesture that twists his lined face into something grotesque.

"Son, what can I do for you today?" Boris grumbles, boredom etched into his features. His voice is raspy with intrigue; despite how he tries to look, his voice always gives him away.

“The Yakuza,” I state, seeing how he wants to play this game.

A smile of a master chess player spreads across his closed lips. “Yes? Talented fellows. Better allies, more of a headache as enemies.”

“Your deal with them,” I press, keeping my tone steady. “What was it?”

Boris leans back slightly, his eyes gleaming with that familiar, unsettling spark. "Their endgame is control, Nik. As it always is in this business. They respect power, and right now, they see a potential weakness in our line."

"Do they see it? Or did you tell them that?" I snarl and he lets out an incredulous laugh.

"I am in a cage, under constant supervision. How can I tell anyone anything?" He's smiling, and that smile irritates the fuck out of me, and I turn to not show him how much I want to punch him in the fucking face.

I click my head to the side and lean forward. "Do you take your son for a fool?" His eyes narrow and I flash a shining smile as his disappears. "Boris, we know you have some ways of communicating, or you set things to go into motion the minute you disappeared."

"Your dear old Dad is one smart cookie, huh?" He spits out the question like it's venom. Boris's lips curl into a smile, revealing yellowed teeth. "The Yakuza have their orders."

I narrow my eyes, losing my cool and wrapping my hand around his neck, squeezing hard enough to hear a tiny wheeze that eases some of my stress. "What orders, Pops?"

"How's the heirs coming?" Boris snarls and I push him back onto the floor. He grabs his neck coughing. "Heard you had some fun at Johanna's."

I run my tongue over my teeth, narrowing my eyes at him. "That is none of your fucking business."

"I can't let you bastards continue to spread, can I?" he asks as if the question is rhetorical. Boris stands, his movements slow but deliberate, the cruel smile never leaving his face, then lowers his voice to a whisper, "The Yakuza will wipe out any heir you have. They won't back down unless they see an heir from my lineage taking the throne."

My jaw clenches, a cold fury rising within me, but I hold my ground. "Nadia or Aleksandr could be your children."

"I doubt that, but this isn't about them." Boris walking closely, his voice a violent melody. "This is about you, being alone like you were meant to be. You fucking abomination."

Without warning, I lunge at him, landing a punch that sends him sprawling. I don't stop, raining blows until Boris is a bloody mess on the floor. Each strike is met with a grunt or a gasp, but he never pleads for mercy. Despite the whirlwind of emotions coursing through me, my body doesn't stop until he's lying on the floor, bloodied and broken. As I stand over him, panting with adrenaline pouring through me.

Breathing heavily, I glare down at him. His face is bruised and bloodied, yet there's still a glimmer of that twisted satisfaction in his eyes. "This isn't over."

"When they let me kill you, it will be a slow fucking death, and you will die with no one by your side in a gutter like you fucking deserve."

I spit on the floor, staring at his bloodied smile, and as I storm out of the room, Aleksandr is waiting outside, his gaze silent as he flickers over my split wrist and bloody shirt, but I don't stop, just call over my shoulder, "Make plans with the Italians at *Johanna's* for tonight. We need all the allies we can get."

25

GWEN

The club tonight is more feral than normal. All the girls are wearing maid costumes with little bells and we are serving drinks and food tonight for a special evening. I start behind the bar with Hudson, helping him make drinks since the bartender called out and no one else knows how to make a Manhattan or Cosmo, including our manager Oscar.

Hudson slides over to me with a shaker in his hand, wiggling his eyebrows. “Ready for your big night?”

I place a maraschino cherry on top of the tequila sunrise, and I slide the drink down to a lady at the end of the bar. “I am ready for all the big tips. And please, I don’t mean yours.”

Hudson laughs, pouring out his shaken Martini for the same green eyed man who nuzzles up Kim every night. “I’m just saying if I was shaking ass for a room full of men, including my boss who I am fucking, I’d be nervous as hell!”

“How can I be nervous when I look this good?” I smirk, doing a little twirl that allows my ruffled black and white maid skirt to spin around me. The dress barely covers my ass and the top of this dress has buttons to give a little peek-a-boo of my breast if I wanted to. "Besides," I hum. "Nik isn't even here."

I know this because I haven't felt his eyes on me all night, but Hudson clicks his tongue and nods in the direction of the other side of the room. "Oh, the boss is here and he has friends tonight."

I look over, my heart pounding in my chest as I stare at him. His slick back dirty blonde hair and intricate tattoo crawling up his neck, the lights showcase him in pieces. His pink lips, that he licks before letting out a low laugh showing off his white teeth. His arms, flexing in his black long sleeve t-shirt and matching black jeans. His shoes are black timberlands which is so completely New York of him that I smile, but as fast as I admire him, my world crumbles down. Nik didn't notice me, and Nik always notices me. Even before he cut Jordan's pinky off in my honor, he noticed me. My stomach plummets as I think about what Kim said earlier.

It's like he lost everything. Was I a part of everything? Did my absence break him, even if it was only for a few months? I look over at Hudson. "I'm going to talk to him. Can you hold down the fort for the next twenty minutes?"

"Or the next hour if things go right?" Hudson smirks, wiping down a glass.

"Maybe longer?" A playful giggle escapes my lips as I circle the bar, Hudson's howls echoing in the background. The slick sweat on my hand causes it to slip against the polished surface, but I quickly wipe it on my apron and smack my lips to combat the dryness in my mouth. Weaving through the crowded dance floor, I slowly make my way towards Nik, my heart beating rapidly with each step. The pulsating music fades into a distant hum as all of my focus is fixed upon him.

Before I can even approach him, his intense gaze locks onto me. Waves of heat radiate from his eyes, drinking in every inch of me as our gazes meet.

But before I can close the distance between us, a large figure steps into my path.

“Excuse me?” I snap, trying to look past the man, but he blocks my gaze, folding his arms over his chest.

“Boss said no. He will talk to you when he has the time.” The bodyguard growls even deeper, but before I can tell him where to shove his shitty attitude, I hear Oscar calling my name from next to the main stage.

I glare daggers at the intimidating bodyguard, my jaw clenched so tightly that I fear it may shatter. With a huff, I spin on my heel and march towards the stage, where Oscar eagerly awaits me. He gestures frantically for me to join him, his excitement palpable.

As I approach with fire in my eyes, Oscar's smile widens even more. He opens the back curtain for me, urging me forward as he whispers in my ear, "That's the look I want to see! Knock them dead!"

“Oh, I intend to,” I mumble under my breath as I position myself at the slit of the curtains, just like Kim and I practiced earlier. The anticipation and adrenaline coursing through my veins is almost overwhelming.

Oscar grabs the microphone with a booming announcer voice, his words echoing throughout the venue. "Ladies and gentlemen, give a warm welcome to our newest Johanna performer - she's bold, sassy, and has curves like a backroad. Get ready for Cinnamon!"

The crowd roars as my stage name is announced, and I take a deep breath before poking out one leg from behind the curtain as a tease. The spotlight illuminates me in a warm glow as I saunter onto the stage, the music pulsating through my veins and guiding my movements. The crowd's cheers and whistles fill the room, fueling me with a rush of exhilaration. I sway my hips to the rhythm, letting my body move with a fluidity that brings everyone's eyes to my hips, as I rub my hands up and down my body. I can feel everyone's eyes on me but no one's eyes are hotter than Nik's. They sear through me and I can practically feel the anger radiating through him.

As the music thumps in sync with my racing heart, I glide around the pole, each movement precise and alluring. I allow my gaze to lock onto Nik's business partner, a smug grin playing on his lips as he watches me intently. He leans over to Nik, whispering something as he points to me, and Nik's jaw rolls with irritation he doesn't show anywhere else on his body.

Nik mouths to me, "Stop it."

But I ignore him, flashing a coy smile. I intensify my performance, making sure to give his associate more attention than necessary. When I unravel my maid's skirt, I throw it point blank at the man next to Nik and he catches it with a wink. I return in earnest. As I pop each button on the top of my costume, I act as a tease, giving a full view to Nik and his associate before tossing my top to Hudson, leaving me in a lace black set, knee-high stockings and five inch heels, along with a bell that rings every time I move.

Nik mouths to me, "Get down, now."

I smile as if the lights are too bright to see him and blow a kiss in his direction. The music wraps around me like a second skin, guiding me as I dance for the leering crowd. But my eyes never stray far from Nik, who walks closer to the stage with clenched fists and a dark look in his eyes.

As the song reaches its climax, I descend from the pole with a sensual grace that leaves the audience breathless. Ignoring the cheers and whistles that surround me, I focus solely on Nik's seething gaze. His anger fuels me as I drop down into a split, swing around. The man with Nik howls in excitement as I run my hands through his hair, catapulting his arousal even higher. With a seductive smirk, I spin around and give the man a peck on the cheek before arching my back and crawling away towards Nik and his associate.

Nik's nostrils flares as he whispers, "Don't you dare." But I blink innocently as I swing my legs off the edge of the stage and open them right in front of the associate.

I lean in close to the man and whisper, "Hi, baby."

A wicked glint dances in his eyes as he chuckles, relishing in the attention he's receiving. My gaze falls on Nik and I can't help but shiver at the crystalline hardness in his icy blue orbs. Fear creeps up my spine, but I push it aside, determined to make my move. With a seductive stretch, I arch my back and let the bell around my neck chime with each deliberate movement. But before I can reach the man, Nik grabs me roughly, his biceps bulging with tension as he effortlessly lifts me off the ground. The crowd boos, and I growl under my breath, "Let me go, Nikolai."

"No," he retorts, his grip on me tightening. "This is what you wanted, right, Gwen?" His shoulders bunch up with fury as he gives my ass a hard smack. "You wanted my attention."

"I wanted to talk, not get manhandled like some caveman." I

struggle against his hold, but his fingers dig into my thighs with bruising force.

With a single fluid movement, he kicks open the door to the bathroom and slams me onto the sink. "Are you trying to provoke me, Gwen? Trying to drive me mad?" His voice is a low growl, his blazing eyes burning into mine.

His rage radiates from him, and I can't help but be taken aback by his intense reaction. “I was just-”

“Just what?” he cuts me off sharply, his voice dripping with venom.

My own voice trembles as I whisper through clenched teeth, “I wanted to talk to you.”

He pries my legs open with a force that makes my bones ache, his fingers digging into my flesh as he catches my chin in a vice grip. His voice is low and menacing as he growls at me, “Oh so you flirt with the head of the Italian mob because you want my attention?” I try to look away, but he forces me to meet his gaze. “My little brat almost makes me start a fucking war in the middle of my club because she wants to talk to me?”

My throat tightens as I struggle to speak. “I didn't want you to start a war.”

He scoffs, his lips brushing against mine. “It's not your decision, little brat. If that man had touched you,” he leans even closer, sending shivers down my spine, “I would have put a bullet through him without hesitation.”

“Nik-” I jump but he cups my cheeks in his hands.

“No, Kotik,” Nik says sternly with a small nod and a hint of a smile. His voice is firm but gentle as he continues, “It's time for you to be a good girl and take your punishment.” I feel a shiver run down my spine at his words, my heart beating faster in anticipation.

He leans in and presses his lips against mine, the intensity of his kiss taking my breath away. I feel intoxicated by the taste of his tongue, my head spinning with desire.

When he pulls away, I whisper, "Yes, sir."

Nikolai steps back, his eyes darkening as he watches me. "Strip," he commands, his tone leaving no room for argument. My hands shake slightly, my heart pounding in my chest, then reach behind me to unhook my bra. The cool air hits my skin as it falls away, followed by my panties. I stand before him completely exposed, my body tense with a mix of fear and excitement.

Nik's gaze rakes over me, his eyes burning with intensity. "Turn around," he orders, his voice deep and commanding. I do as he says, my back to him, my hands instinctively crossing over my breasts. "Hands down," he snaps, and I drop them to my sides, feeling vulnerable under his scrutiny.

He steps closer, his presence overwhelming. I feel his hand on my shoulder, guiding me to bend over the sink. The cold porcelain presses against my bare stomach as he positions me, my legs spread wide.

His fingers trace the outline of my sex, teasing the sensitive flesh before delving inside. I moan loudly, my body arching towards his touch. Nikolai watches me with a predatory glint in his eyes, his actions deliberate and calculated.

"Beg for it," he demands, removing his fingers and stepping back slightly.

Torn between humiliation and desperation, I hesitate for a moment before whispering, "Please, Nik...punish me."

Satisfied with my response, he steps forward again, his hardness pressing against my backside. "That's right, Gwen. You deserve every bit of this."

Without warning, his hand comes down hard on my left cheek, the sharp sting making me gasp. Before I can catch my breath, he spanks the other side, the sound echoing in the quiet bathroom. Tears prick at my eyes, a mix of pain and submission coursing through me.

"You need someone to put you in your place, don't you, Kotik?" he asks, his voice calm yet authoritative. My cheeks warm at his nickname for me, as another swat from his hand swipes across my left cheek.

"Yes, sir," I manage to choke out, my voice trembling as heat flutters across my ass and wetness pools at my center.

"Don't worry, Kotik, I will teach you," he replies, his hand stroking the reddened skin gently before delivering another sharp slap. "You will be a good girl and learn, won't you?" Each hit sends waves of heat through me, my body responding in a confusing blend of pain and pleasure.

"Yes, sir," I whimper against his hold. Nik's hand moves upwards, sliding beneath my stomach to cup my breast roughly. His thumb finds my nipple, pinching it hard between his fingers.

"Nik," I gasp sharply. Sparks of pain shoot through my body right to my clit. It feels so good. I want him to do it again.

"You like that, don't you, Gwen?" he taunts, his breath hot against my ear. "You like being treated like this. Like my little slut."

The word *slut* rings in my ears, and I moan. He pushes two fingers inside me, his thumb rubbing my clit in slow circles. I arch my back, pressing myself against his hand, my breaths coming in shallow gasps. His eyes are dark with lust as he grips my hips, lifting me onto the marble counter beside the sink once more, his fingers still inside me. “Spread your legs,” he commands, and I obey, opening myself to him.

Shame rushes through me. This isn’t like me. I have two fucking degrees. I was top of my class at Georgetown. There is no way I am the type of girl to like being disrespected and to want to obey the dirty things Nik says, but I do. I want him to use me. I want to be his.

Nik lines himself up, his cock hard and ready. He enters me slowly, watching my face for any sign of discomfort. I bite my lip, my body adjusting to his size, the sensation both painful and thrilling.

“Look at me,” he orders, his voice gruff. I turn my head to meet his intense gaze, my black curls cascading over my face and down my back, partially hiding the want in my expression. “I want to see your face as you feel every inch of me inside you," he murmurs, beginning to move, his thrusts deep and deliberate.

“Good girl, baby. Keep those eyes on mine.” I cling to the countertop, as he pounds into me, smacking my ass sharply. I bite my lip to keep from calling out. The pain he inflicts only heightens my arousal, making me yearn for more. Nik seems to sense this, his grip tightening as he pushes me further against the sink.

"You belong to me, Gwen," he grunts, his pace increasing. "Only me." I moan at his words, chasing my building orgasm as I brace myself against the mirror and the sink.

His pace increases as he thrusts deeper into me. Each movement is harsh and unrelenting, pushing me to the brink of both agony and ecstasy. I can feel my body responding despite the pain, my muscles contracting around him in involuntary waves.

His hands grip my hips, pulling me closer as his thrusts become more forceful. My body responds eagerly, arching against him as the pleasure builds inside of me. I cling to him, my nails digging into his back as my inner walls clench around him.

"Give in to me," he growls, his voice laced with desire. "Let me see you fall apart for me."

His words push me over the edge, and I feel myself unraveling in his arms. Every nerve ending tingles with pleasure as I ride out the waves of ecstasy crashing through me. "Nik, fucking hell!"

His gruff, desire filled voice chuckles in my ear, "I'm right with you baby." Nik's own release soon follows in hot spurts, and he collapses on top of me, our bodies intertwined and breaths mingling.

"You're mine, Gwen." He wetly kisses the curve of my neck. "Fucking mine. Don't you fucking forget that."

In the daze of my orgasm and the high of being in his arms again, I say the stupidest thing I could have possibly said. "Yes, sir."

26

GWEN

The minute the words leave my lips, a gust of cold air swipes across my spine, and I know I'm screwed. Nik's eyes darken to that mystical deep blue that feels like looking straight down into the Atlantic Ocean, but instead of fear, my heart races at the prospect of jumping in, of being his. Fuck! Why the hell did I say that? "Yes, sir?" Have I lost my mind? Or is the dick that good that I say things I can't possibly mean?

Nik's breathing heavily, staring into my eyes, and unlike with Mason, I don't feel brave around Nik. I feel human. I feel the need to run, to get away from the man who has shredded my maid costume, fucked me in his bar's bathroom, and now stares at me like he would worship the ground I walk on if I gave him a chance.

"How the hell am I supposed to go back to work when most of my uniform is still on the main stage?" I want to snap at him, but my breath comes out breathy and drunk with lust.

He leans forward, his nose brushing mine with a small laugh that sounds like he's blowing dust off his vocal cords. "Who said anything about you going back to work?" he mumbles against my skin.

My back shoots straight when his head lolls to the side, and he hovers over my collarbone. He peppers kisses over his hickeys and bite marks as he continues to speak. "Your punishment is not over."

"Excuse me?" I jerk back, my head bumping against the mirror as I scoot further up the counter, trying to put some distance between us. "You just punished me, Nik. Playtime is over."

I move to close my legs, but Nik keeps his hands firmly on my inner thigh. His tight grip makes me suck in a sharp breath as heat pools between my thighs, and fuck, maybe I don't want playtime to be over. But the darkness of his eyes makes me think that I don't want to play with him anymore. He clicks his tongue at me disapprovingly. "You think this is a game, Kotik?"

"Two people fucking whenever the fever of the night takes them?" I snort, before sighing and leaning up against the mirror, as if my stomach isn't fluttering with a horde of butterflies I intend to kill by the end of tonight. "Yup, sounds like a game to me."

A wicked smile curls across his lips, and from this angle, he looks like the devil reincarnated. "That's your problem, Kotik. You think I'm just having fun. That you're like any other girl that I can just get tired of and throw away."

His eyes flicker down to my lips as I gasp. My eyes shoot to his pink tongue swiping across his bottom lip, and my voice comes out shakily. "Aren't I just a game? Isn't this just for fun, Nik?"

His smile falls off his face. A growl crawls up his throat. "Kotik, you are more than just a game. You are everything I have ever wanted. You are like an addiction to me," he purrs, his hand gripping my waist as he pulls me closer to him. "You've made me into a fucking addict, chasing the high that is you. Never feeling high enough, so I take dose after dose trying to get back to you."

Jesus Christ. My mouth is dry as I search his eyes for a lie or exaggeration, and even though his eyes don't speak of dishonesty, I still call him out. "Bullshit, Nik."

"Are you calling me a liar, Gwen?" he growls, his face snarling right in front of mine.

"No," I whisper, too afraid to speak. "But you're exaggerating because you want what you can't have."

His right hand slides down my stomach, his fingertips grazing the mound of my pussy, and it takes everything in me not to shiver at his touch. "You don't think this pussy is addictive? You don't think this pussy is intoxicating?"

Two fingers slide across my very sensitive clit and trail between my folds. Against my better judgment, I inhale sharply, gripping the edge of the counter as I turn to look away from him, but Nik pinches my cheeks between his other hand and pulls my face to his. "You think this is what? A cat and mouse game? Just something to pass the time?"

His eyes dart across my face as he slides a finger inside my sore pussy and smiles at how I sharply inhale through my nose. "I am not the type of animal that hunts for fun, Gwen." His fingers curve inside me, and I gasp, trying to catch my breath. "I'm chasing you because this sweet pussy, this delectable body, and this smart mouth of yours that needs to be filled has me acting like a fucking addict."

He swiftly takes two fingers out of me and plunges them into my mouth. An explosion of cum and honey runs across my tongue, but I don't dare close my eyes. I keep them trained on Nik's drunken stare as he pushes his fingers back so far in my throat that I gag. "I do not play games when it comes to you, Kotik."

He pulls his fingers out of my mouth, and I gasp. "Nikolai, you can't just—"

"I can't just do what? I can't have you just because you say no?" Nik moves his hand from my cheeks to my chin, pinching tightly as he tilts my head to be aligned with his. His ocean eyes drown me as he whispers, a breath away from my lips, "You keep saying no, yet you keep ending up with my cock inside of you. Funny."

"Nik," I scold, narrowing my eyes at him, but he just flashes that boyish smile.

"Gwen, you don't get it. You are making me go through withdrawal. An addict going through withdrawal can't be held responsible for what they do," Nik whispers against my lips, and a flurry of butterflies in my stomach goes mad. I want to jump his bones, give him his high. Admit that despite all the fighting, I'm addicted to him too. I want to drown in his embrace. I want to submit to his will and be his because there is nothing that feels more natural to me. But instead, I harden my face.

I scowl. "You are responsible for all of your actions, withdrawal or not."

Nik's shoulders hunch up as he lets out a heavy sigh, his fingers tapping impatiently on the counter next to us. He looks around for a moment before grabbing his phone off the counter. "What are you doing?" I ask, trying to peek at his phone, but he quickly backs up and begins furiously typing a message. “Nikolai?”

He finally looks up at me with narrowed eyes, his lips drawn into a tight line. “Nik,” he corrects me sharply.

Suddenly, there’s a knock at the door. My heart pounds in my chest as Nik quickly moves to block me from view with his body. He opens the door and exchanges words with someone outside before turning back to face me, holding clothes in his hand that he received from one of the guards. His expression unreadable, he meets my gaze and says, “You’re coming with me.”

“The hell I am!” I snap, crossing my arms over my chest.

Nik stalks closer to me, his nostrils flared as he tosses the clothes onto the counter next to me. “Either you get dressed and come with me willingly, or I drag you out of here naked and screaming while I shoot every man out there that lays an eye on you. Your choice.”

His eyes are now a piercing blue, and the mere thought of the potential bloodshed makes my chest tremble. A small part of me feels excited by the idea of Nik ruthlessly taking out anyone who sees me naked, but the rational side of me —the part that studied law and knows that impulsive behavior like this would make a great case for an insanity plea—makes my mouth go dry. I silently nod as I pull the cotton white t-shirt and gray sweats into my lap. The woodsy scent of Nik drifts off the clothes, and I turn to look at Nik with a smirk.

“What?” he interrogates me as his head lolls to the side.

“Of course you would wear gray sweatpants,” I comment, sliding his shirt over my head.

"I don't normally hide the goods, but if you want me to, I will." His smile is lazy, but his eyes are trained on me expectantly.

"Don't tell me you let your addictions control your life," I tease.

He doesn't respond, just smiles to himself for a moment as I shimmy off the counter and grab the sweats. As I step into them, I can't help but think about everything Nik just said. He's right—there's something about him that has me entangled, something intoxicating.

I play with the string around the waist of the sweats and pull tight. Nik watches me closely, his eyes darkening as I struggle to adjust the sweats around my hips. "Why are you looking at me like that?" I ask, finally meeting his gaze.

He chuckles softly, shaking his head. "Because, Kotik, you are drowning in my sweats. It's adorable." Nik turns to leave the bathroom, and I stumble, following behind him out into the hallway as I slide my kitten heels on from the maid costume.

"Nik, where are you taking me?" I whisper-yell as the smooth jazz of Kimberly's set flows across the club. When he rounds the corner into the main club, I grip his arm, attempting to pull him back, but it's like the wind pushing against a mountain. "I'm not going anywhere with you until you tell me where we're going first."

Nik turns around, shaking his head. His voice is a low, velvet growl as he says, "Sweetheart, you don't have a choice."

Fucking hell, despite my ass burning every time the fabric of his sweatpants touches my abused skin and my pussy sore from how roughly he fucked me only minutes ago, I still want him. My heart pounds in my chest as I look him over, trying to find some annoyance or hatred deep within me, but I can't. But as Nana Rose always said: fake it until you make it.

I raise an eyebrow, crossing my arms again. "And you expect me to make it easy for you to drag me to your dungeon and be your little live-in sex slave with the rest of your women? No dice. I won't do it."

Nikolai gets in my face again. His features darken, illuminated by the flashes of white and pink light across his face, making him look dangerously beautiful. "I don't have other women, Gwen. I only have you, and if I want you chained to my bed on the constant brink of orgasm, you will do it."

I take a deep breath, trying to compose myself because, fuck, that sounds amazing. "And why is that? Why do you just assume I'll let you have me anyway you please?"

"Because I'm not bargaining with you anymore. You're mine. You said it," he growls, gripping my arm firmly.

"I said it with your dick balls-deep in me. That doesn't count, Nik," I counter, leaning into my right hip as I cock my head at him with a smirk.

"If I have to keep my dick in you for you to be mine, I'll do it. If I have to keep you chained to my bed so you don't go anywhere, I'll do it. Fuck, if you need to be on your hands and knees with a fucking collar on, then just say the word," he snarls, his voice low and commanding.

His jaw clicks under the light, nostrils flared as if he's on his last nerve. And if I test it, if I keep trying to fight him, he'll have me crawling after him like a fucking dog. I take a deep breath and bow my head as if in submission.

His hand flies across his face, and a breath I didn't realize he was holding escapes his lips so quietly that if I wasn't so attuned to every fiber of his being, I would have missed it. He caresses his hand down my face and threads his fingertips through the curls of my hair. As my eyes meet his, I gasp, "Nik."

Nik bends down, his forehead resting gently against mine. "Let's go home, Gwen."

Before a snarky comment can leave my mouth, he threads his fingers with mine and leads me out of the club.

27

GWEN

Nik is winning. Nik has me to himself and despite me wanting to keep him safe, keep him away from me, this man has walked into the pits of hell and he doesn't even know it. A part of me wants to cuss him the hell out and tell him that he was a fucking idiot for being so attached to a random one-night stand. I mean I know I am pretty, and a little feisty in a way that makes most men excited, but I am not worth this. I am not worth him losing his life.

The drive to Nikolai's apartment is a blur of honking cars and flashing lights as he navigates through the chaotic city streets. Despite the chaos, his hand remains firmly planted on my knee, providing a sense of comfort in the midst of the frenzy.

As we pull up to one of the most extravagant buildings I have ever seen, valets and doormen rush to greet us, addressing him with reverence as "Mr. Petrov". The opulence and luxury of the building is palpable, from the sparkling marble floors to the chandeliers hanging from the ceiling. I question in a breath of awe, “Is all of this necessary for an apartment?”

That rich kid, entitled smirk spreads across his lips as he firmly places a hand on the small of my back and whispers, "Only the best for my Kotik. Only the best."

That horde of butterflies I have yet to truly massacre in my gut springs to life again. *My Kotik*, fuck, that does things to me that it shouldn't. His need to possess me is something I need to reject, no matter how weak my knees are at the nickname.

The elevator ride up to Nikolai's penthouse is filled with a tense silence. The unresolved tension between us hangs heavily in the air, and we both know it. As we rise higher, my mind races with thoughts, uncertainties, and a series of plans to make him get tired of me or learn to hate me. Only for his safety and the safety of our children, I need to stay on high alert. I need to keep my walls up, even though he is the best at chipping them down.

The elevator doors slide open, revealing a space so grand and polished that I almost forget to breathe. The grandeur of Nikolai's penthouse is overwhelming—sleek, modern design and floor-to-ceiling windows that offer a jaw-dropping view of New York City. My heart races as I take in the glittering skyline, a mesmerizing sea of diamonds against the dark backdrop of the night sky.

My eyes scan every inch of the luxurious space, from the polished marble floors to the intricate artwork on the walls. But I know I can't let myself be awestruck. Not here. Not with him.

My heels click against the polished dark wood floors as I enter. The living room feels spacious and welcoming, despite its sleek and minimalistic design. The tall ceilings enhance the expensiveness of the penthouse, only making me feel more out of place The blend of natural materials adds warmth to the space:

deep, rich wood paired with crisp, white walls remind me of apartments I've see in magazines. The furniture is modern, featuring clean lines and muted shades of gray and navy that almost makes me feel dirty.

I take a deep breath, trying to keep my composure as I move further into the penthouse. I wander over to the windows, letting my eyes drift over the breathtaking view of the city. The lights shimmer like stars, and for a moment, I feel a pang of something I can't quite name. Longing? Awe? Fear? Maybe a mix of all three.

“Impressive, isn't it?” Nikolai's voice rumbles from behind me, low and smooth.

His intense gaze follows me as I turn to face him. He leans against the doorframe with a casual air, but his eyes tell a different story. They hold that same hunger I've come to know so well—the one responsible for the fluttering butterflies in my stomach whenever he looks at me.

"Nice place," I comment calmly, trying not to let on how much his gaze affects me. “Though it's a bit much, don't you think?”

He smirks and pushes off the doorframe, sauntering towards me with the grace of a predator who knows his prey is within reach.

“Ah, but you know me. I always go big,” Nikolai purrs, his smirk turning into a full-blown grin that doesn't quite reach his eyes. He reaches out a hand to brush a loose strand of hair away from my face, his touch sending a shiver down my spine. “Besides, I like the finer things in life. And you, my dear, are about to experience just how fine they can be.”

I can feel the heat radiating off his body. My heart hammers in my chest, betraying the calm facade I try to maintain, but I continue to fake my annoyance.

"Is that so?" I reply, arching an eyebrow as I take a step back, putting some much-needed distance between us. "Well, forgive me if I'm not easily impressed by material possessions."

I roll my eyes as I move away from him into the corner of the room. I keep my eyes on the glittering skyline of New York, trying to distract myself from the way he makes me feel—like I am on the edge of a cliff, teetering between falling into him and running far, far away.

My words are sharp, but Nikolai doesn't flinch. He's already moving, closing the distance between us with those same slow, deliberate steps that make my pulse race.

"This is your home now, *Kotik*," he whispers, the intensity in his voice cutting through the space between us. There's a flicker of something in his eyes—hope, maybe even longing. It's almost enough to make me waver.

But I can't let him get that close. Not yet. I take a solid step back, holding his gaze with a narrowed glare. "Don't get any ideas, Nik. I'm not someone you can just pin down like this. I am not your possession that you get to dictate and control. I do not live here."

He closes the space between us. His hand snakes around my neck, pulling me into his orbit. "It's not just about the possessions, *Kotik*. It's about comfort, control...security." His voice dips lower, smooth and deliberate, as if he's drawing out each word to test my patience.

"Security?" I scoff, still staring out at the city lights as if I can will myself not to look at him. "I'm sure that's what all of this is about, right? Keeping me safe or...keeping me close?" I glance back at him, daring him to deny it.

A smirk tugs at the corner of his lips, but there's something in his eyes that's dead serious. "Why can't it be both? You belong here with me, Gwen. I can give you everything—safety, comfort, whatever you need. You wouldn't have to worry about anything. All you'd need to focus on is us."

His words send a thrill through me, my heart racing as I try to process them. My body instinctively moves closer to him, and I tilt my head up to meet his intense gaze.

My lips brush against his as I whisper, feeling the warmth of his breath against my skin. "Is this your plan? To keep me hidden away in your luxurious penthouse like some kind of prized possession?" I pull back slightly, my voice shaking with emotion. "That's not how a real relationship works, Nik."

He chuckles softly, but I can hear the underlying tension in his voice. "So, we're in a relationship now?"

"Not if you keep me locked up in here." I push him back as I say the words. "Then this becomes a hostage situation."

"I am only trying to lock you up because you have mastered the art of disappearing, *Kotik*." He leans in closer, snaking an arm around my waist. "I just want you close. I want you where I can take care of you, where I know you're safe."

I tilt my head back, letting out a breath I didn't realize I was holding. "Nik, you can't protect me from everything. And you sure as hell can't control every part of my life." I keep my voice firm, even as my heart pounds wildly in my chest. "I need freedom. I need to know that I'm choosing to be with you, not because I have no other choice."

"Then choose to be with me," Nik pleads, searching my eyes for a response.

"Nik, it's not that simple." I sigh, looking down, but he pinches my chin between his thumb and forefinger, pulling my face up to him again.

"No, Gwen. It is that simple." He searches my face once more with his gaze before dropping his head and resting his forehead against mine. "Being with me could be as easy as breathing, *Kotik*."

I suck in a sharp breath and hold it, not wanting the next words I feel to leave my mouth. "I know, Nik."

"Then why do you make this so difficult?" he pleads, his eyes shut tightly as he speaks. I don't respond, and after a while, my lungs burn and my eyes tickle with tears.

A heavy breath leaves his lips and flutters over my face, and I want to tell him everything, but before I can, he laces his fingers with mine and whispers, "Follow me. I want you to see something."

I let out the painful breath in a sharp exhale as Nik leads me up the winding staircase, the soft glow of the chandelier illuminating the way. Each step creaks beneath our weight as the silence between us stretches on forever. As we reach the top landing, he pauses and turns to look at me, hesitating for a second before saying, "You were meant to be here with me, Gwen."

Without another word, Nik pulls me gently towards a set of ornate double doors at the end of the hallway. He pushes them open, revealing a master bedroom that is every bit as luxurious as the rest of the penthouse.

But it isn't the grandeur of the room that makes my breath catch in my throat. It's the sight of the space that has been meticulously set up for me. He lets go of my hand as I make my way deeper into the room.

The bed, fit for royalty with its soft, luscious linens and oversized pillows, is adorned with a throw blanket in my favorite color: emerald green. Opposite the bed, a small door stands ajar, revealing a stylish adjoining room that serves as a wardrobe.

Inside hangs a collection of clothes—his suits and casual jeans on one side, and on the other, a selection that seems to have been chosen specifically for me. The pieces exude effortless chic with just the right amount of edge. There are combat boots, ripped jeans, elegant high heels from Louboutin, alluring floor-length gowns that I doubt I will ever have an occasion to wear, and even a leather jacket that feels soft like butter to the touch.

Everything in there feels as if I've chosen it for myself, but before I can really question him, I exit the wardrobe and see a section of the room with a mahogany desk and a comfy pale green loveseat that looks like the pink couch from my old apartment with Nana.

"What is this?" I demand, but the question comes out in a breathless gasp as I walk closer to the area.

The desk sits against the wall, its surface adorned with neatly placed pens, highlighters, and post-its, alongside an iPad ready for use. Above the desk hangs a floating bookshelf, showcasing a collection of books handpicked for me—from fantasy novels I mentioned during our one night together to an Italian cookbook and law textbooks for my studies.

Every detail is meticulously thought out. It's almost as if Nikolai has gone out of his way to create a space uniquely mine, nestled within his own world. My heart hammers in my chest as I repeat my question one more time. "Nik," I whisper, turning slowly to look at him because I don't want to freak out more than I already am. "What is this?"

Nikolai strolls deeper into the room, his hands casually tucked into his pockets. He looks around as if seeing the space for the first time. "Our room, obviously."

"Our room?" I echo, my voice tinged with disbelief. "What do you mean by ours?"

"A bedroom for you and me," he replies, as if it's the most natural thing in the world. "Where else would you sleep?"

I stare at him, trying to process the sheer audacity of it all. He's set up this entire space for me, assuming—no, expecting—that I'll just move in and live in his room like some kept woman. Like I'm his possession.

"You're out of your mind if you think I'm just going to—"

"To what?" he interrupts, stepping closer. "To accept what's already yours? To live here with me, as we both know you will?"

I clench my jaw, refusing to let him steamroll over me. "I never agreed to this, Nik. I never agreed to be yours."

His expression darkens, but there's something else there too—something softer, almost vulnerable. "Gwen, you belong here. With me. This is where you're meant to be. Look." He turns me back to the little study space. "You can go back to law school. Dedicate all your time, be back at the top of your class. Or you can run Johanna's. Or you can cuddle up on this couch right here and read your novels all day. Shit, you can write one."

"Nik." I shake my head against his chest. "I can't just... Why?"

"Because I want you here, with me, and this will make it easier."

I turn around, placing both palms firmly on his hard chest. I try not to think about how hard his heart beats against his chest, against my hand. I look down at where I'm gripping his shirt in my hand as I whisper, "I need my own space, Nik. I can't just... I need somewhere that's mine, where I can breathe."

His eyes narrow, and for a moment, I think he might refuse. That he'll use that stern voice that makes my panties wet and my knees weak and say no, you're going to stay here with me, in this room, and I may crumble. If he demands I stay in this room where he just did the most romantic thing I have ever experienced, I won't make it out of here as my own person. I'll be his, happily. I'll have to put him in danger because I'll want him, need him too much to ever let him go, even if it's for his own good.

But then he surprises me by nodding slowly. "Fine. You can have your own room."

I blink, not expecting him to give in so easily. "Really?"

"Yes. You can have this room." He sighs, running a hand through his hair. "But on one condition."

Here it comes, I think. Here comes the line that makes me say, screw it, and jump into his arms. "What's the catch?"

"You sleep in my bed five nights out of the week. The other

two nights, you can have your space." His voice is firm, leaving little room for negotiation.

Five nights? That's a compromise, sure, but still a significant demand. I cross my arms over my chest, trying to think it through. Can I live with that? Can I do that and still save myself? Can I still save him from the danger of Mason? And would that be enough time to hide the existence of Gio and Mia from him until I know we're all safe?

"You're not really giving me much of a choice, are you?" I ask, narrowing my eyes at him. My heart is pounding against my chest feverishly.

He shrugs, his lips curling into that devilish smirk that always sets my nerves on edge. "It's the best offer you're going to get, Kotik."

I huff out a breath, knowing I have to pick my battles. "Three nights," I counter, lifting my chin defiantly. "I get my own space for three nights a week."

He raises an eyebrow, clearly amused. "You're negotiating with me?"

"I was a top law student, Nik. Bargaining is second nature to me."

He chuckles softly, his eyes gleaming with admiration—or was it amusement? I can't tell with him sometimes. "Alright, Gwen. Three nights."

It's a small victory, but a victory nonetheless. I nod, trying to hide the relief that washes over me. "Good. Then it's settled."

He takes a step closer, his voice lowering to that husky tone that always makes my knees weak. "But don't think for a second that you're free from me those nights, Kotik. You may have your space, but you're still mine."

The way he says it sends a ripple of goosebumps across my skin. I'm playing a dangerous game with a man who could so easily consume me, body and soul. But as I look into his intense oceanic eyes, I know one thing for certain—I'll do anything to keep him safe, even if that means losing the one man I think I could love.

"Don't worry, Nik," I reply, my voice in that evenly confident lawyer tone. "I'll remind you of that when I'm the one calling the shots."

His grin widens, and for the first time, I see a flash of something more in his eyes—respect, maybe. Or perhaps it's just the thrill of the challenge. Either way, I steel my shoulders and look at him head-on.

Nikolai leans in, his lips brushing against my ear as he whispers, "I look forward to it."

28

GWEN

The first night, I kicked Nikolai out of my room. He had the nerve to pout, his sharp eyes narrowing as he assessed me, gauging how serious I was. But he listened—probably calculating that letting me win this small battle would just ensure his victory in the long run. He left, but not without a final glance over his shoulder, a smirk tugging at his lips like he knew I'd eventually come crawling back. I hated that he was probably right.

After the door clicked shut behind him, I collapsed onto the bed, curling into a ball. I gnawed at the inside of my cheek until I tasted blood, the metallic tang mingling with the guilt gnawing at me even more ferociously. The guilt felt like a weight pressing down on my chest—suffocating, relentless. Because even if Nikolai knew, in some twisted way, that we were on the same side—both of us fighting for a version of "us"—he'd still see me as the enemy.

He didn't realize the real battle wasn't against him, but against demons from my past. Against Mason. I was the only one with the vantage point to keep everyone safe, even if it meant locking myself up in this castle built from my father's debts. But how could he ever understand that when I was hiding so much from him?

I barely slept that night. Every time I closed my eyes, I'd see flashes of what I was doing to him—hiding his children, pretending to be someone I wasn't, making him believe I didn't want him. And for what? Just to buy time so I could pay off Mason and disappear? The logic was sound, but the emotional toll was unbearable.

The second night, I fell asleep on the couch before Nikolai got home from a business meeting. I woke up wrapped in a cream blanket, my head resting on his lap, his hand halfway through a caress in my hair. He was fast asleep, looking almost innocent. In the morning, I told him I counted that as a night of him not being in my room. He playfully said he should've let me freeze on the couch.

Later, Taylor called, threatening to file a missing persons report if I didn't respond. I joked that Prince Charming had stolen me away to his dragon's lair, but Taylor didn't find it funny. He demanded lunch on Sunday, and now I have no idea how to tell Nik without him insisting on tagging along to sulk through the meal—or worse, threatening Taylor for daring to touch what he considers his.

Tonight, I decided to keep myself occupied with logic exercises from the LSAT, sitting cross-legged on the plush cream rug in my room. It was the kind of challenge that distracted me from counting the five grand I'd saved up—cash hidden away in secret compartments, safely out of Nikolai's sight. At this rate, I could be done paying off Mason in four, maybe five years. By then, the twins would be eight or nine. I'd be in my mid-thirties. Would Nik still wait for me? Maybe I'd dramatically reveal our kids to him on their sixteenth birthday—or leave a note explaining everything once I'm long gone, escaping to California to avoid his wrath. A wrath that only grows the longer I keep this secret.

But deep down, I know I'm playing a dangerous game. Nik is patient, but that patience has limits, and every day I keep this secret will chip away at the trust he's already unsure of. It's like a time bomb ticking away, and I can't help but wonder how much longer I have before everything explodes.

"Fuck," I growl when I realizing that I did the math wrong. I lean back into the plush carpet, wishing Nik would have let me work at *Johanna's* tonight; maybe then I could blow off some real steam.

Surprisingly, Nikolai hasn't stopped me from working at Johanna's, though he hovers around the bar area 90% of the time and refuses to let me take private shows where the real money is. He even joked that if I was that desperate for cash, he'd pay for a dance himself. But that's the thing—I want to tell him sooner than in five years. That's why I've been pushing to work every night shift I can.

When Nik wasn't dragging me into dark corners to fuck me senseless, the customers tipped well—surprisingly well, considering they were Wall Street types who assumed money could buy anything, even people. But at least they weren't as handsy as you'd expect, probably out of fear of Nik. That was one perk of being his girl, I guess. It gave me just enough room to breathe while I silently counted every dollar, inching closer to freedom with every shift. So that me and him had a real chance in hell together, not this pretend shit we were doing now.

A soft knock at the door pulls me out of my thoughts. My heart jumps to my throat, half-expecting it to be Nikolai, but it's not. When I open the door, I'm met with Mary, Nik's maid—a woman in her late fifties with kind eyes, bright red hair and a politeness that is in direct opposition to Nana which only makes me miss her more. She offers me a small, tight-lipped smile and a hot pink box with a large sage green bow on it in her hands.

"Ms. Gwen," she greets politely, stepping further into the room. "Mr. Petrov asked me to bring this to you."

I blink at the box, my annoyance and reluctantly my excitement spiking. "What is it?"

She carefully places the box on the bed, her hands smoothing over the satin ribbon before stepping back. "It's an outfit he's chosen for you for tonight." She wiggles her eyebrows along with a note.

Of course, it was. Typical Nik, always trying to control everything, including what I wore. I already feel my temper rising, my jaw clenching as I move to open the box.

I gently remove the neatly folded note from the box and set it aside on my bed before finally looking at the dress inside. My breath catches in my throat as I take it all in. The gown is a stunning creation, floor-length and black with subtle sparkles that catch the light perfectly. The material is sleek, elegant, and undoubtedly expensive - the kind of dress you'd see on a red carpet.

As my fingers brush against the soft fabric, a wave of nostalgia washes over me. It reminds me of the dress I wore on our first date - the one that drove Nik wild all night long. I can feel his heated gaze once again as my hand traces the same slit that he couldn't keep his eyes off of. He knows exactly what he's doing by choosing this dress for me. I take a deep breath placing the dress back in the box, and turning my attention back to the note.

I SNATCH IT UP, UNFOLDING THE PAPER WITH AN aggravated flick of my wrist.

Get dressed, Kotik. We have plans for you to be in my bed tonight. Don't keep me waiting.

I crumpled the note in my fist, resisting the urge to throw it across the room. Nik's bossiness was infuriating, as much as his knack for romantic charm. It was like every time I thought he was the most romantic guy in the world, he tried to exact power over me and show that he had the upper hand. What Nik didn't know is that his romantic gesture was so telling of how much I drove him wild.

Mary clears her throat, clearly sensing the tension as a devious smile spreads across my lips. "If you need any assistance, Ms. Sharp—"

"I don't," I cut her off, my tone sharper than I intended. She sighs sharply, and I feel a twinge of guilt, but I quickly brush it aside with a large smile on my face as I turn to her. "Tell Mr. Petrov I will be ready in an hour. I am going to knock his socks off."

A brighter smile crosses Mary's face, and I pity the admiration dancing in her eyes. She doesn't know that I intend to bring Nik to his knees tonight. If he wants me to look good for him, I will look drop dead fucking gorgeous.

29

NIKOLAI

I stand at the base of the grand staircase, dim lighting casting shadows that stretch like dark tendrils across the marble floor. My hands are shoved in my pockets, fingers tapping rhythmically against my thigh as I wait for her. The anticipation is a slow burn in my veins, simmering into something darker, something primal.

Tonight is not just a date—it's a battlefield, and I plan on winning. When Gwen descends those stairs, she walks right into my trap. I see how she pushes my buttons, testing the limits of my patience. But tonight, I remind her exactly who she belongs to. By the end of this night, she'll be begging for me, her every defense shattered. She will be putty in my hands, an obedient little sub on her knees for me.

The sound of Gwen's heels clicking against the marble stairs pulls my attention. My breath catches in my throat as I take in her appearance, and I curse myself for ever buying her that dress.

She glides down the stairs with the grace of a queen walking to her throne, each step a promise of the night ahead. I can't help but mutter, "Чёрт возьми, она чертовски великолепна" under my breath, the Russian curse spilling from my lips as I take in the sight of her.

She is a vision—a dangerous one. The inky black gown drapes and clings to her every curve like a second skin, as if it were tailor-made by the devil himself. A daring slit slices up to her hip, teasing with just enough skin to leave one's imagination running wild. My imagination is running wild; it almost looks like she isn't wearing anything underneath. The idea of that alone makes my blood heat.

Her lips are painted a deep, sinful red, drawing attention to their fullness and inviting the gaze of all who see her. The smoky darkness of her eyes only adds to the mystery and allure of her presence. Her curls are styled with precision, each strand falling perfectly into place to frame her face in wild, soft tendrils. She exudes an air of power and confidence, like the queen of death—here to drag me to my grave, and I'd willingly go.

I'm so caught up in taking her in that I almost miss the sly smile curving on her lips. "Pick your jaw up off the ground, Nik," she says, her tone laced with a teasing edge.

I shake my head, trying to regain my composure. "You're killing me, you know that?" I reply, my voice smooth but laced with a hunger I can't hide. "You look so beautiful, I don't even want to take you outside. No one should see how good you look but me."

I can't help but curse again, this time louder and more fervently. "Господи, котик, это чертовски безумно," I mutter, the curse heavy with my desire. As she slides her hand into my open palm, my thoughts teeter between getting her out of that dress right now and remembering we have reservations.

Her grin widens as she twirls effortlessly, giving me a full view of the dress—if you can even call it that. A dress with a slit that high should not also be backless. It is fucking criminal, revealing so much skin I feel my control slipping. "Что ты со мной делаешь," I mutter, this time louder and more fervently, the curse heavy with my desire.

Her eyes sparkle with mischief as she leans in even closer. "What does that mean, Nik?" she asks, her breath warm against my ear.

Her giggle is like a sweet poison, intoxicating and maddening all at once. What I said roughly translates to 'What are you doing to me, Kotik,' but instead of telling her the exact translation, I lean in closer, placing both of my hands on her hips and whispering against her lips.

"It means," I murmur, my voice a low growl, "that you're driving me out of my mind. You look so fucking irresistible I can barely keep my hands off you."

Her lips curl into a sultry smile. "Well, that's exactly the effect I was going for." She trails a teasing finger down my chest, her touch electric.

A growl emanates from my chest, but she ignores it and laces her fingers with mine, pulling me toward the elevator.

"Let's get this date started before you end it," she says with a smirk, but there's a glint in her eyes that tells me she knows exactly what she's doing.

She guides me into the elevator, pressing the button for the lobby as the doors slide shut. But before they close completely, she leans in, her voice a sultry whisper. "You were right."

I arch a brow, intrigued. "Right about what?"

She meets my gaze with a slow, seductive smile. "I saw it in your eyes when I was walking down the stairs. You don't think I'm wearing any underwear right now."

"And?" I snarl, keeping my eyes trained on the elevator doors slowly closing in front of us.

"And you would be right, Niky." She leans up, her breath fluttering over my cheek and her breast grazing my arm as she playfully whispers. "I am totally commando."

The doors close, and I'm hit with a wave of heat so intense it takes every ounce of willpower not to pin her against the wall and ruin her perfect lipstick. My fingers twitch at my sides, itching to tear that gown off her and claim what's mine.

But tonight is about control—hers and mine. And I've never been more determined to show her who really runs this game.

"Gwen," I murmur, looking down at her with the most casual gaze I can muster, the tension between us thickening with each breath. "You're playing a dangerous game."

Her eyes glitter with challenge as she leans back against the elevator wall. "Good. I love danger."

DRIVING WITH GWEN BESIDE ME IS AN excruciating test of my self-control. Her movements are subtle yet deliberate—crossing her legs, shifting in her seat, every slight adjustment of her body only heightens my desire. Each time she shifts, her dress reveals just a hint more of her smooth skin, making it harder not to drag her home and hoard all of her beauty for myself. *Fuck* buying this dress.

I white-knuckle the steering wheel as I drive. It's all I can do not to pull over and claim her right there in the passenger seat of my Ferrari, but then we would have to have dinner with her looking freshly fucked, and I don't know which is worse: her looking this good with or without my cum dripping down her thighs.

Tonight is about control. My control, and I can control myself around her, even if it's sparingly.

As we enter the elegant lobby of *Le Bernardin*, I place my hand against the small of Gwen's exposed back. My lips twitch in satisfaction at the way she shivers at my touch. I guide her through the restaurant, where the opulent décor and dim lighting set the perfect mood.

The hostess's smile widens as soon as she spots us. "Mr. Petrov," she greets, her voice softening as she flutters her lashes. "Your table is ready. Right this way."

I barely nod in acknowledgment, but I catch the way Gwen tenses beside me, her posture stiffening and her tongue running across her inner cheek. My Kotik, jealous? The idea sends a ripple of satisfaction through me. "Jealous, are we?" I whisper into her ear.

She scowls, burning holes in the back of the hostess's head as she leads us through the dimly lit restaurant. Gwen's gaze darts to the side, her jealous ebbing into discomfort, wary of the lingering stares we attract.

"Are people staring at me?" she asks, rubbing her forearm nervously.

I look around the restaurant, feeling my eyes become as black holes as I focus on one guy who is staring at Gwen so hard that his date hits him and walks away. He is lucky she got his attention before I did because I would have killed him for the heavy gaze he has on my girl. "Do you want me to make them stop? I'll give you their irises as a gift."

"You're jealous." She snorts, throwing my words back at me as blush rushes to the apples of her cheeks. "It's okay if they look, as long as they don't touch."

My body bristles at the thought. "It is not okay that they look, but trust me, I'd be dead long before anyone got close enough to breathe the same air as you, let alone touch you."

I slide my hand down her exposed back, leaving a trail of goosebumps in my wake, and draw small circles along her spine, my lips gently leaning in to kiss her temple. She whimpers quietly, and a warmth bursts in my chest.

When we reach our secluded table, draped in crisp white linen and surrounded by the glow of candlelight, I pull out Gwen's chair for her. "Relax, kotik," I murmur, my fingertips running back up her spine as she sits. I lean in close, whispering in her ear, "You are mine, and I will always protect you."

Her eyes meet mine, softened by a hint of vulnerability that she quickly masks with a small, playful smirk.

Gwen gracefully lowers herself into her chair, the slit of her dress parting just enough to tease. My gaze lingers on her, the urge to take her right here almost overwhelming, but instead, I unbutton my jacket and slide into the seat across from her.

With the combination of the male gazes I feel trained on the body that belongs to me and the fact that Gwen's dress has my imagination running fucking wild, I immediately regret not buying out the entire place. Here I thought we could have a normal date that doesn't end in me giving her another finger for her collection.

I keep my eyes on Gwen as I speak. "We'll start with a bottle of F. Raveneau Les Clos 2015 Chablis, and for appetizers, we'll have the Montauk shrimp and the oyster-uni."

Gwen raises an eyebrow, looking between the hostess and me as she whispers her protests, "Nik, I haven't even looked at the menu yet."

I give her a roguish wink, my confidence unwavering. "I like you too much and know you too well to let you order for yourself."

A soft blush creeps up her cheeks, and she quickly looks away, her fingers fidgeting with the edge of her napkin.

"Right away," she says with a polite nod, taking note of our order before leaving us in the dimly lit, elegantly decorated dining room.

I lean back, crossing my arms as I regard her with a smirk. "I think you're enjoying teasing me tonight. You've been playing this game all evening, and it's not lost on me."

Gwen's lips part in a playful grin. "Nik, I would never."

Her tone is light, almost innocent, but the glint in her eyes betrays her mischief. She tilts her head slightly, her voice dripping with faux sincerity. "I'm just here to enjoy the evening, and if I happen to catch your attention, well, that's just a bonus."

I lean in closer, my gaze locking onto hers with an intense, challenging look. "Oh, really? Because it seems to me like you've been deliberately pushing all my buttons tonight."

Gwen's smile widens, and she places a hand over her heart in mock offense. "Well, how could I not push your buttons when you look so cute when you're annoyed?"

Her nose scrunches in that cute way that makes me want to make her do it again, just because I know that fake look of annoyance belongs solely to me.

I give her my deadest glare and she smiles poking my left cheek with the tip of her pointer finger. I playfully nip at her wrist, but before she can fully retract her arm, I grab her wrist and curl the edges of my mouth into a smile. "Moya lyubov," I whisper against her soft flesh. "No one calls me cute."

Her pulse beats faster against my lips, only making me smile more. Her breath comes out as a combination of snark and lust, all breathless and needy. "Maybe more people should. You are-"

"Handsome," I correct before she can say cute again. "Sexy. Fine. All acceptable adjectives."

"I was going to say you are full of yourself; let's add more adjectives for your minions to inflate your ego with, shall we?" She yanks her wrist out of my hand, her eyes trained on me. "Cute. Annoyed. Cocky. Asshole. I like the sound of those."

"Kotik, you can call me whatever you want as long as you are mine." I give her my best cocky grin, leaning back in my chair as I spread my lips into a winning smile.

Gwen rolls her eyes, covering her face with her opened menu. "You know just because you cum in someone doesn't make them yours."

"It does when I cum in you," I counter, and she growls, peeking at me from over the top of the menu.

"Nik," she scolds, keeping her eyes trained on the menu.

A waiter returns, expertly pouring two glasses of white wine before nestling the bottle into a sleek silver cooler beside our table. As he steps away, I shift closer, unable to take my eyes off Gwen as she lifts her glass to me. "A toast." She smirks.

"To what, Kotik?" I tease and she purses her lips with a knowing smile.

"To you learning the difference between possession and affection," she purrs, raising her glass to her lips with a cheshire grin.

I laugh deep in my chest as I raise my glass to hers. "Good luck with that, Kotik. You see, I prefer the kind of affection that leaves its mark."

"Of course, you do," she rolls her eyes as she whispers her words under her breath, and I pull my glass back slightly.

"Kotik, don't make me teach you proper manners in this restaurant," I growl, and her eyes narrow on me as her back arches into the table. She fidgets slightly in her seat, and I lean forward with my glass almost touching hers. "Now do you want to try to say your toast again?"

She gives me a tight smile as she speaks. "To stubborn men and the women too smart to fall for them."

A scoff-like laugh leaves my lips as I tilt my glass to hers. Never break eye contact even as both take a sip. "Let me make an addendum."

"You can't change the toast after we've drank," she teases, and I shrug.

"It's just you and me we can bypass that," I whisper in a low, husky voice. "Now I think we should toast to stubborn women who secretly love being chased."

"I don't like being chased." She scowls as I lift my glass lazily in my hand and point it at her. She keeps her glass in her hand, but just out of reach of my glass.

"Kotik. You might fight me, and argue, and try to outrun me, but you know you can never really outrun me." I drop my voice again and lean in. "And deep down you like that you can't outrun me."

I wink and watch as she tries to take a deep breath without me noticing. She looks away from me and her lips touch the rim, delicately, but a small droplet escapes, trailing down the corner of her mouth.

Without a second thought, I reach out, catching the droplet with the pad of my thumb. Her eyes widen slightly as I bring my thumb to my lips, tasting the wine that clings to my skin. The sweetness lingers, both from the wine and the subtle essence of her. I can't help but smirk as her cheeks flush, a mixture of surprise and something else swirling in her gaze.

"Do you have to do that?" she asks, a hint of playful annoyance in her tone, though her eyes betray her curiosity.

"Do what?" I drawl, clicking my head to the side as I stare at her.

Gwen's lips thin as heat rushes her cheeks. "Do really sexy things like I don't know, sucking the wine from the corner of my mouth off your thumb."

A laugh boils in my throat as I lean in even closer, my voice dropping to a hushed whisper as I hold her gaze. "You, my dear, are like ambrosia. I can't let even a drop go to waste."

The words roll off my tongue slowly, deliberately, and her eyes follow the slow flick of my tongue.

Gently, I reach across the table, lacing my fingers through hers. Her hand is warm, fitting perfectly in mine. "You taste like heaven," I murmur, brushing my thumb across her knuckles. "And I'm the lucky one who gets to indulge."

"Well fuck." She huffs, shifting in her seat.

The waiter returns with our appetizers, setting down both plates before leaning over and pointing to the shrimp first. "Sorry for the interruption. On our right here, we have the Montauk shrimp and to the left, we have our oyster-uni. The chef said that he is excited to have you in attendance, Mr. Petrov, and would like to make you a special entree."

I look over at Gwen as I say, "Sounds delicious."

"I will let him know you agree." He gives a courteous nod before stepping back.

She delicately spears one of the shrimp and takes a bite. The moment the flavor hits her tongue, a soft moan escapes her lips. Her eyes flutter shut for a brief second, savoring every note of the dish. I grip the edge of the table, trying to hold back a groan as I lean closer, the words leaving my lips in a low, restrained growl.

"Careful, kotik," I warn, the roughness in my voice unmistakable. "You can't make sounds like that here."

Her eyes snap open, and she meets my gaze, feigning innocence. "Like what?" she asks, playing coy as she tilts her head slightly, her lips quirking into a teasing smile.

"Like you're already begging for dessert," I reply, my voice laced with a mixture of amusement and desire.

"Well, dessert is the best part of dinner," she coos, picking up another shrimp with a naughty smile.

But I reel in the tension quickly, straightening in my seat as I take a sip of my wine. "As much as I enjoy watching you enjoy yourself, there's more to tonight than just this game of ours," I say, allowing a pause before adding, "I organized this date for a reason."

Gwen's brow furrows slightly as she dabs at the corner of her lips with a napkin. "A reason? And here I thought you took me out to wine and dine me."

I set down my glass and lean in, enjoying how the candlelight illuminates her features as I speak. "I brought you here to spark a deal. I know how much my little lawyer loves negotiation."

Her eyes light up as she studies me, a faint smile on her lips. "What kind of deal are we talking about?" she asks, shifting in her seat with excitement.

"I do not want to keep running in circles anymore. I know you are mine, Gwen, and I think you should admit that," I say.

She sighs, humorlessly. "And how are you going to make me declare that, Nik? You already have me locked up in your penthouse like some New York damsel. What else could you want?"

You. I want Gwen to want me. To stay with me willingly. I don't want to have to track her to the ends of the earth. I don't want to have to keep dragging her back to me kicking and screaming, but I would. I would keep searching for her until my last breath. I don't want her to resent me, but with Gwen, being honest about how I feel hasn't worked, and like any good businessman, I know now it's time to pivot.

"If I make you cum in the middle of this restaurant, by the end of tonight, you have to admit that you are mine and give us an actual shot," I murmur, looking at her over the flame.

Excitement, desire and something sinister sparks in Gwen's eyes as she negotiates with me. "Now what do I get out of this if you can't make me cum?"

"I'll let you go back to living with your frat boy," I growl, not wanting to show all of my cards but hating that one in particular.

"Oooh temporary freedom," she mocks. "What about something real? Like ten grand."

"Kotik, if you want ten grand, I'll just give you ten grand," I say nonchalantly, picking up my wine glass with a flourish. "Or do you want to skip the game and just admit that you are mine now?"

"See, bargaining my freedom is pointless. You will find a way to drag me back to your lair," she says, and I hide my smirk behind my wine glass. My girl is as smart as she is gorgeous. She could run circles around most people, but not me.

"Why do you need ten grand?" I ask pointedly, staring at how she nibbles the corner of her glossed lip for a second.

"For a money shower." Her voice squeaks slightly, and I know she is lying.

"Kotik," I warn, and she looks down at the appetizers for a second, contemplating her next move.

"If I win," she whispers, "I'll tell you."

She looks up at me with demure eyes, and I can see something dark, maybe even fearful cross over her hazel eyes. I lean forward, searching her gaze. "Gwen, are you in trouble?"

She looks away from me immediately, sharply biting the middle of her bottom lip before looking back at me. "Lose if you want to know," she whispers, and I lean back in my chair with narrowed eyes.

If I win, I'll have her, but she will still be at this distance. She will always be a flight risk, because I might never know what makes her run. If I lose, I'll have her secrets, but from the way she avoids my gaze, I can feel in my bones that I won't have her anymore.

This is a lose-lose situation, but lucky for her, my odds still give me a piece of her, even if they are crumbs. I'll collect every drop she will give me willingly. Reaching my hand across the table, I give her a dazzling smile. "Deal."

She places her small hand in mine, giving me a firm shake, the word coming out of her mouth so quietly I almost miss it. "Deal."

30

GWEN

We just made a deal. A fucking lose-lose deal. My hand stings in Nik's hand, his palm eclipsing mine with his coolness, easing my heat.

Nik stares at me as if in both options he wins something worth less than what he'll lose. It's the same look my opponents during debates in law school used to give me -- hopefully hopeless, full of contradiction.

This whole deal is that reckless kind of false hope. On one hand, I need that money. It's a sliver of hope I am desperately holding on to. If I get all the money I need, plus some for interest, Mason will accept defeat and let me go. It's the only leverage I have left to keep Nik and I's kids safe.

If I win, I get to be free of the burden of keeping Nik in the dark about his children. I should feel relieved, but instead, dread coils tightly in my gut. Because I know what's at stake. If I let him in, if I tell him about the danger I am in and the kids, he may never forgive me for hiding his children from him and putting them in danger.

For a brief moment, I almost tell him. I almost spill everything about Mason, the kids, the money. I don't know Nik to be forgiving, even if he is kind to me, and the fear that I crossed the line, one I can never recover from, forces me deeper into my silence, and instead I made a deal that only divine intervention could keep me from losing.

To not be able to cum, with this man so close to me, would be the will of some higher power, and how could I refuse the intervention of a deity bigger than me? I would have to tell him, even if I know he would hate me.

Nik shifts his seat closer to me, his back blocking me off from the rest of the restaurant, and a devilish smirk on his lips. His lips curve into a sly smile. He plucks an oyster from the tray between us and brings it to his lips. I can't help but follow his movements as he slurps the shellfish down, his Adam's apple bobbing with each swallow. A low groan of satisfaction rolls over his throat. My heart races at the sight.

My gaze follows his fingers as he sets down the empty shell and turns his gaze back to me, his eyes glinting mischievously.

"Your turn," he says huskily, picking up another oyster with his fingers and holding it idly in his hand.

I turn my head, looking at the brown paneling against the wall, trying to avoid his gaze. "I've never had an oyster before," I whisper.

He leans in closer, gently cupping my chin as he pulls my gaze back to his. "Want me to show you how it's done?" he murmurs, his voice low as his breath tickles my lips.

Without waiting for an answer, he picks up another oyster, holding it up between us.

I can feel my body burn as I watch him guide the shellfish to his lips once more. He pauses, looking at me with a playful glint in his eye before slowly sliding the oyster into his mouth. The way his lips close around it forces me to squeeze my thighs close as my bare pussy slicks itself with desire. *Goddamn traitor.*

"Eating an oyster is all about the swallow." Nik's gaze stays locked on mine, his smirk deepening as he notices my reaction. The heat in the air is palpable as he leans in closer, the space between us shrinking until I can feel the warmth radiating off him.

"No chewing," he murmurs, his voice dropping to a velvet purr. His thumb traces my lower lip, drawing a shaky breath from my lips. "You just need to relax and let it slide right down your throat."

My breath hitches as he brings the oyster closer to my mouth, his eyes never leaving mine. The cool shell brushes my lips, as he instructs me. "You'll want to gently twist the oyster between your fingers, so that the hinge of the shell pops open. Be careful not to cut yourself on the small tip of the shell."

I hesitate, biting my lip nervously. But before I can overthink it, Nik tilts the shell just enough for the oyster to glide onto my tongue with a slick flick of his wrist.

"Good girl," he whispers, his eyes darkening as I close my lips around the briny flesh. His hand lingers at my jaw, thumb brushing my cheek as I swallow. The rich, salty flavor fills my senses, but it's the way he watches me—like I'm the most enticing thing in the world—that has my heart pounding.

He leans even closer, his breath hot against my ear. "How does it feel, Kotik? You like it?"

A soft hum escapes me as I nod, the sensuality of the moment making it impossible to think straight. Nik's fingers stay at my jaw, guiding me gently as I follow his lead.

"Now tell me," he says, his tone husky as his thumb traces the line of my jaw, "you're soaked between those thighs, aren't you?"

I bite my lip, trying to compose myself, but the rush of heat pooling low in my belly is impossible to ignore. "Maybe a little," I manage, my voice breathless.

I feel Nik's cool hand on my thigh under the table, his fingers tracing slow circles that send waves of goosebumps across my skin. The restaurant buzzes around us, the clink of cutlery and murmur of conversations filling the air, but all I can focus on is the cooling nature of his touch.

"Watching you swallow, Gwen, has to be the sexiest thing in the world," he murmurs, his voice low enough to avoid detection but filled with intent. His fingers inch higher, brushing against my slickness running down my thighs.

I bite my lip, trying to maintain a polite face, instead of showing the tiny tremors his touch releases up my body. "Nik, I swallow every second of every day." My voice comes out breathy as my thighs fall open for him under the table

"I know," he growls, the rasp in his voice rolling across my neck. "You love to torture me, don't you, Kotik?"

His hand runs across my lower lip, and a small whimper escapes me. His satisfied grin kisses my cheek as the waiter approaches with our entrees.

Nik pulls back, watching me as the waiter sets down our plates, the rich aroma of steak and roasted vegetables filling the air. "Enjoy your meal," he says before moving on.

Nik whispers, his other hand reaching out to toy with the stem of his wine glass, "Focus on me."

I try to comply, leaning back in my chair as his fingers work their magic. The world narrows down to the sensations he's creating, each stroke building the pressure inside me. I can feel myself growing wetter, my body betraying me as it responds to his skilled touch.

“That's it,” he encourages, his voice a seductive purr. "Let go for me, Gwen."

My resolve wavers, the pleasure overwhelming as he quickens his pace. I squeeze my eyes shut and bite my lips so hard, I can feel the copper in my mouth as I fight against the urge to moan aloud. The restaurant noise fades into the background, replaced by the sound of my own ragged breathing.

“Look at me,” Nik demands, his fingers speeding up slightly.

I open my eyes, meeting his intense gaze. “Tell me you're mine,” he breathes, his fingers resuming their rhythmic motion.

The words stick in my throat, pride warring with the pleasure coursing through me. I shake my head slightly, unable to form the words just yet.

Nik smirks, clicking his tongue as he pushes pressure on my clit. “Stubborn until the end, aren't you?” He leans closer, his lips brushing against my ear. “Don’t worry, Gwen. I am going to make you say it soon, I promise you that.”

His confidence is intoxicating, his fingers relentless as they push me closer to the edge. I grip the tablecloth, my body trembling with the effort to stay silent. The pleasure builds, wave after wave crashing over me, threatening to consume me entirely.

"Almost there," Nik murmurs, sensing my impending release. "Just a little more, Kotik."

I arch my back, a soft gasp escaping my lips as the first tendrils of climax begin to weave their way through me. The intensity grows, his fingers working in perfect sync with my body's demands. I feel myself teetering on the brink, the world dissolving into a haze of the sensations he gives me.

"That's it," he coaxes, his voice a soothing balm amidst the storm. "Give in to me, Gwen."

With a final, desperate surge, I surrender, my body convulsing as the orgasm rips through me. I bite down hard on my lip to stifle a cry, my hands gripping the table so tightly my knuckles turn white.

Nik withdraws his hand slowly, watching me with a satisfied smile as he pushes his two fingers covered in my release inside of my mouth, and I suck on the tips greedily. "I win," he declares softly, pulling his fingers out of my mouth with a slow pop.

"Well, Gwen?" Nik prompts, his eyes gleaming with triumph. "What do you say?"

I swallow hard, meeting his gaze with a mix of defiance and resignation. "I...I'm yours," I whisper. Nik's groan makes the hair on the back of my neck stand at attention, as if I inherently know badly I have fucked up.

His hand reaching out to cup my cheek tenderly. "Good girl," he praises, his voice thick with emotion. "Now, let's enjoy our meal, hmm?"

I grab my fork and nod numbly, submitting to my rightful place.

31

NIKOLAI

F*uck.* I want to make her say it again. *I'm yours.*

I watch as Gwen takes another fork full of the chocolate tart, her eyes avoiding me as she swallows the dessert. I lean in again, murmuring, "Say it again."

Her back stiffens, but she covers up her tense body movement with an exaggerated eye roll of fake annoyance. My voice drips heavily in her ear. "Don't you dare roll your eyes at me." She sucks in a sharp breath. "Now, say it."

"I'm yours," she whispers.

A wide smile spreads across my lips. "Now finish your dessert, so I can have mine."

As soon as the elevator doors to my penthouse slide shut, a palpable tension fills the small space. Without hesitation, I push Gwen back against the mirrored wall, my hands roaming her curves with a hunger that's been building all night. Her name escapes my lips like a prayer, "Kotik," and she responds by parting her soft, inviting lips beneath mine.

The taste of her is like a potent blend of rich wine and her own unique essence, addicting and intoxicating. She moans quietly into my mouth, igniting a fire within me that has been simmering all evening. My hands grip her hips with need as I press her tighter against my body, desperate for every inch of her skin to touch mine.

"Nik, please. I can't wait," she whimpers against my lips.

I lean back slightly to look at her, my hand sliding between the slit of her dress to rub over her hip before cupping her ass possessively. "Can't wait for what, Kotik?" I whisper huskily in her ear. "My dirty little cat can't wait until we get upstairs to fuck?" She lets out another whimper as I grip her ass painfully tight.

Her fingers tangle in my hair, tugging just enough to make me melt under her touch. Our kisses grow more frenzied and consuming, devouring each other like time is running out. The world outside the elevator seems to fade away as our bodies entwine, seeking more and more pleasure from one another. With a low growl, I lift her up so that her legs wrap around my waist, deepening our embrace.

The moment the elevator doors slide open, the heat between us intensifies, turning our kiss even more fervent. My hands move to the small button holding the dress against her neck, unhooking the dress and pulling it down to expose her full breasts and chocolate nipples. "My naughty girl, had no underwear on all night?" I growl as her cheeks flush. "You will be punished for that."

She gasps, looking at me with wild eyes. "What? Why?"

My grip tightens on her ass as I growl, walking us towards my living room couch. “For making me lose my mind all fucking evening.”

She giggles as I kiss a trail down her neck, her skin warm and fragrant beneath my lips, and she whimpers softly.

Dropping her onto the couch, I move placing one knee between her thighs as I start to unbutton my shirt. My gaze locks with hers, seeing the hunger mirrored in her eyes, a primal connection between us that sends a thrill coursing through my veins when a pale box catches my eye.

My body stiffens, frozen in fear as my gaze darts between Gwen's fierce eyes and the lavender box resting on the armchair. A chill runs down my spine as realization washes over me like a wave of ice-cold water. "Gwen," I mutter, my voice trembling with unease. "Get upstairs."

Gwen shifts under me, her brows furrowing in confusion. "Nikolai, what's wrong?" Her voice is tinged with worry. She doesn’t understand, and I can’t explain it to her—not without revealing just how deeply this darkness runs. She would never understand why a man would deliver his children pieces of their mother, and I couldn’t blame her if she ran.

Fear flashes across Gwen's face as she quickly obeys, covering her chest and scrambling away from me towards the stairs. As she disappears into her room, I am left alone with the ominous presence of the lavender box and the weight of my own darkness looming over me.

I can feel the threat hanging in the air; my movements are a methodical panther like crawl as I make my way closer to the soft silk box. What would it be this time? Her right foot with her signature gold anklet still wrapped around the joint, or her head with her face still twisted in fear? Or maybe it would be her blue eyes that match mine?

My presents from daddy dearest have always been worse than my siblings, with an extra splash of depravity since I am the only one who knows of our mother's infidelity, and I have embarrassed him by being head of his beloved mafia anyway.

I am the stain that he can never scrub out, therefore I deserve more of his depraved mind than the others. A mind that matches mine, in a way that almost tricks you into thinking I am his son.

My fingers tremble slightly as I open the delicately wrapped box as if it is a Christmas present. The satin ribbon falls to the ground in a graceful twirl as I gently lift the lid, revealing the fragile contents within.

There, resting on a bed of delicate pink silk, lies a piece of my mother. Her lifeless right hand, once so full of warmth and love, now lays still against the soft fabric. Despite the nauseating scent of her decomposing flesh that fills my nostrils, I cannot bring myself to pull away.

The first time my father did this, it was her engagement finger, complete with the large ring she wore with pride bloodstained on her finger, a paternity test, and a note that called me a bastard. I screamed, practically pulling my hair out as I grabbed at her decomposing flesh. I couldn't sleep for weeks and felt as if I was dying a slow death.

That's how I found out about her infidelity and that father murdered her. He told me that from that day he disowned me and that I was to disappear from New York, never to return. Jokes on him, though; the mafia had already wanted him gone and now I have the motivation to do so. That is only thought that helped me feel alive again, making Boris want to die.

But upon the fifth time receiving a piece of her, my body numbs and it almost feels like these parts are of a stranger. I focus in on a delicate, diamond-encrusted Tiffany watch tightened around her purpling wrist. Its face sparkles in the dim light, mocking me with every glint.

I move the hand slightly revealing a note underneath, written in that familiar sharp scrawl that haunts me.

"A gift for your lover."

I clench my jaw, shoving into my large coat pocket as I yank out my phone. "Lock down the building," I bark into the phone as soon as the head of security picks up. "Search every floor, every corridor, every entrance. I want cameras checked, and I want to know how the hell this purple box got into my fucking apartment."

"Yes, sir," a security officer responds, as I make my way to the elevator and punch the ground floor button.

The tightness in my chest only grows as I stalk out of the elevator.

My mind is racing with a thousand questions and possibilities, each worse than the last. *A gift for your lover?* How does he know? How the fuck does he know about Gwen? Who told him? Who the hell is watching me? I punch the ground level.

My blood runs cold as one thought rings out above the rest *—he knows about Gwen*.

It would be safer to take a car, but the distance between my penthouse and my office is three blocks and I am too on edge to sit patiently in the back of a car.

I yank my phone out of my pocket, impatiently dialing Aleksander's number as I grit my teeth.

“Nik,” he answers evenly.

I growl into the phone. “I got her right hand and wrist with her missing Tiffany watch.”

“Okay. Now we have about 45% of her body back.” His voice is matter-of-fact as he speaks. The typing of a keyboard rings across the line.

“Alek, he knows about Gwen,” I growl. The elevator doors slide open, and I stalk out onto the street, heading towards my office with a single-minded determination.

"Okay," Aleksander replies calmly, his fingers already clicking away at a keyboard. But I can feel my control slipping as I snap back at him, forgetting that he doesn't understand emotions like a normal person. He's been diagnosed with sociopathy since he was 13, so threats against someone I love don't register to him like they do to me. He doesn’t know how to act like he cares right now.

“Call Nadia,” I bark into the phone, "Tell her he threatened Gwen. Meet me back at the office in twenty minutes." I hang up before his emotionless tone can infuriate me any further.

My hands clench into fists, nails digging into my palms, as I struggle to contain the rage and fear churning inside me. I am practically running down the street as I make my way to my office, my gut telling me that something is wrong. One thing I know about Boris is that he would not come after the king if he didn’t plan on a fucking headshot.

I push through the glass doors of the modern, sleek building that houses my office and Boris's cell. The receptionist greets me with a warm smile, but I barely acknowledge her as I head straight to the stairwell door. Impatiently, I wait for the scanner to recognize my retina and fingerprint before granting me access.

The door slides open with a soft hiss, revealing the dimly lit staircase leading down to our secure underground facility. I skip steps, jumping down the stairs to the basement. As I push open the doors, A rush of cold air hits me like a slap in the face.

The corridors are eerily silent, every shadow seeming to crawl with warning. I don't hesitate as I make my way to the far end, to the cell where Boris has been locked away—where he *should* be locked away.

But when I reach the heavy metal door, there is no guard, and the door is slightly open in a way that most would ignore, but I know before flinging it open, my worst fears have come true.

The cell is empty.

The cot is untouched, the steel chains lie on the floor like discarded snakes, and there's nothing—*nothing*—except that single, taunting piece of paper taped to the wall. I rip it down, my heart pounding in my ears as I read the words written in blood.

"Gwen is a beautiful girl, and I have always told you it is not nice to hide your toys. Time to share."

32

GWEN

I haven't moved since Nik barked at me to go up the stairs. Hours have passed, and the morning sun beats at my exposed back, but I can't bring myself to change my outfit or do anything besides stare down at this door, mentally urging him to come back and tell me everything's okay even if I can feel that something is wrong. Even if I feel ill just thinking about the look in his eyes.

What changed? One moment his hands were gripping my hips, pulling me into the curve of his body, and then I was running up the stairs stumbling over my feet, locking my door, and then sitting here.

What if he discovered the truth about Mason, Gio, and Mia before I had a chance to tell him? What if someone has already exposed me, and Nik is just dragging out my inevitable downfall? Anxiety floods my senses and now this dress that had Nik on his knees for me feels like sandpaper against my skin. I yank at the dress, trying to pull it off of me even if it means ripping the seams.

In my panic, I walk over to the wardrobe, my fingers brushing against the cool walls as I pull out one of his pristine white t-shirts. As I slip on the soft fabric, I am immediately overwhelmed by the scent of cedar and leather that clings to it, flooding my senses with memories of him. I find myself pulling at the fabric as if trying to bring him closer to me.

I sink to the floor, pulling my knees into my chest, tears burning in the back of my eyes. If I drowned here surrounded by the phantom embrace of him, it would be too soon. The vibrations of my phone break me out of my spiral, and I find myself crawling over to my bed and pulling my phone into my hand.

Kelsey's name flashes across the screen, and I choke back a sob. Mia's sweet face shines over my screen. She has chocolate on her face and a huge smile as she screams, "Mommy! Mommy, Mommy!"

"Hello, sweetheart," I coo as she positions the phone farther from her face. Gio pokes his head in the camera, his black hair flopping over his eyes. "Gio, buddy you need a haircut."

"Uncle David tried but he looks scary with scissors." Gio grimaces as he bumps into Mia and shoves himself into the camera a little better.

"Mommy, when are you coming?" Mia interjects, her bottom lip poking out as she pouts.

"Soon, baby," I lie, giving her a soft smile as I push a strand of my hair behind my ear. "How's home schooling?"

"Aunt Kelsey doesn't know how chimps develop friendships,"

Gio complains and the echo of teeth sucking invades the speaker.

"They did not teach us that in elementary school!" Kelsey yells off camera and I giggle.

Gio rolls his eyes, huffing, "Mom, please come back."

Kelsey crawls up behind the twins, noogieing Gio and kissing Mia on the cheek. Kelsey bats her eyelashes in the camera and uses a baby voice that sounds very close to Gio's. "Yeah, Mommy, when are you coming home?"

"Very soon, babies," I coo, an unexpected gust of laughter leaving my lips as I play along.

Guilt twists and tightens in my chest; the weight of my secrets gets heavier by the minute and threatens to crush me the more I gaze at their faces. Mia's tousled dirty blonde locks frame her face in these wild, loose curls that remind me of Nik early in the morning when no one is paying attention. And Gio's piercing oceanic eyes seem to hold the entire world in them, just like his father's. It's as if you can drown in him, or float to the heavens.

Nausea rises in my throat because despite my children never meeting their father, they possess so much of him to the point that I can't help but feel guilt the more I realize I am the only thing keeping them away from him. Mason is a threat, sure, but I could have told Nik before someone else did, and now he hates me. Now, I am sitting in this room waiting for him to scream at me, because what else could have him not talk to me for going on 13 hours now, besides that he knows and he is trying not to hate me.

A knock at the door jolts me out of my thoughts and I brighten my smile as I look at my children and Kelsey one more time. "I love you and I will see you all very soon, my loves."

They all say "Love you, bye", in unison, waving frantically in the camera as I hang up. The knocking increases and my back is bone straight as I look at the pale door, prepared to meet my fate.

I clear my throat, yet my voice comes out broken and shaky as I say, "Come in."

The door opens, revealing a disheveled Nikolai. His hair is no longer in his professional slick back with a stubborn curl on his forehead; rather it is a mess, thrown about on his head like he just got into a fight. He is still wearing the clothes from last night, his black button up wrinkled and untucked with buttons missing. His jacket is tossed over his shoulders, and he has a gray filter over his face that almost makes him look sickly.

When he enters the room at first, he doesn't speak. It doesn't even look like he breathes. Instead, he just stares at me, his eyes roaming over my body from head to toe as if he was scared he wasn't going to see me again. I take a cautious step forward, my hand reaching out to touch his face and he flinches from me. His eyes immediately dart to his muddy loafers.

A choked breath gets caught in my chest and the ball of salt rotates in my throat, begging for me to spill my secrets, beg for forgiveness and tell this man that I think I may love him, that I want him. That I need him. I whisper his name, "Nikolai."

"Kotik," he responds in a drunken whisper. "Let me just look at you."

I freeze, my eyes darting back to his, unable to make any sense of the words that just left his mouth or the way he looks at me. I feel like he can see through me, or like he is looking at me for the first time, but his gaze on my body makes my stomach roll. I want to give him this. I want to allow him to take his fill of me before he kicks me out onto the street, but I can't stand his eyes burning me to a crisp like this. The intense heat of his glare makes me want to itch, scream, cry, but instead I blurt out the only thing I know to say.

"Nik, I love you." The words escape before I truly know what I'm saying and even then, I keep the word vomit coming. My eyes avoid his widened gaze, and I look at my bare feet, in front of his muddy loafers. "I have for a while, and I know it has taken me so long to say this. But I mean it when I-"

His hands fly over my mouth. He stops my rambling and my eyes widen as they lock on his. And now that he is so close I can see how haunted he looks. He looks like he met with the grim reaper and barely made it out alive.

"Gwen," he sighs, and a layer of despair spreads across my skin, thick and unmoving. "Please, just stop."

The tears I've been holding onto sizzle and spill down my face, mixing in with the metallic and dirt taste on his palm. "Gwen," he whispers. "Before you pour your heart out to me, we need to talk." A choked sob leaves my lips, muffled by his hand, and my tears are falling so hard down my face that his face is blurred. "Because after I tell you about what was in that box, you may not want to deal with me anymore, and I couldn't blame you."

My eyebrows knot as he releases my mouth and brings his other hand up to cup my face. His thumbs wipe the tears as they stream down like rivers. My voice comes out as a hiccup as I ask him, "What do you mean?"

His breath is unsteady as he holds my face tighter and he takes a deep breath through his nostrils. "We need to hide you, okay? You can't work at the club, or travel without bodyguards or me."

"Wait a minute. I tell you I love you and you lock me away in a fucking tower, are you serious?" I jerk back from him, anger flying through my body like a grenade without a pin. "No, I refuse to let you run my life, Nik."

"Kotik," he pleads, and I jerk away from him, shaking my head the tears threatening to fall again.

"No, Nik," I growl. "Fucking no, I don't care what you found out. You cannot fucking do this to me."

"Listen to me. You're not safe," he snarls, his hand reaching out to me, but I dodge it, wanting all the space between us I can create.

"Bullshit," I snap. "You know, I thought we were past this. That you knew I was my own person, that you knew that you couldn't keep me locked up."

"Gwendolyn," he barks, and I seethe at my full government name, at the way he yells, at the heat in his eyes, and something in me fucking snaps.

"No, I don't care how much I love you. I'm not doing this." I stare at him with hardened eyes, and I grab my phone off of the floor and growl out my next words. "I'm leaving."

"No, you're not." He matches my anger, his eyes wild and crazed. A sharp, hard exhale leaves his lips as he runs his hand roughly through his hair. "If you want to leave, you're going to have to kill me to do so." I jerk back at his words, not wanting to show him any more weakness than I have, but unwilling to commit such a crime, especially to him. "Now sit down and listen."

Against my better judgment, my back straightens and I am sitting on the edge of the bed, looking at the open wardrobe door, the law books scattered on the floor, the sun fully rising outside of my window, anywhere but at him.

After a moment, he sighs, and the bed dips and creaks next to me. I feel his body shift as he leans forward and places his elbows on his knees, taking a deep breath before speaking the words that make my stomach drop. "My father wants to kill you."

I always knew loving Nik would feel like drowning, but this feels like a tidal wave pulling me under. I suck in a sharp breath, but I don't speak and he continues in a low, hushed voice.

"Yesterday in that lavender box was a piece of my mother."

I pull my bottom lip between my teeth, my lungs burning as the waves draw me further into the sea. "What do you mean, a piece of your mother?" I whisper back, looking at his tense frame from the corner of my eye.

"I mean my mother's right hand and wrist with her limited edition Tiffany watch still on it." Nik states everything so matter of fact that I forget I am supposed to be angry and turn to him. A part of me wants to see a smile on his face, because he has to be joking, because no one would be cruel enough to send him pieces of his mother.

But there is no smile. Instead, his eyes drop and a small tremor runs through his body. I snake my hand between his clasped palms and scoot closer to him, our knees touching and my arm brushing against his chest.

"You can't go anywhere because I don't know where he is, and he will kill you to get to me. To destroy the one good thing I have left in this world." Nik's voice comes out like this is some manic dream he can't will himself out of.

"Why would he do this to you?" The minute the question comes out I feel stupid, inconsiderate because what child knows why their parents are so cruel? There is no father in their right mind who would ever do this to their child. I could never imagine tormenting Gio and Mia with throwing away one of their millions of drawings, let alone sending them pieces of their father.

"I am not Boris's biological child." He rushes out the words as if this is the first time he has ever said them.

"So this random man is tormenting you?" My ears are so hot, I can feel them burning my skin, and my hands itch with the need to rip Boris to pieces.

"No, Boris is my mother's debt collector of sorts."

"Well then, pay him off, Nik, you have the funds, don't let him do this to you!" I grip his hand tighter, pulling it into my chest, my voice a strangled plea as I try to catch his eyes on mine, but he just bites his bottom lip and looks away.

"My mother was in debt trying to keep her club open and Boris took advantage of that. He told her that he would pay off all of the debt she acquired, and back then my mother would've done anything to keep the club open; it was her dream." He licks his lips slowly and squeezes my hand tighter.

"So she agreed?" I urge him along and he lets out a laugh that sounds humorless and almost mocking.

"Agreed is an understatement," he murmurs. "The deal was that she provided him with children to be the heir to the mafia. They would have a marriage of convenience rather than love, but Boris was still so territorial of my mother, used to treat her like property and beat her so badly she was in the hospital a couple of times."

"So he was an abusive prick? Now instead of paying him off, I vote to kill him."

"When I was younger, I used to try to fight him off of her, but I was a kid and he was a grown man, so I did nothing but get a busted lip and a broken arm." Nik scoffs, and one hand releases mine so he can rub down his face, before he hunches back over and continues.

My heart beats painfully in my chest, and I can't help picturing a younger, helpless version of Nik, trapped under the weight of a monster whose only way to make him a man was to beat it into him. If I ever get my hands on Boris, I want to make him feel the fear Nik did as a child. I want him to suffer and bleed.

"What the fuck?" I twist my face, wanting to stare into Nik's eyes but he avoids me, and stares at his split knuckles. "He broke your arm? How could he? You were a fucking child."

"He was priming me into the next head of the mafia. It didn't matter that I was a child."

"Yes, it did. Nik, how could your mother put you in danger like this?"

"Don't blame her. My mother didn't have many ways to fight against him. Her only strategy was to shame him by ensuring that none of his children were actually his." He bites his bottom lip and then looks at me with a broken, lazy smile. "So my father is psychotic, and he knows I am not his, and he is pissed that I am the head of the mafia."

I look away from him, pulling my bottom lip into my mouth and nibbling on the dead skin there. He makes so much sense now, his obsessive need to hold on to what he claims as his, to control every piece of his world because everything was ripped out from under him back then.

"Look, that's a crazy story, but how does that end up with you getting your mother's hand in a box?" I snap, my anger at Boris cresting, and I feel like I want to strangle that man to death for hurting Nik when he was too young to fight back.

He speaks in a hushed tone as he says, "If I resign from my position, I can give my mother a proper burial before she decomposes beyond recognition." He continues, "There's a question if Nadia and my other siblings are actually Boris's children. If Nadia is his, he wants to arrange her marriage to another Russian in order to keep the Petrov name alive. And if Aleksander turns out to be his child, he wants him to kill me and take over the throne, just as Boris did to his own brother years ago."

I feel numb, and all I can see is Mia and Gio, our children, smiling, laughing and then dead, killed for the sins of a grandmother they would never meet. My body aches with guilt, and panic gnaws at me. I am forcing him to be in the dark about his children because of Mason who seems like child's play compared to the monster Boris is.

The world feels like it's closing in on me; my fear suffocates me and my chest tightens with every breath. The thought of Boris harming our children as a way to punish their grandmother, a woman they will never know, fills me with unfiltered rage.

If I tell Nik about our kids and their potential danger, it could destroy him. He would never forgive me because now he has to think about protecting himself, his siblings, me and two unknown children. And yet, if I keep this secret from him, perhaps he won't be able to protect them from Boris at all.

Fuck, I waited too long and now Nik can't know about the twins until Boris is dealt with, and even then, it may be too late; Nik may already be dead.

"Shit," I comment, because that's the only thing I know how to say besides you have secret children we need to protect. I look down at our feet again. I bite my inner cheek hard enough for the copper taste to invade my mouth and give me a different pain to focus on, one I can soothe.

"Either outcome where Boris doesn't die before telling my siblings the truth, I am dead. You cannot let the previous leader of the mafia live. So, either Boris, or Aleksander, or Nadia's new husband will kill me and become leader of the Russian mafia."

"Don't say it like it's that simple," I choke out a gravelly sound from my throat.

"But it is that simple." He takes a deep breath, shifting away from me. "There was a time I thought I could just let Boris kill me and save everyone the grief."

He lets go over my hand and stands, his back towards me as he continues to speak, "But then I met you and I had someone to live for. After you, I became selfish."

"Nik, look at me," I whisper and he turns slowly, his eyes look like hot glass on the edge of shattering.

"So no, you can't leave, because if you die, I die." His voice is firm as he speaks and my heart flutters so hard, I can't breathe. Instead, I stand, run into his arms and give him the best kiss of my life.

33

GWEN

With a soft sigh, Nik leans into me, his lips meeting mine in a kiss that immediately overwhelms me. I wrap my arms around his neck and pull him closer to me like I can mold my body with his. Our mouths move together, in effortless sync, and before I can get lost in him, he pulls back. "Gwen, wait."

"No." I lean back in to pull him back into our kiss but he grabs my waist tighter and searches my face with frantic eyes.

"Gwen, listen to me." His voice is barely above a whisper, rough around the edges as if each word costs him. "I can't let you go. You have to let me protect you because the thought of losing you..."

The tremor in his voice cracks something inside me, and I grip his shirt, holding him even closer. "You won't lose me. I'm not going anywhere, Nik."

I snake my arms around his neck, bringing my lips closer to his, our breath mingling together. I speak softly against his lips as I run a thumb over the tense line of his jaw. "You're not alone in this. I know you've been carrying this weight for a long time, but you don't have to do it alone anymore."

I lace my hands in the back of his hair, and he exhales deeply, relaxing under my touch. I pull his lips to mine, and he kisses me like I am the oxygen he breathes. Our tongues explore each other's mouths, and he tastes like the last drop of heaven.

Our hands roam freely, mapping out each other's bodies like we are trying to memorize each other by touch. He cups my face, his calloused fingers pressing into my cheeks, pulling me closer, deepening the kiss.

The taste of him is addictive, sweet and tangy, like ripe fruit. I can hear the faint sound of our breathing, mingled with the rustle of clothing as we fumble to remove the barriers between us.

My hands fumble to unfasten the rest of the buttons on his shirt, revealing bruised tan skin that glows in the morning sun. As I slide the top off his shoulders, I pepper kisses along his chest, paying special attention to every purpling bruise and fresh wound that marks his body.

He lets out a low groan as my lips trace the marks. His fingers tangle in my hair as I continue to explore the map of bruises and scars that adorn his body. My fingertips run over his pulse, beating harder under my touch, and he tugs on my hair, bringing our lips together once more.

His hands race to the hem of my shirt, yanking it over my body, exposing my breast. He immediately pinches one of my nipples, rolling it between his rough fingers. I moan into his mouth, "Shit, Nik."

I pull away from our kiss, and My eyes drift down, savoring the sight of him as my fingers graze the waistband of his slacks.

With practiced ease, I unzip them, feeling the tension in the room thicken. He kicks off his shoes and socks, pulling his slacks and boxers down in one smooth motion.

I take a step to the side, circling him slowly, my gaze trailing over every inch of his gloriously naked body. My eyes linger on the ridges of his muscles slowly purpling, the strength he carries even when he's at his most vulnerable. His broad shoulders, the defined lines of his chest, the sharp dip of his waist—I drink it all in, admiring the man that calls himself mine.

I pause behind him, my breath catching as I trace the curve of his back with my eyes, down to the hard planes of his hips.

As I come back around to face him, I bite my lip to keep the sob from escaping as my eyes trace over the bruises and scars that mar his body. A surge of nausea rises within me at the sight of the marks left by those who have hurt him. Every fiber of my being wants to cry, to heal every wound and make him whole again.

I gently guide him to sit down on the bed again, refusing to let him close himself off. Kneeling between his legs, my hand rests on his cheek, and he kisses my wrist with patience. As I look into his glass eyes, I whisper, "Let me take care of you tonight."

He shakes his head with a soft smile on his face. "You don't have to."

"I want to, just wait here." I gently brush my lips against his skin before making my way to the adjoining bathroom. My hands tremble with fear and fury as I turn on the faucet and plug the tub, a volatile mix bubbling just beneath the surface. I want to scream, to lash out, to burn this world to the ground if it means I can get my hands on Boris.

I would stop at nothing to ease the agony that consumes him, to grant him even the tiniest taste of retribution, to give my children a chance at meeting their father.

I take a deep breath, forcing myself to focus on the water filling the tub, steam rising in delicate tendrils, but images of a broken and bloody Nik swirl through my mind, and my fury rises again. The dread is the only thing that gnaws the anger away from me—if Boris ever learns about our children, he will kill them.

My fists clench, nails digging into my palms as I imagine every way I could make that monster suffer. But I push the dark thoughts aside. I grab some lavender oil out of the cabinet and sit on the edge of the tub as I pour some of it into the water.

I dip my fingers in the water, testing the temperature until it's just right—warm enough to soothe, but not too hot to overwhelm. I want this moment to be one of comfort, one where we can both let down our guard, even if just for a little while.

When I return to the bedroom, Nik is sitting on the edge of the bed, staring at the floor. His broad shoulders are slumped, his hands resting loosely between his knees.

"Nik," I call out softly. He lifts his head, and the exhaustion is etched into every line of his face. "Come on, the bath's ready."

He doesn't speak, just nods and stands. When he reaches me, I take his hand, intertwining our fingers, and lead him into the bathroom. I guide him to the edge of the tub and he steps in, the water lapping gently at his waist as he sinks into its warmth. I follow him down, perching on the edge of the tub, grabbing a washcloth and dipping it gently into the water.

"So, I am assuming *Johanna's* is your mother's club?" I whisper, dabbing the cloth against his face, wiping away the tension that seems to cling to him like a shadow.

"When she owned the club, it was called Vivi's." He snorts, a small smile dancing on his lips. "I changed it to her name the first chance I got."

"What's wrong with Vivi's? I like the name."

"Another reason my mother would have loved you." He chuckles as I continue to glide my fingers down his back. "She thought Vivi's sounded like a fun place, but the club itself looked ridiculous."

"How so? *Johanna's* looks so elegant now."

"It used to be covered in fake tulips. My mom adored flowers, but she had a bad pollen allergy so her solution was plastic flowers." He lets out a small laugh before gazing off into the distance and then clearing his throat. "But it looks much better now, and my mother's name was Johanna. It just seems like a more fitting name for the club."

"I agree that Johanna is a great name, but Vivi's sounds like a good time." I poke his nose with the washcloth. A hesitant smile spreads on his lips quickly and disappears just as fast.

Nik leans back against the tub's edge, his eyes closing as I continue to run the washcloth over his skin, trying to ease the tension that's still coiled tight in his muscles. We fall into an easy silence, just the sloshing of water and the light strokes of the washcloth across his body.

"You know, I was named after my grandmother," I say quietly, my voice barely above a whisper. "Her name was Gwendolyn, too. My mom used to talk about her like she was some perfect, elegant lady—someone to admire. But the truth is, she abandoned my mother when she was just a kid."

"What do you mean abandoned?" Nik shifts to look at me more clearly with furrowed brows and his lips in a hard line.

"It's the curse of the Sharp girls, we have babies that we can't raise. The pressure of motherhood gets to them and they leave." My voice gets quieter, my mouth drying as I realize that I left my children, that I am no better than my mother. My voice cracks slightly as I speak. "My mom thought she could handle it, that she could break the cycle and be a good mom. But when things got hard...she ended up doing the same thing her mother did. She left me, too."

The words hang in the air, and I feel a sting in the back of my throat. I focus on the rhythmic motion of the cloth against Nik's skin. Nik reaches out and gently catches my wrist, stopping the motion of the cloth.

"Come here," he murmurs, his voice softer than I've ever heard it, and I slip between his legs, the warm water enveloping me. He leans in and places a tender kiss on my temple before pulling me closer, wrapping his arms around me from behind. I lean back into him, resting my back against his chest. "I will never abandon you," he whispers in my ear.

"But I already abandoned you once."

"I won't let you do it again," he whispers in my hair. "You will stay, and we will be great parents one day."

His words punch me in the chest, the guilt suffocating me, and I feel like I am drowning again.

My body leans against his solid chest, closing my eyes as I soak in his belief in me. "I wish I had even a fraction of the faith you have in me," I whisper.

His hand rests on my bent knee, his thumb tracing soothing circles as he speaks with conviction. "When you see yourself the way I see you, there will be nothing that can stand in your way, Kotik, not even me."

Tears prick at the corners of my eyes as I nod, biting my lip and fighting the urge to share everything with him right here and now. I just have to hold on a little longer. Once Boris is dealt with, I'll introduce him to the kids. I will tell him about Mason and the debt. I have to, because Nik deserves to know his children, and they deserve to be in the family Nik believes we can give them.

"But until then," he kisses my shoulder, "we can always practice, make sure we get our first born done right."

34

GWEN

Nik's voice is low and husky as he whispers in my ear, "Don't worry, Kotik, practice makes perfect."

His hands glide down my arms, guiding them to rest on the edge of the tub. His touch sends shivers down my spine, and I feel his arousal pressing against my lower back.

"Nik," I breathe out, turning slightly to meet his gaze. His eyes lock onto mine, and the weight of my secrets threatens to spill over. Tears well up in my eyes, but one of his big, calloused hands trails up my arm while the other wraps around my waist, resting on my stomach. I nearly break under the weight of everything I'm holding in.

Seeing my tear-filled eyes, he pulls me closer. "Kotik, don't you dare cry. There's nowhere you could hide from me. I will always be there."

His voice is laced with a confidence that tightens the knot in my throat. His words cut deep, making it clear that running isn't an option, even as dread twists my stomach at the thought of him discovering our children. But instead of telling him the truth, I lean in, letting him capture me in this moment. Our lips meet in a tender kiss, the taste of him mixed with the faint sweetness of lavender.

As we kiss, I shift my position, twisting around and straddling him in the tub. The water sloshes gently as I move, the warmth of it enveloping us both. Nik's hands find my hips, steadying me as I settle onto his lap with his cock bobbing slightly above the water in between us. He breaks the kiss, whispering against my lips, "What are you doing, love?"

I slap on my most mischievous grin, pushing down any sadness that wells in my chest and say, "I think for our first, I should be on top, don't you think?"

His eyes darken to that Atlantic blue that makes me want to drown in him, and he tightens his grip on my hips, bringing my core right on top of his cock. He rocks my hips, sliding me over himself, once...then twice, and I can see the growing wetness between my legs, and trust me, it has nothing to do with the tub.

"Show me, Kotik," he murmurs, his voice thick with desire. "Show me how we're going to make our first born."

I grip the base of his cock, and he lets out a sharp exhale. I rub the tip of him against my slit, right to my entrance, and without hesitation, I sink down on him. I throw my head back and forget to breathe as I fill myself with his cock, no reprieve or ease, just me plunging down and ripping a moan out of myself as his thick cock consumes me. "Shit," I whine, shimmying myself down, making sure I don't miss a single inch of him.

"Fucking hell," Nik groans, his nails digging into my hips as he draws me closer adjusting the angle inside me so he is kissing my G-spot like the fucking tease he is. "You're going to be the death of me, Gwen."

With my eyes hidden behind my curls, I lean forward. One hand digs its nails into his chest while the other grips the edge of the tub tightly. Even with bruises scattered across his body, he still looks like the Nik I fell in love with five years ago: his messy hair and lazy smile. I remember this exact position on a hotel floor when we couldn't make it back to bed. In a cruel twist of fate, I realize that this is probably the same position where Nik gave me Gio and Mia because when we're in this position, he hits that spot that makes my walls milk everything out of him.

"Remember this position, Nik," I whisper, rocking my hips slightly.

"Kotik," he hisses out his warning, but it's too late. My breasts are in his face, and I am already grinding my hips up and slamming back down on his cock. "Shit."

The water around us ripples with each movement, the sound of splashing and our moans almost musical in the quiet room. I close my eyes, focusing on the sensation of Nik inside me, the way he fills me, constantly teasing my g-spot every time I slam back down onto his cock. His hand grips my ass, forcing me to keep him inside.

"Nik," I whine, trying to shimmy up.

"Where are you going, Kotik?" He pushes my hips back down and thrusts into me. "Stay right here, so I fill you the fuck up."

Nik's breath is hot against my ear as my body trembles as he holds onto my waist, pounding into me, and I obey his command not wanting to move in case I miss any of this pleasure. "Such a good fucking girl, Kotik. You want to be filled with my child, don't you?"

"Yes," I groan. Every time he bottoms out in me, my eyes see stars and my body tingles so much I barely feel his skin under my fingertips. "Please, Nik, please fill me up."

"Fuck, dirty girl." His hand trails down my back, gently caressing, drawing a line down my spine as he guides my movements. I rock my hips in rhythm with his thrusts, each movement more deliberate, more passionate than the last.

The sound of our bodies meeting is drowned out by the splashing water. My hands grip the sides of the tub, my fingers leaving imprints as I push myself harder onto Nik's cock.

"Yes, like that," Nik encourages, his voice strained with effort. "Take me deeper, Gwen."

As if responding to his command, I adjust my angle, allowing Nik to hit that sweet spot inside that sends waves of pleasure coursing through my body. I gasp, my head falling back as I lose myself in the sensation.

Nik takes advantage of my exposed neck, peppering kisses along my skin, his teeth gently nipping at my flesh. I am on the edge, ready to jump over. Nik growls against my throat, "You are going to take all of me, understand?"

"Nik, I..." I start to say, my voice breaking as I tries to express the flood of emotions within me.

"Shh, Kotik." Nik's hand moves to cup my face, turning me to look at him. "You are going to make me a father, right now."

The tears threaten to fall again, but before I spiral, Nik's pace quickens, his breaths coming faster as he nears his climax. I can feel it building within him, the tension coiling tighter and tighter until it explodes. I cling to him, my body tightening around his cock as I ride the wave of pleasure alongside him.

"Gwen, I'm...I'm close. Come with me."

His fingers slide to my clit, and a whine leaves my throat as I grip both of his shoulders and match his thrust. "That's it, Kotik, make me give you everything."

My body rings with desperation as my movements become erratic, driven by instinct to make it over the edge, to let him become a father, again, and that thought to make Nik a father again causes the tears to finally fall, mixing with the lavender water around us, and my orgasm rips out of me, crashing over me like a tidal wave, covering my sobs in a moan.

With one final thrust, Nik spills himself inside me, his body shuddering with release.

I collapse on his chest, the water still sloshing around us as we catch our breath. Nik's arms wrap tightly around me, holding me close as if afraid I might slip away. "Kotik," he whispers against my hair. "I love you too, and our future little juniors."

I avert my gaze from him, and the tears stream down my face like rivers. I'm grateful that his chest is already wet, otherwise I might have spilled out my soul to Nik if he noticed the tears.

35

GWEN

I haven't been alone in two weeks. Nik won't let me. It's either him, or an unnamed guard who isn't allowed to smile at me let alone have a conversation, and forget about me dancing at *Johanna's.* He closed it down until further notice, told everyone to look at it like an overly paid holiday, and believe me when I say he is overpaying everyone not to ask any questions.

I haven't seen Taylor in a month now; he's nervous and constantly texting me to send him pictures with newspapers with the date visible so he can make sure I am alive. He doesn't trust Nik, and who can blame him?

Nik is essentially a ghost now. I only see him at night, when I am halfway asleep and he tells me that he just needs to hold me tonight. I don't argue. I never argue with him anymore, because he is exhausted and has new bruises every time I see him. Besides, the guilt is killing me.

Every night, I bite my tongue until it bleeds just to keep me from telling him the truth. Every day, I spend my time wandering this massive penthouse trying to figure out a way to tell him the truth. Today is the first day I just decided to show him, because there are no words that equate to looking at the daughter with your hair and the son that has your eyes. It seems easier to do that than to figure out what to say to him.

I lean outside of my bedroom door where a heavily guarded man stands, staring silently at the opposite wall. He looks down at me from the corner of his eye.

"Hey?" I whisper.

He doesn't respond and just grunts. "You know it would be easier to talk to you if I knew your name?"

The guard huffs, shifting in his position. "Okay let me guess," I continue in a sing-song voice. "Brett...Kendall...Lyon?"

"No, what type of name is Lyon?" he snaps, rolling his shoulders back and keeping his eyes trained forward.

"A fun one. But could you tell me your real name? Please?" I bat my eyelashes, smiling at his stone cold face.

"Roshin."

"Oooh Roshin. I like it!" I beam. "Now Roshin, can you get Mary for me? It's important."

"Sorry, miss, can't move unless you move."

"I know that, but I can't really exit my room right now in this predicament." I dart my eyes down to my pants, and then back at him with shy eyes.

"Oh," he comments uncomfortably. "Don't leave this room."

"You have my word." I smile tightly and watch as he marches down the hallway and out of sight.

I tightly close my door, holding my phone in my hand, knowing I have about ten minutes of privacy before Mary knocks on my door and Roshin is back in place. I bite the bullet and call Kelsey and Taylor on a group Facetime. Kelsey answers on the second ring with David smiling in the camera.

"The guilt is eating me alive," I blurt out, and both Kelsey and David's faces twist.

"Woah, back up a bit," Kelsey says with furrowed eyebrows. "And start at the top."

Taylor finally answers the call, sweat dripping down his face as he runs at full speed on a treadmill. "Hey, don't spill the tea without me!"

I take a deep breath and close my eyes as I continue speaking. "I have to tell Nik about Gio and Mia. Kelsey, you have to bring them here to us. Nik's father is trying to kill me, and I'm afraid he will go after the kids too. But I can't protect them because Nik doesn't even know they exist. And Mason is probably still searching for me at the DMV area, because you know he's not so bright, so it doesn't matter that he's on our tail because he's just one small fish compared to Nik's father Boris, who is like a fucking shark."

"Okay." Kelsey swallows, looking at David. "Did you get that?"

"Kind of?" David questions.

"What the hell, Gwen?" Taylor snaps as he slows down to a brisk walk.

"Okay, so Taylor's got this," Kelsey comments, shifting on the couch.

"Tay, I love him, okay? I know this is bonkers."

"Bonkers!" Taylor scoffs. "This is downright insane, Gwen. You need to get out of there."

"I can't. Nik is the only one who can protect all of us, trust me."

"What, is Nik the fucking president?" Kelsey chimes in, rolling her eyes.

"No, he's the head of the Russian mafia," I spill without even thinking.

Everyone is silent for a second, even Taylor slams down on the stop button on his treadmill and stares at me. Then in unison they all scream, "What?"

"He has the power to protect us," I whisper.

"What the fuck, you're dating the head of the Russian mafia? The FBI has been trying to take them out for years!" Taylor barks.

"Yeah, are you sure you want to introduce your almost six year old kids to their father who may kill you for hiding them!" David yells.

"He won't kill me, he loves me," I counter. "But you have to believe me, this is the only way to keep us all safe. The man after Nik is unhinged and if he finds out about the twins, we're dead, please."

I tighten my grip on the phone, ignoring the sweat that's gathered in my palm. My nerves are shot. I've kept this secret for so long, and now it's all crumbling in front of me. Kelsey's wide-eyed expression doesn't help; she's usually the one with a calm head in a crisis, but even she's at a loss for words. David leans in closer, trying to read my face through the screen.

"Kelsey, I need you to bring Mia and Gio to New York," I say, trying to keep my voice steady. "I'm hoping Taylor will be gracious enough to let you guys stay there until I can get Nik there to meet them."

"Gwen, are you out of your mind?" Taylor snaps, still winded from his run. "Do you hear yourself? You're about to drop two kids into the lap of a mafia boss and hope he just...what, melts into a puddle of fatherly love? He's dangerous!"

"He's their father, Taylor," I retort. "They deserve to know him, and he deserves to know them. I can't keep this up any longer, not with everything going on. Boris is out for blood, and if he finds out about Gio and Mia before Nik does, we're all dead."

Kelsey inhales sharply. "You really think that bringing them to Nik is the best way to keep them safe? What if this backfires? You're betting on his love for you, but what if he sees this as a betrayal?"

"I've thought about that," I admit, pacing the room again. "But this is our only shot. The kids can't stay hidden forever. The longer I wait, the more danger they're in. And Nik... he's been good to me, Kelsey. He'll understand why I kept this from him. He's ruthless to his enemies, but to the people he cares about? He's different."

"Different?" Taylor scoffs. "He's mafia. You think love is gonna override his instincts to control everything around him? He's already got you locked down, isolated. What happens when he finds out you've been hiding something this big?"

"Taylor, if this man loves her, he won't hurt her even if this is a betrayal. She is the mother of his kids, that affords her some leniency," David responds cautiously.

"He won't hurt me," I say firmly, even though a part of me is still terrified of that very possibility. "I know him. He's not going to turn on me for this. But if I don't tell him, if Boris gets to him first, then there's no coming back from that. The only way out of this mess is to face it head-on."

Kelsey rubs her temples, clearly stressed. "And what do you expect me to do, Gwen? Just pack up the kids and fly to New York, knowing I'm walking them into a mafia family reunion?"

"Yes," I reply, desperate. "Just for a couple of days. I need to get them here, and I need to have this conversation with Nik face-to-face. Once he knows, once we're all on the same page, I can figure out the next step. But I can't do that until he meets them."

Taylor crosses his arms, his brow furrowed. "And what if he doesn't react the way you expect? What if he tries to take the kids? You know damn well the mafia doesn't play by the same rules we do."

"He won't," I say with a conviction I wish I fully felt. "He's not that kind of man. He'll be shocked, sure, maybe even furious at first. But he's been talking about wanting kids, Taylor. He's already soft with me—this will change things for the better. He's wanted this family; he just didn't know it was already here."

David sighs and leans back on the couch. "Kelsey, you're not really considering this, are you?"

Kelsey looks torn, chewing on her bottom lip. "I don't like it, but Gwen's right about one thing. Those kids won't be safe if Boris gets to them first. If Nik is the only one who can protect them, then we have to make sure he knows."

"Thank you," I say, relieved that at least one person understands. "I promise it'll just be for a few days. Once Nik meets them, we'll figure out the rest."

Taylor shakes his head. "You are putting everyone into danger. Me. Kels. David, your kids."

"I know, but I need you to believe in me, Tay," I whisper, biting the corner of my lip and he stares into the camera with a defeated look on his face.

"Fine, but if anything, and I mean anything feels off, if those kids are in danger, I'm coming to get them, and I won't care what Nik or his goons have to say about it."

"Deal," I say, grateful. "I'll make sure everything's ready at my end. Kelsey, can you get them here by Wednesday?"

That gives me three days to prepare. She nods reluctantly. "I'll pack up their stuff and we'll be on the first red eye on Tuesday."

"I owe you both," I reply, wiping my eyes. "I know this is insane, but it's the only way to keep us safe. I'll handle Nik—I just need you to trust me."

"We do," David responds. "Just stay safe."

A sudden, urgent knock at the door startles me and I quickly say goodbye before hanging up the phone. Mary's unruly red curls peek in through the crack in the door and she gives me a sympathetic smile.

"I heard Aunt Flo came for a visit," she says softly.

"Oh no," I shake my head dismissively as I wave her inside. She closes the door tightly behind her, shutting out the world beyond. "Can you help me set up a surprise for Nik? I need some supplies."

36

GWEN

With my bare hands, I dig into the damp soil, feeling the coolness and moisture of the earth on my skin. Mary has been by my side for the past two days as we carefully arrange a row of garden boxes on Nik's balcony, right off of his office, on the first floor of the penthouse. The air is filled with the soft hum of the city below, and the vibrant colors of pink, yellow, and white tulips make a beautiful mess in front of me.

These are the same types of flowers that Nik's mother had throughout the club when it was called *Vivi's* instead of *Johanna*'s. I tried to match the colors of *Vivi's,* but I could only find limited photos of the club on Google, so most of the garden comes from my imagination.

I take a moment to lean back on my heels and wipe the dirt from my palms onto my jeans, admiring the neat rows of planted tulips. I can't help but imagine Nik's reaction when he sees them - perhaps a flicker of surprise, or even a rare genuine smile. Thinking about it warms me from within, even though I know it will be short-lived.

The garden still has some empty corners, but it's coming along nicely. I move over to the last corner, determined to fill it before tonight. I want to show Nik after dinner, hoping that in some small way it will bring him peace before I inevitably shatter his world even more than it already is.

The sharp ring of my phone cuts through the tranquility, snapping me back to reality. I quickly wipe the dirt from my hands, fumbling to pull my phone out of my pocket. The screen flashes with an unknown number, and for some reason, my skin turns cold.

"Hello?" I answer cautiously.

"Is this Gwendolyn Sharp?" The voice on the other end is cold and professional, with the clipped tone of someone delivering bad news.

"Yes, this is her." I fix the phone to be in the crux of my neck and slide my bottom to the concrete to sit criss-cross in front of the garden. "How can I help you?"

"This is Officer Meyers from the Maryland Police Department."

My mouth runs dry.

"We have a deceased individual we believe to be Rosalina Sharp."

I can't fucking breathe. I feel sick to my stomach.

"We've been unable to reach her son, Randolph Sharp, so you're listed as the next of kin. We need you to come in and confirm her identity."

I'm numb. The world around me blackens, and I swear there is nothing keeping me from jumping up and free falling off of this balcony.

"I—I can't do that right now." My voice cracks, and I clear my throat, trying to regain some composure. "I'm not in Maryland."

"I understand, but you have 72 hours to identify her. If not, we'll have no choice but to bury her as a Jane Doe."

"Jane Doe?" I whisper.

"Unidentified woman. She will be buried in the porterfield."

"Oh," I respond mindlessly. "How did she die?"

"Ma'am, I cannot disclose sensitive information over the phone."

"Please," I whisper so low I can barely hear myself.

"Homicide," the officer whispers back.

My throat tightens, and I barely manage to whisper a thank you before the call ends. The weight of it hits me all at once, and I drop the phone into the dirt. Tears sting my eyes, and I bite down hard on my lip, willing myself not to break down.

No. No, this can't be happening. I refuse to fall apart right now, not when the weight of my world is crashing down on me. Nana Rose, my rock and constant source of strength, gone in an instant. If she's truly dead, then it must have been Mason's doing. The scream that rips from my throat is raw with pain and anger, threatening to consume me whole.

I can't help it; my dirt filled nails scrape at my skin as another sob escapes me.

I can't. I can't fall apart right now. Nana Rose can't be dead, she was as healthy as a horse. At 72, she barely broke a sweat during our weekly yoga sessions and I damn near passed out from exertion. She had years to live and if she's dead, then it was Mason. I can barely hold in the scream that escapes my lips.

My dirt-covered nails scrape against my skin as another sob escapes me. I can't stop myself from doing it; the action is involuntary, as I feel myself burning at the stake.

The guilt is overwhelming, because Nana's death is my fault. I should have let Nik protect her. If I had been honest from the start, I wouldn't be forced to go identify her remains now or risk her being buried in some unmarked grave on a disease-ridden island off the coast.

This can't be happening, it's impossible. I refuse to believe it until I see her lifeless body with my own eyes. But I can't even do that.

Every step outside of this building, let alone New York, puts me, Nik, our children at risk. Nik's father is still out there, and Mason is relentlessly pursuing me.

I inhale deeply, blinking rapidly to push the tears back. I have to keep it together. I focus on the empty corner of the garden, because if this was a memorial for bodies Nik and I would never see again, then it's only right for Nana to be here.

All I have are fucking tulips, but Nana's favorite was her yellow Roses that her father planted in their garden as she grew up. She used to say yellow roses bring hope for tomorrow. It's the least I can do for her. I press the dirt, carving out an even square out for her, letting the repetitive motions of planting calm me, even though my hands are trembling.

When the soil looks ready, I brush the dirt off my jeans before standing up. My heart feels heavy, but I force myself to square my shoulders.

I need to find Mary and tell her to buy me yellow roses. I need to call Kelsey and ask if she can leave the kids at Tay's and identify Nana's body with me, but worst of all I need to look Nik in the eye and tell him I am the reason my nana is dead.

I walk inside of the study, about to make my way towards the kitchen when I hear voices—Nik's, along with two others that I don't recognize.

I quickly wipe my eyes and take a deep breath, schooling my features into something that looks cheerful enough. I can't let him see that I've been crying. Not now. I follow the voices down the hallway, the sound growing clearer as I approach his living room. When I round the corner, I plaster on a bright smile. "Sorry, am I interrupting something?"

Nik's gaze snaps to me instantly, his eyes narrowing as they take in my appearance. I can see the suspicion flicker behind those steely blue eyes. "Why do you look like you've been crying?"

"Jesus, Nik, can you say hi first." A woman with butt-length honey blonde hair and eyes that sparkle darker than Nik's smacks him in the chest as she looks me over.

I shake my head quickly. "It's nothing. Just got a bit emotional over the surprise I have for you, actually." I hope the distraction works.

He studies me, not fully convinced, but lets it slide for now. "We'll talk about that later," he says, still watching me intently. Then he gestures to the two people standing beside him. "Gwen, this is Nadia, my sister and second-in-command, and Aleksandr, our fixer."

Nadia is tall and sharp-eyed, with a cold elegance that makes it clear she doesn't take any nonsense from anyone.

Her princess-like features contrast against her black leather knee-high boots, ripped black skinny jeans and a lace black top under her kiss-ass leather jacket. She offers her hand and a deadly sweet smile. "You're a gorgeous girl, no wonder Nik's been blue balled since the last time he saw you."

"Oh." I shake her hand, looking over at Nik from the corner of my eye. "I thought he was lying about the five year dry spell."

"Trust me, we wish he was. He's a dick when he hasn't fucked." She rolls her eyes.

"Oh yeah? So what's your excuse, Nadia?" Nik taunts and she flips him off.

Aleksandr studies me from a distance, his sharp chocolate brown eyes dart over my frame and when he has gotten his fill of me, he nods once in acknowledgement, and I nod back, wary.

"Nadia and Aleksandr will be moving in," Nik says, looking around the room.

"Welcome to Nik's penthouse," I say with as much warmth as I can muster, trying to ignore the shattering of my heart.

"Our penthouse, Kotik," he corrects, wrapping his arm around my shoulders and kissing my temple.

Nik has been in meetings since eight tonight, and because he's home, Roshin is nowhere in sight, neither is Nadia or Aleksandr. I am alone for the first time in forever, in Nik's black cashmere hoodie that smells like cedar, smoke and home, in the middle of the living room reading the same two lines of a Virgina Woolf book.

"One cannot bring children into a world like this. One cannot perpetuate suffering, or increase the breed of these lustful animals, who have no lasting emotions, but only whims and vanities, eddying them now this way, now that."

It's as if Woolf can see me. My children are probably in a taxi to the airport, on their way to a doom of my own creation. In less than 24 hours, I'm about to introduce them to a father who'll love them but might never forgive me for hiding them from him. A man who might resent me. I keep imagining the way Nik's going to look at me after he finds out.

His eyes will flash that dark blue; confusion, hurt and resentment will burn until any love he has for me burns out in his pupils. He will never forgive me for my crimes, and even now, I want to keep them hidden.

I can't shake this feeling that I am dragging them into a world that they should never be part of. Nik's world is filled with violence, people are treated like pawns, and everyone is selfish. The animals that stalk these shadows are men who are ruled by greed and primal instincts, who would destroy everything in their path for a fleeting sense of control.

I want to protect them from this, to give them peace, love, and a childhood I never seemed to have, but regardless of want, I am pulling them into the darkness because Nik has already consumed me in him. I am selfish for this, for loving a man so dangerous again. I should have learned from my high school sweetheart, Mason. Instead, I upgraded from hometown gang leader to Mafia Boss.

A scoff leaves my lips and I close the book, not wanting another one of Woolf's haunting lines to see through me again, not tonight. I am not even a fan of her work. Nana was. Nana loved Virgina Woolf, thought they were cut from the same cloth. A woman tired of a man's world breaking free of it. I am not that, not anymore.

My throat tightens, and my eyes begin to water. Fuck, here it goes again, my grief hitting me in the chest -- taking what little bit of strength I have left within me. Leaving me a shell of myself.

I performed during dinner under Nik's squinting gaze. I performed on this couch reading, knowing he would peek down from the meeting room upstairs every ten minutes or so. I perform now, pulling his sweater around me tighter, believing that his scent will run the demon away, but this time they don't run far enough.

"Gwen," Nik's gruff voice snaps me out of my trance, and I look up at him with an easygoing smile.

"Yes?"

He pauses, staring at me from above, and again he asks the question I keep internally begging he stops. "Are you going to tell me what's wrong?"

"Nothing's wrong." I smile, pulling my feet underneath my bottom. "Well, besides your father hunting us and me going stir crazy in this house."

He nods sharply, disbelieving. I bite my lip, internally begging him not to demand I tell him the truth. I can only lie when he doesn't command me to be honest, and I can't be honest right now. "Come take a shower with me."

"Sorry, can't scrub your back tonight." I shrug, showing him my book. "I'm reading."

"Right." He looks off for a second before looking down at me with a mischievous smirk. "Well, be done with that by the time I get out of the shower. I want my favorite dessert tonight."

My stomach flips, and my cheeks turn blossom a soft pink. "Don't let me get cold. I heard I am best served hot."

A lazy smile spreads across his lips before he turns around and disappears down the hallway. When I can't hear him anymore, I let the fake smile drop off my face as I scurry to my feet and start to walk in the opposite direction.

Looking cautiously over my shoulder, I turn towards the emergency staircase passing some of the guards and placing my finger up to my lips to shush them.

"Ma'am, I can't-" One of them tries to stop me, but I knock my elbow into his rib cage and give him a deadly sweet smile.

"Sorry, on the phone. I need privacy." I sidestep him, my hand pressing against the door knob of the staircase when he places a palm on my shoulder. "If I were you, I would stop touching me because if Nikolai sees your hands on me, that will be the last time they will be attached to your body."

The man snatches his hand back to his body, caressing it as if I just bit him. "Ma'am I can't let you down that staircase; you're not allowed to leave the penthouse."

"Look, I get it, I'm in danger but I need a minute, no guards, no one breathing down my neck, just a minute where I can be alone and feel normal for a second." My eye darts between his gaze and the man behind him. But before they can say no again, I continue. "I won't leave the building, I promise."

One more cautious glance. And then the guard takes his position back against the wall. "Twenty minutes, Miss, and then we are coming for you like it or not."

I give him a tight smile. "Thank you, boys."

I push into the stairwell and slip my phone out of my back pocket, quickly dialing Kelsey's number. I skip casually down the stairs, taking my time down the forty flights of stairs. Kelsey answers on the third ring, her voice shooting over the speaker. "If you were calling me to tell me not to come to New York, it's too late, we're already through security and Mia already has a matcha latte."

I snort, knowing that Gio is probably pinching his nose away from her because he hates the smell. "What's Gio drinking?"

"Your son is weird, he got iced black tea, no sweeteners, or juice, just plain black tea, totally not normal," Kelsey whisper-yells into the phone. In the background, Gio's muffled voice can be heard protesting, while Mia's high-pitched hello echoes in the background. My heart swells at the sound of their voices, anticipating seeing them again.

But then I remember why I had to call Kelsey, and a sickening feeling settles in my stomach. I was going to introduce the twins to Nik, but when was I going to tell them that their grandma had died? They would notice when she wasn't here for Thanksgiving, or Christmas, or when there were no sloppy kisses on their cheeks for their birthday. They would ask for her and I would have nothing to say. I don't know how to tell two five-year-olds that they will never see their nana again. And I know I could never tell them it was my fault.

"Hey Kels, can you leave David with the kids for a second? I have to tell you something." I continue my way down the stairs, listening to her shuffle away from the children.

"What's up? If you seriously don't want us to come to New York City, I was just joking. We will literally turn around and go back home," she rushes out, but then takes a deep breath and continues. "But the twins really miss you, G. They want their mom."

"It's not that, just-" I pause, pushing open the other emergency door at the ground level, and entering a surprisingly empty lobby. It's weird, unsettling even, but I pushed that thought aside as I make my way to the back corner of the lobby where I will have enough privacy.

"After you land, I need you to drop the twins off at Taylor's and then drive down to DC." I perch on the arm of a chair, nervously tapping my foot against the floor.

Kelsey groans. "Why do you want me to drive down to DC? After a four hour flight? Why?"

"They found Nana Rose's body," I blurt out before I can stop myself. The words feel heavy and cold on my tongue, making everything more real. The ball of salt that keeps building and unraveling in my throat churns again. "The cops need me to identify her. I can't do it alone, Kels. I can't."

"Gwen, what the hell? When did this happen?" Her voice comes out in a croak as if she's on the verge of tears.

"If you cry, I cry. And if I cry, I won't stop so please don't cry," I plead and listen as she sharply clears her throat.

Before she can respond, the hair on the back of my neck stands up and I feel something cold and menacing standing behind me. "Kelsey, hold on."

As soon as I open my mouth to respond, a chill shoots down my spine and I feel a menacing presence looming behind me. Before I can even turn around, a hand covered in cloth clamps over my mouth, cutting off my scream. The scent of something sharp and sickly sweet invades my nostrils and just then, panic sets in as I thrash against the strong grip, but it's no use.

A raspy voice grates against my ears as he whispers, "Don't you worry, gorgeous. We are going to treat you just fine."

I take a deep breath, ready to scream my heart out, but then everything goes black.

37

NIKOLAI

"Repeat that," I demand, my voice cutting through the thick tension like a blade.

Nadia sits on my bed, hunched over her knees, her grip tightening around the knife in her hand. The gleam of steel catches the dim light as she spits out the words again, each one laced with venom. "Boris is striking a deal with the Yakuza to smuggle him out of the country. He's desperate, and they're his only option."

Rage coils in my chest, sizzling off the leftover shower droplets along my skin. The bastard's always been a snake, but this? This cuts to the bone. The alliance between the Russians and the Japanese had always been fragile, a ticking time bomb ready to explode at the slightest provocation. And now, Boris is setting the match.

"No one makes deals with the fucking Yakuza," I snarl, the words like gravel in my throat. My fingers itch to grab something, break something.

Aleksandr leans against the window, unnervingly calm, his shadow stretching long across the room. His eyes are hard, calculating, but there's a resignation there that only fuels my fury. "It makes sense," he mutters.

"The hell it does," I snap back, pacing the floor, the towel around my waist nearly forgotten. I can feel the tension building in my jaw, muscles clenched so tight it feels like they're about to snap.

Aleksandr's gaze is cold as ice as he speaks, his voice mocking. "The enemy of my enemy is my friend."

I stop in my tracks, locking eyes with him. "The Yakuza aren't a group that makes a deal that big without something bigger in return."

"He'll be lucky if they get him out of the country alive, let alone to Russia." Aleksandr's even tone grates against my skin, and a part of me wants to punch him in the face for being so fucking calm.

"Old man's lost his mind," I mutter almost to myself as I make my way into the walk-in closet and search for clothes. "He knows how volatile this is. If this gets out—"

"It won't get out," Nadia growls, followed by the sure sound of my comforter being sliced open with her knife. The room is silent for a moment, besides the clink of my hangers knocking against each other.

"Are you saying that you finally agree to let us kill Boris?" Aleksandr questions, and I pause my searching throughout the closet to hear her answer.

Nadia's voice comes out small, cautious just like she sounded as a child. "Yes...I mean...I don't know."

"Well, when you figure it out," Alek responds in a bored tone, and I continue to look through my clothes.

I carefully retrieve a dark, charcoal-colored hoodie from my closet, along with a well-worn pair of black jeans and black timberland boots. I sit on the bench in front of the wall-length mirror and take a deep breath before facing my reflection. My eyes widen in shock as I take in my disheveled appearance - tangled hair, dark circles under my bloodshot eyes, and pale skin. I look like shit. I am running on fumes, barely able to function, and I don't know if I can keep running around like this to capture Boris.

I haven't slept more than four hours this week, barely eaten anything, but the ache of not being inside Gwen for the past two weeks is like a knife twisting in my gut, leaving me raw. I am on my last sane nerve before it pops and I become the man I never wanted to be.

Funny enough, this is the type of man Boris wanted me to be. A man gone insane for vengeance just like he is, and I don't know how he looks so well rested. I pull my clothes onto my damp skin, adding a cashmere t-shirt and underwear under the all black attire.

I wipe my hand across my face and make my way back into the bedroom. "If Boris is in bed with the Yakuza, it means he is desperate enough to be sloppy; we got him right where we want him."

I don't stop to look at my siblings; instead, I leave the room knowing they will follow. "We need to move Gwen to a safe house. Nadia?"

"Don't worry, I got her," she responds, keeping up with my pace.

"Alek, I need you to find Boris's trail even if it is a footprint. I want to know the last place he breathed," I order and Alek responds with a curt grunt of agreement. I turn the corner, starting down the stairs, looking over to the couch and seeing that Gwen is absent and her book sits idly closed where I last saw her.

"Gwen," I call as I hit the last step. The murmurs of my guards catch my attention.

A hushed whisper yells, "What do you mean she is not in the lobby?"

Another voice whispers back, "I did a floor by floor sweep. I don't know where she went."

The cold knot of dread coils tighter, hardening into a fist in my gut. "What the hell are you saying?" My voice is sharp, lethal, and it silences the murmuring guards instantly.

Nadia moves in beside me, her eyes scanning the room with a predator's intensity. "She wouldn't just leave without a word. Where was she last seen?"

My mind races, piecing together fragments of the last hour. Gwen in my hoodie, curled up with her book, pretending everything was fine. The way she smiled—too easy, too forced. I should've seen it. I should've known she'd run away again.

"Where is she?" I growl, every muscle tensing as I turn on the guards.

"She—she said she needed a minute alone, sir. She promised she wouldn't leave the building, just needed some space," one of the guards stutters, clearly terrified.

I feel something dark and violent crack open inside me, a red haze blurring the edges of my vision. "And you believed her?" The words drip with venom. "You let her out of your sight?"

The guard's face pales, his hand trembling as he clutches his gun. "I—I thought—"

"I don't pay you to fucking think," I snarl, cutting him off. My heart pounds against my ribs, each beat filled with the icy dread. "I pay you to know where she is at all times. Now I'll ask again. Where is Gwen?"

"Nik, let him go." Nadia's voice eases under the hot burn of anger, crawling under my skin. My eyes stay on his fear filled pupils as I release my grip on his throat and he gradually drops to the ground out of my eyeline.

I close my eyes for a split second, forcing the rage down, forcing myself to think. Gwen's gone, and every second that passes is a second closer to losing her for good. No, I won't let that happen. I can't.

"Alek, sweep the building, all exits. Now!" I bark the order, and without hesitation, Aleksandr bolts into action.

"Move it," Aleksandr commands, shoving two guards towards the emergency exit with such force that they stumble.

My eyes lock onto the guard who let her slip away, and I can feel my blood boiling with rage. "You're coming with me." My voice comes out in a dangerous low growl. "And if we don't find her, you'll wish you were never born."

The guard's face pales as he stammers out a response, but I don't give him any more attention as I storm toward the elevator, every nerve in my body on edge. The thought of Gwen in the hands of someone else—of someone using her against me—makes my blood run cold.

Nadia is hot on my heels, and she places her hand on the sliding doors, her eyes narrowing in on me. "Nik, if you catch him. You can't...you can't-"

"And what do you think I should do, Nadia?" I lean forward, looming over her with sharp eyes, eclipsing her in my shadow. "You want me to let daddy dearest go? Let Gwen die? Give him a free pass to Russia?"

"No," she grinds out, avoiding my gaze, nostrils flare as she darts her gaze from side to side. "Nikolai, he's our father."

"No," I snarl, knocking her hands off of the sides of the elevator. "That is *your* father, and when I catch him, there will be less of him left than our mother."

I back up, keeping my hardened gaze on her as the elevator doors close in her face, but before they can slam shut, her pain-filled scream cuts through the air, "Nik!"

There is a part of me that wants to run to her and beg for forgiveness, promising I won't kill her father, but right now, with Gwen so far out of my reach, no piece of me bleeds for her, because Gwen has already bled me out.

"Last time she was seen was in the lobby," Aleksandr says, spinning his laptop to face me as we walk down the seventeenth floor hallway, because when my guards said they swept the building, I didn't fucking believe they'd do it properly. They went from the top down and went from the bottom up.

"Where in the lobby?" I move the bed of a twenty year-old couple who are currently being occupied by my head guard

Roshin who regrettably was on his scheduled sleep break during Gwen's disappearance. A fucking mistake that I would never make again.

"She was on the arm of the couch in the corner, then the video skips."

I grab Alek's wrist and he turns back the video to Gwen talking on the phone one second and then the lobby being empty the next second.

"We also found her phone," Alek adds, his voice rough. A guard behind him holds it up like it's some sort of consolation prize, but all I can focus on is the blank screen, the reflection of my own fury staring back at me.

"She was right there," I mutter, more to myself than to anyone else, my eyes locked on the screen. "Right fucking there."

I force myself to look away, my thoughts clouded as I am trying to figure out where I can ground myself, see clear enough not to get her home safely.

I tear my eyes away from the screen and grab her phone, dialing the last number she called which unsurprisingly was Kelsey. It rings once, twice, and then goes straight to voice-mail. I curse under my breath and try again, the repetitive drone of the unanswered call like a hammer to my skull.

Voicemail. Again.

I try once more, a cold sweat breaking out on my forehead. Nothing. Just that same damn voicemail. I'm gripping the phone so hard I'm surprised it doesn't shatter.

As we approach the lobby, my eyes scan the space with the precision of a predator. I'm looking for anything—any sign, any clue that those idiots might have missed. And then I see it, placed gently on the middle of the seat where Gwen once sat on the arm of the chair, chatting to Kelsey on her phone—a satin lilac box, almost identical to the last one with pieces of my mother, except for the ivory silk ribbon tied around it.

My breath catches in my throat, and I step forward, my breathing coming out sharp and heavy, beating in my ears. The box burns in my gaze. It's taunting, and it's for me. I know it before I even touch it.

"Nik, don't-" Alek barks.

I push through, and pull the ribbon loose with trembling fingers, the rage in my chest tightening into something cold and lethal. The box opens with a soft, almost innocent click, revealing its contents.

A chunk of Gwen's curly black hair.

I stare at it, the dark curls resting on the pale satin like some twisted trophy. A note is tucked beneath the hair, its edges crumpled as if someone had clenched it in a fist. My hands shake as I pull it out, unfolding the paper with a kind of dread that seeps into my bones.

The words are scrawled in a jagged, almost mocking script:

Next time, I'll send you her scalp. Let me leave in peace, or you'll have her in pieces.

For a moment, I can't breathe. The world narrows to just those words, and the strands of Gwen's hair tied in an emerald green bow. Her favorite color. Just how fucking long could he have been watching her?

A low, primal growl builds in my chest, rising up until it rips from my throat in a roar of pure, unfiltered rage. I slam the box against the wall, the satin and ribbon scattering across the floor as I turn on my heel.

"Gather the heads of our alliances. I need to make a deal."

38

NIKOLAI

"I don't fucking care that tonight is the governor's ball; shut it down or he won't make it to tomorrow," Alek growls into the phone. "No, Thomas, that wasn't a threat it was a fucking promise."

Aleksandr clicks off his phone, stalking back to the conference table in the Petrov building. Our eyes lock with those of the ruthless leaders of the Irish, Polish, and Italian mobs. None of us has our security and Nadia has been missing since I said I'd kill our father.

"Gentlemen, I have invited you here for a favor." I lean over the table, my fingertips spread in a tense web.

"You didn't invite us, Nikolai, you dragged us out of our houses with guns and threats," says Dante, the head of the Italian mafia, a man with pitch black hair and a constant low gaze that makes him look more predator than human.

"My apologies, Dante," I comment, squeezing my eyes shut as I keep a trained gaze on the table in front of me.

"This better be good," Mr. Doyle, the head of the Irish Mafia comments, adjusting his navy blue robe.

"Boris has taken someone very important to me," I say, my voice strained as I stand up straight, cracking my knuckles—a nervous tic I haven't succumbed to since I was twelve.

"The curly black haired girl?" Jakub, the head of the Polish mob answers nonchalantly and I narrow my gaze on him.

"What do you know about her?" I growl, taking small steps towards his seat.

"Oh come on now, Nikolai, you are not the only one who keeps tabs on everyone," Jakub taunts, reclining back in his chair as I make my panther stroll closer to him. "But I swear I know nothing of her missing."

I stop two steps in front of Jakub as I continue to speak. "I need the forces of everyone to find out where Boris is and where he has taken her."

"And in return?" Dante questions.

"Anything," I snap back, looking over in his direction.

The doors burst open, and Nadia in her normal all black attire, just covered in dirt with a strong stench of metallic, storms in, her eyes puffy and her face red. "Sorry to interrupt the sausage party," she says with a teasing grin, before her eyes narrow in on me. "But I couldn't see how this conversation could happen without me, so I'm here," she snaps, her tone laced with sarcasm as she drops into a chair and kicks her boots onto the table.

"Nadia," I warn.

"Now, Nik, don't worry about me. I'm just here to make sure you don't murder my father, since you disowned him," she counters, and my stomach twists. If only I could disown the bastard, but he is not even my father to abandon.

"Now is not the time," I growl, my voice deadly, but she ignores me, her gaze sharp as a knife as she meets my eyes.

"I don't care what time it is. Matter of fact, I think now is the perfect—" she starts, but Aleksandr cuts her off, his voice a bark.

"Nadia, go," he commands, his tone leaving no room for argument.

She jumps to her feet, both hands placed flatly on the table, her jaw tightening as she smiles something ruthless. "Make me, psycho boy."

Aleksandr tenses to the point he looks statuesque and I step closer to Nadia, growling through my teeth. "Both of you cut it out!"

The door creaks open again. This time, Lily steps in, her satin night set clinging to her frame, the matching robe trailing behind her like a whisper of silk. All eyes, but mine, fall on her innocent frame.

"Lily," Aleksandr says, his voice dripping with irritation, "Go home, and change."

"Excuse me, Aleksandr, but I have a job," she retorts, her chin lifted in defiance.

Doyle leans forward, his voice a lazy drawl. "Yeah, let her stay, Aleksandr. She can hang with the big dogs, can't you, doll?"

Aleksandr's eyes flash with anger. "If you want to keep breathing, Doyle, you'll mind your business."

Lily raises a hand, taking a cautious step closer to Aleksandr who keeps his eyes trained on Doyle. "Woah, okay," she whispers, standing on her tip-toes to catch Aleksandr's eye line. "No need to fight. I'll go home and change," she reassures him, her voice soft but steady.

He nods tightly and sighs, and Lily turns to look directly at me. "But, Mr. Petrov, there's a woman in the lobby waiting to speak with you. She won't leave until she does."

The room falls silent, the weight of her words hanging in the air. I look between my siblings and the mafia leaders, the tension crackling like a live wire. "Handle things here," I order Aleksandr, and then I look at Nadia. "You come with me."

"You don't give me orders, Nikolai," Nadia snarls, but I zero in on her, my gaze cold and unyielding.

"Now, Nadia." Without waiting for a response, I stride out of the room, towards the lobby.

I hear Nadia's reluctant footsteps behind me, and I push forward, the anxiety gnawing at me with every step.

"Sorry, Mr. Petrov, I tried to tell them no, but the girl threatened to skin me alive," Lily squeaks as we approach the lobby. My heart pounds so loud in my chest a pain rings in my rib cage, but I push it aside as I round the corner.

Kelsey and David—Gwen's best friends—stand there, their faces etched with worry. I recognize them from pictures and the light stalking I had done into Gwen's background when we first started dating. While Kelsey is fiercely protective of Gwen and a complete spitfire, David is calm, coolheaded and the only thing that pushes him over the edge is when Kelsey and Gwen are in danger. He had been like this since they were kids.

Kelsey stomps forward, her face red in anger. "Where is she?"

"It's nice to meet you too, Kelsey," I respond in an almost bored tone as I extend my hand for a handshake.

"Cut it, partner. Where is our Gwen?" David snarls, standing like a protective dog behind his woman. I would have cut his tongue off for calling Gwen his if I didn't already know their history.

"David." I nod, turning back to a nose twitching Kelsey, lowering my voice I say. "Gwen is missing, but I have it handled."

"Missing?" Kelsey snaps, poking my chest. "What the hell do you mean by missing? You were supposed to protect her."

I can feel my gaze darken, and I take a step back like I've been punched.

"Hey, back off," Nadia snarls, removing Kelsey's french tip acrylic off of my chest, moving to stand between Kelsey and I. "We will get her back."

"Auntie Kel, what happened to Mommy?" The voice of a scared little girl forces my gaze to drift down, and I notice two small figures huddled close to David, looking up at me with wide eyes. A boy and a girl. A girl calling Gwen her mommy.

A deafening ring fills my ears, drowning out all other sounds as I fixate on the little girl in front of me. Her golden curls cascade down her face, framing eyes that are an exact copy of Gwen's hazel brown orbs. My gaze shifts to the boy standing next to her, his jet black hair falling in untamed waves around his face like a shroud. And then it hits me like a freight train - recognition. My breath catches in my throat because those ocean blue eyes and that dirty blonde hair... No, it can't be.

Before the words can leave my lips, before I can process this revelation, Kelsey snaps me out of my trance. "Mason is a gang leader Gwen's father owes money to and she has been on the run from him. That's the guy who took Gwen, has to be."

"Mason? Nik, did you know about Mason?" Nadia questions.

"Whose children are these?" I say in an almost deadly calm way.

"Shit." David coughs, looking down at the two. The girl clings to Kelsey, her small hand gripping her skirt tightly. The boy stares up at me, his eyes filled with a mix of curiosity and fear and his fists stuffed into his jean pockets.

"Gwen was going to tell you," Kelsey whispers, holding onto the little girl tighter.

"No fucking way," Nadia scoffs looking between the two children and me.

"Nikolai," Kelsey says in an unsure tone. "Meet your children: Mia and Gio."

39

NIKOLAI

"What do you mean his children?" Nadia snarls, stepping closer to Kelsey.

I don't respond, my eyes trained on the two cowering young children, who eye me with caution and confusion. They're so young, so vulnerable.

Gio grips his sister's arm protectively as he silently moves to stand slightly in front of her. I stare into his eyes, watching my own suspicious expression spread across his face, like he understands the weight of the world on his tiny shoulders. *Fuck,* he's my carbon copy—his protective instincts, the way his eyes narrow suspiciously, the same way mine do when I sense danger.

And then there's Mia. She laces her fingers with his. Her eyes run across my body from head to toe, as if she wants to remember what I look like to identify me in a future line up. *Shit,* while Mia looks like Gwen, she also looks like my mother.

"I mean these are Gwen and Nikolai's children," Kelsey snaps, her voice cutting through the fog in my mind.

As Kelsey says the words, my world seems to shatter around me. My breath hitches, and Gwen's face flashes in my mind, an unfamiliar anger rises in my chest, but it's quickly swallowed by an overwhelming flood of disbelief and something else—joy. Joy? I can't even recognize it at first, buried under the layers of betrayal and fear. How could she keep this from me? My own flesh and blood, hidden away like a secret shame.

"Please." Nadia lets out a harsh laugh. "As if he would have a child in this world and not know about it."

"Are you calling me a liar?"

My eyes bounce between both the twins, and when Mia's eyes lock with mine, she pulls at Kelsey's skirt harder hiding like she is scared I will hurt her. I flash Mia a small smile and she furrows her brows, looking so much like my mother it fucking hurts.

"Does a dog bark?" Nadia retorts, her grin sharp, but her voice falters when she catches the tremor in mine.

"Nadia, she looks like Mama," I whisper. My voice is so quiet, almost as if I'm afraid saying it out loud will make them disappear or make this more real than it already is.

Nadia looks down at Mia, whose lower lip is quivering in fear and her eyes have a shimmering crystal gloss covering them. "Не может быть!" she gasps, dropping down to her knees in front of the little girl.

The disbelief in her voice mirrors the storm brewing inside me. There's a part of me that wants to shout, to rage against the unfairness of it all. How could Gwen do this? How could she say she loves me and not tell me we have children? Did she not trust me that much? But there's something else too—an instinctual need to protect them that's clawing its way to the surface, eclipsing all other emotions.

Gio steps closer to me, his wide eyes filled with confusion. He steps closer to me, and instinctively, I bend down to his level, my face inches from his. He places a palm on my cheek and tilts his head to the side. His eyebrows furrow as if he's trying to make sense of this, of me. He studies me, the warmth of his palm anchoring me to him.

"You have eyes like mine," he whispers, his voice so innocent, so pure. It breaks something in me.

I nod, covering his hand with mine. "Nadia," I call out, still staring into Gio's eyes, but she doesn't respond and my breath hitches when Gio's thumb moves cautiously across my cheek.

"You know," Gio begins, his voice soft, yet direct like his Uncle Aleksandr, "monkey dads and their sons do this thing to feel closer." He pulls his hand back and gently strokes my cheek again, this time in a smooth motion from my jaw to the apple of my cheek. "They touch each other like this, on the back, or the head, or the arms. It helps them feel safe and loved."

My chest tightens like I am being crushed by the weight of an elephant. It's like a part of me I never knew I was missing came home, and my disbelief, and joy are being eclipsed by fear.

I blink, absorbing his words, feeling a warmth spreading through my chest, mingling with the confusion and disbelief that's been swirling inside me since I first laid eyes on him. "Safe and loved," I repeat, my voice a little hoarse.

Gio nods, a small, serious expression on his face. "Yeah. It's like their way of saying, 'I'm here for you. Everything's going to be okay.' It helps them stay calm, too."

A lump forms in my throat as his tiny fingers brush against my skin. I reach out, hesitating only for a moment before I gently stroke his hair, my fingers brushing through the soft waves. "Like this?" I ask, my voice barely above a whisper.

He smiles, a small, reassuring smile that seems too mature for a child his age. "Exactly like that," he says, leaning into my touch.

I inhale deeply, a part of myself feeling complete in a way that terrifies me. I never knew I was missing this, and now that Gio and Mia are here, the thought of losing them paralyzes me. I hold his cheek in my hand and call out to Nadia again, "Защити их, Надя."

"Yes, Nik. I will protect them," she responds, her voice filled with a fondness I have never heard in her voice before. My eyes flicker to her tucking a hair behind Mia's ears. "I will do it because they are innocent and do not deserve to suffer for your sins."

I stand up slowly, my knees weak, and turn to face Kelsey. "You are under the protection of the Petrov family. My sister will take you all to the safe house in the Hamptons."

As I head back to the conference room, where the other Mafia leaders are waiting, I can feel the tremor in my hands, the way my breath catches in my throat. When I round the corner, I pause, inhaling a deep breath and gripping the wall, hoping to God no one can see how shaky my breathing has been since Gio, my son, touched me.

GWEN

I have never been religious and right now I regret that.

NANA ROSE HAS ALWAYS CHASTISED ME FOR NEVER going to church, never getting the twins baptized, never securing my soul for the best afterlife possible. She'd always say, "You will be scared at death's door because you have no faith in what's next."

I GUESS YOU WERE RIGHT, NANA. I AM AT DEATH'S door hoping he won't be home, or at least be in the mood for a bargain. But, you know, Nana, you were wrong, heaven isn't pearly white with gold gates. It's just gray, a little empty with this throbbing feeling that makes my head hurt. I thought you said there was no disease or pain in heaven. I thought you said there was peace.

I mock Nana in my head, but just as the white light parts through the gray of purgatory, my eyes flutter open. So, joke's on me—I wasn't dead yet, and Nana still isn't here.

The cold, damp air bites at my skin, and I slowly blink the grogginess out of my eyes. The pounding in my head only intensifies as the light seeps into my vision. It's harsh, almost blinding, and every flicker of brightness feels like a sledgehammer to my skull.

My wrists are raw from the rope tied around them, bound tightly behind the metal chair that digs into my skin, making my whole lower body ache with a deep, dull pain. The seat is hard and unyielding, and my butt is so numb that it feels like I'm sitting on pins and needles. My mouth is parched, every breath a struggle against the dryness that scratches at my throat, but my lips are sealed shut by duct tape, trapping my desperate gasps for air.

I blink, trying to clear my eyes, but they're sticky with the remnants of tears that have dried into a crust, making it difficult to open them fully. It feels like I've been crying for hours, my vision blurred and stinging as if the tears had mixed with salt. My ankles, tied to the chair's legs, are the only part of my body spared from the harsh bite of the ropes, cushioned by the soft fabric of my sweatpants, but even that small mercy does little to ease the overwhelming discomfort.

I want to scream, to thrash against these bindings, but my body won't cooperate, and slowly, I remember the last time I did that. The first time I woke up, I screamed for Nik and was met with a pink-haired man who quickly silenced me with a sharp jab to my arm. The cold burn of the sedative spread through my veins as I fought against it, but my vision blurred, and darkness swallowed me whole.

This time, I inhale deeply, trying to cool my nerves, but all I can smell is the metallic blood mixed with the cedar of Nikolai and it makes me want to cry. Fuck, Nikolai is probably tearing the city apart looking for me.

Somewhere in the fog of my mind, I cling to the hope that Nik will come, that he'll find me before it's too late. I picture him storming through the door, fury blazing in his eyes, and it gives me a flicker of strength, just enough to keep my heart from sinking completely into despair.

I force myself to take shallow breaths, in through my nose, out through the small gaps the duct tape allows. The air is stale, heavy with the scent of mold and dampness, but I need to keep breathing. I need to stay conscious. For him. For our kids.

I can feel my heart stop beating when their faces flash in my mind. Mia's golden hair and Gio's dark blue gaze. They are probably sitting in Taylor's house waiting for me to come, to hold them, to tell them I love them. Panic rises in my throat. I don't remember the last time I told them I loved them.

If I can't stay alive for me, I damn sure will stay alive for them. I wiggle against my restraints, trying to ignore the searing pain in my wrists. My fingers scrape against the rough ropes, and I try to find any slack, any possible weakness in the knots. I twist my wrists, feeling the sting of the raw skin tearing further, but I can't stop. There has to be a way out of this. I just need a chance, a single moment to—

A door screeches open above me, the sound sharp and grating, forcing my body to go rigid, my pulse hammering in my ears as footsteps echo down the stairs. Each step sends a fresh wave of panic crashing over me, and I try to shrink into the chair, to make myself as small as possible.

The footsteps stop, and I hold my breath, every muscle in my body tensing in anticipation. My heart is pounding so hard it feels like it might burst out of my chest.

Then a shadow falls over me, and a man steps into view. He's tall and muscular, his presence dominating the small space. His hair is streaked with gray, a stark contrast to his dark, predatory eyes.

He tilts his head, looking at me with an unnervingly polite smile. "Ah, you're awake," he says, his voice smooth and cold. "Now the fun can begin."

I flinch at his words, a fresh surge of terror flooding my veins. He takes a step closer, and I fight the urge to recoil, to scream, but my voice is trapped, strangled by fear and the tape over my mouth. All I can do is stare up at him, wide-eyed, as he leans down, his eyes gleaming with a sickening anticipation.

"Don't worry," he murmurs, his breath hot against my face as he reaches for my lips. "We're going to have a lot of fun together."

He rips the duct tape off of my mouth, and I scream.

40

GWEN

"You have terrible taste in men, Gwendolyn," the salt-n-pepper man comments as he folds the duct tape in on itself. I swipe my tongue over the bleeding skin, my mouth filling with the copper taste.

I spit out the bloody, thick saliva on the floor, and cough out, "When a man is shit, you blame their father."

The man laughs to himself, disappearing into a dark shadow of the basement. "And what do you say when the man is good?"

"His mother must have been a saint."

The man's laugh is loud, cruel and almost sinister as he returns back into the light with a closed water bottle. "Well, you can't blame me for Nikolai. I am not his father."

My eyes widen. Is this the man who has been sending Nik pieces of his mother? Is this the man that has Nik on high alert, barely sleeping or eating? This man who has the body of an ex-military sergeant and the aura of a serial killer?

The man unscrews the water bottle in front of me, and then places the tip to my lips. I open my mouth and greedily drink the lukewarm water as if it was the nectar of the gods. After three big chugs, he pulls the water bottle away and flashes me his cruelly piss yellow teeth. "Be nice and you get more water."

"Before I start being nice," I rasp out. "Are you the guy who likes to cut up pieces of his ex-wife and send them to his children?"

His smile spreads to show the sharpness of his teeth. "You can call me Boris, sweetheart."

"Well, sweetheart." I smile before sucking all the salvia in my mouth and launching it onto Boris's chest. "I'm not so nice to scum."

Boris doesn't flinch. Instead, he chuckles, a full-fledged belly shaking laugh. His eyes flash with a dangerous glint as he leans in closer, his breath warm and fetid against my face. His grin widens, revealing a glint of cruel amusement. "I can see why Nikolai likes you."

In a swift, jarring motion, his hand rises, and before I can react, it crashes against my cheek. The force of the slap snaps my head to the side, and I can feel the sting spreading, a fiery line of agony that pulses with every breath he breathes in my face.

My cheek throbs, and a coppery taste floods my mouth, mixing with the lingering warmth of the water I drank moments before. I can't help but wince, the sharp pain radiating through my jaw and into my skull.

Boris's laughter fills the air, rich and unbothered, while my eyes water from the sting. "You're a bitch just like his mother."

I click my head to the other side of my body, the weight of my head after that hit feeling too heavy to move. “Oh, I get it.”

“You get what?”

“The type of man you are.” I let out a drunken laugh. “You’re the type of man who lacks the emotional intelligence to use his words, so you hit because you’re too caveman to talk.”

Boris’s eyes darken with irritation, and in a blink, his fist is hurtling toward me. The punch connects with brutal force, slamming into the side of my face. It’s a solid, bone-crushing impact that sends a wave of shock through my body. The force of his punch is like a sledgehammer, crashing into my cheekbone and forcing my head to snap sideways with a sickening crack.

The pain is immediate and intense, a blinding burst of agony that leaves me gasping for breath.

“Want to keep talking, sweetheart?” Boris mocks.

I spit out a lump of blood from my mouth and give him a lazy smile. “Come on, sweetheart, I thought we were just getting started.”

“You and Nikolai have the same problem.”

“That we both can’t stand you?” I cock an eyebrow.

“No, you have distractions that keep you from your goals.” He pulls up a chair across from me, crossing his arms over the back of the chair. “You, a stellar lawyer, fails because her gambling addicted father owes money to a gang. A gang that put a price tag of hundred thousand dollars on your head to track you down and you being given back to their leader Mason.”

"I knew you were a bad guy, but sex trafficking is a new low, don't you think?"

"Don't worry about me, love. Mason didn't specify if he wanted you dead or alive," he teases, and I swallow a dry lump in my throat. "I'd prefer for you to be dead."

"Is that what you do when you don't get your way with a girl?" I counter. "You kill her?"

"Gwendolyn, I am not one of your boyfriends." His knuckles run down my swelling cheek as he speaks. "You can't manipulate me. I feel no guilt for my crimes."

"How original!" I deadpan as I pull my face away from his touch. "A villain who is proud of his crimes."

"If you give me a reason to kill you, I will, but until then." Boris pulls a phone out of his pocket and points the camera at me. "Smile for Nikolai while you still can."

41

NIKOLAI

In exchange for more than half of the Russian territory and a couple of favors I would have to find a way out of, the Italian and Irish mafias agreed to shut down the city. The Polish mafia on the other hand, well, they don't have a leader anymore. By the time I made it back into the main room, Aleksandr had killed him as an example, or for making a crude comment about Lily. Either way, it didn't matter. The Polish were small compared to the Bratva in New York, so their revenge for the death of their leader would have to wait.

When I asked about the gang in DC that Gwen's father owed money to, Dante already had the Howlers gang on his payroll. Mason was a means to an end, costing more than he was worth and I was given the green light to dispose of him accordingly.

It had been three weeks since Boris left me with my mother's hand and one week of Gwen being held hostage, and I had only gotten a total of six hours of sleep. My body pulsed with exhaustion, but I pushed it to the side because we were finally outside the entrance to Howlers' headquarters where Mason could be keeping Gwen.

We were one step closer to rescuing Gwen and bringing her back home. One step closer to finally uncovering the truth about why she would keep my children away from me. And even if this lead turned out to be a dead end, I would still have accomplished something valuable: not only would I potentially bury the lead that Gwen could be here instead of with Boris, but I would also make sure Mason paid for his threats against the woman I love and the mother of my children. It was all still a win-win.

I slam through the door, the frame splintering under the force of my entry with Nadia right behind me. Aleksandr stayed at home with kids because Mia insisted on giving him a makeover. If one of my siblings wasn't watching Gio and Mia, I wouldn't feel at ease leaving them behind while I traveled to Washington D.C. in search of Gwen. However, Nadia was adamant about coming with me to confront Mason, so that meant Aleksandr had to stay in New York with the twins. When we left, Aleksandr had a gun strapped to his chest with red lips and sky blue eyeshadow, and a confused expression that also looked like a plea for help.

The rancid stench of cigarettes and sweat assaults my senses as I storm into the dingy house doubling as an underground UFC club. All the men look at me with hard eyes, and a particularly ugly man with one eye spits at my feet.

"Eh," the ugly man with a thick Hungarian accent rang through the house. "What the fuck do you think you're doing here, pretty boy?"

I offer him a wide, devilish smile and speak with the carefree bravado of a man who owed the ground he stood on. Nadia stands with a shotgun sitting on her shoulder, more for show because men like this normally didn't see her as a threat and there is nothing that angered her more than that. “I am looking for Mason.”

“Yeah?” a big, burly man with thin lips and a bald head questions, his four-finger hand leaning against his knee. “Who’s asking?”

“Ah, Venom.” I walk up to him, swinging my knife open as I make my way over. “I thought you would remember me, pal. You know I still have your finger?”

I wiggle my eyebrows, teasing him, and three guys hold him back when he lunges for me. I wink at him. “Don’t worry, babes, we'll play later.” I look around the room again, screaming at the top of my lungs. “Mason!”

“Mr. Petrov,” a man's voice rings from up the stairs, and I see the skinny bastard wiping his bloody hands on a cloth as he enters the room. “It’s not normal that I get a visit from a man of your caliber. To what do I owe the pleasure?”

“You wouldn’t happen to know where a curly-haired girl named Gwen is?” I ask, flipping the knife in and out as casually as I could muster.

“You mean my girl?” Mason’s eyes narrow as he clicks his head to the side, standing on the last step of the stairs. His hands are still pink from someone else's blood. My body runs cold and my smile turns cheshire.

“Your girl?” I question with a flicked eyebrow, keeping my composure. “Don’t make a fool of yourself, Mason. You and I both know she’s mine, but if you don’t understand that, I could surely beat it into you.”

Mason giggles. He fucking laughs in my face. “You won’t get within five feet of me before one of my men kills you.”

"See, that's why I have her." I point to Nadia who stands behind me, casually popping the gum in her mouth.

"And what's a little girl going to do to us?" Venom chuckles, clinking his glass with a green haired boy next to him.

I glance back at Nadia and give her a subtle nod. In one swift movement, she lunges at Venom, grabbing his head and slamming it into the glass he was previously tapping on so arrogantly. Blood spurts out from his broken nose as he staggers back, letting out a guttural scream that only brings satisfaction to my smirk.

Nadia's hand moves with lightning speed, pulling out a silver blade from her boot. She plunges it deep into Venom's gut, twisting it with a satisfied smirk as his screams turn into gurgles and blood pours from his mouth. With precision and ease, she slashes his throat in one fluid motion, creating a spray of crimson that paints the air in front of us as Venom crumples to the ground.

Nadia stands over Venom's body, wiping her blade on his shirt with a casual disdain, as if she was polishing a spoon. I turn my gaze back to Mason, whose smug grin has vanished entirely.

"Nadia," I say, my voice cold and steady, "has a way of getting the point across, don't you think?"

Mason swallows hard, looking over at his men, who eye Nadia with caution as she picks her shotgun back off of the floor and places it back on her shoulder.

"Now," I continue, my voice dropping to a dangerous whisper, "I'll ask you again, Mason. Where is Gwen?"

Mason's eyes dart around the room, and he rolls his shoulders back, staring at me head on. Instead of answering, Mason sneers, his lips curling into a twisted grin. "You think you scare me, Petrov? You think I'm just gonna roll over and give you what you want? No, Gwen is mine, so fuck off."

I tilt my head, assessing Mason with cold, calculating eyes. He's either a fool in love, unbelievably stupid, or just that unlucky. But it doesn't matter to me. I will kill him all the same. With a casual shrug, I lift my hoodie off, roll my neck to the side, and let out a low, menacing growl. "Since you insist on being difficult," I spit out each word like acid, "your entire sorry excuse for a club will have the pleasure of witnessing me beat you within an inch of your life."

I don't give him a chance to respond. I close the distance between us in a heartbeat, my fist connecting with his jaw in a brutal uppercut that sends him stumbling back. His men don't dare intervene; they know the consequences would be lethal. Nadia pops her gum with a smile on her lips.

Mason recovers quickly, wiping the blood from his mouth with the back of his hand. His eyes narrow with a mixture of fury and determination. "Really, Petrov? A sucker punch?" he spits, lunging forward.

I duck under his first swing, but he catches me off guard with a quick jab to my ribs. The pain radiates through my side, but I shake it off, retaliating with a hook that connects solidly with his cheekbone.

I don't allow him to breathe as I deliver a series of rapid blows, each one more punishing than the last. Blood sprays from his mouth as I smash his face with my knee. His cries of pain are music to my ears, and I smile as his shattered face looks at mine.

The room is silent except for the sickening thud of my fists connecting with flesh and bone. I can feel the rage boiling inside me, the fury that has been building ever since Gwen disappeared, ever since I met my children, since Boris killed my mother. Every punch I land is for them, for the terror he put her through, for the danger he placed my children in.

Mason's face is a bloody, swollen mess by the time I finally stop, barely recognizable. He gasps for air, his chest heaving with the effort to stay conscious, his breath coming in ragged, shaky bursts as he falls to the ground

"Where is she?" I demand again, my voice low and lethal. My hand grips his hair to pull his face back up to me.

With blood dribbling from his mouth and his teeth loose in his gums, Mason finally breaks. "Boris...a man named Boris has her. She's...she's in the warehouses in the South Bronx."

I lean in close, my lips brushing his ear as I whisper, "Good. You did one good thing with your useless life."

The words barely leave my mouth before I drive my knife into his chest, and growling against his ear, I twist it slowly as his body convulses in agony. "This is for threatening *my* woman."

His eyes widen in shock, the life draining out of them as I pull the blade free and watch him collapse to the floor.

For a moment, I just stand there, breathing heavily, letting the adrenaline that ran through my veins sizzle to a simmer. All the energy I had, the thread keeping me standing and giving me the strength to beat the crap out of Mason, seems to snap, and before I can stop it, three weeks of exhaustion catch up to me.

My eyes drop to the blood pooling around Mason's lifeless body. I turn to face his men, who are frozen in place, and I can feel their eyes locked on me. I drop to my knees, my head spinning and my body heavier than it has ever been.

Nadia steps forward, her shotgun slung over her shoulder,

"Now," Nadia says, her voice cold and unyielding, "either you fall in line with Dante and his men and leave here alive, or you stay and die here and now. Choose wisely, boys."

The room is silent, save for the sound of the men shuffling nervously out of the house. I close my eyes, listening to the footsteps and whispering to myself *she's almost home.* "Nikolai," Nadia whispers, her finger curve around my shoulder.

The front door slams and I let out a breath I didn't know I was holding. "Ты устал, брат," she whispers.

"I am fine, Nadia." I take a deep breath, not willing to open my eyes even as Mason's blood seeps into the fabric of my jeans. "The South Bronx, we need to."

"No, you need to go home and rest. Your men will search the warehouses. You can sleep for the next couple of hours." Nadia's voice is firm, almost motherly, and that makes me smile and groan.

"Буду отдыхать на том свете," I whisper, finally opening my eyes to stare at the empty wall in front of me.

"You will be dead sooner than you need to if you don't rest. You have been going without sleep for three weeks."

"Why do you care?" I mutter. "I thought you hated me."

"I do, but you cannot fight our father in your current state. He will kill you and Gwen. Besides if you are going to die," she bends down into my ear, "I want to be the one to kill you."

The helicopter lands in the backyard of my Hamptons villa. It was a two-hour plane ride from DC back to New York, followed by a conversation with Nadia about the layout of warehouses in the South Bronx. I don't even remember the details of the conversation. I'm not even sure how I got here; my mind is a haze of exhaustion and rage, memories of blood and Mason's lifeless eyes blending into the dark void that has consumed me since Gwen disappeared.

As I step into the dimly lit hallway, the silence is almost suffocating. The house is too quiet, and the weight of everything presses down on me. My body aches, my knuckles are still bruised from the fight, and all I want is to close my eyes for a moment. But before I can even think of sleep, I hear the soft patter of small feet on the hardwood floor.

"Daddy?"

I freeze, turning to find Mia standing at the top of the stairs, clutching a worn-out stuffed rabbit to her chest. Her wide eyes look at me cautiously and she sucks her bottom lip into her mouth like Gwen does when she's nervous.

She takes a tentative step down the stairs, her little face scrunched up in thought. "Uncle David said you are my dad."

A lump forms in my throat, making it difficult to speak. I nod slowly. "Uncle David was right. I'm your dad." The words feel foreign, unreal, but her face lights up with a smile that melts away some of the darkness inside me.

"Why are you up so late, солнышко?"

"I was waiting for you," she says softly, taking another step closer. "I made you something. It's a present."

My heart aches as she reaches into the pocket of her pajama pants and pulls out a crumpled piece of paper. She hands it to me, her little hands shaking slightly. I take it, unfolding it carefully. It's a drawing—me, Gwen, Mia, and Gio, all holding hands, with the words "I love you, Daddy" written in shaky letters at the top.

"I always wanted a daddy," she says, her voice so innocent, so full of hope.

I feel a pang of guilt, realizing how much she's missed out on because of me, because of everything. As much as I want to find Gwen, a part of me, a very small part, is so mad at her I am scared to see her again. I swallow hard, forcing a smile.

I feel the weight of exhaustion bearing down on me as I kneel in front of Mia, her innocent eyes filled with a trust I don't deserve. I gently take her tiny hand in mine, the drawing she made crumpling slightly in my grip. "I'm here now, Mia. I'm not going anywhere."

She tilts her head, studying me and then scrunching up her nose as her tiny fingers pull at my cheeks. "You look tired."

I let out a soft chuckle, brushing a stray curl behind her ear. "I am tired. I've been having some nightmares."

Mia's eyes widen, and her nose scrunches in disgust. I immediately regret saying nightmare, but she twists her lips in thought and then holds out the well-worn rabbit almost as big as she is that she has been holding at her side.

"You need Mr. Floppy," she says earnestly. "He helps with bad dreams. Mr.Floppy makes everything better. "

I pick her up, cradling her small frame against my chest, carrying her back up the stairs to the room she shares with Gio. I smile, touching the ear of the rabbit. "Are you sure you don't need him?"

Mia nods sleepily, resting her head on my shoulder. "I don't need him anymore because I have you."

Something sweet bursts in my chest and I pull her closer to my chest in my arms. "Thank you, Mia," I whisper, pressing a kiss to the top of her head. "You're a brave girl."

"Just don't lose him! He's my best friend." She yawns.

"I would never. I promise. I'll take good care of him," I say, gently pushing open the door to the bedroom where she and Gio are staying. The room is dimly lit, the soft glow of a night light casting shadows on the walls. I lay Mia down in her bed, tucking the blanket around her small body. She snuggles into the pillow, her eyes already drifting closed.

"Goodnight, Mia," I whisper, leaning down to kiss her forehead.

"Goodnight, Daddy," she murmurs, her voice barely audible as sleep takes over.

I stand there for a moment, watching her, feeling a strange mix of emotions—relief, love, fear, and that ever-present guilt. I quietly close the door behind me, leaning against it for a second to steady myself.

Then my phone buzzes in my pocket, pulling me back to reality. I pull it out, a sense of dread washing over me as I see the message notification. I swipe the screen and feel my stomach drop. It's a photo of Gwen.

Her face is battered, one eye purple and swollen, a cut running across her cheek. I seethe with rage, but before I can break the phone in my hand, another message follows immediately after:

Ready for a trade?

42

NIKOLAI

"If he wants to strike a fucking deal, then make the fucking deal," I snarl through my teeth.

"No," Aleksandr snaps, hunched over the opposite side of my desk. His eyes are sharp and deadly, grilling me to the spot. "He wants his freedom or your death."

"He has Gwen, so we make the fucking deal." My voice rings of finality, but the laughter from Nadia forces Aleksandr and I to snap our necks in her direction.

Nadia sits side saddle in a chair, filing her nails with an annoyed look on her face. "Oh, don't look at me. I didn't hide your children for the last five years and then weasel my way back into your life just to get myself kidnapped."

"Watch your mouth." I slam my hand on the table, growling out my words.

Nadia's eyes narrow on me and feral sneer spreads across her lips. "Make me, сука."

"Enough." Aleksandr steps between Nadia and I, breathing heavily with a look of apprehension on his face. "We cannot make a deal if that means he gets his freedom. It's that simple."

"And letting Gwen die is not an option," I counter.

"So we kill him," Aleksandr agrees.

Nadia stands with a look of horror on her face that makes me roll my eyes in annoyance. "No."

"No?" I lean closer to Nadia with narrowed eyes. "So what do we do, Nadia? What do you fucking want me to do, if I am not allowed to murder the man who has my woman looking like this!" I toss my phone onto the table with the picture of Gwen bloodied, with a swelling eye and a busted lip.

Nadia doesn't look down at the phone and flares her nostrils at me. Her voice comes out softer than I expect it to. "He's our father."

I swallow dryly and look down at my hands. "He is your father."

Nadia sighs. "Nikolai, please."

"No," I cut her off. "He is not my father. He may not be yours either."

"What are you talking about, Nik?" Aleksandr questions evenly, his shoulders rolling back with tension.

I pause, running my hands together, avoiding both of their eyes.

"Spit it out, Nikolai," Nadia seethes.

The room is thick with tension, the air practically crackling around us with charged energy. I glare at Nadia, her words echoing in my mind like a curse. *He's our father.* The phrase churns in my stomach, and I want to swallow the words back, just say I am bitter and consumed with the grief of missing Gwen, but I can't bring myself to lie when the truth is so close.

"He's not my father," I repeat, my voice low and cold, my tone grates against the fury simmering just beneath my skin. "He may not be yours either."

Nadia's expression shifts from annoyance to something darker, more volatile. Her eyes narrow, her fists clenching at her sides. She leans closer to me across the desk, her lips twisted, fury dancing across her eyes.

Aleksandr's voice cuts through the silence, calm but tight, like he can't breathe. "What the hell are you talking about, Nik?"

I take a deep breath, my hands rubbing together as if trying to cleanse themselves of the truth, like this is my sin and not our parents'. The words stick in my throat, heavy and bitter. "Mother… She cheated on Boris religiously. He found out, tested to see if I was his, and when I wasn't, he killed her for it."

"Shit," Aleksandr whispers but it is barely audible due to the sound of Nadia's hyperventilating.

Nadia's face contorted with rage, her body trembling and her stiletto nails dig into my mahogany desk. "You're lying!" she hisses, stepping closer to me, her breath coming in sharp bursts. "Are you fucking insane, Nik? Do you even understand what you're saying?"

I lift my head to meet her gaze, my heart pounding in my chest. "I'm not lying. Boris found out she was unfaithful, and he killed her. That's the truth. He may not be your father."

Nadia's eyes blaze with fury, her nostrils flaring as she struggles to contain the storm inside her. "So you've been lying to me all along?" Her voice is venomous, each word dripping with disdain. "How long have you fucking known?"

I slowly blink before whispering, "Three years."

"Господи!" she gasps, shaking her head silently. "You know, I expect this from Aleksandr because he doesn't know any better. He can't feel what we do, but you? You knew all this time and kept quiet. You kept us in the dark while our mother rotted in a box somewhere, and for what?"

"Nadia-" I whisper, trying to get out an apology but she continues.

"You did this because of the fucking Bravta. I can see it in your eyes." Nadia sucks her teeth, placing her hand against her head.

"One of you would have to kill me. If the truth came out and either one of you were the rightful heirs, you would have to kill me, Nadia. You know the rules."

"I would have never killed you!" she screams. "We would have found a way."

"Nik is right, Nadi. He's right," Aleksandr whispers, peeking at her from the corner of his eye. "We would have to kill him, or we have to kill Boris first. If anyone finds out, they will deem us weak and kill us all. This needs to die here."

"Alek, he...you can't expect me to-" Nadia stutters.

Aleksandr's voice is calm and measured as he speaks. "We're not talking about whether we're bastards or not. We're talking about life or death.

"We're talking about how to save Gwen." His gaze shifts to me, his expression calculating. "Nikolai, focus. We cannot let Boris go free."

“And letting Gwen die is not an option,” I counter, my voice hardening.

“So we kill him,” Aleksandr agrees, his tone flat and devoid of emotion.

“No!” Nadia’s voice rings out, her hand slamming down on the table. Her outburst draws our attention, and I can see the horror etched into her features. She’s not just angry; she’s terrified. “No,” she repeats, her voice softer this time, almost pleading. “He’s our father.”

I shake my head, my jaw tight. “He’s not our father.”

Nadia’s breath catches in her throat, and for a moment, she looks like she’s going to break. But then she squares her shoulders, her eyes burning with hell fire. “You can’t take him away from me, Nik. You can’t take away the chance for me to know if he’s truly my father, or Alek’s.”

“We can’t take that chance, Nadia.” My voice is firm, leaving no room for argument. “He’s too dangerous. We don’t know what he’ll do if he’s free.”

Aleksandr’s voice cuts through the tension like a knife, cold and precise. “Enough. We’re not making a deal with Boris.” He pauses, his gaze shifting to me.

“Ok, so we track him and kill him.” I nod.

“No.” Aleksandr's smile is sinister. “We’re going to make a deal with the Yakuza.”

I blink. “The Yakuza? How are we going to do that?”

Aleksandr’s expression remains unreadable, his tone clinical. “I know where Sho Matsumoto, the son of the head of the Yakuza, is. There’s a rumor that there’s a bounty on his head, and Sho owes me a favor.”

I narrow my eyes at him, suspicion gnawing at me. "We're going to trade one man's life for another? That's your plan?"

Aleksandr's gaze doesn't waver. "This isn't about Boris, Nik. This is about getting Gwen back. Sho has connections, power that we can use. If we do this right, we can save Gwen and capture Boris long enough for DNA tests." Aleksandr's gaze flickers back to Nadia. "But father or not, we can't keep him alive any longer than necessary."

The room falls silent, the weight of Aleksandr's words hanging heavy in the air. I can feel every fiber of my being screaming that this is wrong, but then I see the image of Gwen, her face bruised and battered, and the fear and desperation claw their way to the surface.

Nadia looks up at Aleksandr, her voice barely more than a whisper. "And if Sho doesn't help us?"

Aleksandr's smile widens, the shadows in his eyes growing darker. "He doesn't have a choice."

My eyes flicker to Nadia, her hands trembling but her jaw set in determination. I turn to Aleksandr, trying to read his stoic expression for any hint of doubt or fear. But his face is like a marble statue, giving nothing away.

"Fine," I finally say, my voice hollow. "But if this goes wrong, we're all dead."

Aleksandr's smile fades, his gaze steely. "Then we better make sure it doesn't go wrong."

GWEN

I know nine days have passed. How do I know this? Because Boris has lunch with me everyday. A ham and cheese sandwich with mustard and mayo, wavy Lays potato chips, and water everyday like clock work. If I don't eat with him, then I don't eat at all.

He's even upgraded my basement to include a cot and a long metal chain that lets me move about six feet in all directions. I can only walk to the stairs, a bucket that acts as my bathroom and a small table with two chairs where we have lunch together everyday.

Every lunch starts and ends the same way. He asks me questions about myself, and I respond with questions about Johanna, Nikolai's mom, which normally results in him knocking me out via a punch to the face or an injection.

Boris comes down the stairs with our normal lunch, two flute glasses, and a green glass bottle with gold accents.

I cross my legs on my cot, looking at him from the corner of my eye. I sigh. "Are we celebrating something?"

"I'm celebrating," Boris says in a melodic tone, placing the glasses down he beckons me over.

I make my way over to Boris with a bored expression and the music of my chain rattling against the concrete floor as I sit in my plastic folded chair. "You didn't come here because you thought I'd be happy for you, did you?"

Boris slides me my sandwich and laughs. "You can be happy for you, because I just sent Nikolai that picture of you last night."

"Excuse me?" I sit up bone-straight. "You took that a week ago, why send it now?"

"Because I've made it so he has to agree to my terms, and your boyfriend is so infatuated with you, he will walk right into my trap." Boris smiles smugly as he pops the cork to the champagne.

"Trap? Boris, what did you fucking do?"

Boris's laughter echoes in the cold, damp basement as he pours the champagne, his every move deliberate and unhurried, as if he's savoring the moment.

"You see, your precious Nikolai and his siblings think they're clever," he says, handing me a flute of champagne as if this were some casual celebration. "They are probably planning on using their connection to Sho Matsumoto to plot against me."

"Who's Sho Matsumoto?"

"He is the heir to the Yakuza, or he was." Boris shrugs, opening up his sandwich. "Until he betrayed his uncles during a deal and was exiled out of Japan."

"So they are going to trade Sho for me; seems like your plans are falling through, B." I smirk, twisting my lips in satisfaction.

"I already made that deal with the Yakuza, darling." Boris's smile spreads so large I can feel it invading my chest. "In exchange for my escape, or better yet the throne to the Bratva, I will give them Sho, dead or alive."

I stare at the glass in my hand, the bubbling liquid mocking me. "You're using your children as pawns. They won't hesitate to kill Nik or Sho the minute they see them, will they?" My voice trembles, and I hate that he can hear my fear.

Boris smirks, lifting his glass in a mock toast. "Exactly. Killing two birds with one stone, as they say. Once they're out of the way, I'll be back on top, reestablished as the head of the Bratva, with the Yakuza at my back."

A wave of nausea washes over me as I struggle to keep my composure. "You're a horrible father. How fragile is your ego if you're doing all of this just because your wife cheated on you?"

His eyes darken, but the smile never leaves his face. "This isn't about ego, Gwen. This is about preserving a true Russian heir. One who isn't tainted by infidelity. One who isn't fathered by a fucking American."

My breath hitches in my throat. "You know who Nikolai's father is?"

"I do, but he's a little harder to get closer to. I need the Bratva to kill him, and he knows I'm coming." Boris smiles to himself and I can see how his eyes twinkle. My stomach rolls.

"You sent him her head, didn't you?"

"You know me so well, Malyshka." He leans forward on the wobbly, plastic table. "If you play your cards right, I might even take you as my next wife."

I recoil in disgust, nearly dropping the glass. The thought of being tied to this man in any way is enough to make me want to vomit. "I'd rather die."

Boris chuckles, as if amused by my defiance. "At this point, you might, so not a far fetched dream to aspire to."

Just as he raises his glass to toast, his phone rings. He glances at the screen, and his eyes light up with twisted amusement. "Speaking of the devil," he murmurs, before answering. "Nikolai, how nice of you to call."

My heart leaps into my throat. Nik. He's calling, and he has no idea what he's walking into. I can feel the panic rising, but I force myself to stay calm, to think of a way to warn him without giving away too much.

Boris listens to whatever Nik is saying, his expression smug and condescending. "Yes, yes," he says, waving his hand dismissively, as if Nik's words are of no consequence. "I'm sure we can come to an agreement."

Then, to my shock, he hands me the phone. "Here, talk to your boyfriend. He's so eager to hear your voice."

I grab the phone with trembling hands, desperate to hear Nik's voice, even if it's only for a moment. "Nik? Nik, are you there?"

"Gwen." His voice is like a balm to my frayed nerves, and I can't help the tears that spring to my eyes. "Are you okay?"

"I'm fine, Nik, but listen to me—" I take a deep breath, trying to keep the panic out of my voice. "You need to be careful. Don't worry about me. They don't care if Sho is dead-"

Before I can say anything more, Boris snatches the phone out of my hand, his face twisted in anger. "You are such a predictable stupid bitch," he snarls, before slamming the phone down on the table.

The sound echoes in the room, and before I can react, his palm connects with my face, sending me crashing to the floor. The world goes black before I can even register the pain.

43

NIKOLAI

The rumble of the engine hums beneath us as the SUV cuts through the dark streets, headlights slicing through the night. I sit in the passenger seat, staring blankly out the window, my mind a chaotic mess of thoughts. The city blurs past, and all I can think about is Gwen. Her voice, the desperation in it, the warning she tried to give me before Boris cut her off. The fact that our children are sitting at home waiting for us.

Aleksandr is driving, his hands gripping the wheel with a controlled precision, eyes focused on the road ahead. He's always been the calm one, the methodical one. But even now, I can see the tension in his jaw, the way his knuckles whiten slightly as he steers.

In the backseat, Sho Matsumoto sits silently, his gaze flicking between Aleksandr and me. He knows exactly what's at stake, probably more than either of us. The Yakuza wants him, and we've promised to deliver him. But Gwen's words echo in my head—*they don't care if Sho is dead*—and that changes everything.

I turn to Aleksandr, my voice low, almost a whisper. "We need a new plan."

Aleksandr's eyes shift toward me for a split second before returning to the road. "You're saying we abandon the deal with the Yakuza?"

"No," I shake my head, trying to clear the fog of uncertainty. "But we can't just hand Sho over. If they don't care if he's dead or alive, they'll shoot us on sight."

Aleksandr is silent for a moment, considering. His mind is always working, always calculating. "Sho, you didn't tell me they wanted you *dead* or alive."

Sho leans forward, his voice calm, almost eerily so. "If your son killed all your trusted guards in an attempt to eradicate the family line, wouldn't you want me dead too?"

Sho's black hair is cut into a mullet-like style, loose waves framing his face and trailing down the nape of his neck, where a collage of black tattoos reside. The lazy smile that plays on his lips is a permanent fixture, but it's the kind of smile that never reaches his eyes. When he leans back in the truck, I follow his movements in the rearview mirror, getting flashes of him and Nadia from the headlights of passing cars.

Nadia sits across from Sho in the SUV and continues to sharpen her knife with an eyebrow lifted in interest. "All? You killed them all?"

"You always have to leave one alive to send a message." Sho smirks back.

Nadia sucks her teeth. "The murder is enough of a message. Leaving one alive is foolish."

I stare at Sho through the rearview mirror, watching as his eyebrow piercing catches the light when he shifts, a small but sharp piece of metal that adds to his rugged appearance. There's always a look in his eyes—sometimes it's deadly, sometimes it's humorous, but it's always calculating, always aware. Even now, as he gazes at Nadia with that flirtatious glint, his eyes are sharp, taking in every detail, every flicker of emotion on her face. My blood rings and I curve my fingers into the palm of my hand, because if he even thinks about touching Nadia, he won't have to worry about the Yakuza killing him. I will kill him.

His broad shoulders are loose, and he leans back with a confident air, one arm draped casually over the back of the seat. "I'm not a ninja, Hime. I'm not in the business of being silently deadly."

"If they don't care if he's dead, why don't we kill him now?" Nadia leans towards him, her eyes narrowed on Sho's casual yet smug smile.

"You want to kill me, Hime?" He raises his eyebrows in a teasing manner, and Alek clears his throat.

"Sho, what's the new plan?" Alek deadpans.

"Let them shoot." He shrugs.

A muscle in my jaw twitches. "Let them shoot? That's all you got?"

"Aleksandr knows me. I have to want to die for them to kill me."

"I don't care if they kill you, Sho. I care if Boris kills Gwen," I growl, turning to look at his bored expression.

"Aw, I'm hurt Nik." Sho's tone is playful, his dark eyes bore into me. "I have something up my sleeve. We will get Gwen out safe. And then my debt to you is repaid, Alek."

"Not even close," Aleksandr says, his voice cold and certain. "But think–a huge dent if Gwen makes it out alive."

"If?" I growl.

"When," Nadia says with certainty.

I close my eyes for a moment, trying to steady my breathing. The thought of losing Gwen is enough to make my blood run cold. I can't let that happen. I won't.

"We'll need to be ready for anything," I say, opening my eyes, meeting Sho's in the rearview mirror.

Aleksandr nods, his expression unreadable. "Then let's get the weapons and make sure we're not the ones who end up in the ground."

THE TRADE OFF IS SCHEDULED FOR DAWN IN STATEN Island next to the floating barges of trash. Nadia leans against the SUV, her face twisted and hands tucked deeply in her leather jacket. "It fucking stinks."

"It smells like New York." Aleksandr rolls his eyes, an AK 47 lazily draped across his lap as he hangs out of the side door of his truck. It smells like rotten fish and vomit, but with the sweet tinge of vanilla. I can't tell if the vanilla is true or if my mind is playing tricks on me because Gwen is so close to being back in my arms.

Sho is tucked in the backseat of the SUV, sliding doors wide open, tossing a grenade in the air and catching it despite Nadia telling him to stop four times around. She clicks her jaw and the fifth time is coming. "Sho, you're going to get us all killed, stop fucking throwing that grenade."

"Hime, I told you if the pin is released I have about fifteen second to through it into the ocean. We'll be fine." He yawns, tossing the grenade once again.

Nadia steps up into the SUV. Aleksandr lets out a low whistle as she leans over him with fire in her eyes. I smirk, popping the gum in my mouth. Twenty minutes until I see Gwen, might as well have a show first. Nadia rips the grenade out of Sho's hand, pulls the pin and tosses it into the Alantic.

No one flinches when the explosion causes some of the water to splash the floor around us, and Sho smiles in Nadia's face like he just won the fucking lottery. It makes me want to punch him in the face. "Nadia, if you wanted to get my attention, you didn't need an explosion, just sit in my lap next time."

His tattooed fingers curls around her right hip, but before I can say anything, Aleksandr growls and Nadia pushes one knee into Sho's crotch. Nadia flashes him a sickening sweet smile as she pushes her knee deeper until Sho winces in pain. "Milyy," she purrs, leaning so she is a breath away from his lips. "The next time I am in your lap, I will be making you a eunuch."

His grip on Nadia's hip loosens as she shoots him a venomous glare before swiftly extracting herself from his grasp.

Sho coughs and leans forward out of the SUV, looking at me with a foolish smile. "I think I may be in love with your sister."

I bristle, a growl escaping my lips as I look him over. "You really have a death wish, don't you, pridurok?"

Sho flashes me a toothy smile that makes me growl, but before I can punch him in the face, three black SUVs pull up to the dock and my heart stops beating.

Sho leans in close to my ear, that same smile on his face and says, "Well, let the fun begin."

The car barely comes to a complete stop before Boris is flinging his door open, bearing his yellow teeth with the flourish of an executioner. Sho dips back into the SUV, probably to find himself another grenade. Aleksandr straightens his backs with the AK 47 hanging on his shoulder pointed at Boris's car. Nadia plays with her signature knife and has three guns attached to her body. And as a sign of fake good faith, I have one gun tucked in my waistband. Everyone has on bullet proof vests and if I didn't know that there were probably twenty men waiting to kill me, hidden all around this dock, I would have more faith in us.

"Nikolai," Boris whistles. "What a ragtag crew you got here."

"Only the best to kill you, Boris!" I give him a shining smile and open my arms like I was showcasing a glorious event and not the downfall of the three other killers next to me.

"So that's your plan, Nikolai. No deals or negotiations?" He shrugs, looking back at the members of the Yakuza slinking out of their cars. "You just want me dead?"

"I couldn't care less if you live or die, Boris. Where's my girl?" I snarl, looking towards the car.

Boris laughs to himself as he slides the door open to his black car and Gwen is kicked out onto the ground, followed by a colorfully inked man grinding his teeth. Guilt crashes through me, sharp as a blade to the gut, the second I lay eyes on her. Gwen's barely recognizable—just a shadow of herself, battered and broken because I wasn't there to stop this. I want to tear my own heart out for letting her get to this point.

Her hoodie hangs loose, like it's been through hell with her. The sight of her—on her knees, wrists bound, bruises darkening every inch of her skin—makes the blood roar in my ears. My fists clench so tight my nails cut into my palms, but I welcome the pain. It's nothing compared to what she's been through.

Her lip is swollen, split, and the corner of her mouth trembles as she breathes. The bruises around her eye have turned deep shades of purple, her skin marred with the evidence of every blow she took because of me. Blood, dried and flaking, stains her cheek, and I can't stop staring at it, my mind replaying the endless ways I'll make them pay.

Sho stiffens beside me, but he's already gone from my mind. All I see is her—on her knees on that cold, filthy concrete dock. And that man...the one who kicked her out of the car like she's nothing. He's going to die first. That's the only thing I'm sure of now.

The murderous fury that bubbles inside me won't let me move. My hands itch for a blade. For blood. To make every one of them suffer, and yet the guilt sits heavy in my chest, knowing this is all on me. I failed her.

The sound of her shallow breaths drags me back to reality. Nadia takes a step forward but I curl my hands around her upper arm and hold her back. The plan is still in play even if that means I have to wait a week for DNA results before I kill Boris. His head, his soul, his pleas for life will be mine.

Boris's yellow smile spreads as he scans over Gwen's sagging body. "Sorry for the injuries, Nik. Your girl has quite a mouth on her. You should put it to better use."

My jaw clenches and without thinking, I take a step forward, my eyes burning with fury. With a steely gaze, I meet Boris's malicious grin and calmly respond, "Funny you should mention that, Boris. Because after I'm done with you, the only thing your mouth will be good for is begging for mercy."

Boris laughs and I wonder if that gurgle chuckle he has is similar to him choking on his blood.

"I want to make an amendment to our deal." Boris smiles.

"No," Aleksandr spits.

"Yes, but I want to speak to the king, not the lackey," Boris snarls. Aleksandr seethes, clicking his gun so the red dot shines in the middle of Boris's chest. Boris doesn't flinch, snapping his finger so twenty more dots beat violently on my chest. Bullet-proof vests can't withstand repeated shots to the same location. Twenty shots to my chest and I'm a fucking goner.

With a wicked smirk, I bring my hands up to chest level. "What's the deal?" I ask, trying to hide the growing unease in my gut.

"Gwen for the Bratva," Boris declares, his words sending a surge of fear through my veins.

My blood runs cold as Nadia growls her opposition, "Absolutely fucking not."

"That's not a good deal, Boris. A girl for the crown to the Russian Mafia, real uneven," I counter, narrowing my eyes on the confident click of Boris's jaw.

"I raised him well, didn't I?" he sneers, gesturing to the colorful man who kicked Gwen out of the car. She cowers on the ground, refusing to meet my gaze. Every fiber of my being screams to protect her, to hold her, and tell her for the first time that despite everything, I love her. But she just hunches over her knees on the floor, forcing her knotted black curls to cover her face.

But then Boris speaks again, his voice smooth and calculated. "Let's sweeten the deal, shall we? Leave town with your precious girl and your kids, and I won't kill you as long as you never step foot in New York again."

My body freezes at the mention of my children. Did he just say my kids? Panic rises in my chest as I steal a glance at Nadia, her face drained of color. Aleksandr cocks his gun once more, finger tightening on the trigger.

I turn to look at Gwen, only to see her staring back at me with wide eyes filled with terror. And then it all comes crashing down on me. Boris pulls out his own gun and presses it against the back of Gwen's head, a sickening click echoing through across the dock and clashing against the constant sound of the waves.

"Say no and I'll blow her brains out," he snarls, his grip on the trigger unyielding. "And then I'll hunt down your children and do the same."

My blood boils at Boris's offer, his smug grin taunting me as he dangles the lives of Gwen and my children like a carrot in front of a starving animal. My fists ball up in frustration, my eyes narrowing into slits as I glare at him.

Sho's hand grips my shoulder with a fierce snarl, his eyes blazing with anger and desperation. "If you give him the Bratva, the Yakuza will use him to regain control over both mobs. Nik, you can't-"

I turn to look at him, anger pulsing underneath my skin, but when I speak, I don't address him or Boris. "Mr. Matsumoto, will you change the deal if I break your son's hand?"

A sinister chuckle echoes from the shadowy figure emerging from behind Sho, the sun slowly rising behind him casting an eerie glow on his features. My skin prickles at the sight of Yasou Matsumoto, head of the Yakuza. He gives me a kind smile. Despite the kindness in his eyes and that his first name Yasou means peaceful man, my stomach drops, and my skin pricks at the mere sight of him. The minute I called him, I knew if I was a demon, then Mr. Matsumoto was the devil.

Sho stiffens beside me, realizing the gravity of our situation. He turns accusingly towards Aleksandr, who stands nonchalantly nearby, gun still trained on Boris. "You betrayed me," Sho seethes.

But Aleksandr merely shrugs, as if bored with the entire situation. "I saved your life," he retorts coolly. "You owe me one now."

For a moment, it seems like Sho has accepted his fate. I watch as he closes his eyes and perhaps says a silent prayer. But then, with lightning speed, he pulls out a grenade and pulls the pin out with his teeth.

In a quick flick of his wrist, he hurls it towards Boris and Gwen before anyone can react. The explosion is deafening and fills the air with smoke and chaos. All I can hear is Gwen's scream.

44

NIKOLAI

The explosion roars in my ears, a wave of heat and debris knocking me back. My body slams into the ground, my vision blurring for a moment as the smoke thickens. Gwen's scream echoes through the chaos, and that sound—her fear—drives me to move, despite the pain shooting up my spine.

Sho had his own plans. I should've known. There was no way a man like him would agree to do something like this without an ulterior motive, no matter the code of honor the Yakuza claims to abide by. He was banished from the ranks. He has no honor, no loyalty, and I will kill him for his deceit.

Sho is faster than everyone else. Blood sprays across my face as he slices the necks of men flying across the dock towards us. Aleksandr is hot on his tail, bodies upon bodies falling to the ground in his wake.

"Sho, you bastard!" Aleksandr's roar pierces through the thick smoke, cutting through the chaos. I barely turn in time to see Sho emerge, drenched in blood, eyes blazing with a single deadly purpose. His teeth are bared, his focus sharp, and I know without question who he's looking for—Boris.

If Sho gets to Boris, it'll end the Yakuza's grip on both sides. Killing him would be the final blow, the one that could set us free. But it would also mean losing Nadia forever.

She can't lose Boris. Not after everything. Boris might be a monster, but to Nadia, he's the only parent she has left. Our mother's gone—killed by the same man who raised us, who might not even be our real father. But for Nadia, Boris has always been her father. He was the one who held her as a child, who guided her, even if it was all under the shadow of the Bratva. She can't face the idea of losing him too, not without knowing the truth.

And that's the sliver of hope I have. Nadia hasn't forgiven me for everything—not yet—but there's a chance, however small, that she will if Boris survives. As much as she despises what he's done, she needs answers. She needs to know if the man she's been loyal to all her life is truly her father.

If Boris dies here, that hope dies with him. Nadia will never forgive me, not for this. Not for taking away her last parent before she knows for sure.

"Nadia," I hiss urgently, but she is already moving through the smoke without hesitation.

I scramble to my feet, frantically searching for Gwen. She's still on the dock, crumpled against a mound of debris, but alive. Relief floods through me, but it quickly fades as gunfire erupts all around us. The sound echoes in my ears like thunder, and I instinctively dive for cover as bullets whiz past, tearing through the air where I was just standing moments before.

Reacting instinctively, my hand reaches for my gun and I return fire, determined to take down as many of them as possible before reaching Gwen's side. The sharp crack of each shot reverberates in my ears, and I watch with satisfaction as two of Boris's men drop to the ground, their bodies crumpling in an instant.

Through the haze, I can see Boris—still standing like a man possessed, barking orders to his men. His wild eyes lock onto Gwen, his gun following his gaze. My stomach tightens in rage.

But before I can act, movement flashes in the corner of my vision. Two of Boris's soldiers emerge from the smoke, one to my left and the other on my right. They're closing in fast, their guns raised and ready. Instinct takes over, my body moving before my mind can catch up.

The first soldier lunges from the left, his figure a dark blur through the fog. I pivot sharply, dropping to one knee as his weapon cracks just above my head. The bullet whistles past, missing me by inches. Without wasting a second, I shoot. My bullet catches him in the chest, and he collapses, his weapon falling from his hands. He lets out a guttural scream, crumpling to the ground, but I'm already moving.

The second soldier charges in from the right, swinging the butt of his rifle toward my head. I twist my body just in time, feeling the air shift as the metal grazes past my cheek. The soldier follows up with a punch, but I parry his strike, catching his wrist and twisting it sharply. He grunts in pain, dropping the rifle, but he's still fast—his knee slams into my ribs with brutal force, sending a sharp burst of pain through my side. I stagger, gasping for air.

My vision blurs for a moment, but I force myself to focus. I slam my elbow into the side of his head, the crack of bone against bone echoing in the smoke-filled air. He stumbles back, dazed, giving me just enough time to grab him by the front of his vest. With a savage growl, I throw him to the ground, hard. He tries to rise, but before he can regain his footing, I drive my knee into his chest, pinning him to the ground.

My gun comes up, and I press it against his forehead, my finger hovering over the trigger. For a second, I meet his eyes, wide with panic, and then I pull the trigger. The shot is muffled by the smoke, but the effect is instant. His body goes limp beneath me.

I'm panting, my heart thudding in my chest as I rise to my feet. The dock is a battlefield, bodies littered around me, but I don't stop to count.

"The deal is off, Nikolai! She dies now!" Boris bellows, his gun aimed directly at Gwen's vulnerable body.

Everything seems to slow down as if time has frozen. With every ounce of strength left in me, I lunge towards Gwen just as Sho hurtles himself in the air and crashes into Boris. A searing pain rips through my thigh from a bullet that tears into it, causing me to stagger and nearly collapse from the intense heat radiating from the wound. Before I can fully recover, another shot strikes my shoulder with brutal force, propelling me sideways and sending waves of agony through my body. Then a third slams into my vest, the force nearly sending me to the ground again. The vest holds, but the impact leaves me gasping for breath.

"Gwen," I let out a gut-wrenching moan, clutching the gaping wound on my leg. My vision blurs with red as I see her trembling form reach up to touch the back of her head. With shaking hands, she brings her blood-covered fingers into her line of sight and my heart pounds with rage.

"Nik," she chokes.

I grit my teeth, pushing through the pain, and fire back, unloading my clip toward Boris's men, trying to create some space. "Stay down!" I manage to gasp out, biting my lips so hard from the pain, the taste of metal invades my mouth.

Sho and Boris wrestle each other, their bodies colliding with explosive force, my eyes desperately seek Gwen's.

Through the haze of smoke and blood, I see her, huddling by the SUV, holding her head as she violently shakes. Ignoring the agony coursing through my leg, I sprint toward her, firing over my shoulder as I grab her, hoisting her up.

"Nik," she cries into my neck.

I growl back, "Hold onto me and keep your head down."

The adrenaline pushes me forward, every beat of my heart pounding like a drum as I run across the dock, firing over my shoulder. Nadia is right by my side, a whirlwind of lethal precision, shooting her gun and breaking the necks of anyone who dares to come close. The sound of gunfire echoes in the air, and though we're making ground, we're far from safe. I can hear Boris's men regrouping, the shuffle of their footsteps creeping closer, a ticking time bomb waiting to explode.

But none of that matters—not right now. Not when Gwen clings to me, trembling from the terror still coursing through her. Her body feels fragile in my arms, shaking with adrenaline and fear. I hold her tighter, as if I can shield her from everything that's happened, everything still to come.

When we reach the SUV, I place her into the backseat, my breath coming in heavy bursts. My eyes rake over her body, taking in every bruise, every cut, every ounce of pain she's endured. Despite it all—despite the blood, the dirt, the exhaustion dragging her down—her chest rises and falls in shallow but steady breaths.

She's alive.

For a fleeting moment, the world goes silent. The chaos around us, the gunfire, the shouts—it all disappears. It's just me and Gwen. My heart stutters in my chest as I look at her, my black hoodie hanging loosely on her battered frame. Her hands, once bound, are now free, though her knuckles are scraped raw. Her lip is swollen, her black eye a painful reminder of everything she's been through. Her hair, tangled and greasy, falls in disarray over her face, hiding her tired eyes.

But she's alive.

Relief floods through me, overwhelming and fierce, and I can't stop myself. My hands, still shaking, reach out to her. I gently push the hair away from her face, careful not to hurt her any more than she already is. My fingers tremble as they brush her skin, and all I can think about is how close I came to losing her.

"Gwen..." I whisper, her name barely leaving my lips. My voice cracks with the emotion I can't hold back. She looks up at me, her eyes wide and filled with tears that spill over her cheeks.

"Nik, I am so sorry," she whispers, her voice small and broken. I know what she's apologizing for—the twins, leaving the apartment, everything. But I don't care. I shake my head.

"Not now," I murmur, moving one of her knotted curls behind her ear. "Just keep your head down and stay here."

"Nik," she protests, trying to move forward, but I stop her with a gentle hand on her shoulder. The fear in her eyes rips me apart, but I can't let her put herself in danger again.

"Stay here, Gwen," I growl, the desperation lacing my voice. She recoils slightly, retreating further into the back of the SUV. I should pull away, should slam the door and get back to the fight—but I can't. Not yet.

Before I can stop myself, I lean in and capture her lips with mine. The kiss is fierce, raw, and filled with everything I've been holding back—fear, relief, guilt, and love. Her swollen lips tremble against mine, but she kisses me back, her fingers curling into my shirt as if holding on for dear life.

In that moment, nothing else matters. Not the gunfire, not the chaos, not the danger waiting for me outside. Just her. Just this.

When I finally pull away, my forehead rests against hers, and I whisper, "Stay safe, Gwen. I'll come back for you. I swear."

Without waiting for a response, I pull back, my heart hammering, and slam the door shut, locking her inside.

Before I can return back to the fight, a vicious crack echoes through the air. I whip around to see Aleksandr pinning Boris to the ground, his arm twisted at an unnatural angle. Boris howls in pain, thrashing beneath Aleksandr, who's ruthless in his movements. Another sickening crack follows, and Boris's kneecap shatters under Aleksandr's boot, rendering him completely helpless.

"You're done," Aleksandr growls, towering over him. He grips Boris by the collar and starts to drag him across the dock towards us.

But the fight's far from over. Sho lunges at Nadia, and she meets him head-on, her eyes blazing with fury. They clash in a blur of fists and blades, and I can barely keep up. Nadia's fast —faster than I've ever seen her—but Sho's not holding back. He's in it to kill, and every blow between them feels like a death sentence waiting to be delivered.

I force my body to move, pulling myself toward them, every muscle screaming in protest. I need to help Nadia, but then I catch sight of something far more dangerous—Mr. Matsumoto, standing calmly in the chaos, his eyes locked on me.

This ends now.

With my good arm, I draw my gun and stagger toward Matsumoto. He doesn't flinch as I press the barrel of the gun to his temple, his calm demeanor unwavering. "Call them off," I snarl, my voice low, barely containing the rage boiling beneath the surface.

His smile doesn't fade. "Or what, Nikolai? You think my men won't kill you dead right here, right now?"

"I'll blow your fucking head off," I snap, pushing the barrel harder against his skull. "Besides, if you're dead then the heir to the throne is Sho, right?"

Matsumoto's jaw rolls in anger but I push the barrel firmer against his temple, barking loudly, "Call them off."

My voice echoes and the fighting slows. Nadia's got Sho pinned to the ground with Aleksandr's help, both of them holding him down as he thrashes in a desperate attempt to free himself. Boris is unconscious, his arm and knee shattered beyond repair, leaning against the door of our SUV.

Everything hangs in the balance.

Matsumoto tilts his head, almost like he's amused. "And if I do not? What will you do then?"

I don't answer. The click of my gun's safety being released is all he gets in response.

The dock falls eerily silent, save for the distant crash of waves and the labored breathing of those still standing.

"If my siblings or I die, then you lose all sway in the Bravta. Boris will be dead regardless of your move and no one else in the family will make a deal with the Yakuza," I spit on the ground.

"Otōsan!" Sho barks from across the dock but Matsumoto doesn't even look in his direction. Instead, he swipes his hand once across his chest, and all his men return to a soldier's stance, stiff with hands locked behind their backs.

"We will be taking Sho," Matsumoto says, looking at me from the corner of his eye.

"No. Sho has a life debt to Aleksandr. We will be cashing that in now."

Matsumoto shakes his head in disappointment, but he doesn't spare a glance at Sho or me. He turns away, my gun still trained on the back of his head. After a few steps towards the towncar I didn't even notice was there, he pauses and looks at me over his shoulder. "A lesson for you from a father who doesn't want you dead. Next time you pull a gun on a man like me, kill me, no deals, no hesitation."

45

NIKOLAI

Right after the Yakuza left, Nikolai collapsed and was dragged into the SUV where I waited, trembling next to an unconscious Boris. A Japanese man with piercings and tattoos who Aleksandr referred to as Sho sat chained to the door while Nadia held a gun to his head.

The next couple of hours are a blur of us rushing to the Italian Mafia's safe house where a doctor met us and took care of Nikolai. Once he was stable and both prisoners were secured, we made our way back to the mainland and swiftly placed a drugged up Nikolai in his bedroom in Manhattan. It's been almost fourteen hours since the stand off with Boris, but I can't move. I haven't left his side once, even when everyone told me to take a shower, to eat, to see the twins. I just shook my head and stared at Nikolai.

Even as Taylor, Kelsey and David cried, telling me that they were so worried and that they loved me. I mindlessly hugged them back and then made my way back to Nikolai.

I am staring at him right now, sitting at his bedside, watching his chest rise and fall with each shallow breath. My hands clean with hand sanitizer and a pack of baby wipes by my side. At some point, I will need a shower. I will need food, but that can be dealt with after Nik wakes up.

Sweat glistens on his brow, and I reach over, gently wiping it away with a baby wipe in my hand. His skin is clammy, his face drawn tight with pain, and it kills me to see him like this—broken, battered, barely holding on.

"I'm so sorry," I whisper, my voice trembling. "This is all my fault."

The words hang in the air, unanswered, but I don't stop. Maybe he can hear me, maybe not. It doesn't matter. "You almost died because of me. I should've—" I stop, choking on my words. *I should've told you. I should've told you everything.*

My hand lingers on his forehead, tracing the lines of his face, and I can't hold back the tears any longer. They fall, hot and silent, as I sit there, watching him fight for every breath. "I don't know what I'd do if I lost you."

For a long time, it's just the sound of his breathing, steady but too shallow. I wipe away more sweat, brushing his hair back from his face. He's so still, it's unnerving. I lean forward, resting my forehead against his arm, praying for him to wake up. To give me any sign that he's still here with me.

As if hearing my silent plea, there's a faint movement beneath my touch. His fingers twitch against the sheets, and then, slowly, his eyes flutter open. At first, it's just a flicker, his lashes barely lifting, but then his gaze meets mine, and he smiles—a small, tired smile, but a smile nonetheless.

"Hey," I whisper, my voice cracking. Relief washes over me so fast it feels like I might drown in it.

He blinks at me, his lips parting, but no words come at first. I can see the pain in his eyes, the exhaustion, but somehow he still manages to lift his hand and reach for mine. I take it, squeezing tightly.

I wipe away the fresh tears that spill down my cheeks, trying to pull myself together. "I—I need to tell your siblings. Let them know you're awake." I stand, about to turn toward the door, but his grip on my hand tightens. "Nik?"

"Wait," he murmurs, his voice rough, strained. "I need to tell you something."

My stomach drops, and a wave of nausea ripples through me. If he wants to yell at me about the twins, or about leaving the penthouse knowing the danger we were in, that can wait until I've at least seen him awake for five minutes. "We can talk about it later, okay? You should rest. I should-"

"No." He squeezes my hand again, his eyes locking onto mine with an intensity that makes my heart skip. "I need to say this now."

His words are slow, deliberate, like he's fighting against the weight of unconsciousness pulling him back under. I sit back down, anxiety prickling at the edges of my thoughts. "Nik, you're hurt—"

"I love you."

The words hit me harder than any blow. I freeze, staring at him in disbelief. "What?"

"I love you," he says again, his voice firmer this time, though still laced with pain. "And it killed me...to think...that you could've died without me saying that."

I can't breathe. Tears burn my eyes, blurring my vision as his words sink in. He loves me. After everything—after the secrets, the lies, the danger—he loves me. And I almost lost him without knowing.

I try to speak, but my voice catches in my throat. "I...I love you too."

I can see the relief wash over him, a small smile tugging at the corners of his mouth, and for a moment, it's just us—no chaos, no danger. Just us.

The door creaks open, revealing two hesitant figures in the doorway. Mia and Gio stand there, looking almost unrecognizable with how much they had grown since I last saw them. Mia held onto her favorite stuffed rabbit, Mr. Floppy, tightly as her wide eyes take in the sight before them. Beside her, Gio nervously clutches Nadia's hand and his sharp gaze seems to size up the situation. His concern is evident as he takes in my greasy hair, swollen eye, and bruised face.

"Sorry, I couldn't keep them away any longer." Nadia offers me a small smile, releasing Gio's hand in my direction.

"Mama?" Mia's voice trembles, staring at me like she's trying to figure out what happened.

I wipe at my tears quickly, forcing a smile. "Hey, baby." I open my arms, and they rush to me. As soon as they crash into me, I finally feel like I can breathe again. I pull them close, kissing the tops of their heads. "I've missed you both so much."

"We missed you too," Gio murmurs, sounding quieter than usual, his arms looping around me tightly. Mia presses her face into my side, her grip on Mr. Floppy firm.

Gio pulls back slightly, inspecting me, darting between myself and Nikolai. His face is calm, but his eyes are sharp, and I can tell he's piecing things together. "Mama...what happened to you?"

"I'm okay," I say softly, brushing hair out of his face. But his eyes remain fixed on me, unconvinced.

Mia, still clinging to my side, turns her worried gaze to Nik, who lies pale and weak on the bed. "Is Daddy okay?" Her voice is a whisper, trembling.

I freeze. Daddy. My heart pounds. Nik's eyes flick from Mia to me, a small, pained smile tugging at his lips despite his exhaustion.

"Yeah, Daddy's going to be okay," Nik says, his voice gentle and hoarse.

Gio, still watching me, frowns deeply. "You're hurt too, Mama. How do I know you're okay?" His voice isn't demanding, just practical, like he needs proof before he can relax.

I sigh, holding his gaze. "I'll explain everything to you, I promise, but right now...I'm just so happy to see you both."

He doesn't look satisfied, but before he can press more, Nadia steps in, her voice gentle but firm. "Why don't I take these two for some ice cream?"

Gio doesn't move at first, still focused on me. "I don't want to leave yet. You haven't told me anything."

I swallow, reaching out to touch his cheek. "I will, Gio. I'll talk to you about everything. Just give me a little more time."

His eyes search mine before he finally nods. "Promise?"

"Promise."

Nadia gives me a soft look, then turns to Gio and Mia. "Come on, you two. Ice cream sounds pretty good right now, right?"

"Ice cream!" Mia's face lights up, and despite himself, Gio gives a small nod, letting Nadia take his hand.

They rush to Nik, kissing his cheek. "Get better soon, Daddy," Mia whispers.

Nik smiles, ruffling Gio's hair. "I will."

I stand frozen, watching them leave. Nadia glances back before stepping out with the kids. "You two talk," she says quietly, leaving me and Nik in the quiet aftermath.

As soon as the door closes behind them, I turn to Nik, my breath coming fast. "What...what was that?"

"What?" Nik asks, his voice tired, as he tries to sit up. His body protests, and he winces.

"They called you—Nik, they called you dad." My voice cracks, my hands trembling as I stare at him. "H-how do they know? How do you know?"

Nik watches me for a moment, his face unreadable. Then he lets out a sigh.

I feel like the floor drops beneath me. "But you didn't know—"

"I know now," he cuts me off, his voice soft but firm. He shifts slightly, groaning at the movement, but his gaze never leaves mine. "I've known for weeks now."

I open my mouth to protest, to explain, to justify the secrets I've been keeping, but Nik shakes his head, struggling to get out of bed. "Nik—wait—"

"I don't want to hear it right now," he says, his tone final.

He stands, slowly, wincing as he moves toward the bathroom. I follow, my pulse racing, but he doesn't turn around. He's moving stiffly, clearly in pain, but I can't let this go. "Nik, please—"

He pulls his shirt over his head, tossing it aside before stepping into the bathroom. I linger by the door, watching as he turns on the shower. The steam begins to rise, filling the small space with heat and humidity. I know I should leave him alone, give him space to process, but I can't. I can't let him walk away from this without understanding what's going through his mind.

He steps under the water, and before I realize what I'm doing, I follow him in, fully clothed. The warm water hits me, soaking my hoodie, but I don't care. I stand there, watching him through the mist, my heart pounding in my chest.

Nik finally turns, his expression softening when he sees me. His hand reaches for mine, pulling me under the spray with him. The water beats down on us, but all I can feel is his warmth, his presence, the weight of everything between us.

"Nik, I just didn't know how-" I start up again, but his hands grip my soaked clothes, pulling me closer to him. His eyes search mine for a second, pleading. A surge of relief rushes through me, and a moan escapes my lips.

Nikolai growls, pinning me against the door of the shower. His lips are on mine, firm and punishing.

Nikolai's hands grip my wrists as he pushes me against the door of the shower. His lips crash onto mine, forcing them open with a roughness that sends shivers down my spine. I try to push him away, but his strength overwhelms me. My body betrays me as I involuntarily respond to his touch, my heart racing and my skin tingling. His kiss intensifies, his tongue eagerly exploring every inch of my mouth with a desperation that mirrors my own.

I try to pull away, to say something, anything, but his hands are everywhere, gripping my waist, my hips, my shoulders. He's relentless, his need overwhelming any resistance forming in the back of my mind. My hands find their way to his chest, feeling the steady thump of his heart beneath my fingertips. It's fast, erratic, just like mine.

His fingers trace the bruises on my skin, lingering on each one as if trying to memorize them. I flinch at his touch, the memories of my kidnapping flooding back in waves. But instead of pulling away, he presses closer, his body molding to mine as if he could absorb my pain. I open my mouth, but his stormy eyes lock with mine.

"Shh," he whispers against my lips, his voice hoarse and strained. "Don't."

I nod, unable to form words, my throat tight with unshed tears. His hands move lower, slipping under my soaked hoodie to cup my breasts. I arch into his touch, a silent plea for more, for every part of him I've missed in the last couple of weeks. He responds by kneading my flesh gently, his thumbs brushing over my nipples until they harden against his palms.

His mouth leaves mine, trailing kisses down my jaw, my neck, pausing to suckle at the sensitive skin below my ear. I shiver, my body trembling with need and fear and something else I can't quite name. His teeth graze my earlobe, making me arch closer to him, moaning and desperate for more.

"I thought I was going to lose you, Kotik," he murmurs, his voice thick with emotion.

His words wash over me, filling the void where my voice should be. I want to tell him how much I've missed him, how much I've needed him, but the words stick in my throat. Instead, I press my forehead against his, our breaths mingling in the steamy air.

His hands slide down to my waist, lifting my hoodie over my head and discarding it on the floor. I stand before him in nothing but my soaked bra and dirty sweatpants, exposed and vulnerable. He takes a step back, his eyes raking over my body with a mixture of awe and sorrow.

"I thought I was never going to see this beautiful body again," he says softly, his fingers tracing the outline of a particularly dark bruise on my ribs as his jaw rolls, tension roaming through his face.

I shake my head, tears welling in my eyes. I reach out, cupping his face in my hands, pressing a tender kiss to his lips, even as he wraps his fingers around my waist so tight I gasp for air.

He presses his naked body against mine. The contrast between his warmth and the cool tile behind me forces me to mold my body deeper into his. Our bodies fit together perfectly, as if we were made for each other. His erection presses against my stomach.

His hands roam over my back, his fingers digging into my skin as if anchoring me to him. "You can't leave me, Gwen, never."

"Never," I repeat, but he places a hand over my lips, silencing me. His hands slide around the waistband of my soggy sweatpants. Keeping his eyes locked on mine, he pushes them down my legs, leaving me standing in only my soaked underwear.

His eyes roam over me like the very first time. A groan leaves his lips as he whispers, "Ты меня когда-нибудь убьёшь!"

He slides two fingers in my underwear, my body immediately bucking at his touch. His palm muffles my moan, but he doesn't stop. Instead, he deepens the pressure, his fingers exploring every inch of me with relentless precision. My breath hitches, and I feel myself growing wetter, more desperate for his touch.

Nik's gaze never wavers from mine, his eyes dark with intensity. He withdraws his fingers, letting them trail down the inside of my thigh before hooking them under the elastic of my soaked underwear. He yanks them down, exposing me completely to the cool air of the shower.

My legs tremble slightly, but Nik's grip on my waist keeps me steady.

He circles my clit with his thumb, applying just the right amount of pressure to make me bite my lip to stifle a cry. His other hand moves lower, his fingers slipping inside me with ease. I gasp, the sensation overwhelming, and Nik takes advantage of my momentary lapse in control.

He thrusts his fingers deeper, his movements rough and unrelenting. I arch my back, trying to find some semblance of balance, but Nik's hold on me is too strong. He angles his fingers just right, hitting that perfect spot inside me that sends my body into a spasm. I can't stop it.

"Shh," he whispers, his voice barely audible over the sound of the running water. "No noise, Kotik."

Nik's thumb returns to my clit, circling it with a maddeningly slow rhythm. His fingers inside me quicken, matching the pace of his thumb. I bite down on my lip harder, trying to keep the moans trapped in my throat.

But it's no use. The pleasure is too intense, too overwhelming. A soft whimper escapes my lips, and Nik's eyes darken further. He leans in close, his breath hot against my ear.

"Bad girl," he murmurs, his voice low and dangerous.

Before I can react, he pulls his fingers out and lifts me off the ground. My legs instinctively wrap around his waist as he carries me to the tiled wall of the shower. He pins me there, his body pressed firmly against mine, and I can feel his hardness pressing against my core.

Nik's hands move to my thighs, gripping them tightly as he positions himself at my entrance. He looks into my eyes, searching for something, though I'm not sure what. Then, with a suddenness that takes my breath away, he thrusts into me.

I gasp, the sensation of being filled so completely overwhelming. Nik doesn't give me a chance to adjust, pulling out almost completely before thrusting back in with even more force. The impact against the tiled wall echoes loudly in the small space of the shower, but neither of us cares.

Nik's thrusts are hard and fast, each one driving the breath from my lungs. He pounds into me with a ferocity that leaves me clinging to him for dear life. My nails dig into his shoulders, and I can feel the muscles beneath them tensing with each thrust.

My own orgasm is so close, teetering on the edge, but Nik's hold on me is unyielding. He doesn't let me fall over that precipice just yet.

"Don't you cum until I tell you," he growls in my ear, and I buck in frustration, my release only building.

I tighten my grip, my legs locking around his waist as he continues his brutal rhythm. The water cascades over us, mixing with the sweat and the tears that have begun to fall from my eyes. But I don't care. All I can focus on is the way Nik feels inside me, the way he owns me completely.

I gasp as his fingers find their mark. His thumb presses harder against my clit, drawing small circles over the ball of nerves. The pressure builds, and I can feel the tension coiling tighter and tighter within me. The sensation is almost too much to bear, and I bite my lip to stifle a moan. Nik's eyes never leave mine, his gaze intense and unwavering.

I scream, my body convulsing around him as wave after wave of pleasure crashes over me. He follows seconds later, his own release washing over him, his body shuddering with the force of it.

He holds me like that in his arms for a couple of moments, his breath washing over my face, and I wrap my arms around his neck, pulling him in close. I move my head so our noses nuzzle together. "I love you, Nik."

Silence fills the air as he refuses to reciprocate my words, instead slowly withdrawing from me. His fingers trail down my body with a lingering touch that sends shivers down my spine. As I am lowered to the cold tile floor, Nik's hands steady me, but it is his piercing gaze that holds me in place.

In an instant, his warm embrace turns into a cold grip as he cups my face in his hands. I sniff, trying to keep my tears at bay, but they fall and he wipes them away. His voice is laced with pain and anger as he speaks.

"I love you, Kotik," his voice is strained with emotion, "so much that I would move heaven and hell for you. But you..."

He pauses, searching my eyes with a mix of pain and betrayal. "You don't love me enough to tell me the truth."

My heart constricts at his words. "Nik-"

"I can't trust you, Gwen."

All warmth leaves me as his hands fall from my face. "I can't." His jaw tightens, and before I can speak, he turns and walks out of the shower. I stay under the stream until the water turns frigid, alone and empty without his comforting presence. That night, I lay alone in our bed, haunted by his words. I don't get any sleep.

46

NIKOLAI

A month has passed, and I've kept my distance from Gwen. I want to say it is not intentional, but I know it is. I can't seem to bring myself to be near her, not without feeling the weight of everything she's hidden from me—the twins, my own children. The betrayal gnaws at me every time I look at her, even when her eyes pulse with apologies. I just can't seem to do it.

Gwen keeps trying to talk to me, but if it is not about the twins or her recovery, I shut down the conversation. I don't know how to tell the mother of my child that her secrets have broken a part of me I don't think can recover.

Instead, I focus on Mia and Gio. My interactions with them are easier, simpler. They don't ask why I'm avoiding their mother. They don't understand the storm that's been brewing inside me since I found out the truth. But it's there, burning in my chest, simmering every time I catch a glimpse of Gwen's tired eyes watching me from across the room.

Every night, I hear the soft padding of Mia's feet as she sneaks into my study, asking me to tuck her into bed, and every night, I rush to their sides, thinking it will make up for all the nights I wasn't home for. She tells me about her day, about the games she played with her brother, and Gio gives me one fun fact about primates every night from his studies. The kid is a mini genius, and Mia's voice is filled with innocent joy. I can't help but let the knot in my chest tighten when I think about all the years I've missed, all the memories Gwen kept from me.

I don't know if I can forgive her.

"The DNA results are in." Nadia's voice slices through my office, and I jerk my head up from the unsigned paperwork on my desk to see her and Aleksandr staring at me.

"And?" I clear my throat, leaning back in my leather chair.

Nadia strolls over, tossing the results on top of my paperwork and slumping into the chair across from mine. "We waited for you to open it."

Aleksandr's eyes flicker to the balcony and then back to me. "When did you get a garden?"

I look out the double doors. With the Yakuza on our ass, Sho being a demanding prisoner, the Italian coming to collect on their favors, getting to know the kids and my avoidance of Gwen, I didn't notice the garden.

I shrug. "I don't know."

"Gwen did that." Nadia yawns. "It was a surprise she started before the kidnapping. She finished it a week ago."

I pull a switchblade out of my top desk drawer and fling it open as I grab the DNA test. "How do you know that?"

"I talk to her. Speaking of which, when are you going to talk to her?"

I swallow, sliding the knife across the top of the letter.

"You're dragging this out," she says, her voice low but pointed.

"I'm not ready," I finally mutter, shimming the letter out of the envelope.

Nadia scoffs. "You're never going to be ready. You think you're punishing her by avoiding her? All you're doing is making things worse—for you, for her, for the kids."

I crush the letter in my hand, my eyes shooting to hers, my voice hard. "She kept my children from me."

Nadia doesn't flinch. "She was on the run, Nik, and then she finds out her baby daddy is a fucking mafia leader. She was doing what was best for her and the kids."

I suck my teeth. "I could have kept them safe!"

"Oh really?" Aleksandr scoffs. "You think being with a man like you would have been safer for them? Did you keep her safe, or was she not just missing for three weeks?"

I don't respond immediately, just stare down at the white paper in my hands. His words slice me open, and I feel like I am an open wound, bleeding out until nothing is left. I grit my teeth, flipping open the DNA letter. "That's not the point."

"Isn't it?" Nadia leans closer, her eyes boring into mine. "You're angry, and you have every right to be. But if you're going to be mad at her, at least understand why she did what she did. You think being with you doesn't come with its own dangers? You think she doesn't regret every moment you missed?"

I don't want to admit that she's right, but Nadia's voice rings painfully in my ears. I bite my inner cheek, reading over the results. "Congratulations, Boris is your father," I bark, tossing the paper across my desk and exiting out of the sliding glass doors where the garden lays.

As I step out onto the balcony, the cool air hits my face, but it does nothing to temper the fire burning inside me. The garden sprawls out below, neat rows of flowers—roses, tulips, and god knows what else. I barely register the colors or the scents, just the idea that it's there because of *her*. The weight of everything Nadia and Aleksandr said presses down on my chest, and I grip the railing so hard my knuckles turn white.

The DNA results had confirmed what I already knew. Boris is Aleksandr's and Nadia's father, just not mine. It doesn't make any difference, not really. Nadia swore no matter the results she would not kill me for the crown of the mafia. Aleksandr laughed it off, so who knows what he will do now.

I breathe out sharply, trying to escape the storm of rage churning inside me. It's impossible to focus on anything but Gwen—her face, her lies, her secrets. The garden she meticulously planted feels like an insult, too serene compared to the chaos she left inside me.

Nadia's words echo in my mind: *She was on the run, Nik. She found out her baby daddy is a mafia leader.* It's never that simple. Gwen hid my children from me for years, denying me the chance to be their father. How can I just let that go? How can I forgive her for the moments she stole from me?

Aleksandr's voice cuts through my thoughts like a blade. "You think being with you would have been safer?"

I hate that he's right. Being with me never promised safety. Boris killed our mother, and danger has followed me ever since. I've always known that anyone close to me becomes a target, but that doesn't excuse Gwen's actions. She should have trusted me.

I stare at the tulips—bright pinks, cool blues, and vibrant oranges, the same colors my mother loved. Somehow, Gwen discovered the exact shades from when my mother ran Johanna's, calling it Vivi's. The thought of her planting them for me, while I've been keeping my distance, fills me with a hollow ache. It's guilt buried under too much anger to process.

I feel like a fool standing here in this garden she created for me. Then I notice the roses, a stark contrast. I bend down, my fingers brushing the thorny petals.

Nadia approaches, her voice soft. "Gwen planted those for her nana."

"What do you mean she planted them for Nana Rose?" I ask, confusion lacing my voice.

Nadia's gaze is heavy with sadness. "I mean she died two months ago."

The words hit me like a punch to the gut. Gwen never told me. I didn't even know her nana was gone. Guilt washes over me like a tidal wave, threatening to drown me. While I've been consumed by anger, Gwen has been grieving, burying the only family she had left.

"She didn't get to bury her properly," Nadia continues, her voice tight. "She missed the identification window at the police station in DC. She spent the last two weeks finishing this garden instead."

I struggle to breathe, the weight of it all pressing down on me.

Aleksandr steps closer, his tone grave. "Mason killed her a couple of weeks prior to force Gwen back to DC."

My chest burns with fury. I want to tear Mason apart for what he did—killing Nana Rose and robbing Gwen of her last family. I would have killed him sooner if I'd known.

I slam my fist against the railing, the sharp pain grounding me. "Damn it," I mutter. "He killed her. He took everything from her. I should have—"

Aleksandr cuts me off, his voice firm, "You couldn't have known, Nik. We only found out recently."

I want to scream, to break something, to release the frustration consuming me. The weight of everything—Gwen's struggles, the years I missed—crushes me. She's been grieving, planting these flowers in memory of her nana while I've been lost in my own betrayal. The worst part is, I'm unsure if I can support her now. I don't know if I can let go of my anger enough to be there for her.

Nadia's hand rests on my shoulder. "You're angry, and you have every right to be. But if you're going to be mad at her, at least understand why she did what she did."

I clench my jaw, trying to push away her words, but they linger, piercing through me. I do understand, but that doesn't make it hurt any less. It doesn't erase the years she took from me.

"She didn't know how to tell you," Nadia says softly. "She was overwhelmed, trying to protect herself and your kids."

"She doesn't know how to tell me anything," I growl, frustration edging my voice. "How am I supposed to protect her when she hides everything from me?"

"She didn't even tell her friends, Nik. She didn't know how to tell anyone. That's why she sent them home, and asked for security," Nadia whispers.

I swallow. Gwen had sent Kelsey and David back to DC with four armed guards she begged Nadia to ask me for. Taylor, being the legal rising star in New York, refused and said it would be bad for his image, but a couple of my guys tail him from time to time. I didn't know why she sent everyone home so quickly and was too angry to ask. I guess she didn't want anyone to see her like this, but that doesn't excuse anything. Gwen is going to be my wife one day. I want to see her at her best, worst, and everything in between.

Aleksandr and Nadia fall into a tense silence, their eyes still burning my skin.

I look at the garden again—the yellow roses, the tulips. It all feels like a desperate attempt to fix something that can't be fixed. Gwen is trying to make things right, but I've only pushed her away.

I breathe deeply, trying to steady myself. My mind races between anger and the deep sense of loss I've been avoiding. Part of me wants to go back inside, find Gwen, and demand answers. But what good would that do? I already know why she did it, but that doesn't heal the wounds.

My eyes drift back to the garden one last time. It's a beautiful creation born from her grief, just like Gwen.

Swallowing hard, I turn away, feeling suffocated by guilt. I look closer at the tulips next to the roses, the same shade of yellow that used to fill the walls of Vivi's. A lump forms in my throat, and the heaviness in my chest tightens. How much have I missed? How much have I pushed away in my anger?

The image of Gwen planting these flowers for her nana and for me, while I kept my distance, twists my stomach painfully.

Determined, I head into the house, my steps quick and resolute. I find Mia's bedroom door slightly ajar and pause, listening to Gwen's soft voice as she sits on the bed, parting Mia's hair and humming. My heart stutters at the sight.

"Gwen," I say, my voice rougher than I intend. She looks up, surprised, her hands freezing in Mia's hair. Mia turns and gives me a sleepy smile, but I barely notice.

"Can we go for a ride?"

47

GWEN

When mafiosos ask you to go on a ride, it normally means they're going to kill you—or at least that's what the mafia movies say. A ride to your end.

It doesn't matter that my stomach is so twisted I feel like my intestines might snap. I wrap my arms around Nikolai's torso, gripping so tight my elbows dig into my sides. The purr of the motorcycle vibrates through my body, but I focus on the scent of him—woodsy, earthy, and undeniably Nik. If I'm going to die today, that's the last thing I want to smell: him.

The wind whips past as we speed down the empty road. He hasn't said much since we left the house, just told me to get on the bike. Five weeks of silence between us, and now this? My heart races, and not from the speed.

I lean my cheek against his back, breathing him in, letting myself have these final moments. The silence, the waiting, the wondering—it's been killing me slowly. I'd almost rather he just do it already, if that's what this is. End it, put me out of this misery.

I clutch onto him like he's my lifeline, knowing that he can't let me stay in his world or be his mafia queen—not if he doesn't trust me. I don't want to stay if this is what our life looks like, with him shutting me out and me feeling like my life is always hanging in the balance. That's no way to live life.

The rumbling of the bike fades to a low hum as we turn off the main road and enter a thick forest. The trees tower over us, their branches reaching and intertwining to create a canopy above. As we navigate through the winding path, I feel a sense of peaceful isolation settling in and the beauty of the forest washes over me.

Finally, we come to a stop near a small clearing and Nik cuts the engine, causing an abrupt stillness to descend. I release my tight grip on him, feeling the tension leave my body. Nik swings his leg over the bike and stands, surveying our surroundings before walking silently deeper into the forest. I slide off the bike, my knees shaky as I follow silently behind him.

His gaze is drawn to something in the distance, but I can't quite make out what it is from where I trail silently behind him. It's then that I notice the small clearing ahead, dotted with wildflowers and a single stone marker. The only sound now is the gentle rustling of leaves, the distant chirping of birds, and our unsteady breathing.

"Nik." I swallow, my body prickling with nerves. "I know I have a lot to apologize for, but I-"

"This is where I buried the parts of my mother I received," Nik says quietly, his voice rougher than usual. "No one knows about this place, not even my siblings."

I blink, the weight of his words sinking in. He's brought me here—here, where he buries his mother, to kill me. At least it will be sentimental, at least he will remember me.

"Oh," I whisper.

"Her childhood home is across the clearing, but the old bastard who owns it won't let me buy it." He lets out a sad chuckle, and I stare at the tension rippling through his back.

"Nik." I brush my fingers over his shoulder blade, contentment rushing through me at the shiver that ripples under my touch. "Why am I here?"

He turns to face me, his eyes soft but filled with something else —something deeper, darker. "Because I need you to know how much you matter to me. You planted that garden back home thinking I had no place to mourn my mother while you mourned alone."

I drop my gaze to the packed dirt beneath us. Every time I am reminded of Nana, it feels like I have been sliced open. "You know...about Nana Rose?"

Nik's eyes soften as he takes a step closer, his hand reaching for mine. "Nadia told me, but you should have told me. I should have been there for you. You shouldn't have had to mourn her alone, Gwen."

The raw emotion in his voice makes my chest ache. I want to look away, to hide the vulnerability bubbling up inside me, but I can't. It feels like the weight of the last four weeks is starting to lift, but it also feels fragile—like it could all crumble if I say the wrong thing.

"I knew you needed space after everything I did. I didn't want to guilt you into talking to me," I admit, the words spilling out before I can stop them.

His face hardens, a flicker of regret passing through his eyes. "No matter what, you should never feel like you can't come to me. I'm sorry. I never should have let it get that far."

I look up at him, my heart pounding as I try to hold back the tears threatening to spill. "You were dealing with so much, Nik. Your dad, the Yakuza, and the Italians. I didn't want to distract you with my own drama."

"Your safety is never a distraction, Kotik." Nik pinches my chin between his fingers, and I drown in his ocean blue eyes. His jaw clenches for a second and then he whispers, "I know. I failed you. I failed us."

I feel a tear slip down my cheek, and I quickly brush it away, hating how exposed I feel.

Nik steps closer, his presence overwhelming, and the depth of his gaze pins me in place. I can feel the intensity radiating off him—the raw guilt, the pain, and something deeper. Something that reaches out to me despite the weeks of silence, and when his fingertips brush over my jaw, I know I'm a goner.

My breath hitches, and I try to keep my composure, but it's impossible. His touch is soft, so careful, yet his grip on me feels like a lifeline—like if he lets go, I'll slip away forever.

"I wasn't there when you needed me most," he repeats, his voice cracking. "Mason...Boris...I should have protected you from them. They got to you in my own house, in front of everyone, and I—" His eyes darken, and for a moment, I can see the war he's been fighting within himself. "I fucking failed you."

I shake my head, wanting to tell him it's not his fault, that none of this is, but the words get stuck in my throat. Because part of me—part of me knows the truth. That we've both been walking this tightrope for so long, holding everything inside, not letting each other in, and this...this was bound to happen.

Nik's hands tremble slightly as he holds my face, his thumbs wiping at my cheeks even though the tears keep falling. He takes a breath, as if he's gathering the strength to say what's next.

"A selfless man," he says slowly, "would tell you to take the kids and run. To get as far away from me, from this life as possible. And you should. You should leave me, Gwen. For you, for Mia and Gio, it's the right thing to do."

I stare at him, my heart shattering with each word.

"But I...I'm not selfless. I'm fucking selfish, because I can't let you go. Gwen, you are mine. I would rather die than lose you. Do you understand that?" His voice is a low, dangerous growl, but there's a vulnerability in his eyes, a desperation that makes me want to reach out and wrap my arms around him, to tell him I'm his just as much as he's mine. But I stand frozen, caught between his words and the truth we've been avoiding for so long.

He leans his forehead against mine, his breath warm and uneven, and the world around us narrows down to this moment. Just me and Nik, standing in the clearing where he buries his pain and his secrets. Where he's brought me to let it all go.

"I've made mistakes," he says, his voice barely above a whisper. "But I swear to you, Gwen, I will never let that happen again. I will do anything—*anything*—to protect you and the kids."

"I know," I croak through the thickening emotion in my chest.

Nik's eyes tighten like he's in pain. "If you know I will protect you, then I need you to act like it." His fingers tighten slightly on my chin, like he's afraid I'll pull away. "Promise me you'll let me fight your fights. No more secrets. No more doing this on your own. Let me protect you."

My eyes drop to his lips. "And what about you, who's going to protect you?"

"Don't worry about me, Kotik." He hooks his index under my chin and lifts my eyes back to his. "I have the entire Russian mafia backing me."

His smile is a wicked gleam that makes my panties soaked.

"I—" My voice cracks, but I steady myself. "I promise, Nik. No more secrets. I'll let you fight for me, for us."

Relief floods his features, and before I can say anything more, his lips crash against mine. The kiss is fierce, desperate, filled with all the emotions we've been holding back for weeks. His hands slip from my face to wrap under my thighs, and I instinctively wrap my legs around his waist. He cups my ass, pulling me closer until there's no space left between us. I melt into him, feeling the tension, the fear, and the uncertainty of the last few weeks dissolve into this moment.

When he pulls back, his forehead rests against mine again, and he takes a deep breath. "Marry me, Gwen," he says softly, the words so unexpected, so raw, that my heart skips a beat.

I blink up at him, shocked. "What?"

"I know most men ask." He pauses, searching my eyes for something. "But I am telling you to marry me."

His words hit me like a shockwave, and I feel my breath catch in my throat. There's no hesitation, no doubt in his voice.

He's not asking, not giving me a choice—just like everything else with Nikolai Petrov. He takes what he wants, and right now, what he wants is me.

A shiver runs through me, not from fear but from the raw intensity of it all. His grip on my thighs tightens, and the hard press of his body against mine leaves no room for argument. I'm not sure I'd want to argue, even if I could.

"Marry me, Kotik," he murmurs again, his lips brushing against mine. "I'm not letting you go. Not now, not ever."

I should feel suffocated, I should push him away, tell him we need to talk, to slow down. But all I feel is the deep pull in my chest, the part of me that's always been his, whether I wanted to admit it or not. I've fought him for so long, but standing here, in the middle of this secluded clearing where he buries his grief, I realize that fighting him is fighting myself.

I bite my lip, my heart pounding in my chest. "Okay," I whisper, my voice barely audible over the soft rustle of leaves. "Yes."

His smile is pure satisfaction, his wicked gleam returning as his lips crash into mine again, claiming me in a way that sends heat surging through my entire body. He grips me tighter, pressing me closer until it feels like we're one person. My back hits the rough bark of a nearby tree, and I gasp, but the sensation only fuels the fire building between us.

"Say it again," he demands, his lips brushing against my neck. "Tell me you're mine."

I tilt my head back, giving him more access as his teeth graze my skin. "I'm yours, Nik," I breathe, the words slipping out like a confession. "Always yours."

His hands slide under my shirt, his touch searing against my skin, and I arch into him, craving more. There's a frantic urgency between us, as if we're making up for every second we've been apart. His mouth finds mine again, and I moan against his lips, the sound swallowed by the kiss.

"Nik," I manage between kisses, my voice trembling, "I love you."

He pulls back just enough to look into my eyes, his expression softening for a moment. "I love you too, Kotik. There isn't a single atom in me that is not obsessed with you."

My lips are back on his in a heartbeat, and for the first time in my life, I feel like even if I could run, I wouldn't want to because this is the man I love. The man I've always loved.

And now, he's mine.

EPILOGUE

NIKOLAI

One Year Later

"One more time." Mia smiles as I close the *Little Red Riding Hood* book.

"No," Gio snaps from across the room, flashlight in hand as he reads a six grade level mystery book series he is obsessed with. "Dad has read that bad book three times."

Mia sticks out her tongue. "Fourth time's the charm!"

"No, it's the third time's the charm," Gio grumbles.

I place the book down on her nightstand and hold both of my hands out to stop the bickering. "Okay, grumpy pants, flashlight out. Princess, you and Daddy have to go to sleep so how about I check extra long for monsters?"

"Monsters?" Mia whispers, pulling her blanket closer to her chest. "You think there are monsters tonight?"

I chuckle softly, ruffling her messy curls. "There are never any monsters when Daddy's around, sweetheart. But I'll check anyway, just to be sure."

Mia nods, her little face serious as she watches me get down on one knee beside her bed. I make a show of peeking under the bed, shining a small flashlight into the corners, lingering extra long just to ease her worries.

"Nope, no monsters here," I announce, sitting back up and giving her a reassuring smile. "Just dust bunnies."

Mia giggles, her fears melting away as she reaches out to hug me. I kiss the top of her head, inhaling the familiar scent of her strawberry shampoo, and tuck her back in. "Alright, princess, time for sleep."

"Love you, Daddy," she whispers, closing her eyes as she snuggles into her pillow.

"Love you more, Mia," I say softly, brushing a stray curl from her face before standing.

I turn to Gio, who's still hunched over his mystery book, the flashlight casting shadows across his face. "Alright, kid, flashlight out. You need to get some sleep too."

"But Dad," Gio protests, not even looking up from his book, "I'm right in the middle of a big clue! It's the most important part!"

I shake my head, amused. "The clue will still be there tomorrow, Gio. And besides, you'll need your rest for our trip to Thailand."

That gets his attention. His head snaps up, eyes wide with excitement. "Thailand? For real?"

"For real," I confirm, crossing my arms. "We're going to see the monkeys just like I promised."

Gio grins, tossing the book aside and finally switching off his flashlight. “Cool! I can’t wait!”

I walk over to his bed, bending down to kiss his forehead. “Goodnight, son.”

“Night, Dad,” he mumbles, already reaching for his book again. I give him a pointed look, and with a sigh, he sets it back down. “Fine, fine, goodnight for real.”

Satisfied, I straighten up and flick the nightlight on as I leave the room, closing the door behind me with a soft click. It’s a quiet moment, but as I stand in the hallway, listening to the soft sound of my kids settling down for the night, I feel a warmth in my chest I never thought I’d have.

Family. A year ago, the idea of being a father—of having this—felt like something I wasn’t capable of. But now, I can’t imagine my life without it.

I trudge down the dark, silent hallway, the faint flicker of candlelight guiding me towards our bedroom. The sound of Gwen’s restless pacing echoes off the walls, growing louder with each step I take.

I push the door open and step into a world of sensory overload. The air is thick with the scent of vanilla and lavender, the warmth of countless candles enveloping me.

My eyes are drawn to Gwen, standing by the bed in a delicate baby pink satin robe that hugs her curves in all the right ways with a hint of white lace peeking out. Her emerald-green eyes sparkle like precious jewels as she holds out a small pink box to me, her lips curling into a coy smile.

As I gently close the door behind me, she shifts on her feet, nervously biting the corner of her lip. Her eyes light up as I take a step forward.

"What's all of this?" I ask, raising an eyebrow at the pink box placed in front of me.

Gwen's smile widens as she pushes the box closer to me. "Open it."

I do as she says, lifting the lid and revealing an array of delicious-looking donuts. A small note is taped to the top of the box. In Gwen's neat handwriting, it reads: *I don't want to grow this baby bump alone!*

It takes me a second to register what I'm seeing. My eyes widen and flick back and forth from the crumpled note in Gwen's hand to the small, gift-wrapped box sitting in front of me on the table. "Wait...are you saying...?"

Her smile widens even further as she nods, her eyes sparkling with unshed tears. "Baby number three, Nik."

For a moment, all I can do is stare at her, my heart racing and my mind trying to process this unexpected news. A rush of emotions floods through me—shock, joy, and a shit ton of excitement. "We're having another baby?"

"Yeah," she laughs, her voice shaky with emotion. "We are."

I blink, trying to wrap my head around it, the excitement threatening to bubble over, and I let out a breathless laugh, pulling her into my arms. "Holy shit," I whisper, burying my face in her neck. "I'm freaking out."

"Me too," Gwen giggles, wrapping her arms around my neck, holding me tight.

Our laughter mingles, filling the room with a warmth that feels almost tangible. I pull back slightly, just enough to look into her eyes, those captivating emerald orbs that have always held me spellbound. "You're sure?" I ask, my voice barely above a whisper, still trying to grasp the reality of it all.

She nods, her smile softening as she brushes a strand of hair away from my face. "Positive. I took the test this morning. Two lines, just like last time."

A surge of pride and love washes over me, and I feel my chest swell with emotion. "Another little one," I murmur, almost in disbelief. "You're amazing, you know that?"

She blushes, her cheeks tinged with a rosy hue that makes her even more beautiful.

She steps back just enough to untie the sash of her robe. The fabric falls open, revealing the delicate lace of her lingerie underneath. My breath catches in my throat as I take in the sight of her, glowing with a new kind of radiance.

She reaches for me, her hands sliding under my shirt to press against my bare skin. "How do you want to celebrate, Daddy?"

I let out a shaky breath against her lips. "Keep calling me daddy and I'm going to make it rough."

Gwen chuckles, and I groan softly as she begins to unbutton my shirt, her fingers deft and sure. "Take this off," she murmurs, her lips brushing against my collarbone as she works.

I comply, shrugging out of my shirt and tossing it aside. My hands finding their way to her waist, pulling her closer until our bodies are flush against each other. The feel of her, warm and soft, sets my blood on fire, and I can't help but press my lips along her jawline, tasting the salt of her skin.

Gwen tilts her head, giving me better access, and I take full advantage, nuzzling her neck, my tongue darting out to trace the curve of her ear. She gasps, her body arching into mine, and I feel a surge of triumph. "You like that?" I murmur, my voice dripping with desire.

"Yes," she breathes, her hands gripping my shoulders tightly. "More. Please."

I oblige, trailing my lips down her neck, pausing to nip at the sensitive spot just below her ear. Gwen moans, her hips grinding against mine, and I feel the unmistakable wetness of her arousal pressing against my thigh. "Fuck, Gwen," I groan, my own need rising rapidly.

My hands roam over her body, exploring every curve, every dip, memorizing the feel of her. My fingers find the clasp of her bra, and I release the hooks, letting the straps fall away to reveal her perfect breasts. My mouth waters at the sight, and I lean in, taking one taut nipple into my mouth, sucking gently as my hand cups her other breast, kneading it softly.

Gwen arches her back, her head thrown back in ecstasy, her fingers tangling in my hair. "Oh God, Nik," she moans, her breath coming in ragged gasps. "Don't stop. Please."

I alternate between her breasts, lavishing them with attention, my tongue flicking over her nipples, teasing them until they peak. She shudders beneath me, but I show her no mercy, nipping at her until she is panting. "Nik."

Gwen's legs part instinctively, and I stifle a groan as my fingers slip under the lace of her panties, teasing the soft flesh of her inner thighs. "Is this what my dirty girl wanted?"

She bites her lip, nodding. "Yes, please, I need you," she whispers, her voice strained with desire.

“That’s all you had to say, darling.” I smile, stripping off the rest of my clothes and tossing them aside without a second thought.

Gwen reaches for me, her hands guiding me to her, and I position myself at her entrance, my cock throbbing and without waiting, I push forward, slowly sinking into her warmth. Gwen gasps, her nails digging into my back as I fill her completely. “Fuck,” she whispers, her voice filled with awe.

I begin to move, my thrusts slow and deliberate, savoring the feel of her around me. Gwen meets my rhythm, her hips rising to meet mine, our bodies moving together in perfect harmony. “Love you,” I murmur, my lips brushing against her ear.

“Love you too,” she replies, her voice breaking with emotion. “So much.”

Our movements grow faster, more urgent, as we chase the peak of pleasure together. Gwen’s hands grip my shoulders, her nails digging in as she cries out, her orgasm building once more. “Nik, I’m close,” she gasps, her voice trembling with need.

“Me too,” I reply, my thrusts becoming erratic as I fight to hold back my own climax. “Come with me, Gwen.”

With a final, desperate cry, Gwen’s body tenses, her orgasm washing over her in waves, and I follow her over the edge, my own release crashing through me with blinding intensity. We cling to each other, our bodies shuddering with the force of our shared climax, our breaths mingling as we ride out the aftershocks.

I collapse beside Gwen, my chest heaving with exertion. She turns to me, her eyes shining with love and contentment, and I pull her into my arms, holding her close. "Best celebration ever," I murmur, my lips brushing against her temple.

"Agreed," she replies, her voice sleepy and content. "Maybe I should tell you I'm pregnant more often."

I chuckle, kissing the top of her head. "Don't tempt me, Kotik. I want at least three more kids out of you."

POST EPILOGUE

NADIA

"Open wide, baby." I lean in close to Sho's face, a trickle of blood falling over his cheek and the fucker has the audacity to lick his lips and smile at me.

"Normally," he coughs, "that's what I say."

His skin glistens that beautiful sheen you only get from victims who can withstand the pain, and if he didn't just betray me and my family, I would be tempted to kiss him for being such a good boy for this entire session.

"Not with me, baby." I grip his jaw with my hand, squeezing the sharp edges into my palm. If he bleeds, I bleed, and how delicious is that?

"I bet I could make you say ahhhh," he sings, flashing his bloody teeth at me.

I push his head to the side and lean back from in front of his face. The metal chains dig into his stained t-shirt. The muscles in his biceps protrude from how tight the cuffs around his wrists are, but despite there being no chains holding his legs open, he sits with his back straight, legs spread, eyes a dark hooded mess, and all I can keep thinking is, he would be perfect for me to use.

Sho's head lolls into his chest, but he doesn't wipe that cocky smile off his face. Instead, his tongue flicks the ball of his lip ring and he covers up the next cough with a chuckle. "I can see what you are thinking, Hime."

"Oh?" I purr, sliding my chest against his. The tip of my lips running across the shell of his ear. "What am I thinking?"

"You think you could top me." His lips curl to the left side of his mouth, and the glittering of his eyes as he side glances me has my core tightening.

"You look like a bottom right now," I whisper. "All helpless and tied up in my basement."

I run my stiletto nails sharply down his arms, moaning at the roll of satisfaction that drips from his lips. I can't help myself. I want to poke my tongue out and taste him, get this small piece of him.

"I am only here because I want to be, Hime. Trust me." His breath flutters over my shoulder, and before I know it one hand is free, wrapping my waist length hair around his fist and pulling me across his lap. The bloodied smile shines over me. He looks like something out of the heavens. "If I don't want to be tied up, I won't be."

Thank you for reading Nik and Gwen's story, if you enjoyed it kindly leave me a review to help me succeed. Coming soon is Nadia's story stay connected by joining Vivy's exclusive reader group.

Join here to receive exclusive content.

HERE IS YOUR NEXT READ, XANDER AND MEL'S LOVE story, an InstaLove Romance with a secret pregnancy...

FOR FUCK'S SAKE.

It takes a lot of willpower to keep the groan from escaping the tight clench of my lips. I had a lot more willpower to keep my eyes from shamelessly roaming over her curves.

The young woman in front of me is wearing a neon green bikini, cut so high it barely covers the lush curve of her ass. Her blonde hair in light waves covers her face as she giggles.

"I'm telling you, Gianna, one more minute and I would have drowned in his spit." She bends over to spread her towel on a pool chair, and I almost choke. This isn't even fair at this point. To look like her and tempt me in the enemy's den.

Who is she? Fuck. I shouldn't even be here, but I can't look away.

The younger girl sits next to her in a similar yellow ensemble and jokes, "Talk about a bad kisser. I hope my first kiss isn't all saliva and chin."

"I swear it doesn't even count as a first kiss." She leans back on her chair, and I can't help the words that escape my lips.

"Well, if you want a do-over, I promise I've never gotten any complaints." Her eyes shoot in my direction, looking like a deer in headlights.

She sits up, shakes her hair out of her face, and shoots me a confused look. "Um, excuse me. Who are you?"

How the hell does she not know who I am?

I walk closer, making sure not to look down at her breasts as I hold my hand out, a wry smile on my face. "You first."

She places her hand cautiously in mine, "I am Melissa Sedric." Holy shit, this only gets worse.

She's a Sedric. "I'm Xander. My father has a meeting with the head of the Sedric Family."

A look of alarm skirts across her face, and she pulls her hand away. So, she *does* know who I am. "You're Xander Amory."

"In the flesh."

Melissa moves closer to Gianna. I smile at how skittish she is. Smart girl.

Our families have been at each other's throats for as long as I can remember. No one knows how the conflict started, but everyone knows it must end one way or another.

"Xander," my name sounds amazing on her lips, "why are you here?"

She cranes her head to the door I'd used. A guard is standing right by it, and she looks surprised to see the guard still standing there.

Maybe she'd thought I'd snuck in. I'd have kept the hell away if I had known they were here.

"Well, you can only listen to two grown men argue for so long." I'd left for a moment of reprieve before I snapped at two of the deadliest men I knew.

The bickering was stupid. We need each other. I don't see the fucking need to deny that.

I keep my eyes firmly on hers, fighting the urge to roam my eyes over her softly glowing skin, the curve of her lips caught between her teeth, and the small scar right on her shoulder where it seems she'd had a fall.

Gianna leans over and looks me over. "Ego will do that to you. Tell me, Xander, do you have a big ego?"

Melissa's eyes bulge out of her head, and she looks at Gianna as if she has lost her mind. "Gianna!"

"When your sister finds out, I'll make sure she reports back." I wink at Melissa, and she shoots up, red blooming along her cheeks. Before she can retort, Daniel's voice breaks in, and she sits back down, a relieved smile parting her full lips.

"There you are; I was wondering where you'd disappeared to!"

Why couldn't he have waited just a second longer? I give her a strained smile and turn towards Daniel, her brother.

He jerks his head at his sisters and smiles softly at them. It's the first time I've seen him smile that way.

"Sorry Xander intruded on you two. I'll take him away now."

"Boo! He was just getting interesting." Gianna pouts as she leans back to sunbathe.

He rolls his eyes. "Trust me, he's boring." Daniel looks at me and nods towards the door. "Neither of our fathers might leave that study alive if we don't get in there soon."

I spare one more glance at Melissa, watching as she nervously nibbles on her pink, plush bottom lip before walking towards Daniel. I can tell she's still looking by the muffled giggles, and it gets louder when we skirt the front door and take a side door into the house.

"Let them kill each other. We'll take our rightful place as the heads and promise not to kill each other." I half-heartedly laugh, and Daniel scoffs.

"Interesting proposition, but you realize both families will be out for blood. There would never be any peace. Best friends, or not."

I suck my teeth. Daniel takes the stairs two at a time, his footsteps stomping over the marble back to the study.

I am itching to end this argument, so I walk ahead of him. So far, I have control over the legal part of the business at Amory Corp. Soon, I will enter the darker part of the corporation, and I want to show I am ready for it.

Daniel turns back to wink at me. "They asked that I bring you in. I'm sure it won't be long now."

I grunt and follow him back to the study, where my father is pacing the length of the large room, his fists bunched at his sides. He waves a hand towards Sedric who is sitting behind his desk, leaning back like he doesn't have a care in the world. "Daniel, did you know your father lacks the grit to run this empire?"

Daniel shrugs, an angry light in his eyes that doesn't reach his voice. "I'm certain you were just about to tell him that. And considering you're in the man's house, you might want to tone it down."

Father continues to snap at Sedric, and I know from his tone that there will be no resolution today. They're too angry to see the bigger picture, and I'm frustrated because that's all I can see.

The legal side of the Amory Corp. teaches you how to be level-headed, and the darker side teaches you how to be ruthless. My father spends too much time in the dark.

"Amory, I'll have your head above my fireplace!"

"Want to bet?!"

I roll my eyes. "If we cannot be civil, then we need to call it a day."

Sedric pauses, looking me over, and so does my father. "Your son is right."

My father sighs. "Tomorrow?"

"Sunday. Outside the church. Even the playing field," I suggest. Both men grunt in agreement. "Great. Bathroom, then we leave. No more shop talk while I'm gone."

Annoyed, I exit the study and go down the stairs, pass by the kitchen, and find the restroom. I use the bathroom, staring at a huge picture of a 1950s woman bent over a toilet bowl with her hand over her lips in a shocked expression.

Her soft blonde curls remind me of Melissa. If I did what I wanted to her, she would look like that, breathless, mouth agape, waiting to be filled.

Fuck. I shake my head clear of her because Daniel would never let me close enough even to try.

I wash my hands at the sink, wishing I was home with my brothers or out there at Amory working; it would be so much better than wasting a big part of my day dealing with this bull-shit. I step out of the bathroom, let the door close behind me slowly, walk down the hallway, and almost run smack into her.

Her eyes widened, and she froze right in front of me. Her blonde hair is wet and matted to her head in loose waves.

She's wrapped in a large blue towel. It's short and barely covers her thighs. Without meaning to, my eyes roam over her frame wishing to unwrap her like the present she is.

She scrambles for the folds of the towel but it's already sliding down her sides, her bikini winking out and providing a stunning view of her breasts still snug, and almost slipping from her now wet bikini.

She gasps and I take a step forward, my cock already growing. She pulls the towel over her breasts and exhales a shaky stream of air. "Jeez, that was close."

Not close enough. Her green eyes are staring up at me, half a smile tipping her lips as a blush invades her cheeks. I'm itching to invade her space. The way her eyes rise to mine makes it look as though the sun is rising.

Soon, she starts giggling. My brows furrow and I tip my head back. "What's funny?"

"You should see your face. You look like you've seen a ghost. Come on, I don't look that bad!"

"No, you look that good."

Her laughter turns into a cough, but all I can focus on is the way she licks her lips and gasps. I lean forward so her face is right up against mine and our breathing rolls together in the air.

"Why did you have to be outside the bathroom, right now?"

She licks her lips and sparks flow over my warm skin. "We wanted some fruit," she whispers, as though scared to break the spell between us. I don't know what it is, but I have a death wish because I kiss her.

At first, she stiffens, but I firmly place my hand on her hip, pulling her into my body and she relaxes, opening her mouth for me. I take advantage of the small opening nipping on her bottom lip.

She shifts closer, her breast pushing against my chest. My hand lifts as though of its own accord to her hair, sinking gently into her hair. I anchor my fingers in her hair pulling slightly, and she fucking moans.

The growl growing in my throat pulls me out of the trance and I pull away from her, my forehead leaning against hers as I guide my hand down to cup her neck. She's panting as if she just ran a race.

"What was that?"

"A redo of your first kiss. That's how it should have been."

My fingers brush their way down her shoulders, slide over her collarbone, and lap for a moment around her neck before continuing on to her chest where I stop. She's barely breathing, her chest unmoving under my palm. But her eyes, they're even wider, even hotter, even brighter, and there's a light breaking out in them that burns like the sun, sending streaks of that spreading light right into my chest.

Her frozen stance suddenly brings laughter to my lips. I chuckle lightly, putting my head by her ears and whisper, "That's the kiss you deserved, *Sole. Il mio piccolo sole.*"

Melissa

He kissed me.

Xander kissed me, and it definitely wasn't like Jacob. There was no chin, no excessive tongue.

It was everything I imagined my first kiss to be, but it was from Xander Amory, which means it can never ever happen again.

I walk mindlessly back to the pool, where Gianna is tanning. When I sit next to her, she pokes up with a frown. “Mel, where are the mangoes?”

I look down at my hands, the memory of them pulling Xander’s hair, as I pulled him closer into me flashes across my mind.

“Hello? Earth to Melissa! Where are the mangoes?” Gianna’s annoyed singing causes me to snap out of my daze and I look at her, blush creeping up my neck.

“Um...I must have forgotten, sorry.” I lean back on my chair dismissing her, but she huffs.

“So you were gone for twenty minutes...wait, where is your towel?” Gianna leans over me with humor-filled accusations. “Oh you were naughty!”

“Was not!” I shoot up.

This will be the first secret I keep from Gianna. She doesn't know about Xander. Nobody can.

This is so wrong. It’s wrong how he makes my stomach flip, wrong how easily we fit into each other, wrong how we finish each other's sentences. Everything about this is wrong.

Gianna tsks at me as she shakes her head, pointing her finger at me. “I know you like the back of my hand, Mel. I know you better than you know yourself. So spill, or I go to the security room and start looking at cameras.”

I sink down, knowing this is not an empty threat, “Fine, but you can’t tell anyone. This is a grave secret.” I extend my pinky for Gianna to wrap hers around.

She smiles. "My favorite type of secret!" We both kiss our hands and she tucks her crossed legs underneath her. "Now spill!"

"I kissed Xander, well Xander kissed me." Gianna almost jumps out of her skin with a squeal, causing one of the guards to run over.

"Everything okay here?" The guard looks around suspiciously and Gianna rolls her eyes.

"Don't you know happiness when you hear it?" The guard looks at her confused and stays still until she flings her hands, pushing him forward, "Go away!"

Once the guard is gone, she turns back to me. "Tell me everything, matter of fact, reenact it!"

I cover my head in embarrassment, "G, this is so wrong. Father will kill me. Daniel will kill me."

"Well was it just a kiss, or something more?" Gianna wiggles her eyebrows at me hoping for something more, and even though my body comes alive thinking about him touching me again, I shake my head.

"Nothing more, just a kiss." For both of our sakes, it better be just a kiss...Read Claimed By The Mafia Prince FREE With Kindle Unlimited and available on Paperbark.

ABOUT THE AUTHOR

VIVY SKYS the author of Steamy Contemporary Romance novels, featuring smart, strong, sassy and witty female characters that command the attention of strong protective alpha males, from Off limits, Age Gap, Bossy Billionaires, Single dads next door, Royalty, Dark Mafia and beyond Vivy's pen will deliver.

Follow Vivy Skys on Amazon to be the first to know when her next book becomes available.

Printed in Dunstable, United Kingdom